WITCH AND WOMBAT

BY CAROLYN CUSHMAN

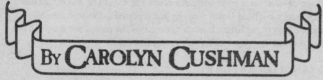

WARNER BOOKS

A Time Warner Company

WARNER BOOKS EDITION

Cover design by Don Puckey
Cover illustration by Jody A. Lee
Hand lettering by Carl Dellacroce

Warner Books, Inc.
1271 Avenue of the Americas
New York, NY 10020

 A Time Warner Company

Printed in the United States of America

First Printing: May, 1994

10 9 8 7 6 5 4 3 2 1

WELCOME TO CLUB MED(IEVAL)!

++

Hali: What's the fantasy world coming to? Witches have jobs, too, and Hali's latest assignment is to play tour guide to a pack of naive mortals!

++

Bentwood: You can put a troll in the executive suite . . . but he'll still have the heart of an evil highway robber . . .

++

Bernie: An overly familiar familiar who wants to be a crow . . . a raven . . . a black cat . . . *ANYTHING* except—a wombat!

++

Leo: Being a heroic warrior's fun . . . until it's time to really *be* a heroic warrior!

++

Tracy: When the going gets weird in the Magic Kingdom, this high school student's weird words are golden!

++

Oliver: Seeking the girl of his dreams, he may find himself in a dream as well.

++

Jamison: When an obnoxious critic faces himself, what he finds is disgusting and amazing . . . or maybe just disgusting!

++

CHAPTER
1

O NE of the first tenets of witchcraft is that a witch needs a proper hut. Shaking her head at the gleaming white walls of her breakfast nook, Hali sat down to breakfast with the latest home improvement guide when the deep tolling of a bell shook the house.

"Visitors!" screeched Hali's familiar, Bernie, a large black crow sitting on the back of one chair beside a setting of birdseed. "Don't get up, I'll get it." He took off through the open kitchen window into the foggy morning beyond.

Just a few feet from the house the fog disappeared, revealing a clear, crisp mountain morning. One solitary grey cloud hovered over the mountain crag on which Hali's house perched, an incongruously neat white A-frame with a blue plastic roof. Witches by nature prefer the tumbledown and rotting look, and Bernie suspected the ever-present cloud was Hali's work, designed to hide the roof, which remained a lively, charming blue in spite of years of spells thrown at it. The cottage had originally been acquired as a stopgap replacement for its predecessor, which had literally tumbled down in a minor magical skirmish.

Though the house had proven amazingly immune to the ravages of wind, rain, and magical fallout, it also resisted all efforts at redecoration, remaining nauseatingly spiffy and bright. Hali had never forgotten the administration's promises to replace it with a proper witch's hut—or forgiven them for failing to do so. Bernie didn't care about the roof as long as it didn't leak, but when work permitted would fly off in search of better weather, leaving Hali to enjoy the gloom of her pet cloud.

Bernie flapped cheerfully into the sky, took a few turns around the bare crag, then swooped down the slopes to the bottom of the hill, where a tired ogre in a grey uniform handed him a stiff envelope.

"Magic Express. Sign here." The ogre held out a clipboard for Bernie to peck. "Why do these witches always build their houses in the middle of nowhere, then put antitransportation spells on them?" the bulky messenger complained.

"You don't think those spells stop their owners, do you?" retorted Bernie with his most haughty caw, designed to depress the pretensions of the nosiest ogre. He took the envelope in his beak and, flying awkwardly, returned to the house on the hill. He landed clumsily on the kitchen windowsill, and dropped the express envelope on the kitchen table inside.

"Magic Express, Hali," he croaked. "No return address. Who's it from?"

"How should I know?" Hali looked up from her copy of *Better Huts and Gardens*, marked the interior decorating article she'd been studying ("Cobwebs: Tried and True, or Tired and Trite?"), and reached over the teapot for the envelope. Lazily, she examined the package without opening it, deliberately ignoring her frustrated familiar as he hopped back and forth on the windowsill.

"Open it, will you?" he begged, bobbing his head.

"Knock it off, Bernie. It's probably bad news from the home office, as usual." She ripped open the package and pulled out a parchment dripping with seals. "Yep. We're hereby ordered to drop everything and report to Bentwood this afternoon."

"So what are we supposed to drop?" Bernie asked. "They haven't sent us any business in ages."

"Maybe that's what we're supposed to talk about. Interesting, though . . ." Hali eyed the summons skeptically.

"Bentwood's signing himself 'Executive Producer' these days. What do you suppose that means?" She tossed the parchment in the fireplace and stretched. "Whatever, I want to have a talk with him myself. He's been promising me a new house for an ogre's age, and I'm just about ready to set- tle for making my own out of gingerbread, except you'd eat me out of house and home."

"Does that mean I can eat the rest of your toast?" Bernie eyed the table scraps warily. "Without getting turned into something icky?"

"Go ahead. I've got to fix my face and get the magic mir- ror ready. If you want to go through with a full stomach, that's fine by me."

For Hali, fixing her face meant the careful application of an ugliness amplification spell, without which she never left the house. As witches go, she lacked a certain fearsome something, though her formidable disposition sufficed to ter- rify the occasional adolescent who wandered her way. Preteens, to her mortification, pegged her instantly as a pushover. If children were unavoidable, Hali screwed her face into her most ferocious scowl, guaranteed to pique the curiosity of even the dullest toddler, but which at least had the advantage of unnerving parents enough that the offend- ing child would usually be dragged off, protesting.

At the other extreme, Hali's most beguiling expression, adopted at social occasions attended by attractive males, tended to send its targets running for their lives. Hali's less- than-respectful familiar Bernie, an enchanted and voluble crow, had more than once opined that Hali ought to try re- versing the two expressions, but since he had to be well-for- tified with liquor (stolen from unattended drinks) to even make the suggestion, Hali remained immune to the idea— and mystified by her lack of success with the opposite sex.

Without magical augmentation, Hali could pass unnoticed almost anywhere, a thin, nondescript woman with just enough of a point to her thin nose and chin to qualify as "witchy." Hali liked to think that her mouse-brown hair snaked about her face, but in reality it hung in limp, slightly scraggly tendrils that only came to life in wet weather, when they suddenly sat up and curled wildly in an uncontrollable mass that made it impossible for Bernie to keep his perch on Hali's shoulder. "Not that I'd want to go stand in a thunderstorm with her, anyway," he'd been heard to sulk, but he admitted when pressed that Hali was at her most impressive when the weather was at its worst.

This morning, Hali was less concerned with looking bad than with keeping the powers that be intimidated, and settled for the basic crone look: shapeless black dress, dull limp hair shot through with grey, lifeless skin, and a slight enhancement to the nose, making a proper beak of it. She refrained from adding a wart to the tip, since Bernie found such protuberances distasteful and tended to show his displeasure by nipping at them whenever he got the chance. An old-fashioned pair of button-top boots with outrageously pointed toes and a scruffy, handmade broom completed Hali's ensemble, and she turned in front of the mirror.

"Perfect. Just the thing for the main office," she commented with a certain smug satisfaction.

Bernie hopped onto the mirror and looked her over. "So where's the pointy hat?"

"Hmmph. Pointy hats are cliché."

"So's the rest of the outfit."

"Watch it, bird. You could spend the rest of your very short life as a slime mold."

"Threats, threats. It could only be an improvement—anything's better than being an ugly crow, or one of you dull, miserable humans."

"If you were miserable it was because you had no taste. This look is classic. And I'm not going to throw you in the briar patch."

"Urrrk," Bernie grumbled, and decided his tailfeathers needed a bit of sudden preening.

"C'mon, bird, we're wanted." Hali held out her arm, and Bernie jumped onto it, walking up to the witch's shoulder. "Ready?"

"As ready as I'll ever be."

Frowning in concentration, Hali held her broom up in front of the mirror, which began to glow with a soft grey-white light. Nodding, Hali stepped into the mirror, which shivered and flexed like a mercury soap bubble as she passed through.

The other side of the mirror opened onto a dark cavern, so deep beneath the ground that not even a memory of daylight could penetrate. Hali pushed through the mirror, which clung to her like a second, silvery skin before parting suddenly, with a violent burst of light. For an instant, the flash lit up the walls of the large cavern filled with walkways, balconies, and doors, hinting at the labyrinthine complex of corridors beyond. The light faded instantly, leaving only an outline around Hali of glowing, molten silver that seemed to drip off of her, sizzling to nothingness on the rocky floor, leaving total darkness. Hali waited patiently for her eyes to adjust, while Bernie moaned quietly on her shoulder.

"You throw up on me and I'll sell your remains to a milliner," Hali threatened. "I warned you not to eat that toast."

"I'm OK, I'm OK," Bernie gasped. "Just give me a second to turn rightside out." He burped and tucked his head under one wing. Voice muffled, he continued to complain nonetheless, ". . . stupid way to travel when you can fly, and why do these stupid caverns have to be so dark—doesn't anybody know about lighting around here? I just can't believe I voluntarily subjected myself to this thing again, and next time I'm flying even if it takes a week. . . ."

"Quiet already, bird. These halls are lighted. You just have lousy night vision."

"And whose fault is that? You're the one who turned me into a crow. I never liked dark, closed-in places anyhow."

"Come on, Bernie, you tried to pick my pocket in a subway," Hali said.

"It was a well-lighted subway." Bernie risked a peek at his surroundings and cawed faintly. He hid his head again, and shivered. "Even an owl couldn't see in this place."

With her eyes adjusted to the dark, Hali could make out walkways limned in a faint luminescence. Moving briskly, she turned to the largest corridor with the most ostentatious entry, a large arch embellished with twining, distorted creatures, their gaping mouths and staring eyes glowing particularly bright. The corridor itself was little more than a tunnel with rough-hewn rock walls, but gradually it squared out, developing smooth, flat walls that met floor and ceiling at right angles. To Hali's astonishment, the corridor further down was lit by track lighting that flooded the hallway with white light.

"Hey, Bernie, check out the new lighting."

"Don't make fun of me," whimpered the crow. "I won't look."

"Seriously." Hali shrugged, forcing Bernie to take his head out to keep his balance. He sat up in amazement, eyeing the walls.

"Wow. Is that wood paneling?"

Hali tapped the wall, and frowned. "Something artificial, but it sure looks impressive. Looks like wall-to-wall carpet up ahead, too."

"What the heck is Bentwood up to now?"

"I'm afraid to guess." Continuing down the seemingly endless corridor, Hali noted the appearance of paintings on the walls, then the addition of a few potted ferns, and a marble statue of an aristocratic elf in hunting gear (complete with antlers). When she finally reached her destination, Hali was only moderately surprised to find a stylish receptionist sitting at a desk that looked more like an oversized fort of walnut and chrome. Dressed for success with a vengeance, the elven receptionist looked down her finely chiseled nose and asked, with distaste, "May I help you?"

"I'm here to see Bentwood," Hali growled.

"I'm afraid that's impossible. The executive producer is very busy at present, and sees no one without an appointment."

"Oh, really?" Hali purred.

"Really. If you wish to make an appointment, ask your immediate supervisor to speak with the sector coordinator, who will schedule you a time, if he decides your problem merits Mr. Bentwood's attention." The elegant receptionist smiled sweetly and turned away.

Determined, Hali started around the desk, heading for the double doors marked Executive Offices, only to find her path blocked by the sudden appearance of a shimmering ward field. "What the . . ."

"Really," huffed the receptionist. "You riffraff can't just walk in and disturb an important producer like Mr. Bentwood. Now go away before I call security."

"You simpering, overvarnished, and undersexed little elf. How dare you talk like that to me? Do you know who I am?" Hali shook her broom in the receptionist's face.

"Uh, oh," said Bernie. Discreetly, he dropped off of Hali's shoulder onto the floor and quickly slipped behind a nearby solid-looking file cabinet, peeping out cautiously to keep one eye on the action. "This should be good," he chortled quietly.

The receptionist waved an elegantly manicured hand. (The fingernails had gold filigree inlays, Hali noted with distaste.) The receptionist called into the air, "Security to Mr. Bentwood's office, please," and smiled smugly as four enormous, club-toting ogres appeared, near naked except for their low-slung studded leather belts, loincloths, white patent-leather brassards, and helmets labeled "Security" perched on their essentially neckless heads. Their huge shoulders filled the reception area to overcrowding, but their short, spindly legs left considerable room down at Bernie's level on the floor, and he briefly debated the possibilities of adding his beak to the coming fray.

"Where's da trouble, doll?" asked the leader, leaning over the reception desk with a murderous grin and a bit of a leer. He scratched himself suggestively under his loincloth. Haughtily, the receptionist pointed.

Hali leaned nonchalantly against the other side of the desk. She nodded genially and the ogres' smiles disappeared. "Oh, shit. Not Hali again!" one moaned.

Hali waved. "Hi, boys. Say good-bye." Two ogres had time to turn but not to run before the transformation hit them, leaving four disgruntled toads in their place. Hali turned to the receptionist and considered briefly before snapping her fingers. "A monkey. You'd make a great monkey." A very ugly bare-bottomed monkey sat in the receptionist's place, and Hali grinned. "Perfect. Be a dear and catch those toads before they get into trouble, will you?" The monkey chittered in dismay, staring at her hands, then at the toads, and back at her hands again, while Hali considered the almost invisible wall that kept her from the door.

"I think I'll leave the wards up. What do you want to bet Bentwood can't undo this from inside?" Hali tapped her broom twice on the floor, then dissolved, turning into a cloud of white smoke that diffused through the barrier, then funneled quickly through the keyhole.

"Hey Hali, wait up!" squawked Bernie. He hopped up to the ward-field wall, and tentatively pecked at it. "Oh, phooey, I wanted to see this." He flew up onto the desk and eyed the monkey. "Well, babe, we've got some free time. Want to see if you can make a monkey of me?" He jumped quickly to save his tailfeathers from the furious receptionist, who shrieked madly and began hopping up and down, bouncing off the walls in simian fury. Retreating behind his file cabinet again, Bernie shook his head. "It's amazing the effect I have on women. What a waste of sheer talent."

Inside the office, Bentwood sat behind a polished desk that could, in case of flood, serve as a raft for all two dozen elves in the secretarial pool. With a mirror propped up before him, Bentwood carefully adjusted the folds of the snowy white ascot that peeked out from the moss-green velvet collar of his terribly sophisticated smoking jacket. His wizened face, bulging bald brow, and protuberant ears, all in the color of slightly mildewed mahogany, sat oddly atop such elegance, but Bentwood felt he had reached the height of sartorial elegance, and his satisfaction showed in the lipless grin that spread literally from ear to ear.

Suddenly he realized that smoke was pouring into his office. Jumping off of his high chair, Bentwood scrambled for the door. The smoke got there first, solidifying in a tall column before the backpedaling troll.

"Eeee-hee-hee-heh-heh." The piercing shriek echoed throughout the oversized office, and Bentwood relaxed.

"Hali, sweetie, nice entrance," Bentwood told the materializing witch. "Great sound effects, too, but you need to work on the makeup. That look is really dated now, you know, and brooms—no one's doing brooms anymore." He backed up as a glowering Hali loomed over him. "Did you notice how that shriek of yours echoed in here? You'd think a rug this thick would prevent that. Remind me to get some acoustical tiling in here."

Hali bared her teeth in a most unpleasant smile, and Bentwood scuttled behind his desk. Holding her broom in a decidedly aggressive position, Hali stalked him slowly.

"Now, Hali, baby, sweetheart—no need to get upset. I've got great news for you. A new job's come up." Hali snarled, and Bentwood waved his hands expansively, talking fast. "It's a great opportunity, on the leading edge—bound to be your big break. Just what you've been waiting for. Believe me."

Hali exploded. "Ha! The only thing I've been waiting for is that new house you promised me, Bentwood. For years you've been promising me, and what do I get? A plastic prefab job you picked up in the Outer Worlds, dirt cheap. I've been Out more than once lately, and I was not pleased to discover restaurants—selling pancakes, yet—that look exactly like my place, even down to that totally pathetic blue roof. You know that Outworld materials are magic-resistant. I can't even get a decent remodeling spell to hold for more than a month. Do you have any idea how embarrassing it is for a witch to have a spiffy white house?

"I've been patient since you told me there's no funds for a new place, business is slow. There's funds for your office, I notice." Hali waved at the room. "This place is bigger than my whole house, and there's enough lumber in the paneling and furniture to keep my fire going all winter. Which is what I'll do with it if you don't come clean."

"Hali, sweetheart, baby, cookie, honey, don't be like this," Bentwood pleaded.

"And what's with all the names? You used to at least be polite. For a troll, anyway."

"It's all part of this new project I've got going," Bentwood explained eagerly. "If you'd just let me explain . . ."

"You know, you were a decent guy when you worked with the rest of us out in the field. Then the white collar crew pulls you out from under that old stone bridge, and you go putting on airs and refusing to listen to your old buddies. Maybe you need to try getting back to your roots for a while."

"Listen, that bridge was the pits. Oh, the slime was great, but having those prissy goats going 'trip-trap, trip-trap' overhead every day was really getting to me. I'm a troll with big ideas, it's just taken time to get in a position where I can act on them.

"Times are changing, Hali. Business is down so low we're facing the biggest crisis ever to hit the Inner Worlds. No one believes in us anymore."

"The folks in the Outer Worlds never did believe, Bentwood. You know that. To them we're nothing more than characters in fairy tales, if that. They have the darnedest ideas about witches, let me tell you. I stopped by for one of their fancy celebrations—Halloween, they call it. You should have seen it. . . ." Hali sat on the edge of Bentwood's desk, pensively gazing into the air.

Though relieved that Hali appeared willing to talk, Bentwood hurried to forestall what promised to be an extended reminiscence. "The thing is, they used to believe, deep down. At least the kids did, the ones who heard the fairy tales and saw themselves as mistreated Cinderellas every time they had to take the garbage out, or the ones who wouldn't go out alone at night for fear of the boogeyman. Now nobody even reads the fairy tales anymore. Everybody watches this new invention, the TV, with its moving picture shows of talking animals and teenaged mutant samurai critters, things like that. No more ogres or trolls—everyone wants aliens from outer space, and they're just Not Our Kind."

"Oh, c'mon, Bentwood, what about that writer, that Tolkien fellow? Seems like most of the kids that have come through my place of late mention him. We suffer in comparison, I gather, but at least they're getting the idea."

"It's not the same. You work with adolescents, and the ones you see represent a fringe group of literate misfits, mostly, and there's just not enough of them. We're losing our belief base in the Outer Worlds, and without that energy we're in trouble."

"Energy?" Hali asked. "What are you talking about? Seems like there's plenty of energy here." She gestured at the glistening postmodern chandelier in the middle of the ceiling.

"Not that kind of energy, exactly," Bentwood explained,

pulling a report folder from his desk. "I'm talking about magic, the essence of magic. Our researchers have borrowed some of their energy concepts and terminology from the Outer World, but the theories work with magic, so far.

"It turns out the magic we take for granted is actually a form of energy, generated by the belief of the Outworlders. For the most part they're not even aware of the energy, so it lies around unused until somehow it gathers here, where anyone with the talent and concentration can use it to create things.

"The catch is, the energy from their imagination gravitates to us only if they've been imagining the right sort of things. The research team thinks this television doohickey is siphoning off our energy. Somewhere a world populated by television characters is forming, even as we speak, and ours is starting to fade. Not enough to notice, but several wizards doing independent research have picked it up. I've been able to keep it quiet, so far, but we've got to do something to reverse this trend. The theorists don't know if we'll just disappear one day, or if we'll find ourselves working as extras in that television world, but either way I won't stand for it."

"So what can you do about it?" Hali asked. "Working between worlds takes a lot of energy as it is, and the time differentials between worlds make it almost impossible. It's really disorienting, you know, going away for an afternoon and coming back a hundred years later. Not so bad going the other way, but still . . ."

Impatiently, Bentwood interrupted. "The tech boys think they've found a way to hold us in sync long enough to do what we need to. That Tolkien fellow's the key, really. As far as we've been able to make out, a whole generation grew up fantasizing over his epic. Somebody else invented a game that let you make up your own adventures of that sort, with dungeons, dragons, elves—even trolls."

"Witches?"

"Not really, from what I've heard, though there's lots of magic-working types in these role-playing games. The thing is, this is as close as people are getting to our kind of world these days, and we do seem to get energy from this bunch. I figure if we can steer the gamers closer still, we've got a chance."

"I don't like the sound of these gamers, Bentwood. Fantasy is a serious business. We're supposed to be helping Outworlders mature by facing their anxieties, acting out their problems. Nothing inspires me more than taking a spoiled brat and forcing her to scrub floors until she starts acting human. A game just won't do that, particularly if the kids get to make them up themselves. It'll be all magic swords and great battles, without the blood and blisters to make it real."

"That's the point—we're going to make it real for them." Bentwood gestured wildly in enthusiasm. "We're going to bring gamers here and show them how grim real fantasy adventures should be."

"I thought that was what we were doing all along."

"Yes, but they haven't been coming to us, so we're going to them. It's all worked out, advertising, teleportation stations, the works. We're going to revive the 'magical shop around the corner' bit, only we're renting a space to give us a permanent center of operations."

Hali shrugged. "Why pay when you can just magic up a store whenever you need one? I thought the big drain was keeping up the connection, not creating the building."

"I don't understand the mechanics, but the wizards in operations tell me they need a fixed, physical anchor for the kind of time-flow adjustments they're doing. We can cross over without losing centuries while we're gone. When we bring kids back here the time flow normalizes, so they can spend days here and be gone only seconds from Outworld."

"So what are we going to do? Run tour groups through in little buses so they can gawk at the ogres and elves in their native habitat?" Hali asked. "Much as I'd love to see the elf lords hawking souvenirs, it doesn't sound practical. I hate to be difficult . . ."

"Oh, sure." Bentwood rolled his eyes.

Hali ignored him. ". . . but *advertising*? Some of those people have really weird ideas about 'fantasy elements' like us, witches in particular, and I really don't think it's a good idea to bring us to their attention. You wouldn't believe the insanity of it all. One visit I made they were running in packs, burning and torturing dozens of perfectly normal people. I just about got burned at the stake myself once when I tried to talk some sense into a rabid preacher. We don't need that kind of trouble."

"Hali, babe, what century were you visiting? They don't do that sort of thing anymore. Well, not often, anyway, and not about witches. I hope." Bentwood shuddered. "I'm more worried about the bad press, but we've got that angle covered, believe me."

"Covered how?"

"We tell everybody it's just another game. See, technology there has gotten so advanced no one understands it all anymore. Stuff like that television might as well be magic. No one knows how it really works, but they all watch it, and just assume there's a scientific explanation behind it. We're going to show them magic right out in the open, and tell them it's a new invention and the mechanics have to be kept secret to keep the competition from stealing our device. The idea was invented by Outworlders, so the credibility's there already."

Hali interrupted indignantly. "You're using an Outworlder invention with magic? Are you crazy? You know their technology is magic-resistant."

"I'm not that stupid," Bentwood huffed. "We're just pretending to be using a technology that doesn't really exist. The Outworlders have this idea, they call it Cyberpunk for some reason, anyway they have this idea that people ought to be able to stick wires in their heads and talk directly to thinking machines called computers. Taken to an extreme, you could create a fantasy world in the mind of the computer, and people could visit through these cyber-connections. We're going to fake the process, putting metal caps on people, with lots of wires, in rooms filled with phony computers. Then we take the caps off, tell them the game is starting, and lead them out the back door straight here. The guys in marketing have come up with a great name for our world." He pulled out a slick brochure featuring a brightly colored castle filled with enough turrets to fulfill the wettest dreams of a mad Germanic king. At the top, in bold, blood-dripping Gothic capitals, it read "Welcome to GRIMMWORLD!"

CHAPTER
2

"**B**ENTWOOD, you're crazy," said Hali. Seated in one of Bentwood's leather-upholstered wingback chairs she looked through the slick brochure that outlined the myriad charms of Grimmworld: dimwitted ogres, wicked witches, princes charming, ladies fair, drafty castles, and dismal dungeons. The slick photographs made even the ogres look good, Hali noted. "This says people can come here and live out their fantasies, having grand adventures just like those games. There's no way we can handle that kind of scenario with any sort of volume."

"That's where you come in, doll. No more princesses in disguise taking up one witch's time for weeks. We're going to streamline the process, taking the kids through in groups. They're used to having companions on their game quests, so no one will think they're being slighted. And I want you to lead the very first group, Hali."

"No," said Hali, firmly. "I want nothing to do with this half-baked scheme."

"Hali, sweetheart, it's a great deal. This is where the future is, and I wanted to let you in on the ground floor. You're the best we've got when it comes to molding adolescents, you're an artist. But what can you do if you haven't got the material to work with? How long has it been since you've had a client at your place?"

Hali considered briefly. "Too long, but taking groups would compromise my standards, Bentwood. I believe in personal attention, trials and labors custom-tailored to each individual's needs. Misapplied torture is worse than no torture at all."

"Think of it as group therapy, sweetie. These aren't the troubled teens you're used to, the ones so depressed or disturbed that their negative energies eat a hole between the worlds.

"These are bored kids looking for thrills, an escape from humdrum reality into the realms of fantasy. What they really need is a dose of our kind of reality to shake them up, right?"

Reluctantly, Hali nodded. "I suppose."

"So all you have to do is tag along while they have their adventures and make sure they don't get killed."

"So much for art," Hali said bitterly. "Look, Bentwood, you've got me under contract, but this project doesn't exactly fit my job description. You want any cooperation from me, you're going to have to make some concessions."

Bentwood eyed her with wary apprehension. "Like what?"

"Like a proper house, of my choosing. The minute I pick out a house, you get it for me, no matter what the price. I'm not looking for a castle, or anything outrageous like that, but I do want quality. Handbuilt and expensive, not one of those cheap magical jobs that fall apart the minute someone casts a spell inside—and definitely not another of those Outworld abortions."

"Sure, Hali, you got it, whatever you say." Bentwood offered his hand. "Deal?"

Hali crossed her arms. "I want it on paper, signed in blood."

"Right, right," Bentwood assured her, crossing to his desk and pressing a button on the intercom. "Miss Silverbeeches, could you come in please?" Hysterical shrieking and monkey chatter answered him. Bentwood turned suspiciously to Hali. "This wouldn't happen to be any of your doing, would it? Would you mind undoing it, please?"

"Oh, all right." Hali waved one hand negligently in the direction of the doorway, which burst open to reveal the flustered receptionist, hanging by one arm from an overhead light fixture.

Eventually, the receptionist calmed down and produced a contract to Bentwood's hurried dictation. Bentwood stabbed his finger with the pointed end of his ceremonial pen, let the green-tinged blood well up into the nib, and signed the new agreement with a flourish. "There, happy now?" he asked Hali. He handed her the document.

She nodded and signed with her own penknife. "Fine. So when do I get to work?"

"Right away. You need to get outfitted. Bernie, too. Where is he?"

Hali looked around the reception area, then pointed a finger at the file cabinet. A spark of electricity zipped from her fingertip and around the bottom of the file cabinet.

"Awk! Ow!" Feathers all on end, Bernie staggered out from behind the cabinet. "Hey, I was just taking a nap. You didn't have to zap me!" he complained, rearranging his ruffled wing feathers with his beak. "It's gonna take me all day to get my feathers properly straightened out."

"Don't bother," said Bentwood. "You're not going to be a bird much longer. Birds are out, these days. You're getting a facelift, Bernie."

"What!" Bernie looked at Hali for confirmation. "I like being a bird. He can't do this to me, can he?"

Hali was busy examining the fine print of her contract. "It does say something about 'an appropriate familiar' here."

"Exactly," Bentwood said, "and appropriate means commercial. Crows aren't commercial; ravens are trite. We've done surveys, and our researchers have determined that the fantasy animal of today is the wombat!"

"What the heck is a wombat?" asked Bernie, crouching low in apprehension, neck feathers all on end.

"Good question," said Hali.

"Well, I'm not entirely sure," said Bentwood, "but they get an automatic response from people. Humorous, you know, like prunes."

"You can't turn me into a prune," wailed Bernie. He

jumped up quickly and landed on Hali's shoulder. "Don't let him do this to me," he begged, hiding in Hali's hair.

Hali picked him off the back of her neck with the ease of long practice, managing to pin both his feet and wings with one hand. "Don't panic, Bernie. He just means the words both sound funny."

Bentwood rummaged in one of the file drawers, and came up with a pair of glossy photos. "There, wombats. That's the ticket."

Hali studied the photos, holding Bernie so he could see. "Looks mammalian," observed Hali.

"Looks like a stupid teddy bear," sniffed Bernie. "I won't do it."

"According to the file notes," Bentwood noted, "it's a marsupial. And you don't have any choice in the matter. This is your big chance to become a star, Bernie, not just an extra but a major player in the biggest production this world has ever seen—Grimmworld!" He rolled out the final word in his best booming troll-under-the-bridge voice, and hugged himself in ecstasy.

"He's really lost it this time," Bernie told Hali. "Let's get out of here before he gets violent."

"Sorry, Bernie, I'll explain later, but we've got to do what he wants for now."

"Oh, right, what did he do, promise you the house of your dreams?" Bernie asked. He eyed Hali suspiciously and apparently found what he was looking for in her face. "You've sold me, your buddy and friend, down the river for a measly building." He struggled frantically, but Hali gripped him firmly in both hands, and shook him lightly.

"Stop that. Just this morning you said you were tired of being a crow. Now hold still and face it like the man you used to be," Hali said, setting him down on the floor, where Bernie cowered.

"I was a coward when I was a man, too," he whimpered, keeping his eyes closed as he waited for the fatal blow.

Hali concentrated on one photo, then set it aside, her brow furrowed in concentration. She stared at the ceiling for a moment, looking for inspiration, then pointed at Bernie. The shivering black lump on the floor grew larger, more rounded, with grey fur instead of feathers. "That's all there is to it. Check it out, Bernie."

The ball of fur uncurled slowly, revealing a button nose, sharp black eyes, rounded ears, and a low-to-the-ground, basically bearish body. "Wow, I'm fluffy," said Bernie. "And I've got hands. Sort of." He examined his forepaws closely, observing the sturdy claws. "Wicked." He tested them by scratching at his belly, then bent over to look closer at his abdomen. "Wait a minute. I'm still male, aren't I?'" he asked frantically, his head between his hind legs.

"You're male, Bernie. Take my word for it."

"Geeze, why am I the one who always gets stuck with the weird transformations? It's not fair," he complained to Bentwood. "Hali's as frumpy as they come, and you don't tell her to change."

"I was just getting to that," Bentwood said cautiously. "Now Hali, baby, I love you, but you really do have to update that look. Basic black is all well and good, but old women, well, they're totally passé. No one wants to look at grey hair and bony noses."

Hali crossed her arms and tapped her foot. A cold wind came up suddenly, and the lights dimmed. "And what, pray tell, did you have in mind instead?" she asked. Thunder rolled through the room.

Bentwood started talking as fast as he could. "It's nothing personal, you can be as convincing a crone as anyone, Hali, it's a great act you've got, but it's time to try something new. Age is out, youth is in, and I had envisioned you in something a bit more . . ." his hands described a generous hourglass figure . . . "*zaftig*, you know? Red hair, too. Red hair is very hot for witches, I understand. Glamorous, exotic, you know. . . ."

"Oh, right, what the stylish succubus is wearing this season." Hali waved her hands and appeared as a long-legged beauty with waving red hair reaching to a tiny waist, a skintight black dress with a very short shirt, a low neckline revealing a bosom so prominent Bernie doubted she could see her feet without bending over.

"Boy, what a time not to be human," he sighed, briefly wondering just what physical features his current form would find attractive. Something round and unbearably fluffy, he was certain.

Hali gestured again and reappeared as her unadorned, somewhat mousy self. "Forget it, Bentwood. I don't object to some minor modifications, but I'm not playing sex symbol. Particularly not if I have to shepherd any adolescent males. If you're selling sex as a part of all this, go get a nymph to be tour guide, I won't play that game."

"But, sweetie, you do it so well. You were perfect just then," Bentwood tried, then raised one hand to admit defeat. "All right, all right, I didn't think you'd agree, but it was worth a try. Look, our designers have some sketches—I told the boys in sales you wouldn't go for their idea. We have some backup designs I think you'll go for. Come on, I'll show you."

Bentwood turned to a small alcove just off the reception area, and pressed a button on the wall. Two doors slid back, revealing a tiny room with a mirrored back wall. Bentwood stepped back and gestured for Hali and Bernie to enter.

Suspicious, Bernie waddled over and poked his nose in. "This is either an elevator or a tiny torture chamber," he decided. "What's with all this Outworld technology around here, anyway?"

"It's showbiz, Bernie," Bentwood said. "We're going all out to impress the moguls. Got to have all the executive trimmings, so they don't get suspicious."

Hali bent down and with a grunt tucked the pudgy wombat under her arm, entering the elevator. "It's all a part of Bentwood's new scheme. We'll explain on the way."

Bentwood slipped into the elevator and went to a panel of buttons that ran from zero down to 666, with one lonely button off to the side labeled with an infinity symbol. The digital readout over the door read 530, and Bernie was startled to realize that he no longer felt claustrophobic about being so far underground. Being a wombat had its benefits, apparently. Bentwood pressed zero, and the elevator started up on the long trip to ground level.

Several minutes later, the elevator came to a stop, the doors sliding open to reveal a large warehouse, empty except for a ceiling filled with scaffolding and lights, and theatrical backdrops hung against the walls. Bentwood led the way to the door. There, stacked against the wall, they found several life-sized cutouts of ogres, trolls, and other of the fiercer and less-desirable denizens of Grimmworld.

Bernie pawed one frighteningly cheerful troll, noting that the figure was painted on half-inch fiberboard. "Okay, I got the idea about bringing Outworlders here for adventures, and making them think it's all an illusion of some sort. So what's with the props? These ogres aren't going to fool anybody."

Bentwood posed next to the troll proudly. "I modeled for this one, and it's very elegant, even if I do say so myself." Completely unclothed, Bentwood's painted figure suggested evolutionary ancestors more like frogs than apes, with translucent, damp-looking skin stretched tightly over a body all arms and legs, connected in the middle by a prominent potbelly in an off-white color that evoked the undersides of dead fish.

Bentwood left his portrait reluctantly. "Anyway, to make the scam convincing, we needed some sort of production facilities, and it had to be impressive. We put together some pictures of stages set with obviously phony monsters being filmed by phony futuristic cameras. The idea is that we stage phony pictures to use as a basis for the computers to work with. I don't know if it really makes sense or not, but the backers seem to be buying it. We've even brought a few in to see the back lot, and they've been really impressed by the size of our operation."

"Back lot?" Hali asked.

"Hollywood talk," Bentwood explained. "What they call the places where they make their moving pictures. Ours is right through here." He opened the door to bright sunlight and sheer pandemonium.

Bernie and Hali followed Bentwood out onto the building's rudimentary porch, and gazed in amazement at a virtual city. In all the chaos, the first thing to catch the eye was the line of giant neon letters that spelled out GRIMMWORLD on the hills above the city. Closer in, buildings of any and all eras of history crowded cheek by jowl with no noticeable concern for period or aesthetics in their juxtapositions. A half-timbered Tudor mansion huddled next to a Grecian temple, which seemed to turn a cold Classic shoulder to the next-door gas station shaped like a pair of giant cowboy boots and hat. Next to an Egyptian pyramid and massive Babylonian ziggurat, a single glass-walled skyscraper posed like an anorexic high-fashion model. Teepees, yurts, and a couple of silver Winnebagos clustered around the larger buildings like chicks gathered about a mother hen.

Everywhere, beings scattered about on apparently urgent errands. All wore human clothing, though the period varied as widely with the clothing as with the buildings. Roman military costume actually suited the ogres, Hali decided, but ruffled flamenco dresses did very little for trolls. Everywhere, workers carried props and more costumes, suggesting further sartorial solecisms in the offing.

"Okay, everybody, take a break," Bentwood shouted, and workers nearby picked up the cry, which was relayed through the streets. Almost instantly the workers disappeared, aside from a few who stopped to chat in the streets. A serious man in white shirt and slacks, horn-rimmed glasses, and headphones came up to Bentwood and proferred a clipboard, which Bentwood waved away. "Sorry, Jim, false alarm. Hali here's part of the staff." The man nodded and walked away briskly.

"This is all part of the act. We don't actually produce anything here," Bentwood explained to Hali, "but it has to look right. Mostly, we got the idea from that Hollywood place, but I guess we overdid it. The Outworlders all seem pretty impressed, even the ones that come from Hollywood. We're gonna get great press when we start bringing reporters in."

Bernie peered at the buildings. "I wouldn't, if I were you. This is as flashy as anything Hollywood ever came up with, but it doesn't look near phony enough. I used to be a bit of a movie buff, you know. I even took a vacation to Hollywood once. Those back-lot buildings are mostly fakes, false fronts with nothing behind 'em. Sooner or later someone's going to want to know how you managed to build so much so well— and where the heck this is. This place looks bigger than Disney World, even."

Bentwood beamed. "It is bigger. That was another of our models, only I figured it could stand to be a bit more substantial. If things go well with the first few test groups, we may open this place up as a theme park. We actually bought a huge piece of swamp for a cover, but the only building we've done there is a huge parking lot, and a fancy gateway with a tunnel that leads straight here, where we can build anything we want, and add a bit of local color with realistic odors and sounds and stuff. If people want medieval, we can give it to them, complete with middens and oubliettes. Those Outworld theme parks with their clean streets and pretty plastic coatings haven't a chance of competing."

"Just don't let any health inspectors in," Bernie muttered under his breath.

"What was that?" Bentwood asked suspiciously.

"Just admiring your planning and foresight," Bernie reassured him. Bentwood's scrawny chest swelled with pride.

"People do tend to believe what they want to," Hali mused. Bernie glanced at her sharply, but Bentwood was lost in his dreams of glory.

"Now you see the brilliance of it all! It'll work, I tell you, sweetheart. Grimmworld's going to be the biggest hit of all time. I can feel it. We're going to be rich in the Outworlds, and the residuals in magic energy will be huge. Comic books, action figures, stuffed wombats with suckers on their feet: I tell you this is going to be a marketing bonanza."

"Gah," Bernie muttered, examining his paws. "No one's putting suckers on my feet and living to tell about it." He flexed his sturdy claws thoughtfully and eyed Bentwood's bare, slightly mossy feet, but refrained from testing his combat capabilities so soon.

Still recounting the various marketing possibilities, Bentwood led the way past a Chinese temple to a two-story building built in blocky but highly functional Bauhaus style. Inside, photos and drawings adorned cork bulletin boards that lined all the walls. The drawings featured Grimmworld residents in a variety of costumes, including a page full of wombats decked out in a wide variety of neckwear including cravats, bow ties, a bolo tie, and even an improbable twenty-seven-foot scarf in multicolored stripes. Hali lifted Bernie so he could see.

"I'll pass on the neckwear, if it's all the same to you,"

Bernie said. "I don't have much of a neck at this point, and most of those things are guaranteed to make walking difficult. The top hat's not bad," he observed of a subsequent sketch.

"No go," said a tall man in an apron covered with smears of paint. He was wiping his hands on a dingy grey cloth, and the smell of paint thinner hung like a cloud around him. "Wombats are burrowers. You'd never be able to keep it on."

"You're kidding," said Bernie. "What else do you know?"

"Not much," said the man, and introduced himself. "John Painter, design staff. About all we were able to dig up in our research is that they're marsupials, largely nocturnal, and live in burrows."

"Well, at least you'll have better night vision," Hali said.

"Yeah, but I think I'm nearsighted," said Bernie, peering at the pictures on the wall.

Hali sighed, wiggled her fingers, and concentrated. Pince-nez glasses appeared on Bernie's snout, and he crossed his eyes trying to see them. "Hey," Bernie complained. "What are these things?"

"Glasses, stupid. Look through them, not at them," Hali told him. "Do they work?"

"Yeah, they do. Couldn't you just fix my eyes, though?"

"I think wombats are supposed to be nearsighted, Bernie. If I mess with the basic plan, the spell won't hold for long," Hali said. "If you want to risk a spontaneous reformation . . ."

"That's OK, I just feel funny with these things perched on my nose."

"They look great, though," the artist observed, cocking his head as he considered. "Cute touch."

"Cute." Bernie moaned. "Familiars aren't supposed to be cute."

"They're not usually wombats, either," the artist observed. "We're breaking new ground here. You could try a monocle, maybe."

Hali turned the pince-nez into a monocle, which promptly fell to the floor and bounced with a fragile ping.

Bernie sighed. "I don't think my eye sockets are built for those things. I'll stick with the first model," he said, and immediately went cross-eyed again as a new pair appeared on his nose. "Give a guy a little warning, will you?" he told Hali crossly. He felt highly undignified, tucked under Hali's arm like a little child. However, curiosity outweighed pride, and as a wombat he was built a little too close to the ground to see much around him.

While Bernie pondered the injustices of the universe, which gave all the power (and good eyesight) to the thoroughly undeserving, Hali and Bentwood followed the artist into a nearby studio. Fashion sketches lined the walls, showing women in a variety of witch costumes that ran the gamut from the basic black of the Wicked Witch of the West to the sparkle and glitter of Glinda the Good. Hali scanned the walls, and Bentwood watched her expression closely.

"See anything you like?" he asked hopefully.

"No," said Hali bluntly. "I think you've got Hollywood on the brain, Bentwood. No one's going to take me seriously in any of these outfits. In their own ways, each is as overdone as the other."

"Hali, sweetie, darling, these are great designs, by the best designers we could get. There's got to be something here you'll accept."

"I like my own look."

"I like being a crow," Bernie commented. "Did I get any say in the matter?"

John Painter looked Hali over. "Now that I see you, I think maybe we were wrong to stick with strictly witchy outfits. You've got the height to pull off something dramatic, a little more in the wizardly line, you know, embroidered robes, big cape with stand-up collar, turn the broom into a tall staff . . ." He grabbed a piece of paper and started sketching furiously. Without looking up, he asked, "What kind of symbols do you like?"

"Moons, stars, magical herbs—easy on the flowers—that sort of thing," Hali answered, looking over his shoulder. "Make the skirt shorter, add some black boots, maybe. I expect to be doing a lot of hiking. I'll be wearing the belt pouch I've got on, so it's got to be a belted look. No, that's too dull, try silver. Not bad." She took the rough sketch from the artist and showed it to Bentwood, who shook his head.

"I can't visualize it. Let's see what it looks like on," he suggested.

Hali concentrated, blurred briefly, and came back into focus with a new look, younger but somehow more dangerous. Straight black hair fell around her shoulders, with a dramatic white streak flowing back from her forehead. Her face looked less sharp, firmer at the jaw, with oddly light silver-grey eyes to add a sinister touch. The dress was simple, but made of a heavy, rich material that draped dramatically over Hali's hips. Subtle embroidery covered the fabric, worked with shining black thread that shimmered when Hali moved. A silver belt hung low on her hips, its intricate design echoed in silver patterns that bordered the wide sleeves and the deep V-shaped neckline. A heavy black cloak hung from Hali's shoulders, held in place with two large circular brooches. The cloak's large collar, heavily encrusted with gold and silver embroidery, stood up to frame Hali's face. In one hand, she held a long oaken staff that reached above her head.

She turned, checking the swing of the skirt. "What do you think?" she asked. "Got a mirror around here?"

"I like the hair," Bentwood said, "but I don't know. It's just not flashy enough."

"Looks good to me," said Bernie. "You look like a high priestess or something. Kind of dangerous."

"There's a mirror in the ladies' room down the hall." Painter pointed the way, and Hali left to check her dress. Bentwood paced the room, looking up nervously when Hali returned looking positively cheerful.

"Not bad," she said. "I like the staff, it's got a real nasty look to it. The embroidery's pretty classy, and the cloak adds real dash—I could get used to this."

"Don't you think it's too bland?" asked Bentwood. "I mean, we want to make a real impression here. How about scarlet or purple instead of black? With a hot pink lining for the cloak, maybe. And those black boots are so boring, sweetheart. How about ruby slippers and striped socks? Now there's an eye-catching ensemble for you."

"Oh, give it up, Bentwood," Hali snapped. "I'll impress the kids more if I don't look like a color-blind refugee from an insane asylum. I've raised my cheekbones and colored my hair for you, and that's about as much as you're going to get."

Somewhat gloomily, Bentwood assented. "It will have to do, I guess. We're running short on time, anyway." He thanked the artist and led the way out of the building and into the twisted streets of the city outside. Hali followed matter-of-factly, swinging her staff and trying different holds. Bernie trundled along in the rear, amusing himself by experimenting with the different gaits made possible by four legs. None of them, however, proved conducive to excessive speed, and thinking too closely about what each leg was doing invariably tripped him up. From time to time Hali and Bentwood turned to shout for him to catch up, and they finally stopped to wait.

"No lollygagging, now. You're going to have to make better time on our trip or you're going to get left behind," Hali told Bernie sternly.

"You should have thought about that before you changed me," Bernie said. "Face it, this body isn't made for speed."

"No problem," Bentwood assured Hali. "With a group of gamers you're not going to be traveling fast, and you might even want to get a pack mule Bernie can ride."

"Oh, great," Hali said in disgust, "you expect me to handle livestock, too?"

"Mules are old hat," Bernie drawled. "I vote we get a llama. Very trendy, really, Hali darling."

"This is serious!" Bentwood shouted, stamping his feet in pent-up frustration. "I won't be mocked by a waddling fur-ball, and you, Hali, will do anything you have to to make this work. I've got your signature on a binding contract, and I'll have you know the unions are backing this project."

"I'd love to know what concessions you made them, too," Hali said.

"They made the concessions," Bentwood announced triumphantly. "I just pointed out that if there's no work to be done, the unions have no power. The leaders were surprisingly amenable to negotiation."

"Yeah, but wait till the rank and file catch on, Bentbrain. They're going to see running groups through as having to work more for the same pay, and as far as I'm concerned they're right."

"This is insubordination," Bentwood shouted, his face turning a deep green. "You don't know anything about the politics of the situation. Just do it, don't ask questions." He stomped off down the road, leaving Hali and Bernie behind to look at each other in confusion. Bentwood finally turned and glared back at the two, hands on hips. "All right, all right, you two, move it! We have to be at the Black Buck Inn in thirty minutes."

Hali looked at Bernie, who shrugged. With a grunt of effort, she picked him up and jogged to catch up with the petulant troll, who continued down the road and out of the makeshift backlot city into the wide grassy meadows beyond.

CHAPTER
3

THE administrative caves had been carved out of the rocky mountains of the Silverrock range, and the backlot city had been placed strategically at one end of a broad plateau that nestled against the foothills. Though rounded by centuries of wear, the edge of the plateau was steep and rocky, and the dirt road out of the city became a narrow path that twisted its way down the slope in multiple switchbacks. Bentwood's awkwardly long arms and legs were surprisingly agile on the rough terrain. He left the trail and headed straight down the slope, pausing only as necessary to prevent mussing his cravat.

At the bottom, the trail widened into a road again, and wandered off into the woods, following a cheerful brook that ran into the pleasant valley below. Appreciative neither of bright sunny days nor of trees (trolls being fond of wet, rocky places), Bentwood hurried along without bothering to look at the scenery. A few minutes later, he arrived at a rambling old inn that looked as if it might have grown there beside the road, its broad thatched roof resembling nothing so much as the toadstools that come up in the warm days after a good spring rain. Hanging from a tall post outside the door was the inn's sign, which showed a leaping black deer on a bright yellow background.

Sulking a bit, Bentwood waited outside the inn, pacing back and forth under the tall oaks that surrounded the building. After a few minutes Hali arrived, somewhat out of breath, her long staff in one arm and Bernie under the other.

"You know, Bentwood, if you'd told me earlier, we could have teleported to that clearing back there," Hali gasped. "Even flying would be easier. This little bugger is heavy." Awkwardly, she let the protesting wombat slide to the ground.

"You know you can't use magic around this inn. It's not stable in this world."

"The inn's not stable in any world—that's its charm. The clearing's not that close; I've used it before, no problem. What's eating you, Bentwood?"

"Yeah," Bernie chimed in. "You've never paid any attention to my insults before. Does that mean I'm actually worthy of your august attention?"

"No!" snapped Bentwood, before he could think. He glared at the smirking wombat, then whirled on Hali. "Why can't you just accept that this will work? It has to work! I've put months of planning into it, then you come along at the last minute and try to tear it all apart." He jumped up and down in a springy, trollish tantrum. "This is my baby, and I won't let you destroy it!"

"All right, all right, Bentwood," Hali soothed. "I know how much this means to you, and I really do believe that our world is in trouble—I just want to make sure that what we're doing is right." She patted him on the shoulder firmly, holding him on the ground. "I'm going to do my best," she swore.

"Now go in the inn and get a drink and calm down," she told the viridian-faced troll. "We've still got time on that deadline." Gently but firmly she steered Bentwood into the inn, and sighed deeply when the door closed behind him. She sat down heavily on the wooden bench just outside the door.

"What was that all about?" asked Bernie, putting one paw on her knee.

"I'll bet you anything he's lying about the unions," Hali

said, absently ruffling his fur. "An energy crisis would have to be a lot more apparent before they'd make any kind of concession, especially if it means more work at less pay—not a popular sort of deal for the bosses to make. If he's been bribing the officials there's going to be hell to pay." She shook her head. "I wish he'd come clean. I have no way of telling if this crisis is real, or if Bentwood's manufactured it as an excuse to go ahead with this project.

"I'm no world saver. All I ever wanted was to have a decent house in the middle of nowhere, do my job, and not bother anybody. Well, most of the time, anyway. A girl's got to cut loose once in a while. Now all we can do is play along and see what happens."

"Could be fun," Bernie offered.

"Yeah, right," Hali said. "Just like the plague."

Bernie tsked. "Attitude, attitude," he said, shaking his head and ducking quickly under the bench before she could swat him.

"Witches are supposed to be crabby," she informed him haughtily. "It's part of the art."

Bentwood strolled out of the inn, draining a large stein. "Mmm, great stumpwater they serve here," he said, then looked at Hali and scowled. "What are you doing sitting about? You should be getting ready."

Leaning heavily on her staff, Hali got up slowly, and looked down at Bentwood from under lowered lids. "Anything you say, boss. Just what exactly am I supposed to be getting ready?"

"Let me show you, doll-baby," enthused Bentwood, already back to his ebullient self. "We've got it all set up back here." Taking Hali by the arm, he led her to a small building off to one side of the inn. Opening the door wide, he gestured expansively. "All the equipment your adventurers need is here, all you have to do is point it out and let them choose for themselves."

Hali eyed the supply shed's contents skeptically. Wall racks held a variety of weapons, each in a wide range of sizes: axes, hatchets, broadswords, rapiers, shortswords, daggers, throwing knives, spears, clubs, staffs, maces, slings, whips, and bows with full quivers beside them. Below this array, shields and armor leaned against the wall.

"Looks like you're expecting a small war," Hali observed. "What about little things like food and clothing?"

Bentwood pointed to a back corner Hali had overlooked. There, dark lumps turned out to be a pile of travelers' packs, already stocked with dry food and water bottles. Several durable cloaks hung from pegs above, and two shelves turned out to hold piles of folded clothing. Hali thumbed through the clothing quickly. "Looks practical. Not exactly exciting, though."

"We'll start them out with just the bare essentials, but each one gets some money. You get them outfitted, spend the night at the inn, and then walk to Fairehaven Town. Two days' easy walk to break them in, then you let 'em loose in the markets, where the real adventure begins."

"What's the objective?"

"You're going to have to wing it, I'm afraid. The whole point of role-playing games is that players get to choose their actions."

"What if nothing turns up? We don't want things to get too dull," Hali pointed out.

"So we throw a couple of ogres at you now and then," Bentwood shrugged. "The contract ogres have no defense against your spells, so there's no real risk. You understand," he told Hali seriously, "the last thing we want is a human fatality. If people think this process is really dangerous, we'll be out of business in no time. It's all a game, no one really gets hurt. Right?"

"Gotcha, Bentwood. Superficial wounds and blisters are okay, though, I hope. No pain, no gain, and all that."

"So long as you can clear them up before the kids go home, sure. No prolonged torture, though. We don't want to scare people off, just give them a few thrills."

"You're taking all the fun out of dungeons," Hali complained.

"You don't fool me," Bentwood said complacently. "Your idea of torture is making someone clean out a septic tank with a spoon, and it just won't sell, believe me.

"Look, I've got to go help coordinate on the other end. We

need to get back to the clearing. That's where the group is going to come through. We figured we'd keep it out of the way, to minimize the initial shock." He led the way back up the road to the first large clearing, a flat, grassy spot surrounded by leafy trees. Bentwood stopped by a large rock set up beside the road, and pointed out some carvings on one side. "The controls are here. Just press the sideways figure eight when I'm in the middle of the meadow. Oh, and Hali, baby—do me a favor? Humanize my skin color, would you, sweetheart? I want to go mingle with the crowd on the other side."

Hali raised one eyebrow. "How about some pants and shoes, while I'm at it?"

"I think he's going to need a whole new body," suggested Bernie.

Bentwood sighed patiently. "Go teach your grandmother to suck eggs, Hali. I've been doing this for some time. There's clothing waiting for me, it's just that I hate all that makeup."

Hali shrugged and concentrated, and Bentwood's dark skin lost its greenish tinge, shifting to slightly warmer tones. Bentwood scrutinized the backs of his hands and grimaced. "I don't know how you humans stand it. Red's such an ugly color, like those revolting rims around your eye, all fire hot and prickly looking. Green's such a lovely cool color—I've always thought my cheeks had the fair bloom of the algae you find in mountain brooks. This, uck," he shuddered.

"It's not easy being pink," Hali admitted. "Are you ready?"

Bentwood braced himself, feet slightly apart, hands behind his back. "Ready."

Hali pressed the button, and Bentwood faded slowly from view.

"How boring," Bernie said critically. "They should add some sparkles and sound effects, whooshing noises maybe, or tinkling bells. Something."

"You know wizards," Hali said. "All technology and no imagination." She found a smooth log, apparently polished by the seats of generations of passersby, and settled herself to wait. "Now all we can do is wait."

"Great," said Bernie. "If you don't mind, I'm going to see about this burrowing business." Hali waved a hand in dismissal, and Bernie trundled off happily toward the woods, flexing his claws in anticipation. In his experience, the best pleasures in life came from following instinct, and his instincts right now were leading him toward a rousing encounter with some nice, soft leaf mold.

Bentwood, in the meantime, materialized in the back room of his new gaming shop, The Troll's Den. Located on a pleasant side street in the shopping district of a major city (Bentwood wasn't entirely clear which one—his grasp of Outworld geography was only slightly better than that of the average American elementary-school student), the shop was long and largely windowless, which suited Bentwood fine. Here in the back, one door led directly into a tiny parking space behind the building; at the opposite end of the room another door opened into the back of the shop. A third door announced the presence of a bathroom, but this tiny cubicle with its dingy fixtures was currently being used to hold the stock overflow, and anyone entering was risking a horrible death-by-bludgeoning in an avalanche of miniature lead figurines and shrink-wrapped gamebooks.

The back room, on the other hand, was immaculate, a maniacal cross between a dentist's office, hair salon, and NASA command center, full of wires and keyboards and blinking lights. Long padded chairs with shiny metal helmets attached lined one wall, facing a row of mirrors that was repeated on the opposite wall. Anyone seated in those chairs was bound to see themselves repeated infinitely in the mirrors, no matter where they looked, and Bentwood was singularly proud of the effect, which, he hoped, would evoke the idea of worlds within worlds. Actually, most Outworlders were reminded of the barber shop, beauty parlor, or fancy restroom where they first experienced this encounter with infinity, but to date no one had ever bothered to mention this in Bentwood's hearing. (In Grimmworld, mirrors were rightly considered dangerous objects, and placing two mirrors opposite each other was known to cause a truly annoying and occasionally deadly effect referred to by wizards as "feedback.")

Bentwood went to a cupboard and pulled out trim white

slacks with suspenders, and a custom-made pair of oversized white canvas shoes. With some effort, he managed to work each gangly leg into the appropriate pant leg, and fastened the belt around his round belly, quickly pulling up the suspenders before the pants could slide down again. Bentwood delicately worked his prehensile toes into the slip-on shoes, and then, with considerable reluctance, removed his elegant smoking jacket, replacing it with a fluorescent green silk shirt, open at the neck, and a white linen blazer. An embroidered badge on the blazer's breast pocket showed the elaborate castle that also graced the brochures, with the legend "Grimmworld" on a banner below. Draping a few gold chains around his neck, Bentwood checked his image in the mirror, and decided he more than looked the part of a successful producer.

Normally, the store had few customers at any time, its musty quiet disturbed only occasionally by small clusters of preadolescent males who pounced on the latest games and packaged scenarios, eagerly discussing the bloodshed potential of the inevitable new-and-improved combat techniques. Older customers tended to slink in quietly and go straight to their area of interest, scanning the fantasy games in particular with the same faint air of guilt normally found in preteen boys at a magazine rack looking at a *Playboy* centerfold. More forthright were the wargamers, confident that their hobby was justifiable as a sort of historical study.

A large part of the store's business went to a minority group that seldom gamed, but bought tiny lead figures and plastic models by the dozen anyway, finding more enjoyment in the process of assembly and painting than in the killing of orcs or in restaging the battle of Waterloo. Some of their better efforts were on sale in the shop: military aircraft hung from the ceiling on transparent plastic fishing line, while assorted fantasy figures and small armies (painted with varying skill) were on parade in a glass-fronted cabinet near the desk.

The shop's official human proprietor sat behind the long counter that ran down one side of the shop. A genial, older man with a flowing white beard, he wore brightly colored T-shirts, generally bearing designs involving skeletons and roses, a variation on the classic *memento mori* theme of which Bentwood approved, though he found the occasional "Grateful Dead" legend vaguely suggestive of necrophilia, which was carrying a good thing just a bit too far.

Today, the store was filled to overcrowding, aisles packed with an impatient audience. Nervous parents accompanied their eager offspring, trying to persuade the younger children that they really had no use for twenty-sided dice molded from brilliantly-colored transparent plastic. Banners hung from the ceiling and shelves, touting Grimmworld as "The Ultimate Gaming Experience" and "A fairy tale come true— Grimmer than you ever believed possible!" Bright lights near the front entrance suggested that the news media had arrived. Bentwood pushed his way through the crowd, stopping just short of the first rank that circled an interviewer and his camera crew. The impeccably groomed reporter thrust his microphone at a young woman, obviously one of the lucky gamers about to try the latest sensation.

"Now, let's ask Tracy Cantero, the only woman in this party. How does it feel to be one of the first to experience Grimmworld?" asked the reporter. "Do you think it can possibly live up to its advertising?"

"I guess we're going to find out," the girl responded. She shrugged, and grinned nervously. "I'm looking forward to it."

Bentwood reached out from the crowd and waved quickly behind the reporter's back. At the signal, a slick young man came forward quickly, and put his arm around Tracy's shoulder, ignoring her irritated glance. "I'm sure they're all looking forward to it," said the PR flack with a wide, ingratiating smile. "This is their chance to make history, as the first gamers to experience the leading edge of computer technology. Grimmworld takes the idea of cyberspace to new heights, creating a world that seems perfectly real to the gamers, with no seams or awkward interfaces to spoil the effect.

"It's been a pleasure talking to you all, but now it's time for our lucky, chosen few to play the game you've all been talking about. Ready, kids?" he asked the grimacing quartet. "Right, let's go then." He waved off the cameras and shepherded the four to the back of the store, where the disappointed crowd was turned away with only a glimpse of the high-tech equipment in the back room. Bentwood just barely managed to squeeze through the crowd and into the room before the door closed with an emphatic click.

An efficient crew, all in white lab coats, surrounded the four gamers and quickly escorted them to the waiting chairs. One woman in glasses, her hair tied back in an efficient bun and carrying a clipboard, stood in front of the chairs and addressed the gamers while the shiny metal helmets were carefully adjusted over their heads.

"I'm Doctor Burkhart," she introduced herself, "and on behalf of the Grimmworld Corporation I want to assure you that the process you're about to undergo is completely painless—in fact, you won't feel a thing. The helmets being placed on your heads generate extremely sensitive, low-energy magnetic fields that interact with your brain waves, allowing our computers to send the images and sensations of Grimmworld directly to your brain. You effectively become part of the world of the computer program—as far as your brain is concerned, Grimmworld is as real as anything you've ever experienced.

"Now, the helmets are in place. Is everything ready?" she asked a technician at one of the computer banks, who gave her a thumbs up. "All right, in a moment we will activate the helmets. You will experience a brief darkness and the game will begin. Ready . . . now." The lights went out.

In the darkness, a voice called out. "OK, they're out." The lights came on again, revealing the gamers unconscious in their chairs. The techs moved efficiently, running wandlike scanners over the gamers, and gently removing any electronic items. From limp arms they stripped all watches, even one stem winder. Then, without a word, the techs turned and left the room by the back door. Bentwood went over to the doctor, who was leaning over the gamers. "All set?"

"All ready," she said. "It's a simple, preset spell. They're set to revive at the snap of a finger." She turned and taped a large note to the mirror. "Shall we go?" Bentwood offered her his arm, and they went to the back door. On the threshold, Bentwood turned and with a grand gesture snapped his fingers, and quietly shut the door behind them.

The gamers lay quietly for a few moments, then Leo Bates opened his eyes. "Hey, nothing's happening," he complained. When there was no response, he pushed the helmet back and awkwardly sat up. Overweight and pasty-faced, with unkempt brown hair, he looked like a large baby who had not quite mastered the art of sitting. One who was pouting at the loss of a promised toy, to boot. "Geeze, what a fraud," he said. "They've gone and left us here and nothing even happened. Get up, you guys, it's over."

"Weird," said Oliver Miller, a tall blonde teen on the next couch. He sat up easily and looked around. "After all that publicity, you'd think they'd have managed things better."

"It's just as I suspected," said the tall thin man. "All talk and no substance. I was hoping to be able to write a scathing review of the game for my magazine, *The Gamesman*, but now it appears I will have to settle for exposing this fraud."

"Hey, you're Richard Jamison, the reviewer," the fat boy exclaimed. "Wow, you're a celebrity! I'm Leo Bates." He put his hand out to shake, but was ignored by the tall critic. "This is great. I've always wanted to write games. I've done some great scenarios. There's this one I've got, based on a game I played. I could tell you all about it, and you could write it up, and we'd make a fortune."

"Undoubtedly yet another routine variation on a tired game. Your ideas hardly merit my attention," Jamison sniffed. "Go away, boy, you bother me."

"Hey guys, there's a note," observed Tracy Cantero, going to the mirror. "It says 'Read Me.' " She pulled it off the mirror and opened it, reading aloud: " 'Knock three times, and open the door; you'll find the world you're looking for.' " She looked around at the others and grinned. "I think this is our first clue."

"Doggerel," Jamison said. "Knock three times—how trite. And the *Alice in Wonderland* reference is hardly original." He pulled a tiny notebook out of his breast pocket and began to write.

"This is a fairy-tale world," said Bates cheerfully. "You've got to expect some old standards. I've been reading up. At least there really is an adventure. I don't think I could have stood it if this had turned out all fake. So far everything feels real enough."

"Hey, we ought to get going," said the tall blonde boy. "Which door do we try first?"

Jamison consulted his notebook. "You must be the Miller boy, Oliver Miller. Seventeen years old, high school student. You got in by winning the tournament at the Southside Fantasy Convention, and then made the first team by lottery. You," he pointed at Tracy, "are Tracy Cantero, the token female, I gather. Fifteen, in private school. Did you pay for the privilege of playing, or did they pay you?"

"I paid my way, and went through the lottery just like everyone else," said Tracy furiously. "I've played dozens of games, and I've been a game master at least a dozen times—and written my own scenarios."

"I've played thousands of games!" Leo interrupted. "Hundreds of thousands. I've worked my way up from first level cleric to paladin and even to god level, twice."

"Leo Bates, nineteen. Entered college early, but thanks to continual gaming you've flunked out of so many classes you may never get past the freshman level. So typical," Jamison sneered.

"Well, how about you?" Tracy demanded. "You're a little old to be living for games, aren't you?"

"Hardly," Jamison said. "I am a writer. I write about games because I consider them a significant development in modern society. Besides, I am only twenty-eight—and I have my Ph.D. in liberal studies. My thesis was on the psychological and sociological implications of role-playing games among maladjusted adolescents."

"Look," Oliver interrupted, "this bickering isn't going to get us anywhere. We'll find out more about each other by playing than by talking. Let's pick a door and get started."

Leo tried the door to the shop, and found it locked. "I guess this one's out."

"Hey," Tracy said. "We're supposed to be a team. You just can't go opening any door you want to. There could be a trap or something."

"Nah, not this early in the game," Leo said smugly.

"Well, fine then," Tracy snapped, knocking on the door to the bathroom, and pushing it as wide as she could. "Yuck. This doesn't look too promising." The others, looking over her shoulder, agreed.

"That leaves the back door—the most obvious egress, I should think," Jamison said, knocking three times with a measured beat, and opening the door to the sunny meadow outside.

CHAPTER
4

STILL seated across the meadow, Hali watched dubiously as the party awkwardly exited the shop door, which appeared to float two feet above the ground. She groaned as Leo Bates tripped on the invisible step just below the doorway, tumbling face first in the grass. "Keeping this group alive is going to be a real challenge," she muttered under her breath.

"Hey!" Leo exclaimed, propping himself up on one elbow and picking at the grass squashed by his fall. "This ground is hard. The grass feels real too. Look, I even skinned my elbow—and the blood looks real!" With a hand from Oliver, he got up and eagerly showed this discovery to the other gamers. "Talk about realism!"

"Hmmph," Jamison grunted. "Hopelessly mundane, no imagination at all. They obviously filmed this little valley somewhere. It's hardly a creative fantasy environment."

Confident she'd seen enough, Hali got up and coughed. "Ahem," she added loudly for good measure, as an argument seemed to be breaking out. "If you've got your feet, we should be getting on. I'm your witch for this adventure, and I suggest you don't mess with me. This is my familiar, Bernie," she looked around for a second, then snapped her fingers. "Right, I forgot. Bernie, front and center!" she called loudly.

A frantic squeal came from the direction of the woods. "On my way," called Bernie, running low to the ground and faster than he'd managed before. He skidded to a stop in front of Hali, and shook his head quickly to rid himself of clinging bits of loam. "Wombat reporting for duty," he saluted, and grimaced when he realized that he'd lost his glasses in the wood.

"That's a wombat?" asked Leo. "Cool, I've never seen one before."

"Whatever it is, it's awfully cute," said Tracy, bending down for a closer look. "And it talks, too."

Bernie gave Hali a deeply wounded look. "Wombats are trendy," he quoted. "Oh, sure they are. And she called me cute! I could just curl up and die."

"Gosh, I'm sorry," said the girl. "I know how you feel. I get it, too. Forget I said it, will you? How do you feel about ear rubs, or are they too demeaning?"

"Oh, not at all," breathed Bernie, looking up at her with the sudden light of adoration in his eyes. "By all means, rub away."

"Bernie," said Hali, "we don't have time for this nonsense." She turned back to the gamers. "As I was saying, I am a witch, and my name is Hali."

"Holly, like in bush?" asked Leo.

"No, Hali as in halitosis," she snapped viciously. Taking a deep breath, she tried again. "Dusk is coming, and we have to get to the inn where we're going to spend the night. Please follow me, this way." With a flourish of her cape, she turned and stalked down the road.

"Boy, a real heart-warming welcome," Leo said.

"Don't let it bother you, she's just touchy about her name," Bernie confided. "It really was Holly, like the bush; all the witches were named for plants, once upon a time. Then the fashion changed, and everyone switched to names like Malevola or Sinestra, Mistress of Darkness. Even a Hagatha, if you can believe it. Hali tried changing her name, but never remembered to answer to the new one, so she finally gave up, sort of. Just humor her." Bernie looked around and realized the others were almost out of sight. "Speaking of which, we'd better run or she'll get really grumpy."

"So, big deal. What can she do to us?" Leo asked, disinclined to run under any circumstance.

"I used to be human," said Bernie, meaningfully.

"Right," said Leo, starting to run after the others, slowing to a shuffling jog after a couple of steps. It was a pace that suited Bernie fine, and the two trundled on down the road, arriving at the inn only seconds after the rest.

Hali raised one eyebrow. "Winded, are you? We'll have to do something about that, won't we." She smiled happily, and Bernie shuddered.

"Yeah," panted Leo. "Seven-league boots would be real nice. I'd even take a flying horse about now."

"I had something a little more basic in mind," Hali said. "That can wait till tomorrow. For now, we need to check into our rooms." She entered the inn and waved her staff at the barkeep, who wiped his hands and came out from behind the bar.

"Hali," he said genially, and shook her hand. "Bentwood said you'd be by with a group. You've got the three rooms at the top of the stairs, just go on up, it's all arranged."

"Thanks, Gordy," Hali said. "Save me a seat at the bar, willya?"

"No problem. I can't wait to hear all about this new start of Bentwood's."

Hali led the party upstairs, and assigned one room to the three males, one to herself and Bernie. To her delight, Tracy got a room to herself, provoking a protest from the men.

"Considering how much this adventure costs, I'd think we would at least get private rooms," Jamison complained. "Three to one room is ridiculous. And what about luggage? I have no nightshirt or toothbrush. I refuse to go to bed without a toothbrush."

"Fine," said Hali, shrugging. "Don't go to bed. Nightshirts you'll have to do without, at least until we get to the city. You'll each get some gold which you can spend as you wish. If you really want to pack a nightshirt all over the countryside after that, no one's going to stop you."

Hali went into her best drill sergeant mode, looking each

gamer up and down with a jaundiced eye. "I don't know what exactly you were expecting, but this is no painless little fairy-tale adventure. As long as you're here, you're in a real world, one with all the rough edges reality can provide, and no one's going to go out of their way to make things easy for you. The sooner you accept that, the better you'll get along. Tomorrow, we'll get you outfitted for travel. For now, the night's your own, and I suggest you make the best of it, but go easy on the ale. We'll be getting a very early start." She turned away, and herding Bernie with her staff, marched into her own room, slamming the door behind her.

"That group's going to be trouble," she said, propping her staff in one corner and shedding her heavy cape. She took off her belt pouch and dug inside, coming up with a hairbrush. "The fat kid's par for the course," she said, brushing her hair in front of the room's one tiny wall mirror, "but what the heck is that adult doing here? He's got one heck of an attitude problem, and he's a bit too old to cure."

"I like the little brunette," offered Bernie. "Spunky, cute—and she'd die before admitting she can't do anything the guys can."

"She'll do okay if she doesn't get in over her head. I suspect the quiet blonde kid's the same. It's just that they're all looking for high adventure, and I hate to think what trouble they're going to manage to get into." She put the hairbrush down, and checked her skirt. "I think I'll set wards around the place, too—don't want our brave adventurers wandering off on their own, now do we?"

"Hey," said Bernie, sitting up suddenly. "I just thought. Should we explain to them about outhouses and chamber pots?"

"Are you kidding?" Hali said. "That's part of the adventure as far as I'm concerned." She strapped on her belt pouch again, and went to the door. "Are you coming down, or do you want to stay up here?"

"I'm coming down," Bernie said decisively. "If I've got to be nocturnal, I'm going to take advantage of it. Party, party, party." He managed a little shuffling dance step out the door.

"Don't complain when you have to get up at dawn," Hali

warned. "You lost your glasses, I notice. You want another pair?"

"Nah, I think I'll go au naturel. It's not like there's much to look at from down here, anyway."

Bernie faced the feat of going down stairs on four legs with equanimity, after a few false starts finally choosing to go down backward. By the time he reached the barroom floor Hali had disappeared outside, and the gamers were arguing noisily at one of the tavern's trestle tables. Bernie waddled up to the bar, then looked up at the bar stools, debating his chances of climbing one successfully. Not very good, he decided. "Excuse me," he said.

"What?" asked the barkeeper, looking around.

"Down here," Bernie called. "I could use a lift."

"Well, well," said Gordy, coming around the bar. "We don't get too many visitors from Oz around here." He hefted Bernie gently and set him down on a stool.

"Oz? The place with the munchkins?" Bernie asked. "You mean it really exists?"

"You look like an Aussie, but you sure don't sound like one," the bartender laughed. "By Oz, I mean Australia. I thought that's where wombats came from."

"Probably is," Bernie said, "but I'm from New York. Used to be human, then a crow, but Bentwood had this idea about wombats being trendy. At least they're nocturnal. Crows aren't much for nightlife, you know. Give me something big and highly alcoholic, with a root vegetable in it."

"One bloody mary with carrot coming up. You want it in a glass?"

"Mmm," Bernie considered, feeling his muzzle to gauge its size. "This is new to me. Maybe we'd better go with a saucer."

Hali came in with a cold gust of night air, and settled on a stool next to Bernie. "Looks like our little friends are enjoying themselves," she observed. "Amaretto sour, Gordy. So, what's the latest gossip?"

"Not much," said Gordy. "Business has been incredibly slow, but I expect you know about that."

"It's slow even here?" Hali asked, surprised. "I figured

you at least would be getting customers, what with the inn popping in and out of the Outworld."

"Either our quaint rustic charm is scaring off the customers, or we're not 'porting between dimensions like we used to," Gordy said. "Seems like we always attracted people in trouble; maybe no one's having serious troubles these days."

"Dream on," said Bernie. "Things never get better there. If anything they get worse."

"Bentwood thinks we're not getting business because no one believes in us, and their belief is what powers our magic," mused Hali. "The kids we usually get want to go to fairyland, deep down. Maybe adults can't let themselves believe in the same way. Instead, at moments of crisis their emotional energy brings the inn to them."

"You mean they just want to drown their sorrows at a magical tavern?" Bernie asked. "That's silly."

"I'm sure they wouldn't put it that way," Hali said impatiently. "It's a weird mix of old childhood longings and new grown-up tastes. If you don't focus magic properly, it has a nasty habit of giving you exactly what you wished for."

"I never get what I wish for," Bernie said wistfully.

"Maybe not what you wish for," Hali said, "but you have a habit of asking for trouble."

"Right," said Bernie. "I think I'll go see how our adventurers are doing." He jumped off his stool with a heavy thump and ambled over to join the noisy party at the other end of the room. Faced with a group of largely novice drinkers, Bernie dutifully warned them of the more potent beverages to be had, and watched with amusement as Leo and Tracy proceeded to sample as many as they could manage. Aside from the gamers' noisy arguments, the inn was quiet, and Bernie soon grew bored. He lasted through dinner, then with another dutiful warning, this time against staying up too late, he wandered outside to experience some real nightlife, leaving the gamers on their own.

Next morning, the birds outside the inn started singing in the half-light before dawn, waking Hali. She rolled over, and kicked the curled-up wombat sleeping on the foot of the bed. "Wake up, Bernie."

Half-awake, he slid onto the floor beside the bed and shook himself. "It's not dawn yet," he complained, yawning. "I only just got to sleep."

"I want to be moving just after dawn," Hali told him. "We have two days to walk to Fairehaven, and we're going to have to take it at an easy pace with this crew. Get them up, and down to breakfast—no dawdling!"

"Yes, ma'am." Bernie saluted with one paw, then waddled to the door and looked back. "The door, please," he said with dignity. Hali waved and the door silently swung open, paused, and then closed close on Bernie's heels.

The gamers were considerably subdued at the breakfast table, and less than appreciative of the Black Buck's superlative breakfast spread.

"Yuck," Tracy said. "Whoever heard of fish for breakfast? Pickled fish at that. Meat, too. Fried ham instead of bacon, and cold roast beef. Haven't they ever heard of cocoa and croissants?"

"Oooh," moaned Leo, one hand clutching his stomach, the other holding his head. "Don't talk about food. I've got food poisoning, I'm sure of it. A place like this can't have good sanitation in the kitchen if it doesn't even have decent plumbing. I'm going to die in this primitive hole." He groaned again and put his head down on the table.

"You're hung over," Oliver commented. "I told you all that ale and mead wasn't a good idea. I'm not sick, anyway."

"Oh, Mr. Pure," Leo sneered. "I get the chance to drink all I want legally, I'm going to take advantage of it. Besides, I've had booze before and all I got was a headache. I'm dying, I tell you. What kind of stupid game kills people by food poisoning?"

"A headache," Tracy said, as if she'd just had a revelation. "Is that why my head hurts? I've never had more than a glass of wine before, I didn't even think I might have a hangover."

"That's why I stuck to the cider," Oliver said complacently, digging into a bowl of porridge. "Hali warned us."

"Children," sniffed Richard Jamison, nibbling tentatively at a bowl of boiled rhubarb. "How can you expect to survive the game if you can't even survive an evening in a tavern? A surprisingly plebeian tavern," he commented, setting the rhubarb aside and taking a chunk of bread. "I certainly won't be recommending this adventure as a gourmet experience. Ah, if it isn't our Den Mother at last."

"And how are we this morning?" Hali said, setting down a plate filled with cold roast beef and fried eggs.

"I'm dying," Leo moaned.

Hali reached over, yanked his head up by the hair, and examined his face. "Hung over?" she asked sweetly.

"No," groaned Leo.

"Yes," chorused the others.

Hali leaned over and tapped Leo's cup. "Drink that. You'll feel better."

"Eeeuw," Leo said, looking into the pewter cup. "It's green and thick." He took a tentative sip, made a ghastly face, but to his horror kept on drinking until the cup was empty. He threw the cup away, gagging. "I couldn't stop drinking it! That's worse than being sick."

"Yeah, but did it make you feel better?" Oliver asked.

"You know, I do feel better," Leo said. "Where can I get some of that roast beef?"

"Maybe you should try the cure, Tracy," Oliver suggested.

Tracy shuddered. "My headache's not that bad."

Hali eyed her suspiciously, then shrugged, and started eating. Fifteen minutes later she shepherded the group outside. The sun was just beginning to peer over the edge of the eastern rim of the valley, and the grass was still heavy with dew. The gamers shivered in the cool morning air, and walked gingerly over the wet grass.

"My tennis shoes are sopping already," Tracy complained.

Hali stopped beside the storage shed and threw the double door open wide. "In here are the supplies you'll need for the next two days. Each of you gets one of the packs, a cloak, basic clothing, and any of the weapons you want."

"Look, broadswords!" Leo pulled one off the wall, and almost dropped it. Exclaiming at the weight, he put both hands on the hilt and started swinging the sword in the close confines of the shed.

"Look out," shouted Tracy, ducking. "You're going to hurt someone."

Staggering under the weight of the sword, Leo ignored her. He swung at an imaginary foe and lost his balance completely, crashing into the wall and bringing down a rack of spears. "That sword's no good," he said, picking himself up and leaving the sword on the floor. "The balance is all wrong. Maybe I'll get one of the battle-axes."

"Oh, grow up," Tracy snapped. She reached for one of the midlength bows and strung it quickly. "I'm going to stick with something I know. I'm glad I took archery classes in school."

"Take a dagger, too," Oliver advised. "They can come in handy." He took a fine rapier and tried a few passes. "I've been taking fencing classes at the community center, but real sword fighting's bound to be different."

"I bet we get the skills to use whatever weapon we choose," Leo argued. "Otherwise, this is going to be a really lame game. How can you get points if you can't kill anything? Right?" He turned to Hali for confirmation.

Leaning against the door with arms folded, Hali rolled her eyes and shook her head with exaggerated patience. "You have the skills you came with," she said. "Nothing more and nothing less."

Leo pouted, but the other gamers accepted this as a basic rule of the game. They explored the rest of the weapons, arguing amiably over the advantages of each, discussed largely in technical gaming terms like "hit points" that had Hali smiling behind their backs. Some practical considerations were brought up, such as a general lack of expertise in the use of edged weapons. Each took a dagger for general use, but there was sharp division on the rest.

Depending on his fencing experience to guide him, Oliver chose a lightweight rapier, the closest thing to a fencing foil available. With some thought, he passed over the plate armor and chain mail, choosing lighter armor made of boiled leather instead. Last, he picked up a small hatchet that fit neatly through one of the extra loops on his pack. He figured it would be good for cutting firewood, assuming the trees weren't sentient in this world, or at least didn't object to the gathering of deadwood.

Without comment, Jamison opted for a bow, a quiver full of sharp-tipped arrows, and a quarterstaff. He picked over the armor with pursed lips, finally settling for long gloves of quilted leather, a padded vest, and a simple metal cap.

Tracy picked a bow and quiver, a staff, and after much deliberation, a sling. "I always wanted to figure out how they work." She weighed a shirt of shiny silver chain mail in her hands, then a heavy leather gambeson, and regretfully took a dull-green jacket of quilted fabric instead. "It looks like a judo *gi*, so it must be good for taking blows," she said, "and it's lightweight. I don't think I could hike very far in any of the other stuff."

"What a bunch of wimps," Leo said. "You're not going to last past the first real battle without any serious armor." After determining that there was no limit to what he could take, he hesitated little. His pile included a large double-headed ax, a round wooden shield with a metal edge, a set of throwing knives, shortsword, metal helmet and gauntlets, and an oversized chain-mail tunic with dramatic leather shoulder pads. Finally, he declared himself ready.

"You haven't got a pack yet," Hali pointed out. "Each of you should have a pack, pick out clothing in your size from the shelves, and grab a cloak."

"I'll take a cloak," Leo said, "but I don't need a pack or extra clothes. I think we should rough it, not wear ourselves out carrying useless stuff."

"Like food?" Hali asked dryly. Leo hesitated briefly, but appeared unconvinced. "Your gold is in those packs," Hali informed him, "and if you don't take the pack, and a change of clothes, you can't keep the gold." This, it turned out, was a winning argument, and Leo joined the others in examining the wardrobes provided for them.

"How drab," Jamison commented, holding up a brown tunic. "I understand the need for an emergency change of clothing, but I do hope you don't mind if we prefer our own clothes to the charms of burlap? Or is this scratchy stuff actually wool?"

"You don't have to wear it if you don't want to," Hali said, "but it's good wool and may come in handy. I recommend you also take one of those linen undershirts, however." She pointed to a nearby pile of off-white garments.

"Undershirt?" Tracy gasped, unfolding a long garment with full sleeves. She examined the drawstring-gathered neckline curiously. "This looks like a peasant dress. I could practically wear it for a nightgown."

"They keep the wool away from your skin," Hali pointed out, lifting her skirt to show an underskirt in dead black, the fine fabric trimmed in silver lace. "Wouldn't do much good if they were short."

"Oh, great," Leo said. "Now you're going to say you want us guys to wear dresses."

"On men they're generally called tunics," Hali said acerbically, "and yours are only intended to be knee-length. Better for walking in, especially if you're not used to long skirts."

"Wow, this is soooo medieval," Tracy enthused, with an ingenuous sincerity that left the others speechless. "I'm going to try mine on." She disappeared into the inn, and Hali diplomatically left the men to their own devices. "We're setting out in thirty minutes," she told them, "so be sure to take care of any last minute business."

"Yes, Mom," Leo muttered rebelliously. Hali turned on him in sudden fury.

"You," she snarled, "had better watch yourself if you don't want to end this game as a toad, or better yet, a slimy albino newt." Her mood seemed to change instantly, and she paused, considering, and smiled in sudden recognition. "You know, you look like a newt already. Sort of pale and squishy, with those slightly protruding eyes. I wondered why you looked so familiar." Suddenly the snarl was back. "Now get in that armor and get that pack organized. Move it!" With a flourish of her staff and a swirl of her skirts, she turned and stomped into the inn, looking for an errant wombat.

The search took her to a small garden behind the inn's kitchen. More specifically, it took her to the compost pile between the garden and the stables, where she found Bernie enthusiastically rooting for the tasty shoots of some recently discarded weeds, incidentally doing considerable damage to the carefully arranged layers of manure, dirt, and kitchen refuse. "Gordy's going to kill us if his gardener catches you," Hali scolded Bernie, who looked up and blissfully licked his grubby muzzle.

"Nah," he said. "This was Gordy's idea. People food doesn't appeal to me these days, not like when I was a crow. I told him I was going to go grubbing in the woods, and he said the hunting would be much better here. He was right, too. They've got carrots, parsnips, rutabagas, sweet grasses, these skinny-rooted weeds, all sorts of yummies. It's all going on Bentwood's bill." Bernie rubbed his paws on a clump of grass to clean them, shook himself, and trundled over to Hali. "Time to go, I take it?"

"They've got fifteen minutes yet, but I suspect they'll do better with a bit of harassment."

They found the gaming party assembled in front of the inn. Quiver and bow strapped to her back and staff in hand, Tracy was showing off her new outfit, which she enthusiastically described as "Robin Hood City." The others had settled for donning their armor on top of their Outworld garb. Leo actually looked impressive. With his helmet's faceplate down, the shield held at chest height, and the chain mail covering him from shoulder to thigh, he looked more like a small, dangerous tank than the overweight fan-boy he was.

"Gee, this chain mail pinches," he complained, and shrugged violently. "It makes my T-shirt bunch up, too. They don't make anything right around here."

"I believe one normally wears padded garments under chain mail," Jamison observed, "not a lightweight cotton T-shirt. Something like Tracy's jacket, perhaps."

"Oh great, now I'm supposed to get out of all this and change my shirt," Leo grumbled.

Hali made her presence known with a small lighting flash and an ominous roll of thunder. "No time, no changes. It's past dawn, and we have a long way to go. Pick up your packs and follow me." She swept past the group, Bernie at her heels, and strode off down the road without looking back.

The gamers scrambled to get their packs. Jamison slipped his on easily, and set off after Hali at an easy pace. Oliver and Tracy stayed to help Leo fit his backpack on over the chain mail and cape, and then shoulder the top-heavy ax. They then jogged after Hali, leaving Leo to shuffle frantically behind.

CHAPTER
5

JUST past the inn, the road—a simple track of packed earth—ran downhill and under the edge of a dense wood. The yellow light of the morning sun barely touched the tops of the ancient maples, highlighting the occasional evergreen that thrust its dark head above the sea of green leaves. Under the canopy the light barely penetrated, and undergrowth was sparse. Last year's faded leaves littered the forest floor, and Bernie shuffled through them happily at the side of the road, scuffling leaves aside to reveal the dark leaf mold, anemic plant shoots, and frantic insect life below. Pleasantly full already, Bernie let all but the most particularly succulent grasses go untouched. Actually, he thought, chewing on a piquant sprout, he would probably prefer something a bit tougher, more chewy. It was always a bit of an adventure, getting used to a new life-form, and, all things considered, Hali had come up with worse than wombats on her own.

The humans in the party were more interested in the larger flora and fauna. The gamers exclaimed over the velvety bracket fungi on the trees, the occasional oversized red and white toadstool, and once a tiny patch of delicate yellow flowers that Hali insisted were violets, whatever their color. Even Jamison professed to be impressed by the quaint scenery with its mossy knolls, delicate ferns, and particularly the backlit view of the trees, their twining branches silhouetted against translucent leaves that glowed green against the brightening sky.

He also found the sound effects quite satisfying. An unseen chorus of twittering birds provided the melody, accompanied by whispering breezes and the sound of running water. The brook that ran beside the Black Buck Inn continued through the forest, looping away from the road more often than not, but always running close enough that travelers could hear it babble, drip, and gurgle the length of the valley.

The group had plenty of time to admire the scenery. The easy pace Hali had planned was fast and furious compared to the crawl forced on the group by Leo's progress, always in the rear. On the rare occasion when he actually pulled abreast with one of the others, he wasted his breath on complaints, which eventually became a steady whine that with the clink-clank of his armor became as much a part of the background noise as the brook, though not half as pleasant.

"I always thought college men were so mature," a disillusioned Tracy confided to Oliver timidly. She was feeling her youth in this all-male party (Hali was too old to count). At fifteen, even a small difference in age can be an insurmountable social obstacle, and Oliver, though at seventeen the nearest in age, seemed unapproachably mature, his fair good looks only making the matter worse. A lifelong city dweller, Tracy also found the woods slightly intimidating, and expected an orc attack with every rustle in the bushes. At first, only Hali's imperturbable expression and Bernie's cheerful (if occasionally unnerving) rummaging about in the leaves reassured her. As the miles passed, though, she began to relax, and despite frequent rest stops found herself worrying more about her feet and her endurance than about monster attacks.

Leading always downhill, the road ran the length of the valley, which gradually narrowed. Toward the end of the valley, the brook crossed and recrossed the road, providing the gamers with plenty of experience in fording streams. At one crossing, wagon wheels had churned the earth to sticky mud for yards on either side of the stream; Hali led the party along a barely worn footpath that brought them to a fallen tree, its bark long gone, that bridged the stream. Like tightrope walkers, the party crossed without mishap, with the one exception of Leo. Overburdened and top-heavy in his armor, he opted to straddle the log and scoot himself across. In the process, he left his battle-ax behind, set down in a bank of ferns and rather conveniently forgotten.

With the ax no longer digging into his shoulder, Leo made better time for a while, but soon his shield became too heavy for the arm carrying it. He should have tied it to his pack, he thought, but the pack itself was becoming an onerous burden. It occurred to him that dark magic might be seeking him out as the only decently armed member of the party, trying to make him strip himself of his weapons. That thought carried him a good ten yards further before he quietly dropped the shield behind a fallen tree. The heavy helmet, now intolerably sweaty, he dumped in a small hollow, casually managing to push some leaves over it with his foot. (Lagging somewhat himself, Bernie shortly came upon the odd scuff marks, and out of curiosity uncovered the helmet, which he left in disgust.)

Leo's pack survived, being too hard to remove, what with the bulky cloak and chain mail. A set of throwing knives were safe, out of reach inside the pack. The finely jointed steel gauntlets, however, found their rusting place in the deep mud at one stream crossing. On those odd occasions when Leo caught up with the rest of the group, his companions found the loss of ax, shield, and helmet hard to ignore, but by unspoken consensus refrained from commenting.

Shortly before noon, the party came to yet another stream crossing, this one muddier than all the rest. On the near side of the stream, they faced a wide stretch of mud marred by hoofprints and wagon-wheel ruts easily two feet deep. The stream itself had spread out to a very shallow eight feet in width. Past it, the far bank looked solid enough, but getting there without wading in the mud looked impossible. Hali left the road and skirted the mud as far as she could, scouting for a clean route. Instead, she found her path blocked by a small swamp, grown up around the stream as far back as she could see.

No trees grew in the stream's immediate vicinity, allowing the gamers a glimpse of blue sky and bright sunlight that made the miniature swamp quite a cheery place. Water gleamed as it ran in tiny ribbons over the mud and around clumps of buttercups and patches of bright green moss. Going as close to the running water as she could without wading in mud, Hali reached out with her staff to test the mud in front of her, and nodded sourly when the end went down more than three feet without encountering solid ground.

"Right," she grumbled to herself. Curtly, she marshaled the gamers and led them back to the rutted road. "This is the only safe place to cross," she warned them. "Even if it is muddy. When you get to the streambed, stay on the rocky parts—don't take any chances. You don't want to get off the path."

"Yuck," said Bernie, testing the mud around the ruts with one tentative paw. "Where are wings when you need them? This stuff's stiff, but not enough. It's going to swallow me alive."

"I'll carry you," Hali said. "Let me get my shoes off." Her boots and black silk stockings disappeared, and she calmly gathered her skirts around her hips and secured them at the waist with her belt, ignoring the gamers, who stared at her bare and bony legs, a little shocked. She picked up Bernie, holding him over her shoulder with one hand. With the other hand, she held the staff, cautiously testing the mud as she went. "You'd think with all the construction going on around here Bentwood could at least get this road fixed," she grumbled. "Peat bogs don't grow overnight."

"Is that what this is?" Bernie asked.

"It's more a puddle with big ambitions," Hali said absently, keeping her eyes on the streambed. Once across, she dropped Bernie on a dry spot on the bank, and bent over to splash water on her muddy legs. With the bulk of the mud removed, she straightened and beckoned. "Come, children," she called a little too sweetly to the hesitant gamers, "a little mud won't kill you."

Tracy and Oliver exchanged dubious glances, but removed their shoes and socks. Tracy followed Hali's example, tying her skirts up out of the way. Oliver rolled his narrow jeans up as high as they would go, just above the ankle. Unwilling to take his jeans off in front of two females, he followed Tracy into the mud with a resigned sigh. Jamison rolled his wider pants legs with precision, finally stopping when they were several inches above the knee. Carrying shoes and socks with one hand, he walked delicately in one of the wider ruts to avoid as much mud as possible.

"Hey, are you guys crazy?" Leo shrieked. "You're not making me wade waist-deep in mud. We can cross easily over here." He walked upstream, away from the ruts, and pointed to the flat stretch of mud.

Sitting next to Bernie on the far bank, Hali stood up quickly. "No, don't," she started to call, then thought better of it. She sat back down, chin in hand, and watched avidly as Leo stepped out onto a small clump of buttercups. He balanced there on one foot, then managed to leap, despite the chain mail, onto a similar clump. At that point, he ran out of buttercups, and made a vigorous leap to one of the bright green patches. He landed on it squarely with both feet—and promptly sank out of sight.

Already on the bank, Tracy screamed shrilly. Oliver, still in the creekbed trying to get his jeans clean, started in Leo's direction, but Hali waved him off. "We don't need two of you in there," she said.

Leo's head and shoulders suddenly popped above the surface, covered in mealy black muck. Bobbing slightly, he managed to work one arm free, and frantically scraped mud from his face. "Get me out of here," he screamed. "It's quicksand! You've got to help me."

"Are you standing on something?" Hali asked curiously.

"Yes . . . I mean no!" he wailed. "There's something down there, but it's too deep. I'm sort of treading water now, but I can't keep it up—the chain mail's pulling me down." Hali doubted he was in danger of drowning, but he was having trouble keeping his mouth clear of the mud.

"Take off the chain mail," Hali instructed, wading back across the stream.

"I can't. My stupid backpack's in the way."

On the nearest stretch of shore, Hali calmly watched him

struggle to talk. "Can you reach your dagger, or did you dump that already?"

"No," gasped Leo, "it's on my belt. I've got it! Now what?"

"Cut the straps to the backpack and get that chain mail off."

"I can't lose the pack!" Leo bleated, with sudden strength. "My gold's in there."

Oliver joined Hali on the bank. "He's nuts. Can't you do anything to help, you know, something magical?"

Hali shook her head, one corner of her mouth pulled back in a twisted smile. "Sorry, kid, that's cheating."

"You can't let him die," Oliver begged. "Damn. Why weren't there any ropes in that supply shed?"

Hali looked at him in surprise. "What a practical idea." She plucked a strand of grass, twisted it in a circle and concentrated briefly. A neatly coiled rope appeared in her hand. She handed it to Oliver. "All yours." She leaned toward Leo and shouted cheerfully, "Hold on, help's coming."

Holding one end tightly, Oliver threw the coil of rope as hard as he could toward Leo. It uncoiled neatly, but failed to fly perfectly straight, falling a bare three feet short.

Oliver swore. "Leo, there's a rope only a yard from you. Can you get to it?"

Leo flailed with his one free arm. "I can't move," he cried, but kept flailing until he managed to turn himself in the right direction. He reached for the rope, but it lay just beyond his fingertips. Grunting with the strain, he kicked out, grasped the rope—and sank in the muck till only his eyes were visible. The rope tightened as Leo pulled his head above the surface. "I lost my foothold," he gasped. "Pull me in!"

Oliver hauled on the rope, slipping on the slightly damp earth of the bank. Tracy ran to help, adding her weight to the effort. Even so, the two made little headway against the mud.

"I can't hold on much longer," Leo wailed.

"You're too heavy," Tracy shouted. "If you don't want to drown, you've got to dump the chain mail."

"My gold . . . I can't . . . oh shit. Hold on, you guys." Leo took a deep breath and let himself sink into the muck, holding the rope with his left hand. With the other, moving as if in slow motion against the mud, he cut the straps to his pack, the ties of the cloak, and the leather straps that held the chain mail in place. He stuck the dagger back in its belt sheath, just in case, and pulled his right arm free of the mail shirt. Desperately, he raised his arm, pushing through the mud, and grabbed the rope. Holding on with both hands, he pulled himself up for a quick breath of air, then sank again, letting go with his left arm and working it out of the mail. Suddenly, he felt at least a hundred pounds lighter. Kicking hard, he got his head above the mud and both hands on the rope. "Pull, guys," he shouted.

Highly relieved, his rescuers put their backs into it, and soon pulled him clear of the mud and onto dry land. Leo rolled over and sat up, clawing mud from his eyes. "I thought I was dead for sure," he panted heavily.

"Told you it wasn't safe," Hali told him. "Get up, we've got to get moving."

"You don't care," Leo accused her. "I could have died, and you wouldn't have done a thing."

"I'm not the one who came here for adventure," Hali snapped, prodding him with her staff.

"You could at least have told me it was quicksand," Leo grumbled, trying to stand on shaky legs with help from Tracy and Oliver. Curious, Tracy picked some mud from Leo's hair and rubbed it between her fingers.

"This doesn't look like sand to me," she said. "It looks more like wet potting soil, the stuff that comes in bags. In movies, quicksand looks more like oatmeal."

"Movies," Leo scoffed. "This stuff is real, and it was sucking me down."

"Peat," Hali said. "It's peat moss. Grows in water and gathers in ponds until they turn semisolid. Deadly enough. Tends to be a bit hard on the skin, too. This pond never was that deep, though. If you'd let yourself sink a little further you could have walked out, though not with that chain mail on."

Oliver stared at her. "You knew that?" he asked, in frustration. "Why didn't you tell us before?"

Hali shrugged. "You wanted adventure, right? Your way worked just as well."

"This is the stupidest game I've ever played!" Leo announced. "I want out."

"You want to die?" Hali asked innocently.

Leo blanched. "What do you mean?"

"I told you. This game is real, as far as you're concerned. You can't get out until the end, unless you die, and death will be very, very real to you when it comes."

"I don't believe this!" Leo pouted. "You can't make me play."

Hali shrugged. "Suit yourself. Sit here long enough and you'll at least starve to death. Otherwise, I think we might as well stop for lunch on the other side of the brook." Holding her staff high, she waded back through the mud, followed by Tracy and Oliver, dragging a protesting Leo between them.

Bernie had waited anxiously during the excitement, frustrated at having to miss the action. Jamison, on the other hand, had felt no need to join in an inept, messy, and, he judged, largely unnecessary rescue attempt. When the rescuers reached the bank, Bernie joined them eagerly, exclaiming over the excitement of the near escape with a wistfulness that made Leo decide it had been an adventure after all. Lunch was quite satisfactory, consisting of fresh bread from the inn with slices of cheese and hard sausage. Tracy and Oliver sympathetically shared their portions with Leo, who declared he'd sweated off ten pounds in the muck.

The sun was shining, grass and flowers lined the stream bank where they ate, and by the end of lunch, Leo had decided that he was the hero of the day, having defeated death in the bottomless bog. Tracy and Oliver humored him at first, but were repaid by hearing their roles diminish with each retelling of the tale. Tracy drew the line when she heard how she'd nearly fainted.

"Some hero *you* are," she snapped. "You've been holding us back all day. Then you got yourself stuck in a swamp, hollered like a stuck pig, and lost all the fancy weapons you shouldn't have taken in the first place. Ate more than half my cheese, too."

"Hey, I've still got my dagger and sword," Leo boasted, drawing the sword and waving it in the air. "That's all we'll need, for sure. They're not going to send anything against us we can't handle—if we die too soon it'd spoil the game and be bad for business," he said, closer to the truth than he suspected.

"He's a regular Clever Hans," Bernie said admiringly.

"Gee, thanks," Leo said, and then the meaning sunk in. "Hey, wait a minute. I've read those stories. You can't call me an idiot. Take it back!"

Swinging wildly, he advanced on the snickering wombat, who waddled and rolled away from the sword and into the brush at the side of the road. Leo followed madly, thrashing at the brush in his path and swearing as his weapon caught in every bush big enough to cause trouble.

"He sure swears like a college man," Tracy observed. Bernie, meantime, jumped out of the bushes and back onto the road, creeping quietly behind the flailing fighter. With a high-pitched scream, he leaped onto Leo's legs just below the back of the knee, bringing him down into a sudden, thrashing heap.

"Help, it's a monster!" Leo screamed. "I'm being attacked. Somebody help me!"

"The deadly wombat strikes again!" Bernie crowed.

Leo stopped thrashing and realized that the rest of the party was laughing. He sat up and put his face in his hands. "Oh, right, laugh at me. I've lost my gold, my armor, and I'm no good at fighting. I might as well chuck the sword while I'm at it." With a dramatic gesture, he tossed the sword over his shoulder and into the woods.

Hali applauded. "Very good. You've got a future in the theater if you can learn to stop overplaying your scenes. Now kiddies, playtime's over, we've got to get moving."

They made better time after lunch. Soon they came out of the valley to find rolling hills, covered with grassy fields and dotted with trees, spread out before them. Hali walked briskly in the lead, pulling ahead of the gamers. Bernie trotted beside her for a while, eyeing her out of the corner of his eye. "Nice, the way that peat bog got rid of the fat kid's armor. Was that your idea, or did it just happen?"

"I haven't any idea what you're talking about," Hali said curtly.

"Fine, be that way." Bernie dropped back in search of more rewarding conversation, and Oliver took his place.

"Would you mind explaining a little something?" he asked.

Hali cocked her head. "What did you have in mind?"

"What's the point of all this? What are we supposed to accomplish here, and when does the game end?"

"What do you want to accomplish?" Hali asked.

"You sound like a shrink I saw once," Oliver said in disgust.

That caught Hali's attention. "A shrink? What's that?"

"You know, a psychiatrist. A head doctor. I was upset when my parents divorced, and my mom dragged me in to see this guy who just sat there and asked me what I thought about things."

Hali decided her Outworld counterparts had made great strides in their technique since the last time she had investigated. "Did it do you any good?"

"Made me mad. Made me decide to solve my own problems. Guess that's good. I quit going after a few visits."

"You ever read fairy tales?"

"Used to. I've been reading mostly fantasy these days, *The Lord of the Rings*, that sort of thing. It's not really the same."

"No, I've gathered that much." Hali debated how much to tell him. He walked silently beside her, but she doubted he would give up easily. "We follow the basic fairy-tale scenario. You've got to overcome a few obstacles, toil at some unpleasant labors, rescue a princess or reasonable facsimile, maybe save a village from a monster or two. You could be here for years, if necessary—but only hours will pass back in the real world."

"What if I decided to rent an apartment in town and just hang out while my gold lasted?"

"One of the nice things about witches is they know how to make things uncomfortable for people when they get a little too happy where they are. One of the primary requirements for the job, in fact," Hali told him.

By this time, the others had pulled alongside to listen. "Can we do magic," Tracy asked, "or is that limited to witches?"

"Witches, wizards, most elves . . ." Hali started.

"Oh wow, elves," breathed Tracy. "Will we get to meet any?"

"If you're very, very unlucky," Bernie chipped in. "They're as obnoxious a bunch of snobs as you're ever likely to meet."

"As I was going to say," Hali said, "lots of different types can work with magic, but it takes an innate talent. Either you've got it or you don't. I do. Magic works differently for some people—wizards have this thing about having a formula for everything—but the basics are always the same. You have to concentrate, visualize what you want, and it appears. Spells, formulae, funny little chalk marks, colored candles, and that sort of thing are all just aids to concentration and visualization."

"Oh, really," Jamison drawled. "Such a simplistic magic system. The designers of this world should have spent less time on the scenery and more time on the fantasy elements. This system makes it too easy for gamers to just walk in and start conjuring whatever they want. Pandering to the lowest common denominator, I suppose."

"It's not that easy," Hali told him. "Like I said, it's a talent. Some people manage to tap into the magic, but can't visualize properly. The result is usually a real mess, hopefully inanimate, but not always. Student witches usually manage to bring at least one household implement to life when they shouldn't. Brooms usually try to be helpful, but chairs and butcher knives can get really vicious, believe me.

"To materialize something, you have to understand it thoroughly. That rope I conjured is an example. My old teacher made me take everything apart and study it thoroughly as an aid to visualization. I even braided a few ropes myself. No matter how hard you study, though, there's always something missing in objects made of pure magic. They're unstable, and have a nasty tendency to fall apart if a spell is cast in their immediate vicinity. Don't try tossing that rope to a drowning wizard—he'd take one analytic look at it and it would fall apart. The best way to avoid the problem is to start with a physical object and only use magic for the window dressing. The bit of grass I used was only a token base, but any little bit helps." Hali shrugged. "I could lecture for hours," she admitted, "but the only way for you to find out if you can use magic is to try it."

"How?" Tracy said.

"Try to visualize something. Anything. Make it small, a pebble or something. Some folks have luck with flame. It's a little dangerous for beginners, but make it small." She plucked a stem of dry grass from the side of the road and broke off the head, leaving a stalk about the size of a cigarette. "Visualize a flame at the tip of this. If you do it right, you might be able to set it on fire, but only for a second. And don't try it unless you're standing on bare ground where there's nothing to burn." She handed the piece of grass-straw to Tracy.

"This ought to be easy," Leo said. "I always did like playing with fire. Mom never let me even touch matches after I burned her car. It was an accident, but she really had a fit." He grabbed a handful of grass and stared at it. "Nothing's happening," he complained.

Hali brought her staff down with a sharp rap on his knuckles, knocking the grass from his hand. "One stalk at a time, if you please, and not now. We've got to keep moving, and even adepts have trouble walking and setting fires at the same time."

This advice didn't stop Tracy and Leo from trying. They stumbled down the road, concentrating on their pieces of straw to the total neglect of their feet. Inevitably, their pace slowed, and they fell behind the others.

"If that Leo kid manages to light a single spark, I'm out of here," Bernie confided to Hali. "Fur burns real easy."

"The only talent he's got is for destruction," Hali told him. "If I thought there was the slightest chance he could work magic, I'd turn him into a frog right away."

CHAPTER
6

As dusk approached, the party stopped for the night in a pleasant willow grove beside a bubbling spring. A fire ring around a burnt patch of ground suggested that travelers often stopped there. Once assured by Hali that the trees wouldn't mind, Oliver gathered a sizable pile of deadwood, and laid a fire.

"This is great. I haven't built a fire since I was in Boy Scouts. Does anybody have matches, or flints, or should I make a bow drill?"

"Pfft," Leo scoffed. "Why do it the hard way when you can use magic? Now that we're stopped, I'm sure I can start a fire. Just give me a minute." Sitting cross-legged beside the fire ring, he grabbed one of Oliver's sticks from the neatly arranged pile and stared at it until his eyes started to cross.

Oliver deliberately repaired the damage to his carefully laid fire and turned to Hali. "I don't want to wait all night for a fire. It's getting cool already. What do you suggest?"

"Well, if you're in a hurry . . ." Hali pointed her staff at the fire, which sprang alight instantly, yellow flames licking hungrily at the dry wood. She bent down and picked up a loose stick from Oliver's stockpile, and held it in the fire until the end caught. Slowly, she lifted it from the fire, gazing into the flame's depths.

Suddenly, she turned and thrust the burning brand at a startled Leo. "Try observing the flame, it might help. You could spend a lifetime studying fire; it has a wild spirit that has fascinated magicians through the ages."

"A wild spirit, nonsense," Jamison said. "It's simple oxidation, a chemical reaction that releases energy in the process. Anyone who's ever taken a class in chemistry knows that."

"Energy again," Hali muttered. "If you know so much, perhaps you could explain further. I've always wanted to meet someone who understood fire in all its variations."

"I only took general science classes designed for liberal arts students," Jamison admitted uncomfortably. "However, considering your ignorance, I suppose my modest understanding can only enlighten you." He smiled in self-deprecation at the pun.

"You know about atoms, I suppose," he continued.

Hali shook her head.

"Even the ancient Greek philosophers had a primitive atomic theory! This is carrying the low-tech background a bit too far." Jamison pulled out his notebook and wrote briefly. "Well, to simplify greatly, everything is made up of tiny particles, called atoms, which combine to create matter. The basic building blocks of matter are called elements, and their atoms combine to make molecules with characteristics totally different from the elements involved. Wood is an organic compound, a mix of carbon, hydrogen, and oxygen atoms. The oxygen molecules in the air—that's what we breathe—like to combine with other elements, if you give them a boost of energy like heat or light. When you burn wood, the oxygen in the air mixes with the atoms in the wood. The oxygen and hydrogen split off as various gases, leaving most of the carbon behind in the form of black ashes. The splitting process puts out energy of its own in the form of heat and light, enough energy to keep the fire going as long as it has enough fuel and oxygen to burn."

"I know that stuff, too," Leo said. "Rust is another form of oxidation. The iron is really burning, but so slow you don't realize it."

Hali tried to visualize the process, but couldn't. "What do these atoms look like?"

"Freaked out solar systems," Leo told her. "A solid lump in the middle with these little electron thingies streaking in circles around them."

"Actually," said Jamison, "that is only the simplest configuration. More complex atoms can be visualized as a dumbbell with a donut around its narrowest point."

"Get real," said Leo.

"I take it you slept through most of your chemistry class," Jamison snapped.

"Jamison's right," Oliver reluctantly told Leo. "I had an introductory science class, and the teacher had a really dopey-looking model, though it looked to me more like a figure-eight hourglass shape with a donut around its middle."

He turned to Hali. "If you ask me, though, the best way to visualize atoms is the old ball-and-stick model, where each atom is just a ball with a certain number of holes in it. You connect the balls with sticks in the holes, but you have to make sure that every hole has a stick in it that connects to another atom. Otherwise, the molecule will be unstable and just fall apart." He took a stick, and sketched three circles in the dirt, connected by two lines. "This is the only one I really remember. The big circle in the middle is an oxygen atom; it has two holes. The little circles are hydrogen atoms, with one hole each. All together, they make a water molecule."

"That's what water looks like?" Hali studied the sketch dubiously. "What does ice look like?"

Oliver looked at the sketch, frowning. "I think it looks the same, but it vibrates more slowly."

"It vibrates?"

"Yeah!" said Leo. "That's the part of chemistry I really like. Molecules vibrate all the time. Gases vibrate the fastest, and have more space between the molecules, but even in this rock here the particles are all vibrating like mad, with lots of empty space around them. I used to wonder why everything didn't just fall apart." For emphasis, he gave the rock a limp karate chop, and it obligingly crumbled to powder on contact.

"I told you the kid had a natural talent for destruction," Hali told Bernie.

"I'm never going to let him pet me again," Bernie said, wide-eyed. "What a talent!"

"You mean, I did that?" Leo asked. "That was magic?"

"That was magic," Hali confirmed. "You visualized particles falling apart, so they did. Try to do it on purpose."

Leo scowled in concentration, reached out, and hit another rock, harder this time. "Ow. It didn't work." He sucked the side of his hand. "Why not?"

Hali shrugged. "You may be trying too hard," she said. "Keep trying, but stick to something small."

"I don't know if that's such a good idea," said Oliver. "Do we really want someone around who can dissolve us with a touch?"

Hali grinned. "It won't come to that. You Outworlders have a natural protection against magic. I could change your form, like I did to Bernie here, but not your basic nature. Even a change in form won't stick unless it's constantly reinforced, or the subject wants it to stick. Bernie here," she gave the wombat an affectionate dig with her foot, "wouldn't stay a wombat if I didn't force him, but he'd be more likely to revert to being a crow than the original human form I found him in."

"I happen to like flying," he grumbled, slightly embarrassed. "So sue me."

"So, even if Leo here dissolved you, you'd still be alive, whatever you looked like, and I could undo it easily enough." Hali picked up a pebble and squeezed it between her fingers, but it remained solid. "This chemistry business sounds useful, like something the wizards would use, but it's really not my style," she commented, turning the stone into a clear, faceted gem that glinted in the firelight. "I'm not much for believing in things I can't see, like those atoms of yours." She tossed the gem aside.

Leo scrambled to pick up the glittering bauble. "Hey, this looks valuable!" To his dismay, it crumbled in his hand, and he wiped off the dust in disgust. "How come I always get the really crummy talents?"

The novelty of camping under the open sky kept the gamers occupied for the rest of the evening. With the fall of night, the air grew distinctly chill, and dew settled on the grass. Without his cape, and wearing only jeans and a light T-shirt, Leo soon began complaining of the cold. Hali refused to conjure him a cape, on the grounds that it would dissolve the minute Leo tried to use his newfound talents. "Besides," she snapped, "it would be cheating."

Though given to skirting rules (or more accurately, tripping over them) in real life, Leo was generally afflicted by a sense of honor when gaming, one of the few things that kept him from being thrown out of any games he graced with his inevitably chaotic participation. (His wild imagination and encyclopedic knowledge of monsters' weaknesses under certain gaming systems also helped.) He accepted Hali's strictures, but that didn't stop him from cadging spare clothes and food from the others.

In the morning, however, Hali was faced with grumbling in the ranks. Stiff from unaccustomed exercise, and a bit sore from sleeping on the ground, the gamers were hardly feeling agreeable.

"There's such a thing as too much realism," Tracy said, stretching to take the kinks out of her legs.

"I quite agree," Jamison said, running through a very efficient set of stretching exercises. "There's no reason at all to spend a whole day on nothing but travel, with no significant action."

"Hey," Leo objected, "I almost died in a swamp. I consider that highly significant."

"The moment had its potential," Jamison admitted, between sit-ups, "but, regrettably, you survived.

"No, I feel that this game was simply poorly designed, with terrible pacing. We should have been given an objective at the start, such as a quest, or even one of those silly errands fairy-tale heroes always go on—selling cows and whatnot. Instead, we're wandering across a very ordinary countryside. I admit, it's well-done, and I'm amazed at the technology involved. The computers must process huge amounts of information at an incredible rate to re-create such realistic surroundings. Too bad they didn't bother to do anything creative with the landscape while they were at it. It's like settling for a photograph when you could have Art."

"Well, I'm impressed by the landscape," said Tracy, "but I don't get out of the city much. I've never been camping before, either. It would be nice to have something happen, though. In most of the games I've played, we would have encountered half a dozen monsters by now."

"In my worlds, I always arrange for lots of encounters just to keep things interesting," Leo agreed. "Otherwise, I just skip over the long journeys."

"But that's not realistic," Oliver argued. "The whole point to Grimmworld is that the adventures are more realistic than ever. We've been spoiled by too much make-believe; until now I didn't realize how much."

"Oh, come on," Leo said. "If I wanted real adventure, I'd answer one of those ads in *Soldier of Fortune* and get myself shot up in some third-world country's latest revolution. This is fantasy. What we're seeing is a bunch of electronic pulses generated by a machine. Why not make it exciting as long as you're making it realistic?"

"My point exactly," Jamison pointed out.

"Okay, I admit that I was looking forward to fighting off some goblins or something," Oliver admitted. "I'm not too keen on getting hurt, though. I don't know about you, but I've got some realistic blisters that are giving me some even more realistic pain."

"Now, there's a man with a realistic attitude," Bernie said. "You'd better show your blisters to Hali before we take off, and she'll fix 'em up for you. She may be sadistic, but right now she's more concerned with making better time today."

"So why doesn't she just fly us there?" Leo grumbled, and Tracy swatted him.

"Magic's cheating, or haven't you figured that out yet?" she told him. "Except for little things that would mess up the game more, like blisters and hangovers, we're on our own."

When approached, Hali provided a jar of sticky, sweet-smelling salve for blisters, recommending all the gamers use it liberally on their feet. She then walked off by herself, deep in thought.

Following the stream that flowed from the campsite's spring, she walked until the grove was out of sight behind a small hill. She dug in her purse, finally extracting a shallow gold pan, and filled it with water from the stream. She set it down carefully on a level spot, knelt before it, and waited for the water to still.

"All right, now . . ." She waved one hand over the surface of the water, and it suddenly shone with a metallic silver sheen. Then the silver dissolved, and a merry, pointed face appeared. "Central Casting," said the pixie.

"Hi Sal, this is Hali. I'm working on this special project of Bentwood's, and I've got an ambitious bunch of amateurs on my hands. I'm looking for an ogre, a real pro who knows how to take a fall. Got anything?"

The pixie looked down at something outside the water mirror's range. "You're in the Silverrock foothills, outside Fairehaven?"

"Right. We're heading into town on the Silverfair road and shouldn't be hard to ambush at all."

"Great. About two hours down the road I can get you George Greytooth, if you don't mind the wait."

"He's the one that does the great pratfalls?"

"Yeah. Any adventurer who can't kill George would have trouble fighting off a kitten. A very small kitten."

"Tell him to prolong the fight a bit, would you? I've got four fighters who haven't a clue, and I'd like them all to get a chance at him."

"Will do," the pixie chirped, and Hali dispersed the image with a wave of her hand.

"There," she muttered to herself. "If they want adventure, I'm going to give it to them."

Slightly over two hours later, Hali was just about prepared to take matters in her own hands, turn the gamers into an interesting set of rock formations, and go home. Low clouds covered the sky, resting foggily on the higher hilltops. Hali and Bernie both enjoyed walking in the brisk morning air, but the gamers found the grey light gloomy. Signs of habitation were limited to distant trails of smoke from unseen chimneys, and the occasional clink-clonk of a distant cowbell.

Tracy was jumpy, Leo cold and whining, and Jamison criticized Grimmworld's magic systems at length, apparently having brooded over the topic during the night. It was obvious, he declared, that since the computers were picking up the players' brain waves, they would read a well-visualized object as "real" and not be able to properly distinguish it from the existing environment. As a result, the computers would simply add the object to the environment they were generating. He felt that calling this effect "magic" was taking a serious program flaw and calling it a feature. In addition, he considered the Outworlders' immunity to magic too convenient, and argued persuasively that it was illogical within the context of the game. All amiability, Hali agreed sweetly that it was unfortunate Jamison was not more vulnerable to her talents.

Suddenly, a giant ogre burst from the bushes beside the road, waving a knobby wooden club in the air and roaring wordlessly. Obscenely fat and hairy, clad only in a large leather belt—and rather blatantly male—the ogre ran at the gamers, who stood petrified in his path. Clumsy on his bandy bowlegs, he waved his club in the air, then brought it down with an earth-shaking thump, barely missing Tracy. She squeaked and turned to run, falling flat on her face. Leo and Bernie had better luck, both diving for the bushes, and Jamison had somehow managed to disappear completely in the first moments of the ogre's attack. Only Oliver held his ground, and he was unable to get his sword out of its sheath. He tugged frantically, but it wouldn't come free, and he didn't dare take his eyes off the ogre long enough to free the weapon.

The ogre roared again, holding his club high over his head. Tracy rolled over just in time to see his club aiming straight at her, and froze in place. The monster roared, stumbled a bit, and miraculously missed the girl. With an agonized scream, the ogre raised his club once more. Still petrified, Tracy watched wide-eyed as the club descended yet again. Her fate seemed certain; even the clumsiest ogre could hardly miss so easy a target a third time.

Hali swore violently, and leveled her staff at the ogre. A blinding beam of light stabbed out, catching the ogre in the chest. It knocked the screaming ogre backward, away from Tracy, who found herself able to move again. She ran for the bushes; the ogre, waving its arms frantically, tried to turn and run for its life, but too late. The light enveloped it, and with a sudden flash of even brighter light, the ogre disappeared.

Sighing heavily, Hali walked over to the spot where the ogre had disappeared, and bent down to examine the ashes left behind. "Sorry, George," she whispered. "That's what you get when you work with amateurs."

"S'all right," the ashes croaked faintly. Hali stirred the ashes with her staff until a small whirlwind rose up and carried the ashes away. She turned around to find the only member of the party in sight was Oliver, who finally had his sword out and was glaring at it in disgust.

"My first battle and my sword gets stuck," he snorted. "I'm a great fighter, aren't I."

Hali clapped him on the back. "You didn't run. That puts you ahead of these guys." She gestured at the bushes. "You can come out now, children," she called sweetly. "The nasty ogre's all gone."

Bernie poked his nose out first. "Glad that's over. I figured I'd better get out of the way before someone stepped on me in the heat of battle." He snickered. "Didn't realize I was in more danger on the sidelines."

" 'Discretion is the better part of valor,' " Leo defended himself as he crawled out of the bushes. "If you don't have a weapon, running away is the only sensible course of action."

"If it were up to you, I'd be dead now," Tracy accused. Trembling, her face dead white, she sat down on the edge of the road and put her head in her hands for a moment, breathing heavily. "I have never been so scared in my life," she said. "I was sure I was going to die."

Jamison emerged from the bushes, casually brushing dirt from his pants legs. "That was a rather pointless little exercise," he commented. "We had no real way to defend ourselves, and I never doubted that if the danger were great enough our nursemaid here would save us."

"That why you ran so fast?" Leo asked. "Why didn't you just stand here and watch the show?"

"I doubt you would be able to understand my thought processes even if I were to share them with you, and I have no intention of explaining myself to a pack of Philistines."

"I understand you well enough," Leo retorted. "You want

to sit back and watch us do all the dirty work. Well, you can just . . ."

Oliver stopped him. "There's no point in trying to see who's the worst coward. None of us made a very good showing, so just leave it."

"At least you stood up to that, that . . . thing," Tracy said. "I never imagined ogres were so disgusting, all those flabby rolls of skin, that mangy hair and . . . naked, like that. Yuck. It burst out of those bushes and I just couldn't move." She turned to Hali. "There aren't a lot of those things around, are there?"

Hali wasn't reassuring on that head, and went on with some pleasure to describe some of the other interesting creatures to be found in the open countryside. Further down the road, however, she paid for her amusement. From the start, she'd envisioned the gamers as sheep to be herded. Now the sheep had seen the wolf and were running scared, bleating constantly while they were at it.

Hali worried more about keeping the players from injuring themselves. Tracy and Jamison had their bows out and strung, with arrows in hand. With difficulty Hali dissuaded them from walking along with bows drawn and arrows nocked. Oliver took the lead with his rapier out, held at the ready, and spent more time staring into the underbrush than watching the road. Even Leo fingered his dagger from time to time. Worse from Hali's point of view, he seemed to depend more on the protection of Hali's staff than on the others' weapons, and dogged the witch's step the rest of the morning.

Too nervous to sit for long, the gamers opted for the briefest of rest stops, and only Leo had any desire to stop for lunch. They ate on the march instead. By midafternoon, they entered more heavily cultivated areas, and even passed a few travelers going the other way. Then they reached the troll bridge.

No truly violent trolls would have been tolerated on a major road so close to civilization, and the elderly keeper of this bridge was well known in the locality as a crusty but harmless curmudgeon, so old his skin had faded to match the lichen-encrusted grey stone of the bridge. Hali had originally planned to let her charges cope with him themselves, and despite some misgivings decided to go with the plan. She dropped back slightly as they approached the bridge, a quaint stone structure that arched neatly over a narrow but deep, slow-flowing river.

Still playing advance guard, Oliver set foot on the bridge first. When a hair-raising screech issued from beneath the bridge, he whirled instantly, ready for action. Almost as fast, Tracy and Jamison had their arrows nocked and ready to fly. So it was that the old troll jumped into the middle of a bristling ring of steel points. His usual outraged demand for payment became a cry of simple outrage, and he jumped up and down in a trollish fury, looking like a cross between an angry frog and a demented spider.

"What do you think you're doing? Put those down, I say. This is my bridge, you can't do this to me in my own home. At least point those arrows somewhere else! Don't you know those things are dangerous? Could go off at any second, the way you're holding them. What are things coming to when an honest troll has to work in fear? Stop it, stop it, stop it!"

Tracy kept her bow drawn, but moved her aim aside slightly. "What are you?" she asked.

"I'm a troll, what do you think I am?" the outraged bridge attendant said. Skinny arms akimbo, he glared at the gamers. "This is a troll bridge. You have to pay the troll to cross."

Hali came up behind the two archers, and leaned on her staff to watch. On her heels, Leo decided it was time to take part in vanquishing the evil troll. Drawing his dagger, he went up and waved the blade in the troll's face. "You're not getting any gold from us!" he declared triumphantly.

"Why are you worried?" Tracy asked. "You don't have any gold left anyway."

"You can't do this to me," the troll squeaked as the knife came closer to his throat. His already protruding eyes bulged out even further. "This is highway robbery!"

"Come on, guys, this thing's helpless," Leo declared. Grandly, he sheathed his knife and walked past Oliver, in the process knocking Oliver's sword aside.

Seizing the advantage, the old troll screamed and jumped on Leo's back, wrapping his bony arms around the gamer's neck. "You're not getting past me!" the troll shrieked. "No human's ruining my six-hundred-year perfect record."

Leo gurgled and grabbed at the troll's arms, but discovered that their spindly length provided the troll with excellent leverage when properly applied. Flailing desperately, he spun in circles. Oliver danced alongside, looking for an opening, but didn't dare attack the erratically moving target. Finally, Leo stumbled into the bridge's knee-height railing, and with a choked-off wail toppled over the edge and into the water, carrying the troll with him.

Tracy and Oliver raced for the railing, bending down to peer over the edge. The river, flowing imperturbably past, seemed to have swallowed the combatants. Scanning the surface as far as they could see, neither Tracy nor Oliver could find the slightest sign of either Leo or the troll.

"He's got his knife," Oliver said, in the tone of one trying to believe in a forlorn hope. "He's still got a chance."

"Underwater?" Tracy said. "Not a hope. That troll looked like it would take to water like a fish. Frog. Whatever." She slapped the stone railing in frustration. "There's got to be something we can do!"

"I suggest we cross quickly while the creature's gone," Jamison said, eyeing the water at the foot of the bridge, bow still drawn and ready. "We've lost one player; there's no point in taking chances." Cautiously, he edged onto the bridge.

Suddenly, a hollow voice called from under the bridge. "You couldn't just pay the usual fee, noooo. You had to try to get by without paying, resorting to violence. Whippersnappers have no respect. You could at least come down here and help me with this great lump."

Tracy and Oliver looked at each other, a sudden hope in their eyes. With a whoop, Oliver raced off the bridge and down the bank, splashing into the edge of the river. Tracy followed just behind, and together they peered cautiously into the dark shadows under the bridge, where they could barely make out Leo's white T-shirt and face, held half out of the water by the crotchety troll.

"No weapons, now," the troll told them. "I won't have weapons under my bridge. If you want your friend, you put those weapons down right now."

Carefully, Oliver passed his sword to Tracy, who set it with her bow and arrows at the top of the bank, out of the wet. "Water's no good for bowstrings anyway," she said.

From on top of the bridge, Jamison stamped petulantly. "This is foolishness. It's an obvious trap. Don't go in there or the troll will get you, too."

"Oh, phoo," Tracy retorted. "If there's a chance we can save Leo we've got to try. If all the troll wants is gold, I say we give it to him."

"That's the ticket," cheered the troll. "Fair pay for a fair day's labor, I always say. You, boy, you take his feet," he instructed Oliver. "My, this fellow's heavy. Buoyant, too; thought I'd lose him to the current for a while there."

Tracy and the troll each took a shoulder, and in fits and starts they managed to work their way up the steep bank to the road, pushing and pulling Leo's soggy body to the top. Though unconscious, he was clearly alive, choking and twitching with every jerk. They dumped him unceremoniously on the road, and the troll pushed him on his side and slapped him hard between the shoulder blades. Water dribbled out of the corner of Leo's mouth, and with a great gasp he started coughing violently and opened his eyes.

"Dad, I'm sorry. I didn't mean to fall off the boat," he said quickly, then suddenly realized where he was and sat up. "What happened? Hey, did I beat the troll?"

"Never in your wildest dreams," cackled the old troll from behind him. The troll slapped Leo on the back again, setting off another series of racking coughs.

The cough kept Leo from acting on his initial impulse to run in terror, and when he could speak again, curiosity tempered outrage. "What's going on here? Why are you just standing around with this monster attacking me? He hit me!"

"He saved you from drowning," Hali interjected. "One bit of advice: Never, ever turn your back on a troll. They're not all quite as accommodating as old Caneback here." She nodded at the troll.

"Accommodating? No need to be insulting, missy," Caneback retorted. "You're associating with unmannered cubs these days, are you? Seems to me you should train them a bit before you inflict them on innocent people."

"Innocent? People?" Leo said, getting up on his feet and gesticulating wildly. "This is a troll. Trolls are monsters. You kill trolls, you don't sit around and chat with them."

"You call us trolls monsters? If I had my way, all male humans would be neutered to keep them out of trouble," Caneback snorted. "Jumping all over an innocent bridge keeper, waving weapons around, just to avoid a little fee. Hmmph." He crossed to Hali and poked her in the chest. "I hold you responsible for this, witch. No more trouble from these brats, and I expect extra for my trouble, too. Now are you going to pay up or not? And none of your fairy-fake-witch-gold, either."

Hali grabbed the troll by one arm and dragged him aside. "You know me better than that, Caneback," Hali said. "We'll pay you the regular fee; you talk to Bentwood about the extra for damages. I'll support you, but it was his bright idea to send armed Outworlders out looking for adventure this way. If we don't hit Bentwood directly in the pocketbook, he's never going to pay any attention to the trouble they cause, and I want you to tell him that. You knew him when he was a nasty little sprat, I figure he'll listen to you."

"Laugh his head silly, you mean. Bentwood hasn't listened to me since he got transferred out from under his bridge. Bad move, that. I know he wanted to get away from those dratted billy goats, but a troll without a bridge loses touch with the basic things in life, like moss and algae, and starts thinking about power and treasure instead. It's gone to his head long since."

"Well, just try, will you?" Hali clapped the old troll on the shoulder, and dug out a small silver coin. "This should cover foot passage for six and a little over."

"Tightwad," the troll mumbled, biting the coin. "I should make you pay extra for the four-legged beastie, but you'd just carry him across and claim free passage for him, wouldn't you." He whirled on the gamers, and started shouting. "All right, all right! Get out of here, all of you. I don't want to see your ugly, pink-cheeked faces around here another minute. Go!" he shrieked, moving threateningly at the gamers, and they got—grabbing their weapons and jogging across the bridge, not stopping until they could no longer hear the howling troll's parting taunts and jibes.

CHAPTER
7

RATHER the worse for wear, the party reached the outskirts of Fairehaven just at sunset. Bernie's stubby legs had given out completely, and Hali carried him draped over her shoulders. The gamers had to carry themselves on dragging legs, bending under the weight of their packs. Under other circumstances, they might have gazed in amazement at the medieval city before them. High walls surrounded a jumble of buildings crowded together so closely that from a distance no streets were visible. Above them all, a square castle dominated the scene, silhouetted nicely against a sky just beginning to show red streaks.

As it was, the gamers trudged wearily toward the great gates of the city, barely noting the odd assortment of buildings alongside the road. Jamison did voice a subdued hope that their accommodations that night might be a bit less tumbledown than the hovels leaning against the walls of the city, but even the seediest inn was starting to look promising. At this hour, few people were on the streets, and even fewer cattle, though evidence of their passing was everywhere, providing a tricky obstacle course for the fastidious in the increasing darkness. Hali hurried the group on, and with a quick word to the guards just preparing to close the gates, ushered the gamers into the city proper.

High, overhanging buildings blocked the last light of evening from the streets. Numerous inns and taverns clustered near the gates, and the street was lit by torches jutting from the walls and bright lanterns hanging over the doors. Straight ahead lay a near-deserted marketplace cluttered with empty stalls, baskets, and carts. A broad ring road led left and right, following the line of the great walls.

Hali led the way to the right, cautioning the party to stay together. Away from the bustling taverns, the lights grew more infrequent, only gracing the more prosperous homes and occasional shops. The party left the ring road, taking first a broad cobbled street, then moving on to a succession of back streets and alleyways that soon had the gamers thoroughly lost.

"Are we there yet?" Leo asked. "I wouldn't mind sleeping on the streets right now."

"We're taking a shortcut," Hali told him. "There's rooms waiting for us ahead, but we've got to hurry."

"Wouldn't it have been easier to take rooms by the gate?" Jamison asked, too tired to be truly sarcastic.

"Why pay for an inn when you can sleep at the castle?" Hali asked, effectively stopping what promised to be a cranky inquisition. As one, the gamers lifted their heavy heads to look at the black bulk of the castle looming above them, and tried to estimate how many more miles of twisty passageways they would have to navigate before reaching their berths.

In a surprisingly short time, they reached the entrance to the castle, a gateway wide enough for four horses to enter abreast. Sweeping gates of painted and gilded iron blocked entry to the wide courtyard beyond. Hali passed the gates, coming to an impressive but more human-sized doorway watched by two guards in gaudy red and gold uniforms. Hali gave her name. It was clear the party was expected; the guards admitted them instantly, and an eager page with a candelabrum rushed forward to guide them to their rooms.

Even Jamison had to admit the rooms were more than adequate. Each member of the party had an individual room, part of a rambling suite. Bernie was particularly pleased to be assigned sole occupancy of a comfy nest of furs in what appeared to be an unused walk-in closet. Although they featured more stone than anything else, the rooms were spacious and elegant, lit lavishly with candles, and hung with rich tapestries depicting daily court activities: dining in state, jousting, hawking in the fields, hunting for unicorns, and harassing the field workers. Tracy forgot her fatigue looking at all the ladies in their fine dresses. "I think these must be the medieval equivalent of fashion magazines," she decided finally. "I would die for this red dress with the droopy sleeves."

Leo headed straight for his bed, a towering structure on a raised pedestal, with heavy brocaded drapes looped on the four pillars that supported the carved wood canopy. As he cared less for the decor than for the prospect of rest, he immediately threw himself facedown on the bed, and almost smothered when he sank into the goosedown mattress. He sat up quickly and pounded the feathers into a more obliging shape, and settled down with a sigh of bliss. The others soon followed his example.

This bliss lasted only minutes before a small army of maids and manservants invaded, carrying kettles full of hot water and huge armloads of clothing. A small, fussy man directed the operations. Dressed in gold and white livery that dripped with clearly nonregulation ribbons of every color, the little man carried an ornate gold staff. He introduced himself as Zhorzhay, the castle steward, and with a will of finest steel had all of the gamers washed and dressed in no time, ready to dine with the king himself.

The garments, styled in the latest castle fashions, delighted Tracy and deeply dismayed most of the gentlemen, who found themselves decked out in colorful striped tights and short tunics of rich velvet and brocade.

With an enthusiasm she normally reserved for chocolate sundaes, Tracy tried on several extravagant gowns in rich fabrics before settling, with the advice of a particularly superior ladies' maid, on a relatively simple dress in red velvet with a clinging bodice and a full skirt that fell in rich folds to her feet. With matching ribbons wound through her curls, and a heavy gold necklace, Tracy felt ready to consort with royalty. Hali forwent the proferred gowns, but took the trouble to dress up her outfit, too. Still in basic black, she magicked her skirts to a dramatic, floor-sweeping length, and added a silver diadem with a moon and star design that was repeated in metal tracings on her staff. Bernie accompanied her, freshly brushed but otherwise unadorned.

However uncomfortable they might have felt, Oliver and Jamison actually cut quite dashing figures in their tunics. Jamison's bright blue velvet tunic was cut in a straight line that showed his slim figure to advantage. Oliver's green and gold striped tunic flared from the hips into a short gathered skirt—so short that only the presence of a pair of puffed shorts made it possible for him to leave his room without blushing. After the initial shock, Leo declared himself quite pleased with his red and green tunic, in what he called "the Henry the Eighth look." He actually considered wearing a gold, pearl-studded codpiece before Tracy and Oliver managed to dissuade him, a difficult task only achieved when they could no longer restrain their hysterical laughter.

"They seem to be mixing their periods somewhat," Jamison observed mildly when the group gathered to be escorted to the dining hall.

"I don't doubt the designers pick and choose from your Outworld fashions as it suits them," Hali told him. "Fashions change constantly at court—the length of men's skirts changes faster than the seasons around here."

A pair of servants bearing candelabra silently led the companions on a winding path through dark halls. The pace was hurried, but there was time for questions, and Hali was in a surprisingly expansive mood.

"I never realized castles would be so dark at night. You'd think they could light them better. Isn't this awfully late for dinner?" Tracy asked.

"King Benton likes to save the daylight for other occupations," Hali told her. "No matter what the time of year, he always dines an hour past sunset. We were expected tonight. That's why I pushed so hard. Benton's a nice fellow if you don't upset his schedules, but once you do, he might refuse to ever see you again, and bar you from the city.

"There's a whole city on the other side of the lake, full of exiles, mostly aristocrats and ex-servants of the king. They call the place Anachronopolis. One of the richer lords built himself a duplicate of this castle, and they've created their own court, and made it a law that nothing there can ever happen on schedule. Makes party-going a bit of an adventure: all you can tell from the invitation is when the party's not being held. Guests make their own guesses as to the correct time, and then show up accordingly, usually late. I'm told it's an art form, but it must be wearing for the hostess to have guests coming anywhere from two days early to a week late."

"I'd be a natural at it," said Leo. "I never get anywhere on time."

Hali eyed him balefully. "Try that here and you'll spend the rest of the trip as a real ass, hauling all our baggage."

"Can I ride on top?" Bernie asked wistfully. "My legs really aren't made for all this hiking."

"Don't count on any ride from me, you animated footstool," Leo snapped. "I never mess up when I'm in a game."

Behind him, Tracy and Oliver exchanged rueful glances. "If it's that important, we'll make sure he gets places on time," Tracy promised.

Finally, they came to a series of splendid rooms, brightly lit by dozens of candles. Servants shone in elaborate uniforms of red trimmed lavishly with gold, with the addition of frilly white pinafores for the women. They bustled about with trays, serving several less-well-dressed figures who lounged around the rooms, sipping drinks and eyeing the gamers enviously, whispering behind their hands.

"Who are all these people?" Tracy asked in a whisper.

Hali eyed the loungers with distaste, and didn't bother to lower her voice. "Them? They're hangers-on: aristocrats currently out of favor, the high lords' bastards, and pretenders. There's always at least a dozen princes from countries that no longer exist, hanging around hoping to charm a real princess into marriage. Real slime-balls."

Bernie nobly refrained from pointing out that her opinion was somewhat biased, since several of these princes had refused to date her in the past.

They turned a corner into a wide, mirrored passageway. At the far end, large double doors opened wide on the castle's great hall. It was a room the size of a double gymnasium, with rows of high, dark windows running the length of the long walls. Halfway up the walls, a wood-railed mezzanine circled the room. On it, at the far end of the hall, musicians labored mightily, but no music reached the gamers. Instead, the sound of the crowd washed over them. It was feeding time, and these social lions were definitely hungry. Hardly a place was empty at the long cloth-covered tables. The tables formed a giant horseshoe with the open end toward the doors through which the gamers entered. At the top of the horseshoe, the tables were elevated on a platform where the king and his family sat above the crowd like actors on a stage. Tumblers performed on the floor in the center of the room, almost completely ignored by the rowdy diners, who joked, gossiped, and schemed at the top of their lungs.

The entrance of the gamers, however, caught the attention of many of the courtiers, who turned in their seats to gape at the painfully embarrassed quartet. Patently unconcerned, Hali followed their servant-guides up the length of the hall, leaving the gamers to stumble and blush their way in her wake.

"Why do they all whisper about us?" Tracy hurried forward to ask Hali in a whisper, not sure whether to be mortified or furious.

"That's what you do at court," Hali responded, not bothering to whisper. "It's all a matter of position and prestige. The closer you sit to the king, the higher your position. Newcomers are always a potential threat, and as for us," she paused smugly for effect, "we get to sit at the high table."

"Don't panic," Bernie reassured the stricken gamers, "the food's just as good up there."

They got to the high table, and were relieved to find their seats at one end, far from the portly king and his tall thin queen. The monarchs watched amiably but merely nodded greetings as the party was seated. Hali sat closest to the throne, next to a downy-cheeked prince with an uncontrollable shock of red curly hair and an unfortunate tendency to blush. Bernie sat on Hali's other side, having been lifted with pompous ceremony onto a pillow-topped stool that brought him nearly level with the tabletop. With an eye to possible trouble, Hali placed Leo beside Bernie, within easy reach. Tracy and Oliver came next, with Jamison at the very end of the table, where he sat with an air of conscious self-satisfaction that made it clear he realized he had the least prestigious seat of the group.

Food was served almost immediately, and Jamison's excessive dignity certainly stood out as the meal progressed. Good manners, as the Outworlders knew them, were largely missing, as were forks and napkins. The service certainly lived up to expectations; a page served each diner at the high table, while the less privileged courtiers below had to share the services of harried footmen. However, the lack of forks meant that diners ate with their fingers, which in turn required the use of sleeves and tablecloth as substitutes for the missing napkins. Oliver and Tracy ate cautiously, surreptitiously watching the nearest aristocrats for guidance, and as often as not finding themselves scrutinized in return. Of the gamers, only Leo truly enjoyed the meal. He displayed a talent for dramatic dining, grabbing the roasted legs of various small creatures, ripping off giant bites that left juices dripping down his chin, and tossing the bones over his shoulder with an enthusiasm that kept the pages behind him on their toes.

The king concentrated on his food, and so did everyone else in the room, to the exclusion of conversation. Tracy addressed a quiet comment to Oliver, and found herself being hissed at by Hali and two pages. Not until the tables were cleared for dessert did the king turn to chat quietly with his queen, and a river of babble ran down the tables as the rest of the diners broke their silence. Limited to conversing with their neighbors at the table, the gamers were both relieved and disconcerted not to be able to converse with the courtiers.

Hali chatted tersely with the voluble young prince beside her, who had strong inclinations toward a career in swineherding. "Pigs are really quite noble animals," he told her earnestly. "You can't imagine how intelligent they can be unless you really get to know them. Besides, I hear it's a great way to meet eligible princesses, and you don't have to worry so much about your clothes and hair."

For dessert, the servants brought new plates, new wines, platters full of cheeses and fresh fruits, and a magnificent array of cakes and flaming puddings. Leo attacked a cone-shaped mound of caramel-dripped puff pastries, and Tracy tried a slice of nut cake, on Bernie's recommendation. Oliver and Jamison shared a fresh apple carved into a delicate swan. Bernie nibbled on a pear that had been similarly sculpted into a rose, but his heart wasn't in it; to his own disgust he craved nothing so much as some nice crisp roots, and debated with himself the possibilities of making a midnight raid on the kitchen gardens.

When the king had finished with his dessert, the servants began clearing the tables. A tall gentleman with a booming voice stood up, and called the room to order. The king stood, and began a speech of welcome. His voice was pleasant enough, but high and slightly reedy, with a peculiarly precise accent. It carried poorly in the big room, which echoed rather nastily in any case. The king faced forward, away from the Outworlders, and as a result they had to strain to hear him. Even when he turned toward them from time to time, with a gracious little gesture, the words seemed garbled. Hali drummed her fingers on the tabletop with some impatience, and the gamers watched her carefully, hoping for some cue if any response should be required from them.

Finally, the ordeal was over, with no response required. The king beamed mightily, waved to the crowd, and offered the queen his arm. Everyone in the hall stood, and simultaneously bowed or curtsied as the royal couple left the hall by a small doorway just behind the throne. The minute the door closed behind them, pandemonium broke out in the great hall. A few diners left the hall, but the majority stayed, clustering in little groups to converse. Immediately, a large number moved in on the high table, surrounding the gamers.

"What do they want?" Tracy asked Hali nervously. "And what did the king say? I couldn't make out a word of his speech."

"I'm not sure he said anything," Hali told her irritably, moving close and raising her voice so she could be heard over the crowd. "Someone told Benton years ago that talking that way made him sound important, so he always uses it for his speeches. I suspect he just goes on and on without really saying anything; he's too lazy and not bright enough to write or memorize a speech. He spent one summer herding goats for me, and hardly said a word. I didn't expect him to get this far, but at the end of summer I played along and gave him whatever magical doohickey he was questing for—I think it was a jewelled rattle—and next thing I hear, the poor kid's won the hand of Princess Griselda of Fairehaven—and the kingdom with her. He was in way over his head, in more ways than one; she's almost a foot taller than he is, and considerably smarter, I'd guess. Must have been desperate for a prince is all I can say, not that I'm one to gossip."

"Huh. Best part," Bernie added from floor level, "is that Benton's still scared to death of Hali and always goes out of his way to be nice to her companions. It's a sweet racket. Ow! You didn't have to kick me, you old witch. If I'm not wanted, I'm leaving." Grumpily, he wandered off, picking his way through a forest of legs in search of a forlorn maiden who might be willing to trade a few ear rubs for some warm, furry company. (So far as he knew, wombats didn't purr, but he was willing to fake it if necessary.)

Left behind, the gamers found themselves hemmed in by curious courtiers. "Oh, there you are," said the tall man with the big voice who had so successfully stilled the room earlier. Silence seemed to follow him, as the surrounding courtiers made every effort to overhear his words. "I'm Lord Silverton, the king's seneschal. King Benton specifically wanted me to tell you all that you are very welcome here in Fairehaven, and to make yourselves completely at home. Just let the servants know if you want anything." He looked at Hali somewhat anxiously. "You aren't going to be staying long, I understand?"

"No, just a couple of days," she answered calmly. "We need to get a few supplies for our trip."

"Wonderful, the king will be delighted to hear that, I don't have to tell you. He always gets so nervous when you're visiting. Well, you understand, goats can leave some painful memories, and that awkward wound in the buttocks . . . well.

He would like to have you all in for tea before you leave; could we set a time?" Tea in two days was duly arranged, and the seneschal disappeared into the crowd.

Anxious aristocrats took his place instantly, all eager to talk to the Outworlders.

"What brings you here?"

"Are you on a quest?"

"How lucky you are, having tea with the king! Are you going to ask him for a favor?"

"Tell us about your world. What do people wear there?"

"Is it true magic doesn't work at all? What do you do for entertainment?"

"Is it true you ride around everywhere on mechanical horses?"

"Why aren't you wearing cosmetics? Do you consider them immoral?"

"Do your parents have big kingdoms or little kingdoms? Are you promised already, or are you looking?"

"Don't men wear beards in your world?" In response to a comment from the crowd, the speaker added, "Well, surely they can't all be sissy-boys."

"Why is your hair so short?" It wasn't clear whether this last was directed toward Tracy or the gentlemen in the party. The majority of the male courtiers had long waving hair that fell at least to their shoulders; the ladies generally wore their hair up, covered with an amazing variety of coifs, but the more elaborate hairdos and occasional knee-length braid suggested that the women kept their hair as long as they could grow it. Tracy nervously wound one of her shoulder-length curls around a finger, and backed as close as she could to the others.

The fashion attacks were daunting, but the high level of misconception behind the bulk of the questions left the Outworlders speechless, not knowing where to start even if they had been able to make themselves heard over the hubbub. Hali scanned the crowd, and finally waved at someone. Then she gathered the gamers and cleared a path through the reluctant crowd, making liberal use of her best drill-sergeant voice and waving her staff about like a cattle-goad.

"Make way. I'm sorry, but we don't have time to talk right

now, no, we must go. Make way, you blithering fop! No, sorry, out of the way. If you must know, we have some business to attend to," she snapped at one persistent dandy with flowing blonde hair and a perfectly exquisite tunic in rose and lime green. When he protested, she waved one hand in his face, and he disappeared. Leaning on her staff, Hali bent down and picked up a small frog, oddly colored with a yellow head and stripes of green and rose running down its back.

"Now, if you don't want to share this fellow's fate, stand back and go about your business," Hali screeched at the remaining crowd, holding the frog high where all could see it. Unhappy but unwilling to argue, the courtiers pulled back, a few in the back grumbling about uncouth witches. Only one young lady refused to pull back, and instead walked up to Hali, chin up and shoulders back, ready to do battle.

"That's my Chauncy you've got there in your hand, and I want him back," she demanded. Hali raised one eyebrow, but rather meekly handed over the frog. "Did the nasty witch hurt my little precious?" the lady cooed to the little amphibian, which was clearly yearning for a kiss. She tapped it gently on the nose in reproof. "That's what you get for bothering a witch," she told it. She looked up at Hali. "He's quite harmless but rather obsessed with questions of fashion and taste—gets terribly rude sometimes. I'll leave him a frog for a little. It might do him good."

Hali nodded, waved a hand in dismissal, and swept on with the gamers in her wake. Across the room, they were joined by an old man with a long white beard, robes heavily embroidered with arcane symbols, and a long rowan staff. "Hali, my dear," he greeted her, clasping her hands and chastely rubbing his cheek against hers. "It's been too long. How's spells?"

"Wow, a wizard," Leo breathed. "A real wizard."

"Hello, Endymion," Hali greeted the old wizard before placing hands on hip and turning to Leo. "And what's so impressive about wizards, when a witch doesn't excite you?"

"Um, well, I didn't mean that, honest. I just, well, you know, witches don't do anything big the way wizards do.

Uh." Apparently aware that he was digging his own grave, he stopped and spread his hands in apology.

Endymion laughed heartily, holding his belly like a sorcerous Santa Claus. "Oh, Hali," he gasped, wiping tears from his eyes, "I see you're still working with the total misfits, aren't you. Come on, let's go to my workroom and talk. I want to know everything about this excursion of yours. What have you heard about the latest discoveries on the energy crisis?"

"Just the little Bentwood told me," she told him. "You know me, I'm not the technical type. Let me get rid of the kids and we can have a good chat."

"Kids!" Tracy muttered rebelliously.

"Misfits!" Leo growled.

"I, for one," Jamison interjected regally, "would appreciate a chance to get some sleep. In a real bed. If someone could direct us to our rooms, I think we could all use some rest."

"Not me," said Leo, following the words with a giant yawn. He blushed, and looked at his feet. "Well, maybe."

"Look at you, you're all dead on your feet," the elderly wizard said in concern. "You've had to sit through one of the king's dinners, too. You should at least lie down for a few minutes. Here, my apprentice will show you the way." He waved to a lanky young man leaning against the nearby wall, and the apprentice immediately jogged over. "Gerhard, show these adventurers to the guest rooms—that is where they've put you, isn't it? That's it." Smiling genially, he waved as the adventurers left, then turned to Hali with a devious grin.

"Gerhard'll make sure they all go straight to sleep," he assured her. "Oh, and nice job with that Chauncy fellow. Many's the time I wished I had more of a knack for that sort of thing. It takes too much time to set up a transformation spell to bother with petty revenge, but he's quite a pest, always bothering me about my beard. I told him long beards are required wear for wizards, but now he thinks I ought to dye or curl it or something." He stroked the beard fondly. "Where's that familiar of yours, and what is he now? Looks like a toy bear."

"Wombat," said Hali. "Bernie's a wombat. One of those weird creatures from the Outworld. Bentwood thought wombats were trendy, so . . ." She shrugged. "He's probably out cozying up to the fair maidens, as usual."

"A fine demonstration that character is independent of form," the wizard said cheerfully. "Come, I've got some lovely apricot brandy upstairs, and we can talk."

CHAPTER

8

AS soon as the gamers started moving about in the morning, servants began bustling about, fetching hot water and fresh clothing. Trays full of food were laid out in the suite's central sitting room. The elegant breakfast, which included flaky sweet rolls, fresh bread and fruit, and a variety of beverages, quite satisfied the gamers. Leo and Jamison argued briefly over the appropriateness of coffee and hot chocolate in a fairy-tale world, but agreed that they were at least preferable to the alternative warm drinks made of sweetened ground almonds (which Tracy quite enjoyed) or the oat-milk with molasses, which Oliver found interesting, though he preferred the slightly effervescent apple cider.

Bernie wandered in, and sniffed at the food disdainfully. Having had quite a successful night of hunting (to the thorough destruction of a row of parsnips, and the gardeners' early-morning dismay), he was ready to sleep through the day, witches permitting. Hali had also had a late night, and woke slowly. She passed Bernie as he headed for bed, and entered the breakfast nook just as the others were finishing, and grabbed a roll and a cup of cocoa.

"So," she grumbled, and yawned. "What are you planning to do today?"

The gamers looked at each other, puzzled. "Aren't you going to tell us what to do? You usually do," Leo pointed out.

"We had to come here so you could outfit yourselves, and we had to keep on schedule," Hali said. "From here on, you're on your own. Explore the castle and town, or go shopping. You've got money—well, most of you have—and Fairehaven has the biggest markets in the region, and some excellent shops. You should watch out for the prices in the shops, though, they tend to be higher."

Tracy, a hardened mall veteran, perked up at the idea of shopping, but asked, "How much can we do with only four pieces of gold apiece?"

"*Only* four?" Hali raised an eyebrow. "A single piece of gold will cover a year's food for your average peasant, though it means living mostly on bread and beans." She paused and sipped her cocoa thoughtfully. "The markets here are notorious, and you're bound to get overcharged. Don't ever pay the first asking price, and shop around before you make any decisions. You should be able to get yourselves plenty of decent trail food, better hiking gear, and even fancy clothes and good boots, though you'll pay plenty extra to get them sewn up in two days. Check the secondhand shops for bargains."

"When we've got everything—what then?" Oliver asked. "You told that seneschal guy we're leaving in two days. Are you coming with us?"

"You're stuck with me for the duration of the game," Hali said morosely, staring blearily into her cup. She'd spent much longer than she'd planned talking over the latest wizardly research with Endymion, and technical discussions and diagrams always made her head ache for hours. "We no longer have a schedule to keep. If you manage to find a good quest or adventure to go on, just let me know. Otherwise, we'll tour the countryside a bit and see what turns up. For today you're on your own." She headed for her bedroom, then stopped.

"One last thing," she said firmly. "Dinner begins promptly at one hour past sunset and you will be in your seats, properly dressed, on time, or else. Make sure that he," she pointed to Leo, "doesn't manage to screw up or we're all going to be out in the cold tonight."

Hali left the room, leaving the gamers to their own devices.

"Maybe we should stick together," Tracy suggested. "We should start by shopping for clothes, if they've got to be made to order."

"I prefer to proceed on my own," Jamison said. "I feel safe in assuming that our taste in clothes, among other things, will be quite distinct." With great dignity, he returned to his bedroom, leaving the others to stare at each other, uncomfortably relieved by his absence.

"Well, somebody's got to go with Leo," Tracy said finally, looking at Oliver. "We promised."

"You promised, I didn't," Leo grumbled. "I don't know why everyone assumes I'm going to be late. It's not like they even use clocks around here. How are we supposed to know what time it is, anyway?"

"It's not that hard to notice when the sun goes down," Tracy said.

"Oh, yeah? Well, how do they decide it's sunset around here?" Leo went to a window and leaned out over the wide sill. In a grand, theatrical gesture he waved at the sky outside. "Do they count sunset from when the sun first touches the horizon, or when it actually disappears, or when the sky really gets dark? And how are we supposed to tell from inside the city, anyway? This isn't fair—they can't give us rules without explaining them."

"We just have to make sure we come back when it starts to get dark," Oliver said patiently. "It was real dark in the streets when we came in last night, and we still had time to get dressed. This isn't that big a city, anyway. I agree we should stick together, though. There's no telling what we might run into. We might want to pool our funds for something big."

Leo agreed. "We need a magic sword for protection, something really tough and easy to use, not like all that unbalanced potmetal they tried to unload on us before." Hacking and slashing with an imaginary sword, he stumbled over a few chairs, bounced off a wall, and headed down the hall to his room.

Oliver and Tracy looked at each other and shrugged. "He won't leave without us. He doesn't have any money," Tracy said.

She and Oliver returned to their rooms and dug out the pouches of gold buried in their packs. The pouches were small and nondescript, made of soft cowhide stained a dark brown. For their size, the four gold coins were heavy. With their new awareness of the value of gold, and used to the company of nimble thieves (one of the more popular roles in fantasy role-playing games), Tracy and Oliver decided to hide all but one of the coins in their shoes, where their lumpy presence was more a reassurance than an irritation. Deciding it was probably better not to call attention to themselves, they dressed in the simplest tunics provided by the castle staff.

Meanwhile, Leo decked himself in a velvet doublet striped in red and green over tights with green and gold pinstripes. He was debating with himself over a red velvet hood and a bright green cap with a feather when the others found him. Sighing, Tracy grabbed one arm, and Oliver grabbed the other, and between them they ushered Leo into the castle halls.

On the way out, the trio saw more of the castle than they intended, having declined the services of a guide. In the daylight, they could see that all the hallways had unglazed windows, or at least keyhole slits, providing light and some indication of their location. Unaware that the castle was built around two large interior courtyards, however, they made several false turns. They found themselves in a small vaulted room that looked like a long-unused chapel, then wandered through a long portrait gallery filled with someone's remarkably unprepossessing relatives, all with snub noses, watery eyes, and double chins faithfully depicted in fussy oils and tempera. Finally, the gamers found a twisting back staircase, lit dimly by widely spaced narrow windows. After a surprising number of turns, and no exits, the stairs led down to the kitchen, where a startled footman in an apron left off polishing the silver to lead the three to the castle's front entrance.

When asked, one of the formidable guards at the gate unbent enough to point out the wide, stone-paved road that ran from the castle to the city's main gates, assuring the gamers that it would pass by the town's shops and markets on its way through the city. From the castle gates, the road ran straight along a row of grand houses, mostly blocked off from the street by high walls distinguished only by the variety of ornaments used at the gateways. To the gamers' relief, this route was a far cry from Hali's back-alley shortcut and much easier to follow, though it wound down the hill in a series of long switchbacks that added at least a mile to the trip.

From time to time, they caught glimpses of the lower city, and mentally marked two large squares, filled with milling crowds, as their probable destination. As they walked, the houses got smaller and more crowded. On the lower levels of the city the street was lined with storefronts topped by second stories that jutted out over the street, never quite managing to block the sky from view along the broad way. Uniformed equestrians and the occasional fancy carriage passed by on the way to the castle; following the example of the other pedestrians, the gamers gave the soldiers and "Cinderella coaches" (as Tracy dubbed them) a wide berth.

The shops had cramped front windows, usually glazed with small panes of green-tinged glass so filled with bubbles and waves that they were only marginally transparent. The better-made windows were filled with disappointing displays that often gave little or no clue to the store's stock in trade. More revealing were the large signs hanging above the doors—a giant shoe at the cobbler's shop, a pair of breeches outside a tailor's, and a guitarlike instrument outside a music shop. Less obvious were the gilded pretzel at a bakery, a peacock outside what appeared to be a lacemaker's shop, and a combined globe and sun over a shop that sold mysterious devices that resembled medical tools, but were constructed most elegantly of gold, fine woods, and tooled leather. A broom and flower hung above a shop full of herbs and dark glass bottles. "Herbs for witches," Leo guessed, as a wrinkled crone bearing a homemade broom pushed past them abruptly and entered the store.

Tracy kept careful track of stores with clothing-related

signs, from bolts of cloth and spools of thread to hats, combs, and giant stockings. Oliver wanted a nonmagical rope, but realized quickly that he had no idea what kind of store to look for; general hardware stores were an alien concept to this city, and it seemed unlikely that a shop could survive selling nothing but rope.

Leo optimistically kept his eye out for a magic shop. Since he had no idea what the sign might look like, he stopped to peer inside the door of any shop with a sign he didn't instantly understand. Shooed indignantly out of one shop that catered strictly to women, the stock in trade still not clear to him, he grumbled, "Someone should tell these people about writing."

"Some of the stores do have written signs of some sort," Tracy pointed out. "We just can't read them."

"Probably the local equivalent of '*Se habla español*,'" Leo groused, squinting at one shakily scrawled notice. "They're all in different scripts."

Oliver agreed. "I've noticed at least three distinct styles— one's all spiky, one's rounded, and there's some blocky stuff that reminds me of Korean. This must be the international district."

Tracy skipped backward, scanning the streets eagerly. "Do you think there might be some elves here?" she asked. "I'd love to see some elves, or even a dwarf."

No such beings were to be found, but soon they came to another curve in the road, which straightened out into an open space easily the size of a football field, filled with hundreds of tight-packed animals instead of buildings. The road ran down the center of this area, bordered on each side by ropes and boards. These makeshift fences closed off pens containing a wide variety of livestock, separated by type. Nearest to the gamers, the backs of the close-packed sheep made a fluffy ocean that surged and fell as the noisy ovines milled about. Shepherds armed with long crooks stood about keeping an eye on their charges as farmers haggled and dug their hands into the greasy fleeces. Across the street, goats bleated and jumped about, knocking heads and generally keeping their herders on their toes. Further down the road, hundreds of cattle moved about restlessly, and past them horses tossed proud heads. Pigs squealed and donkeys brayed, and the warm, musty scent of animals filled the air. The Outworlders wrinkled their noses in uncertain distaste.

Tracy found the presence of cattle particularly alarming, and even the males of the party agreed that these did not look like the placid farm animals pictured on dairy products in the local grocery store. Rather, the beasts were lean but deep-chested, and tall—often taller than the riding horses passing by, and more significantly, so tall that Tracy could not see over their backs at all. Their horns, seldom less than three feet in length, curved slightly, sweeping to the front and coming to alarmingly sharp points. The cattle seemed to come in only two colors, either milk white or blood red.

"This doesn't seem right," Oliver commented. "I thought white cows were supposed to be rare and magical."

"Maybe these are the cattle suppliers to the king," Leo said, and shrugged.

The cows lined both sides of the roads, watching the passersby and placidly chewing their cuds. The city-bred gamers found the constant working of jaws vaguely threatening, and the line of oversized longhorns seemed to go on and on. Finally, they came to the horse pens, where the animals, however large, at least lacked horns.

"Do you guys know anything about horses?" Tracy asked wistfully, eyeing a spirited chestnut stallion as it tossed its head in a magnificent fit of pique.

"I rode a pony at the zoo when I was five," Leo said.

"That's about the limit of my experience, too," Oliver said. "I don't think horses are a good idea, considering."

"I have to ask," Tracy said, approaching the man holding the stallion's lead rope. As assertively as she could, she asked, "How much?"

The man eyed her dubiously, and laughed. "This horse is not for little girls," he said in a heavy accent. "This horse eats grown men for lunch."

"Hey," Leo whispered urgently, grabbing Tracy's arm, "around here they might mean that literally."

"Be serious." Tracy shook off his hand, and addressed the groom again. "I'm just curious. How much for the horse?"

The man shook his head, smiling wryly, but answered civilly enough, "Forty gold."

Somewhat shocked, Tracy thanked the man absently and left willingly at Leo's urging. "If one gold piece is enough to buy food for a year, then forty gold—that horse's worth more than a fancy car!"

"You heard the guy. That horse must be magical. Probably costs a fortune in slaves just to feed it." Leo rubbed his hands in maniacal glee until Oliver punched him in the shoulder.

"Knock it off. It's probably a racehorse or something like that," Oliver said, considering other animals in the area. He walked over to a nearby pen and pointed to a sad-looking, swaybacked creature. "How much?" he asked the bored attendant, who brightened up considerably as he looked the gamers up and down.

"Four silver," he said.

"Don't trust him," Leo said in a stage whisper. "He's got a crafty look."

"So what?" Tracy hissed back. "We don't know what that price means, and we don't really want the animal anyway."

Oliver shook his head, and turned away from the horse dealer, who suddenly showed an interest in negotiating.

"Two silver? It's a good horse, very reliable. Brand new shoes, too." He dragged Oliver closer, and lifted one of the horse's feet for inspection. "One and four, then—you're robbing me, but I know you're a fellow who appreciates a fine animal like this. One and three. Check out these strong shoulders." He slapped the horse on the neck and it shuddered beneath the blow. "One even, then. You won't find a better deal in town."

Oliver shook his head and kept shaking it, pulling free from the over-friendly dealer. With Leo and Tracy close behind, he hurried on down the road. The price went down to four coppers before they were out of earshot, and even so they had the feeling they were well out of a bad bargain.

"Shopping here's not as easy as I thought it would be," Tracy admitted, chewing nervously on her lower lip.

"Come on," Leo said impatiently. "Horse traders are notorious connivers, at least in Westerns. Besides, we don't want any stupid horses."

"I suppose you want to walk for hundreds of miles looking for an adventure," Tracy said. "We're never going to get anywhere that way."

"I'd rather walk than try to ride one of those prancey things," Leo said. "They make me seasick."

"I thought you only rode a pony once," Tracy accused.

"Once is all it takes," Leo said authoritatively.

"There's no point in arguing," Oliver said. "We can't afford good horses, and I don't think we want to buy cheap ones from a used horse dealer, since we don't know what we're looking at. Let's find that other market we saw."

Outside the cattle market, the wide road ran through a bustling shop district, with sellers hawking their wares on the sidewalks. Tracy spotted several promising secondhand shops, and Leo found an unmistakable magic store under the sign of the moon and star. (The crystal ball in the window helped.) Oliver was disappointed, but not entirely surprised, by the general lack of books for sale. Literacy appeared to be uncommon in this city.

Dazzled by the noise and wild array of strange and mysterious objects—such exotica as plowshares and pruning hooks, oxbows and sidesaddles, wire bustle frames and saltcellars—the gamers pushed on. After a few blocks, the street suddenly widened again, and the madness spread out into row on row of open-air stalls, tents, and even blankets on the ground covered with individual merchants' wares.

To the stunned trio it appeared that anything could be bought here. Foodstuffs, from repulsive dried toads to fresh fruits, caught their attention, and they decided to break their first gold piece on meat-stuffed rolls. After eavesdropping to determine the usual price, Oliver made his purchase, haggling briefly and emerging triumphantly with half a dozen rolls and a handful of silver and copper coins.

Emboldened by this small success, Tracy and Oliver settled down to some serious shopping. Tracy splurged on some tooled-leather boots, only slightly scuffed, from a secondhand stall. Oliver found a sturdy rope, and at a leatherworker's stall picked up some strong leather thongs and a moneybelt for his coins. After grumbling a bit about his lack of money, Leo selflessly searched the stalls for items his companions might like, though neither Tracy nor Oliver shared his enthusiasm for such items as a rather dyspeptic falcon, a strictly ornamental dagger, or the heavily embroidered cloak that just happened to be Leo's size.

Trail food presented a new problem. None of the gamers had any idea how long they'd have to go before they could buy more. They had only a vague idea, based on the previous two days' travel, of how much food they would need per day, so they settled for an estimated ten days' worth of dried meats and fruit, and a large supply of hard bread wafers that the seller guaranteed would keep for years.

Leo scoffed at these purchases. "Hardtack and beef jerky. Don't waste your money—we'll live off the land, no problem." He seemed not to notice when the others ignored him, and quite agreeably discussed the keeping qualities of the hard sausages offered at another booth, only objecting when asked to help carry the bulky packages. He pointed out that many of the shoppers carried large baskets such as those sold nearby. While Tracy and Oliver bargained for two of these large carriers, Leo bounded on ahead to look for a nearby magic store.

"The baskets were a good idea," Tracy admitted to Oliver, experimenting with carrying her basket on her hip as the local women did when they hurried to catch up. "Still, I wish he'd help a little. I bet you anything he eats more than anyone else does, too."

"No bet," said Oliver. "Since he's not contributing, maybe we should make him live off the land like he suggested."

Tracy grinned. "It would serve him right, but he'd starve for sure, and then we'd end up carrying him, too. This food is bad enough." She stopped to shift her burden slightly. "Do you really think we can hike far with this much stuff?"

"It won't be so bad if we split it up between us," Oliver said. "Besides, it will get lighter as we go along."

"I don't know. My feet are complaining already."

"If Leo keeps messing up, he might suffer a spontaneous transformation into a four-footed jackass and carry the stuff for us."

"Our luck he'd turn into one of those llamas that spits when you overload it—and he'd have a two-pound limit."

The search for useful magic took longer than the gamers had hoped. A wide variety of fortune tellers worked the markets, reading palms, cards, and tea leaves, or scrying in bowls of water, magic mirrors, and crystal balls. Many dealers sold herbs for magical uses as well as cooking and healing; some even offered love charms and interesting philters and potions. Oliver wasn't interested in love charms, and Tracy firmly refused a potion guaranteed to cause pregnancy. Leo expressed interest at one stall in a surefire aphrodisiac, but the guaranteed product was priced well beyond the gamers' means—even if Tracy and Oliver had had the slightest interest in buying it. All in all, the hunt was disappointing, though Tracy took the opportunity to buy packets of herbs, spices, and a brick of salt, just in case she got a chance to cook on the trail. Sugar was extremely expensive; the locals relied instead on honey and molasses, which Tracy decided were too messy to carry on a hike.

On the advice of several of the herbalists, the gamers decided to try a nearby magic shop. They retraced their steps to the main road and found the shop, a narrow hole-in-the-wall they had overlooked completely before. Glazed with dark panes in different colors, the windows and door revealed nothing of the interior, and the overhead sign was an indecipherable symbol worked in wrought iron. Leo pushed the door open cautiously; a bell tinkled with a hint of mystical echo, and when no more ominous noises issued forth, the gamers entered.

CHAPTER
9

"THIS is the sort of place I've always dreamed of," Tracy said. She peered into the gloomy corners of the shop, trying to make out details as her eyes adjusted to the dusty dimness of the shop's interior. "Anything could be in here."

The space inside the shop was larger than the outside would indicate, but still cramped enough to bring on an attack of claustrophobia. Light filtered through the stained glass of the windows, casting a sepia-toned glow over the stock that gave everything an aura of antiquity, rather than simple shabbiness. Crowded cases and shelves filled the room, and merchandise spilled over onto the floor, making it impossible to move without stumbling into something: a pile of bones, a large box of herbs, or even precious (but battered) books. From the ceiling hung hundreds of dark, shriveled bodies, the mummified remains of unidentifiable creatures in various sizes that made the ceiling seem low and uneven and exacerbated the closed-in, cavelike feeling of the shop. Skulls and skeletons were mounted on the walls: animal, human, and some almost human, but with twisted variations on the form that made them impossible to ignore.

Other objects amid the clutter made their own demands on

the viewers' credulity. A wide variety of arcane devices rested in glass cases, most crudely made from gnarled sticks, bones, hair, feathers, and twisted gut, twined together to serve unfathomable functions, and covered with deep-carved runes. A few homely brooms and crooked staves leaned in a rack at the back, and one case glittered with an array of large natural crystals and a few obligatory crystal balls.

Leo had eyes only for one piece among the marvels: a silver sword that shone with a soft blue light all its own. It was mounted on the wall behind a long counter, in the only empty bit of wall space in the shop. More knowledgeable shoppers would have known immediately that this was the shop's showpiece. All Leo knew was that this was the sword of his dreams—it had to be. Somehow it was calling him.

An old fellow appeared at the counter suddenly, startling Tracy, who thought instantly that she had never seen anyone who looked more like a wizard, albeit a rather shopworn one. Wisps of fine, white hair stood out all around his balding head, on which perched a well-worn pointed cap of wine-red velveteen, covered with slightly threadbare symbols embroidered in gold. He wore an equally worn robe of heavy velvet that hung loosely, but still fell in impressive folds to the floor. When Leo failed to notice his presence, the old man smiled benevolently. "Nice sword, isn't it?" he said pleasantly.

Leo nodded. "It's fantastic. I've got to have it. It's magic, right?"

The old man nodded solemnly, but to Tracy's mind his eyes twinkled slightly.

"What does it do? Does it have a name?"

"It has a name," the storekeeper said, nodding. "That's Backbiter, the famed sword of Robert the Contrary, who used it to rid the countryside of the dreaded Scourge."

"What scourge?" asked Tracy.

"Why Scourge the dragon, of course," the old man replied. "Don't tell me you haven't heard the story!"

The gamers all shook their heads, sensing a story in the offing. This was more like a real fairy-tale adventure than anything they'd run into so far, and they were eager to hear the tale.

"Well, from the very day of his birth, Robert was known to do everything backward. As a baby, he cried when he was happy, and laughed when he was sad. When he grew up, he was friends with people he hated, and made the people he liked miserable. Any jobs he did were always done wrong; ask him to paint your barn red and like as not it would come out black and white, or even green. As you might expect, he wasn't very popular at home, and only marginally employable, so he spent a lot of time wandering.

"One day, he came upon a beautiful young lady, chained to a wooden post just outside a cave. She told Robert that she was a princess, kidnapped by the dragon, and begged him to help her escape. Most young men would have felt obliged to rescue her, but Robert liked the girl on sight and in his usual contrary manner declined to assist her, though he was willing to while the time away with a few kisses and caresses the princess was unable to prevent, bound as she was. However, she had an impressive vocabulary and quite formidable vocal cords, and she made her outrage known in no uncertain terms. The noise woke the sleeping dragon, who slithered out to see what was disturbing his dinner.

"As the princess made it quite clear that Robert was not helping her escape, Scourge was quite friendly, even offering to share his dinner. Robert declined that treat, but agreed to stay awhile and chat. They enjoyed a pleasant visit, once the dragon disposed of the noisy princess in a single efficient gulp, but soon a band of knights rode up. With trumpets and loud-voiced heralds the company announced their intention of ridding the land of its draconic nuisance once and for all.

"Scourge persuaded Robert that the knights would be unkindly disposed toward a collaborator. Robert agreed to help, and the dragon gave him a magical sword with which to do battle. Robert mounted on Scourge's back, and they rushed out to confront the knights. The dragon reared high, flailing its wings and roaring to scare the horses. It was an amazingly successful tactic, normally, but this time most of the knights knew better, and had gone in on foot. Robert waved his sword in the air, lost his balance, and took out a large chunk of the dragon's back with one accidental slash of the sword. Its spine severed, the dragon quickly fell prey to the knights, and Robert was hailed as a hero, and his sword dubbed Backbiter."

"Gee, Leo," said Tracy, "that Robert sounds a lot like you."

Missing the sarcasm, Leo agreed. "He was really my kind of guy, except that part about the princess. I'd have been much more chivalrous. No wonder I felt an affinity for the sword. How did it end up here, though?"

The storekeeper chuckled. "Robert went to court to get his reward, but when he drew the sword to be knighted he accidentally disemboweled the king, a fragile old man who died instantly from the wound. The crown prince was so pleased to finally succeed his father that he decreed the incident an unavoidable accident. Thus, Robert went unpunished, though he never did get knighted, and the new king very sensibly decided that Backbiter should be removed from Robert's possession as a matter of national security. The sword went into the royal treasury for a while, then got sold during a budget crisis. Since then, Backbiter's been through a number of hands, and caused quite a few more accidents, some of them fatal to the owners. The blade cuts through anything without any effort: rock, steel, pillows. You name it, Backbiter cuts it. Makes it a little hard to handle safely. It comes with an indestructible magic scabbard, but even so it's not for careless amateurs."

"I'll be more careful than I've ever been in my life," Leo promised. "How much is it?"

"Young man, I rather doubt your best care would be good enough. For that matter, this sword is priceless."

"Why do you have it in your store if it's not for sale?" Leo asked. "We've got gold. Right, guys?"

Oliver nodded. "We've hardly dented our first piece, so we've got seven gold pieces left, but I don't think that sword is a good idea even if we can afford it."

The old man laughed, though not unkindly. "Seven gold won't buy you a sword like this one, I'm afraid. I paid four hundred for it myself."

The gamers gaped at him, Leo in dismay and Oliver with some relief, while Tracy tried to figure an equivalent price in dollars. She gave up with only the vague idea that it would cost at least a million dollars—peanuts to the U.S. Army, and not out of a rich man's reach, but certainly out of hers.

Leo was more sanguine. "We're adventurers," he declared boldly. "We'll earn it. We'll find treasure, fight dragons for their hoards, anything. If we come back with enough gold, will you sell the sword?"

The storekeeper looked dubious, but nodded. "You come back with five hundred gold pieces, and you can have the sword."

"Five hundred?" Leo gasped in outrage. "It only cost you four hundred."

The old man shrugged. "I've got to make a profit, you know, and pieces like this don't come along every day."

Leo tried negotiating. "Look, isn't there some sort of quest we could go on for you? You know, looking for some rare magical bird or elixir or something? I know that sword is meant for me, I can feel it calling me. My palms itch. This is crazy." He stopped and frantically scratched his left hand. "See? I tell you, I've got to have it."

"Sorry," the shopkeeper said firmly. "You've obviously got a little talent yourself, since you can hear the sword, but that's no reason to go giving you this weapon. Now, how about a magic ring, or an amulet of protection? I've got several here, very reasonably priced, just the thing for novice adventurers." He pulled a velvet-lined tray out of the counter, set it in front of Tracy, and held up a small pendant that showed a snake tied into a three-lobed knot. "Here's one, very popular with the ladies. It glows when you encounter a snake in the grass—reptile or human variety."

Her attention caught, Tracy fingered the pendant. "Sounds useful, but I'm more worried about trolls and ogres. Do you have anything that warns of monsters in general?"

"Well, now." The shopkeeper's nimble fingers picked out a medallion depicting a vaguely human figure. "This glows in the presence of nonhumans with humanoid forms—that covers trolls, ogres, gnomes, dwarves, elves, pixies, whatever. No indication whether they're friendly or not, mind you, so you don't want to jump to any conclusions." He set the medallion aside, and picked up a teardrop-shaped pendant. "This one here is more specific, for larger types like ogres or giants. Now, depending on how much you want to spend, this little gem over here is a bit more expensive, but it tells you whether someone is lying or not; in my experience, liars do more damage than monsters in the long run."

The old man described a variety of charms as the gamers listened intently. Leo stopped sulking over the sword long enough to declare that a courage-boosting ring was a good investment, to which the others agreed with less-than-flattering speed that owed little to the surprisingly low price. Attracted more by its elegant form than by its function, Oliver wavered over a dragon-detecting pendant in the shape of a spread-winged dragon. The shopkeeper asked four silver pieces; with Leo's encouragement Oliver reluctantly offered two, and the pendant was his. Tracy purchased the medallion that detected humanoids, bargaining fiercely even though she figured to get double value for her money. She'd use the medallion not only to avoid disgusting ogres, but also to track down at least one real live elf.

Other items in the shop turned out to be too expensive, or useful only to experienced magic users. With Hali along, the gamers decided, they could survive without any of the costly healing spells. Some ancient leather-bound books caught Oliver's eye. Two were even in English, though an archaic version of the language that would have been difficult to read even if the spelling and script had been standardized. He turned them over in his hands wistfully, but the old shopkeeper warned him that the cheapest cost at least two gold. Oliver sighed, and replaced the books.

"How come you only have two books in English? Don't people around here read?" he asked.

The shopkeeper looked at him quizzically. "People don't, as a rule, except serious scholars and magicians, and English is strictly an Outworld tongue, not much market for it except for some of the works on magic and alchemy—folks get a real laugh from that stuff around here."

"Aren't we speaking English now?" Tracy asked.

"Nah," said Leo impatiently. "Hali put some sort of universal translator spell on us. You can tell if you listen to the sounds when people talk. I figured it out right away; it's a trick they use in lots of sf and fantasy novels. Don't you ever read?"

"I read," Tracy said, somewhat defensively. "I've read *The Lord of the Rings* and some other stuff, but I'm not all that big on fantasy except in games."

"Oh, sure," Leo mocked. "I bet you read romances . . . no, I know, you read horse stories, right?"

Tracy blushed beet red. "I used to read horse stories when I was a kid," she told him. "If it's any of your business, I'm concentrating on reading classics so I'll have a head start in college."

"Ooooh, I'm impressed," Leo said.

Annoyed, Oliver moved to stop what promised to be a rousing, if pointless, argument. With one last wistful look around the shop, the gamers gathered their packages and took their leave, reaching the door just as the bell rang and Hali entered, Bernie at her heels.

"Well, well, well," she said, looking the gamers up and down. Like children caught out of school, they couldn't quite meet her eyes, and shuffled their feet for lack of anything better to do. "How's the shopping going?" Her acid tone implied that she expected total disaster. The trio mumbled hurried reassurances and edged past her and out the door, with fading good-byes.

Hali waited until the door closed behind them, then leaned over the counter and narrowly eyed the shop's proprietor. "I'm in charge of those kids, Ozymandias, old friend. You didn't happen to sell them anything harmful or extravagantly useless, did you?"

The old wizard spread his hands, an expression of wounded innocence on his round face. "Hali, what do you think of me? Would I do something like that, to such a nice bunch of kids?" he asked. "All I sold them was a couple of proximity detectors. Well, a courage booster, too, but you know as well as anyone how effective a placebo can be—if they pay enough it works as well as real magic."

"Did you leave them anything?"

"Sure, sure, they bargained like pros. The fat one wanted Backbiter here, but I wouldn't let someone like him handle this blade for any amount of money, particularly not here in the city where hundreds could die before he managed to do himself in. You should thank me for being so foresighted."

"That kid is so catastrophe-prone he'd probably get along with the sword just fine, but I hate to think of the damage he'd do to everyone else." Hali eyed the glowing sword with a grim expression. "That thing is a menace in anyone's hands. Why don't you get rid of it? You'll never be able to sell it, what with the curse."

"That's the problem," the old wizard said, throwing up his hands. "It's been declared Hazardous Waste. Unless I can find a way to make it permanently harmless, or unload it on some warrior who knows what he's doing, I'm stuck with it. Besides, it looks good on the wall."

Hali quirked an eyebrow. "That's fine, right up to the day some talented shoplifter manages to get a hold of it. At least my crew aren't knowledgeable enough to pull it off, not at this point.

"Anyway, that's not what I came in for." Hali reached into her pouch and pulled out a well-worn map and a marking pen. "Marigold—Uglina she's calling herself these days, can you believe it? I heard one customer call her Ugly Mary, what a nickname—anyway, she tells me you're acting as agent for some of the vacant houses in the area. Bentwood's promised me a house of my choosing as a reward for show-ing this little group a good time here in Grimmworld, as he calls it. They don't have any idea where they're going, so I figure I might as well do a little house-hunting while I'm at it." She looked up, one eyebrow raised. "You didn't clue them in to any good adventures, did you?"

The old wizard snorted. "You think I'd waste a good ad-venture on a bunch of Outworld amateurs? No, no, I didn't tell them anything. The fat one wants to find five hundred gold pieces somewhere so he can buy the sword, but he's going to need more courage than any enchanted ring can give him if he plans to defeat a dragon."

Hali sighed. "Off to seek his fortune, then. I was hoping for something a little more definitive, but it seems like that's the way they all start out."

"Mmmm," the old man agreed. "Now, about those houses.

Did you have anything definite in mind? You're not the sort for gingerbread, as I recall." He leaned over the map and pointed. "Here's a nice one you should look at."

Hali leaned over the map with him, and the two settled down happily to a discussion of real estate.

Glad to have escaped the "wicked witch of the wombats," as Leo put it, the gamers meantime hurried to put a little distance between themselves and Hali. Having seen as much of the markets as they could handle for one day, they headed back toward the castle. As soon as they felt a bit more safe, hidden by the bustling crowd, they slowed down. Tracy in particular made slow progress. Her oversized basket would have made it difficult to thread her way through the crowd at the best of times, but she was hampered further by her determination not to take her eyes off the new amulet hanging around her neck. Chin tucked against her chest, she kept bumping into passersby, apologizing absently before walking headlong into the next pedestrian or sidewalk display.

Starting to feel like a distracted day-care worker, Oliver took Tracy by one arm and did his best to guide her along the side of the street, at the same time keeping an eye on Leo, who alternately lagged behind and bounded ahead, in search of anything that could hold his attention for more than a few seconds at a time. When Tracy stopped dead in the street, just staring at her chest, Oliver was furious.

"We're never going to get anywhere if you don't stop staring at that thing," he started to scold, then stopped when he caught sight of Tracy's amulet. It glowed with silver light, and Oliver would have sworn it buzzed faintly just at the upper edge of his hearing range. He caught Tracy's eye, and grinned at the breathless shock in her face. "Don't just stand there, start looking," he told her, and gave her a slight push.

Together, they scanned the crowds, then realized that their target was behind them, riding up the center of the street, a haughty man with rippling blonde hair, dressed in richly embroidered green clothing and mounted on a milk-white stallion. A closer look revealed pointed ears, ridiculously high cheekbones, and prominent eye ridges that swept up and into the hairline, giving the elf the look of an angry hawk despite his delicate, fair coloring. Others of the elven kind accompanied him, one nearly as well dressed on a dapple-grey horse, and another half dozen, clearly servants, in plain tunics and mounted on velvety brown mules.

"Oh, wow," Tracy breathed. "Elves, real elves. An elf lord even." Without thinking, she put down her basket, stumbled into the center of the road, and waited for the party to reach her. Fortunately, the horses were traveling at an ambling walk, for the riders did not stop, nor even try to go around. Instead, Tracy came out of her daze just in time to jump back at the last minute. She caught herself from falling, then jogged along beside the elf lord.

"Sorry to bother you, your lordship, but are you an elf?" she asked breathlessly. "Well, of course you are, but I've never seen an elf in real life before and I've always wanted to, you know. You're so magnificent, your horses are wonderful. I'd love to talk to you, just for a second. Maybe I could meet you somewhere, if you're too busy right now." Still following, she waited anxiously for a reply.

The elf lord's glance flicked over her ever so briefly, and she held her breath in anticipation, but the elf went back to glaring at the road before him.

"Oh, please," Tracy begged. "I don't have much money, but I'd even pay for a chance to talk to you, give you my firstborn son, anything." Not watching where she was going, she stumbled over an uneven spot, and grabbed at the elf lord's saddle for support. Immediately, he reined in his horse, and glared down on Tracy, who was grasping his stirrup. Aghast at her own presumption, Tracy jumped back.

"I'm so sorry," she gulped. "It was an accident. I tripped."

The elf turned to his elegant companion. "Obviously they don't observe the leash laws in this town," he drawled.

Tracy gasped, and put her hands on her hips. "Well! How rude! I always thought elves had good manners, at least. All I wanted was to talk to you."

The elf lord frowned. "I want this creature out of my way immediately," he said.

"Certainly, Lord Almurran," his companion said, spurring

his horse straight at Tracy. Tracy dodged the horse, but the elf managed to strike her a glancing blow with his heavy riding whip. He reached up for a second blow when a sizzling blast of light caught him in the chest, knocking him backward over the horse's rump and onto the street.

"Yea, Hali," came Bernie's cheerful cry. "Zap the snooty bastards." Stunned, Tracy turned to see the furious witch striding up the street, her staff lowered in ready position. Close behind gallumphed her blood-thirsty familiar, teeth bared in as fearsome a snarl as he could manage, given his round-faced furriness.

"Sorry, O Great Lord El-Murrain," Hali snarled, "this one's under my protection." She planted herself next to Tracy, pointing the end of her staff at the elf lord.

Unperturbed, he eyed her from on high with mild interest. "Well, well, if it isn't that scruffy little witch who stole a rowan branch from the queen's own grove. What was its name? Ivy, or Mistletoe, something like that."

In no way appeased by recognition, Hali warned him, "You lay a finger on any of my charges, I'll turn you into a borer beetle and let you destroy your own groves."

"It's so sad to see such talent wasted on vermin. Talent is as much use to humans as horses are to fish. No finesse, no taste whatsoever," Almurran commented to his companion, who cautiously stood up and dusted off his breeches before remounting. Without comment, the party of elves rode on, but Tracy noted with interest that though they affected to ignore the humans, they gave Hali a wide berth.

The minute the elves passed out of earshot, Hali grabbed Tracy by the collar and pulled her over to the side of the road, where Leo and Oliver waited with the baskets.

"What in the world did you think you were doing?" Hali demanded. "You don't just walk up and accost an elf lord in the middle of the street."

"How was I supposed to know?" Tracy asked, straightening her tunic. "I've never seen an elf before, but I've dreamed of meeting one as long as I can remember. I figured it couldn't be worse than asking a rock star for an autograph."

"Well, you know better now," Hali said.

"Yeah, next time just throw rotten tomatoes," Bernie suggested, ducking behind Oliver's legs to avoid a kick from Hali. "You ask me, those pretty-faced snobs deserve to get taken down a notch or two."

"Those pretty faces hide ruthless minds with a lot of power at their command. Elves have only one use for humans, male or female, and they usually kill their sex partners when they get tired of them. A few perverts keep humans like pets, but it's not a life-style I recommend."

"Rates right up there with being a witch's familiar," Bernie said.

"That reminds me: you haven't done a thing to earn your keep today," Hali told him. "I have more errands to run. You stay with these kids and keep them out of trouble. I know that's like setting the wolf to guard the sheep, but at least you know what will get you killed."

Bernie attempted to click his furry heels, but had better luck saluting with one paw. "*Jawohl, mein Kapitän.*"

Once Hali was out of sight, Bernie got down to business. "Okay, guys, what kind of food have you got?" He approved the durability of the food, but suggested a few additions, including packets of herbs for tea and a small cooking pot with a handle so they could hang it over a fire. "We can raid the castle kitchens for fresh food just before we leave," he decided. "The cook does a mean pastry, and as I recall, she's a soft touch for travelers. I suspect she's never been out of the city, and thinks leaving is as good as a death sentence. It's a pretty common attitude around here."

Food taken care of, transportation was his next concern. As Tracy observed quietly to Oliver, Bernie was second only to Leo in his regard for personal comfort. Determining that they still had more than five gold pieces left, Bernie made a beeline for the stock market, bypassing the horses for donkeys and mules.

"Wouldn't horses be easier to handle?" Tracy asked hopefully.

Bernie spared her a scornful glance. "Horses are big, skittish beasts, and besides that they're expensive to buy and to feed, unless you're willing to waste half the day letting them graze—if you can find open grassland. Donkeys may not be the most willing animals available, but they're thrifty. A good mule combines the better features of both donkeys and horses."

Carefully keeping clear of restless hooves, Bernie examined the animals for sale. He stopped at one pen that held a single donkey and a two-wheeled farm cart. A man in a leather apron and simple farmer's clothing leaned against the cart. He offered no help, but didn't object when Bernie had Tracy grab the donkey by the halter and lead it back and forth, which she proudly managed with only an initial balk by the rather inquisitive ass. "You selling the cart?" Bernie asked the dark-haired farmer leaning against the vehicle.

"Maybe," the farmer said. "What you offering?"

"Depends," Bernie said. "What if we take the donkey off your hands while we're at it? You've got harness for it, of course."

"Maybe. Twelve silver."

"This donkey's pretty small," Bernie said. "How do we know it can pull a cart more than a mile or so?"

"It'll pull," the farmer said, spitting to one side. "Ten silver."

"One gold two?" Bernie squawked. "For a donkey and an old farm cart? I wouldn't pay more than six silver."

"It's awfully cute," Tracy said, stroking the donkey's soft white nose. Bernie swatted her in the ankle, and gave her a look of pure disgust. She tried to undo the damage. "But it's too small. We've got a lot of traveling to do. This little fellow couldn't possibly keep up. I still think we should go with a real horse."

The farmer spat again. "Donkey's a real worker, cart's steady. Man could make his living with a setup like this. Nine silver."

Bernie shook his head sorrowfully. "I couldn't go over seven. Not for a donkey. Especially since we haven't even seen its teeth. It could be on its last legs for all I know."

"One gold, then," the farmer said, stirring himself enough to grab the donkey's head. He stuck his thumb in the side of its mouth, forcing the jaw open. With the other hand, he drew the donkey's rubbery lips back, away from the sharp incisors.

"Well . . ." Bernie mused, eyeing the teeth myopically and

wishing he'd had Hali make him a new pair of glasses. "All right, but you have to teach these three how to harness the donkey, otherwise no deal. Done?"

"Done," agreed the farmer. His lessons relied on hands-on experience, rather than verbal instructions, but after each of the gamers had taken a turn untangling the web of leather straps and tying them on the patient donkey, they felt they had a good understanding of the basic process, even if there always seemed to be one more strap than they could quite account for. Driving instructions were not included.

"We're going to lead the little dustball, not ride," Bernie told the surprised gamers. "This isn't that kind of cart, and we don't want to weigh it down more than we have to. It'll do to haul the baggage, though."

"Don't tell me you don't expect to ride," Leo accused.

"If you haven't noticed, I've got short legs," Bernie responded reasonably. "Without packs, you guys will be making much better time, and I'd just hold you back. Not to mention I weigh a lot less than you do." With that, he got Oliver to lift him onto the flat shelf that served as a makeshift seat at the front of the cart. Tracy, already reconciled to the idea of a donkey instead of a horse, went eagerly to the little creature's head, and taking the lead rope led the donkey and cart into the street.

By the time they reached the castle the sun was low in the sky. The shadows of the tallest towers reached clear across the city, though the sky was still clear blue. The guards at the main gate directed the tired shoppers to an alley that led directly to the castle stables, where an unimpressed stablehand found space for the cart and a small stall for the donkey. Tracy made sure that the little fellow had food and water, and reluctantly left when the others became impatient.

"We've got to name him," she said. "Horses are easy; you can just pick something descriptive, like Blaze or Silver. Donkeys all look alike to me. Otherwise, I'd call him Whitenose."

No one else had any suggestions, so Bernie declared Whitenose the donkey's provisional name, and ushered the trio into the castle to get ready for dinner.

CHAPTER

10

DINNER that night followed much the same pattern as the night before. Bernie had his trio dressed and down early so they could sample the delights of the castle cocktail hour; Hali and Jamison showed up just before the meal started, and as a group they entered the great hall, taking their places at the high table. Rather than an after-dinner speech, a minstrel sang his latest epic lay in a piercing falsetto. The song described the life of the king (including his precocious toilet training), dwelling at length on his ordeals at the hands of a horrible hag that led to winning the hand of the fair princess Griselda. Hali enjoyed hearing herself described as "bony, wizened, wicked, and fell," but after that King Benton's life story went rapidly downhill, at tedious length, including a half-hour listing of the "lawless laggards, lamentably late" who were banished from court for the crime of tardiness. By the time the king rose from the table, the gamers were ready to retreat to their rooms.

"This place looks glorious, and I've never seen such food," Tracy said, "but I feel like I've been bludgeoned by boredom. No one talks about anything but their clothes, or their social status."

"Just like a bunch of girls," Leo agreed, rather unwisely,

and had to run the rest of the way to their rooms to keep ahead of Tracy.

The next morning, the gamers took their time over breakfast, having no pressing plans for the day. With plans of her own, Hali again left the younger gamers to Bernie's tender mercies, with a quick warning. "Don't forget, we're having tea with the king. If you haven't noticed, the castle bells ring every four hours, and they serve tea promptly at the first bell after noon. Ask the servants to show you the hourglasses spotted about the castle, and sundials in the courtyards, and be back here in plenty of time to dress. Benton likes lots of ruffles and frills at tea."

"Yet another anachronism," Jamison noted after she left. "For this teatime ritual we seem to be mixing Victoriana with a basically medieval millieu. I spent considerable time at the markets yesterday, and encountered numerous items that didn't fit into the overall design of the game: paperclips, safety pins, clothing with zippers, rubber balls, even turkeys (strictly a New World bird) at the poulterers, but no potatoes to be seen. Despite a general lack of written materials, I found a few books in English, paperbacks yet, with recent copyright dates."

"We knew they had New World stuff here—chocolate's not native to Europe, either," Leo pointed out.

"The Grimms collected their fairy tales in the 1800s, didn't they? That's well after the discovery of the New World, and into the Industrial Revolution," Oliver added. "That could explain some of those things."

"Zippers are definitely post-Grimm," Jamison noted. "For that matter, why have zippers but no indoor plumbing or clocks? You'd think the king with his chronic obsession would have clocks all over the place. Given the choice, toilets are the first thing I'd import. Those little rooms built out over the castle wall are hopelessly unsanitary, not to mention drafty, and the filth on the walls does nothing for the air quality in town."

"No canned goods, either," Tracy noted. "I remember being surprised to learn in history class that the process was invented in the early 1800s. Everything here is dried, pickled, or salted to death. The king's cooks must be able to get fresh foods to make those banquets, but most folks aren't so lucky."

Bored, Bernie yawned, and said, "I don't know why you're so worked up about it, but there's continual communication between this world and yours. Hali brought me here from New York years ago."

"In that case," Jamison interjected, "I would expect to see far more incidences of modern technology, and more items from our world than a few books."

Bernie tried to explain. "It takes a magic worker to make the crossing, and carrying objects between worlds, particularly metals, is a major project. Organic objects like paper and cloth are easier to transport. Living creatures are easiest, particularly if they want to come. Theoretically, humans can actually dream themselves here temporarily, if they believe strongly enough. Sometimes they stick around long enough to pass on new ideas, if they know enough. Me, I wanted television, but I don't even know how to make wire, much less generate electricity, and that's just the start.

"Also, folks here are traditionalists. They really resist new technologies, particularly ones that make heavy use of metals. Plumbing could be done without metal, I suppose, but the hassles of getting running water piped in are enough to keep the idea from catching on. You'd have to build a high dam and aqueduct, or use pumps to get water to reservoirs in the castle towers, just to get decent water pressure. Paperclips are easy enough to make, but here zippers are luxury items, made by hand, tooth by tooth. I don't know the technical details of canning, but tin cans would have to be made and sealed by hand by the smiths, an expensive process. The local glassmakers aren't precisely into high-quality mass production, either. If you could use ceramic jars, the potters might be your best bet, but would you know precisely what that would require for safe food preservation?"

Tracy shook her head.

"See?" Bernie continued. "That's the sort of thing you're up against here. Wizards keep up on Outworld science, but they like to keep their secrets. Hali's kept an eye on medical developments, too. Among the other things that have caught on you can list aspirin and penicillin, though maybe not quite in the forms you're used to—folks grow their penicillin in jars of moldy bread. Still, with witches around, dentists and surgeons haven't been necessary. If you need serious medical assistance, you just pay a witch to fix you up, though it can get expensive."

"Those who can afford it live forever, I suppose," Jamison said.

Bernie shook his head. "Unfortunately, elves do, or so I'm told, but most humans are quite mortal. There's a limit to what magic can do. The older and sicker the patient, the more power it takes to heal, up to a point where it's impossible. Witches and wizards live an incredibly long time, a side effect of the talent, I guess. A witch's familiar shares her longevity. Live-in lovers do, too, but I'm told their presence saps the witch's powers. Hali's never managed to get a man to stay long enough to test that, though."

"I can't imagine why," Jamison sniffed. "Such a charming personality."

"She's at her crabbiest first thing in the morning," Bernie added. "Imagine waking up next to her, and you sort of get the idea.

"Anyway, some of the hottest ideas imported involve working with people. Organized labor caught on a while back; those ogres actually have a really powerful union."

"Let me guess," said Jamison. "People pay the ogres not to kill them."

"Nah," said Bernie. "They're not into protection rackets. Maiming and killing is their job. You want hired killers, bloodthirsty mercenaries, or really serious bodyguards, you call the ogres' hiring hall. The union regulates their activities to keep free-lance mayhem from annoying the general populace too much. I admit that if the ogres do go on strike they're likely to increase their more undesirable activities, rather than stopping work."

"You mean someone paid that ogre to attack us on the road?" Tracy asked indignantly. "Why would anyone do that?"

Bernie was saved by Leo's quick, if faulty, reasoning. "I bet there're purists who don't want Grimmworld contaminated by our foreign presence. Especially if the game succeeds. There'd be hundreds of gamers tearing up the countryside, chopping down the ogres and dragons, making endangered species of them. Heck, if I were an ogre I'd be against us just on that basis alone."

Jamison snorted. "Grimmworld exists only for the entertainment of gamers. I can't imagine the writers would include a bias against gamers."

"Sure they would, at least in the monsters, so we'd have something to fight," Oliver pointed out.

"Or maybe one of the programmers got creative," Leo suggested. "They're always putting extra 'backdoors' and secret weapons and stuff in computer games."

"Or just possibly it's a bug. It's certainly not consistent with the version fed us through this wombat. A singularly ridiculous vehicle for exposition," Jamison said, scribbling in his little notebook. He closed it with a snap. "Well, all this has been horribly enlightening, but I plan to continue examining the shops. I must say, this town shows considerable attention to detail on the part of the planners, but I have yet to track down any items that would add significantly to our nonexistent quest, though I'm sure some must be scattered about."

"We found a great sword," Leo said, "but we have to get a pile of gold to guy it."

"We got some amulets to detect nonhumans, and a lot of food, too," said Tracy. "Plus a donkey and cart to carry our stuff. What have you got so far?"

"I have refrained from making any purchases," Jamison said. "I prefer to examine all possible options before making a move of such import. Now, if you don't mind, I will be on my way."

The others waited for him to leave before discussing their options.

"Well, he's no loss," said Leo, "but maybe he's got a point about special objects."

"We could spend a year trying to cover all the shops. I vote we check out the castle," Tracy said. "Who knows? We might find something useful lying around in a cellar or something."

Oliver also voted for exploring the castle, and Leo went along with the majority cheerfully enough. At Tracy's suggestion, they started with the stables, where they checked up on Whitenose, who appeared quite happy with his morning hay. Tracy then made the acquaintance of other equine inhabitants of the stables: fine-limbed riding horses, stocky war-horses, and the towering draft horses. Less interested in horseflesh, Oliver, Leo, and Bernie delved into the mysteries of the tack room, which smelled sweetly of leather and saddle soap, with bitter undertones of equine sweat. Pegs on the walls held bridles, horse collars, and complex bits of harness; floor racks held saddles and blankets; cupboards and wooden boxes revealed brushes, combs, ribbons, feathers, bells, and other ornamental paraphernalia.

"If there is a magic bridle in here, I sure wouldn't know it," Leo said.

Oliver agreed. "We'll just have to forget catching a Pegasus, I guess."

They dragged Tracy away from the horses only by agreeing to at least walk by the rest of the stalls, which ran in long aisles along two sides of a small square. Most of the stalls were filled, but none with any horses that seemed the least bit magical. One isolated stall held a huge hart, which threatened any passersby with its magnificent antlers. A groom on guard shooed the gamers away before they could even count the points on the antlers.

Past the carriage house and a blacksmith's forge, the stable block connected to a large courtyard where soldiers exercised. As the gamers crossed, they paused to watch swordsmen hacking at large wooden posts set up at the edge of the parade ground.

"Not much technique to it," Leo said. "Just hack and slash. Maybe I should get another sword."

"Forget it," said Tracy. "I'm not paying for you to toss another weapon into the bushes."

"Hey, that one was defective. We've still got enough money to get a decent sword this time."

"We've got money," Oliver said, siding with Tracy. "You don't." Grabbing Leo by the arm, he dragged him off the field and into the castle. They passed a guardroom and a well-guarded armory, and found themselves in the working part of the castle. Unerringly, Bernie led the group past a series of storerooms and servants' quarters to the enormous kitchen, where he introduced the gamers to the head cook, a fluffy dumpling of a woman who insisted on having them sample a bit of fresh-baked bread.

The kitchen was hung with ceiling racks and hooks that held pans and pots, ladles, and more esoteric implements. Others held whole sides of beef, mutton, and pork, and one four-pronged hook gaily displayed fresh game, not yet skinned: grey hares, gaudy pheasants, generic ducks, and even a pair of bristly hedgehogs. It was worth a quick look, but the gamers quickly moved on. With Bernie in the lead, they visited the buttery, where dairy products were kept cool in troughs of running water fed by the castle spring; a still-room filled with dried herbs and mysterious jars; and a well-stocked root cellar that would have tempted Bernie had he not had good hunting in the night. Down a narrow staircase they found the wine cellars, and amused themselves by thumping on the giant casks (just in case one hid a secret passage) and peering into the darkest, spookiest corners for lost treasures.

Having found little beyond wine and cobwebs in the cellars, they headed for sunlight and took a quick turn through the kitchen garden, a pleasant place filled with neat rows of vegetables, some luxurious herbs, and a row of espaliered fruit trees along one sunny wall—and a vengeful gardener who chased Bernie around the basil patch twice before the galloping wombat retreated through another doorway into the maids' sewing room, the gamers hot on his heels. Bernie shot under a footstool and out the other side, upending one hysterical seamstress and bowling over another before he made it out of the room. Close behind, the gamers found themselves in a whirlwind of angry starched linen and deadly hot irons. Baskets were upended, and more than one sheet sent in for simple darning suffered rips totally beyond repair.

"You know, these fantasy worlds can be dangerous," panted Leo when they finally pulled to a halt behind a staircase at the bottom of one of the towers. He held his palm up ruefully to show a red crease through the center. "Those irons are really nasty. I tried to pick one up so I could defend myself, and the handle was red hot. I should have figured from the giant oven mitts the maids were using."

Concerned, Tracy examined his hand. "Gee, Leo, that was stupid. Now what are we going to do about this burn? It looks serious."

"Nah," Leo said. "I've done worse lots of times. It'll be OK if I don't try to use the hand."

"We'll just have to be careful not to engage any more gardeners or laundry maids in battle, then. Are there any other angry servants around that we should know about?" Oliver asked Bernie.

"Me?" the wombat cried indignantly. "The innocent victim of a gardener's unthinking prejudice against small, furry animals? He must have mistaken me for a gopher. The servants here all know and love me. Though to be cautious I think we should avoid the queen's private garden. Just a precaution, you understand."

"Right."

At Bernie's suggestion, they took the stairs up into the tower. Intended for use by servants, with no frills, carpeting, carvings, or frescoes for entertainment, the broad stairway was nonetheless pleasant to climb, with large windows at every other landing, providing fresh air, light, and some magnificent views of the river and plains beyond the city. Leo counted floors as they passed, three floors as part of the main castle, then another nine as they ascended the tower. The top floor was empty except for a few benches, but wide arched windows provided an excellent view of the countryside in all directions.

"Oh, for a pair of wings," Bernie sighed, going to one of the windows and standing on his inadequate hind legs. "Could someone lift me up so I can see?"

Oliver obliged, lifting the wombat up onto a broad window ledge.

"That's more like it," Bernie said. Squinting somewhat nearsightedly, he nonetheless managed to identify and point out the Silverrock mountains and the foothills where the Black Buck Inn rested, and the gamers finally felt a sense of achievement just in having hiked so far.

"So, where do we go from here?" Leo asked. He scanned the horizon for possible destinations, but failed to spot even a likely town in the bucolic countryside spread out before him.

"Well, we could go just about anywhere, but I suspect Hali will head upriver, unless you guys come up with something better. See those woods up north, and those rolling hills beyond? That's magic country: lots of witches in huts, enchanted animals, that sort of thing. Not too many people live there, just a few desperate farmers and woodcutters. Real fairy-tale material, if you catch my drift."

"Some fairy tale," groused Leo, blowing on his sore hand. "When are we going to find something to do?"

"We should search more of the castle," said Tracy. "Look at it all. We've hardly scratched the surface. What's in the other towers?"

Bernie squinted at the towers. "Let's see: the tallest, pointy one on the city side is the lookout tower, where the guards hang out. The squat, rounded ones are family residences—they get a little extra privacy on the upper floors, and I guess they're easier to guard, not to mention it's handy to be able to park your mother-in-law in her own quarters on the other side of the castle if she gets to be a pest. See that tall, square tower with the dragon weathervane? That's the court wizard's tower, where Endymion and his crew work. It's away from most of the residences, in case an experiment blows up or gets loose. That garden on the side with all the flowers and trees is the queen's private spot; nice place, but the gardener's a real grouch, and the guards can get sticky with intruders. The great hall's between the two paved courtyards, in that big square box with the funny arches on the sides."

Tracy said, "I'd like to see the wizard's tower. Do you think they'd let us?"

Leo agreed. "I'd love to see a wizard at work. Maybe pick up a few pointers myself."

"As long as we ask nicely and don't get in the way, it should be okay," Bernie said cautiously. He led them down, past the third floor. "Nothing but bedrooms crammed full of the lucky courtiers in favor. All the interesting stuff is on the second floor, only here they call it the first floor—the first floor above ground level, I guess. Kinda confusing."

Avoiding courtiers whenever possible, the gamers followed Bernie through some of the less-used halls, passing through long galleries hung with paintings or filled with statues. A rococo music room held a white-painted harpsichord, piano, and gilded harp that perfectly matched the room's decor, though when the gamers tentatively tried keys and plucked strings they found the instruments woefully out of tune.

One unused sitting room lured the gamers in with its avian theme, from the wallpaper birds flitting across the walls to the elaborately carved chairs with backs shaped like lyrebird tails. Stuffed birds filled two large glass-fronted cabinets and adorned most of the furniture. A pheasant stalked the coffee table, big-maned Polish chickens perched on the back of one couch, and two peacocks fanned their tails before the hearth, making colorful firescreens. The cabinets held rare birds, carefully labeled, including a Russian firebird, a green-tailed quetzal, and a rather dull, slightly-singed bird labeled "phoenix." Tracy debated stealing a phoenix feather, on the grounds that it had to be magic, but Bernie dissuaded her.

"You don't want to try stealing in this castle," he said. "This place is completely spellbound. Otherwise, the courtiers would steal every valuable from the place to pay for their wardrobes. If you really want something, ask the king for it at tea, but talk to Hali first. No point in wasting a guest-gift on something useless."

"What do you mean, guest-gift?" Leo asked, suspiciously.

"It's a tradition of the castle. As guests, you get to make one totally ridiculous request. Usually, folks ask for rich trinkets. Only catch is, next time you visit you have to return something of equal value."

"Are we coming back here?" Leo asked thoughtfully.

Bernie grinned. "Probably not. Wouldn't want to wear out our welcome, now would we?"

"Now, wait a minute," Tracy said. "Don't go making any grandiose plans without talking to us, Leo. Bernie, what happens if a prince comes in asking for a princess?"

"There are special conditions for princesses. You can't ask

for married women at all, but the king gets to set a value for a marriageable princess (assuming she's both a subject and a relative) and demand payment up front. You know, 'You can have the princess's hand in marriage and half the kingdom if you bring me Zeeshar's magic jewel-encrusted corkscrew.' That sort of thing."

"That's terribly sexist," Tracy said. "Don't the princesses have any say in the matter?"

Bernie shrugged. "I suspect so, but they keep it quiet. For that matter, crown princes usually get sold off by their fathers for the sake of an advantageous alliance. Younger sons have to fend for themselves, except in a couple of countries where the youngest son gets the throne. It's all crazy; I tried suggesting democracy and equal rights when I first came here, but even the malcontents like having kings and queens—won't consider doing without."

The gamers managed to make it to the wizard's tower without losing too much more time on the way, with Leo in particular lost in thought, contemplating the myriad possibilities of the guest-gift. A timid apprentice let them into the tower, explaining that no major experiments were under way at the time. Five youthful apprentices bustled about, grinding and mixing powders at high laboratory benches. A familiar tall glass structure dominated the center of the room, a maze of tubes and beakers connected by transparent tubing that would have been at home in any mad scientist's workshop. The next room fit the gamers' expectations much better, with somber wood-paneled walls, a stone floor covered with arcane chalk diagrams, and large white and black candles marking various points.

The wizard himself, alerted by yet another apprentice, bustled into the room. "Well, if it isn't Hali's little friends. Come to see where the real magic gets done?"

"Give me a break," Bernie grumbled.

Endymion laughed heartily, setting his belly to jiggling like the proverbial bowl full of jelly. "You witch-folk are so easy to tease, I can't resist. So, what can I do for you?"

"I want to learn real magic," Leo told him. "Can you teach me a spell or something? Hali showed me her way, and it just didn't work for me."

"He dissolved a rock," Bernie said.

"Yes, Hali mentioned that," Endymion stroked his beard thoughtfully. "You didn't happen to keep a sample of it, did you? No, I rather thought not. I've been studying a bit of your Outworld science of late, and I find atomic theory fascinating, but applying it to magic is difficult. I assume you didn't actually split any atoms, but would you say, young man, that you dissolved the crystalline structure, leaving the molecular nature of the rock intact, or did you reduce it to its elemental components?"

Leo hesitated. "I guess the molecules were still intact. I was just thinking of molecules vibrating, with lots of air between them, when the rock fell apart. I haven't been able to do it again, though. I thought maybe using spells would be easier."

"Easier? Hmmm," Endymion considered. "Have you studied a great deal of science?"

"I've taken a class or two," Leo hedged. "What does that have to do with magic?"

"The disciplines are surprisingly similar," the wizard told him. "How about higher mathematics—algebra, calculus, analytic geometry, number theory, topology, that sort of thing?"

"I've taken some algebra, and a quarter of college-level calculus," Leo said.

"Yeah, but did you pass?" Tracy asked.

"Hey, whose side are you on?" Leo asked indignantly.

"Now, now," Endymion said indulgently. He put one hand on Leo's shoulder. "I'm afraid your background doesn't indicate the sort of intense interest I usually look for. Still, you obviously have some talent, and there's that new field called 'chaos theory'—from the name, you'd be a natural at it."

"Whatever Hali told you, I deny it," Leo said. "I've devoted my life to fantasy games. If I haven't been that interested in science and math, it's not because I'm not good at them. I just never realized that they related to magic in any way. That's what I've really wanted to do all my life."

Endymion looked him over seriously. "Well, you're a bit old, but if that's what you really want, I'd be willing to take you on as an apprentice. At least you already know how to read and write."

"An apprentice."

"Yes. You start out familiarizing yourself with the workrooms and equipment. The first year consists mostly of sweeping floors, washing bottles, and suchlike. You work up gradually over a period of seven years."

"Can't you just teach me a quick spell or two to get me started?"

The old wizard sighed. "Young people want everything right away. It's not that easy, I'm afraid. I wouldn't consider teaching you even the most basic spell without the necessary background. It's full apprenticeship or nothing."

"Can you do that?" Tracy asked. "I mean, it would spoil the game, wouldn't it?"

"I think I could persuade Hali," Endymion said. "I'd forgotten about this game business, but times run differently between worlds, so we'd have no trouble returning Leo to the same time as you others, even if he spent decades here. If he masters the mystic arts, he wouldn't age appreciably, which would certainly save explanations, but after that long a time there might be some disorientation on returning to the Outworld, and no telling whether he'd have talent enough to return himself here later. He would have to return to the Outworld eventually—it would spoil the game to have players go missing. Still, I think we could work out the details, if you're willing to commit for the full term."

"Seven years?" Leo gulped. "What if I decide I'm not suited to wizardry?"

"Once you sign the apprenticeship contract, you're committed. If you're truly unsuited to the work I could dismiss you, but you'd still have to either buy out the contract or work off the rest of the time as a bond-servant," Endymion said. He gave Leo a fatherly pat on the shoulder. "It's not an agreement to enter into lightly. Think about it. You can let me know after dinner."

Endymion called one of the apprentices over to give the gamers a tour of the workshops, but their hearts weren't in it, and they soon left, and walked quietly down empty halls.

Suddenly, bells rang out, so close the stones of the castle vibrated with the rhythmic tolling.

"It's noon. Lunchtime," Bernie said. "Let's go raid the kitchen."

With Bernie along to sweet-talk the cook, the gamers secured big bowls of stew to go with the fresh bread. They sat down in a corner of the servants' dining room, and ate quietly.

Finally, Leo pushed his empty bowl aside and sighed heavily. "Geeze, this place is a gyp."

"What do you mean?" Tracy asked. "I thought you wanted to learn magic. If I showed the tiniest bit of talent, I sure would."

"Yeah, but why do I have to be a bottle washer for seven years?" Leo complained.

"You've seen that *Sorcerer's Apprentice* cartoon with the animated brooms, haven't you?" Oliver said. "Washing floors is traditional, I guess, but making sure you know what you're doing before you mess with power makes a lot of sense."

"It's stupid in a game," Leo insisted. "The whole point of games is that they're not real. You get to pick who you are and what you do. If training is required, you bargain with the game master, maybe miss a few turns. You have an objective, magic items, and you don't have to spend months training to use a stupid sword. Here, magic swords are expensive toys, kings and wizards are boring, and even the witches aren't witchy at all."

Bernie felt obliged to support the side. "That's not Hali's fault. She's under contract. The boss wanted something more impressive than the usual old crone, not to mention a wombat familiar."

"There's no boss, there's no Hali, there's no you," Leo told him testily. "It's all a program, in a stupid machine, and we're stuck here with no way to get out. We could be here years, and it's never going to get any better."

"Not if you sulk," Tracy snapped. "Why can't you forget this 'program' business and accept the experience? Fairy tales and other games can skip over the dull parts, but this game promised a realistic experience, and that's what we're getting. We've just gotten to tour a medieval castle and city, the sort of places you couldn't see otherwise outside a museum tour group, trapped behind velvet ropes."

"Even better, we're doing all this in less than an hour of real time," said Oliver. "Think of the vacations people could have, spending years hanging out here when they get fed up with school, or their jobs. My dad's not into fantasy, but I think he'd love this place."

"Everyone's out to get me," Leo moaned.

"You want everything easy, just like Endymion said," Tracy accused. "Maybe you should apprentice yourself to him. You might actually learn to work at something."

Leo scowled and got up from the table. "I know when I'm not wanted," he said. "I'm going back to our rooms. I want to think."

Tracy exchanged a worried glance with Oliver, and got up, too. "I'll go up with you," she said. "I want to try on some more dresses."

"Oh, right. You just don't trust me to find my own way back," Leo grumbled, but he didn't object when Tracy followed him from the room.

"So," Bernie said lightly to Oliver. "What do you want to do now?"

Oliver looked at him and sighed. "Do you mind if I do some more exploring, on my own?" he asked. "I'm getting tired of always being with a group, and I'd like to do some thinking, by myself."

Bernie eyed him carefully, but agreed easily enough. "You're not the type to go getting lost. Just be sure to keep an eye on the time." Amiably, the two parted, Bernie with plans for a garden visit, and Oliver to wander the halls, blissfully alone.

CHAPTER
11

THERE are those who prefer the company of even the most contemptible specimens of humanity, the most suspect of strangers, to their own companionship. Oliver, on the other hand, had learned early to amuse himself with his own thoughts. He felt little need to share those thoughts with others, having found that most people usually laughed at dreams of other worlds, of history and magic come to life. By the time Oliver reached high school, discovered gaming, and met others with similar interests, reticence had become a habit he could break when necessary, but he had never learned to do without a certain amount of solitude. Most role-playing games benefited from the input of several players, but though a single game might take months or even years to finish, the sessions seldom lasted more than several hours, with the odd weekend marathon for the truly dedicated. Without an end even in sight, this Grimmworld adventure promised to go on for weeks, and Oliver was beginning to wish that he could take off and play this particular game by himself.

Intrigued by the workings of the castle, Oliver kept to the ground floor, exploring the various workrooms and peering into the communal living quarters of the lower servants. He stumbled into the laundry room, which opened onto the kitchen garden, where sheets were being laid over hedges to dry. Avoiding the sewing room, he found yet another exit from the garden, this one leading down a stairway into another series of cellars. A pile of torches lay just inside the door, with a flint and steel firestarter nearby. Unable to resist the challenge, Oliver managed to light the oil-soaked torch with the flint, and descended into the murky depths.

A quick glance convinced Oliver that this was where the court banished furnishings that had gone out of fashion. Each successive layer documented a previous fad in castle decor: dark Gothic, early Mayan, Egyptian, Chinese, Louis XIV, Tibetan monastic, Art Deco, and Aztec (a bit blood stained). An extensive use of gilt provided the only recurring theme among the styles. After digging through a number of piles, Oliver decided that the maze of rooms under the castle could have kept a party of fashion archaeologists digging for decades. As it was, his search for the primal fairy-tale decor was terminated by a large stuffed dragon that lay blocking a doorway.

Undoubtedly, many of the glittering objects piled so carelessly together were valuable—some might even be magical—but Oliver despaired of finding any one item to take on a quest. He picked up a small, dusty dragon scale, one of many scattered about near the slightly moth-eaten dragon, and considered keeping it as a souvenir. From what knowledge he had of fairy tales, he guessed that such a minor theft might result in disproportionate magical punishment. Slightly depressed, he dropped the scale and left the cellars by a small staircase he had discovered earlier.

He came out somewhere on the ground floor of the castle. The typical grey stone floor and walls, with window slits high overhead, gave Oliver no clue to his location. The first corridor he took came quickly to a dead end. A little worried about the time, Oliver listened for signs of life, and followed a rhythmic scrubbing sound.

Turning a corner, he found himself in what appeared to be an abandoned entryway, empty of all furnishings but possessing a grand staircase, a sweeping curve of white marble that commanded attention, though it apparently led nowhere, with only a blank wall at its top. Nor was there the large entrance at the bottom that such a majestic stair deserved; the only access Oliver could see was the empty hallway he had just followed.

Kneeling on the stairs about a third of the way up, a maid scrubbed away at this magnificence with a simple scrub brush, splashing water all over the stairs and herself as she worked. Approaching quietly, Oliver realized that the waifish maid was crying as she cleaned, sobbing in time with her strokes. He was tempted to sneak away, but concerned about the time, he cleared his throat and addressed the girl.

"Um, excuse me, I appear to be lost."

The maid whirled, sitting down suddenly as one foot slipped on a wet stair. Eyes wide, she stared at Oliver, her face white where the tears had washed away layers of grime and soot. "Oh my," she gasped faintly. "You're not supposed to be here."

"Like I said, I'm lost," Oliver said. "Are you okay? Let me give you a hand up."

"No, no," the maid said, scrabbling backwards as best she could with worn slippers on slippery stairs.

Oliver stepped back, holding his hands in the air. "Hey, don't worry, I won't touch you. I just need directions."

"I'm not supposed to talk to anyone," the maid told him sadly.

"Aw, c'mon," Oliver coaxed, intrigued. The little maid was actually quite pretty under all that grime, but she was definitely the worst-dressed and dirtiest servant he'd seen in the castle so far. "What's wrong with giving a few simple directions?"

The maid just shook her head stubbornly.

"The king told us we could explore the castle, and to ask the servants if we needed anything, and right now I need directions. Seems to me the king's instructions would supersede any others. Why would they forbid you to talk, anyway?" The maid started crying again.

"Is that why you're crying? Part of it, anyway?" Oliver probed, encouraged by a brusque nod. "Can't you talk about it? You've already talked to me a little. What harm could it do? There's no one here to hear you, and if someone comes

I'll tell them I forced you. My name's Oliver. I'm one of the Outworlders visiting here, a privileged guest, I'll have you know—I sit at the high table for dinner."

"Really?" asked the maid timidly.

"Really," Oliver affirmed.

"Then you've met Princess Ginevra?" she asked.

Oliver shook his head. "Sorry, no, not that I remember. Hali—that's our witch—she's been keeping us away from the royalty, I think. I'm not sure if she's protecting us from them or vice versa. Maybe I'll meet this princess today at tea. Is she a friend of yours?"

The dejected little maid shook her head. "She's my mistress, sort of. Oh, it's too hard to explain!" She started crying again.

Indignant, Oliver sat down on the stairs and put one arm around the crying girl. "Is this mistress the one who told you not to talk?"

"Yes, and she makes me wear these rags and has me work in the parts of the castle where no one ever goes. This is the third time this week she's had me scrub this staircase, even though it doesn't go anywhere. The next time, I'm afraid she's going to make me clean it with a toothbrush."

"It's already sparkling clean," said Oliver. "Why would she make you wash it again?"

The maid shrugged. "She just wants to keep me out of the way."

"Don't you have any idea why?" Oliver persisted.

"I can't tell you."

"I'm not going away until you do. Your mistress doesn't have any right to make you so unhappy." Oliver hesitated, thinking about medieval serfs. "Or does she? The other servants around here look happy with their jobs. I didn't think they got mistreated. Don't you have any rights? Isn't there someone you could talk to? The majordomo, maybe?"

"No, absolutely not! There's nothing I can do. How about if I lead you back to the kitchens? Will you leave me alone?"

"Not until you tell me what's going on."

"If I tell you, will you go away?"

"I want to help."

At this, the maid started crying again. "No one can help. I

don't mean to keep crying like this, but I can't keep going on this way, and I don't know what to do!"

The barriers broken, the story finally poured out in a flood. "You see, she's not really the princess; I am. I was nervous about marrying this Prince Osbert, and my maid Trudy suggested we change places. When I saw the prince, I was glad we had. Have you met him yet? No? Well, he's pasty pale, with limp hair, and he lisps so badly he spits. He's mean, too. I couldn't possibly marry him. He got along so well with my maid, I thought it wouldn't hurt to keep the disguises until I could think of a way out, but now Trudy's making my life miserable. She knows I can't reveal my identity, but she won't let me leave, either. She told the castle servants I have delusions, of all things, and now they watch me all the time so I won't run away."

"Running away won't solve anything," said Oliver, feeling highly protective, but sounding slightly pompous even to himself. At the same time he felt a little nervous about holding a crying princess. "What if you tell them who you are, and refuse to marry the prince?"

"At this point, I don't know if anyone would believe me," she said, cheering up slightly at the thought. "Besides, the bride price and dowry have already been exchanged; if I reveal myself, I won't have any choice but to go through with the wedding, and it's only two weeks away."

"Won't your parents be here for the wedding?"

She shook her head. "Father's got as scheming a set of councilors as you've ever seen; he can't risk leaving the country, and Mother won't travel without him. The marriage was all arranged long-distance, with really bad portraits to show what we looked like. Prince Osbert's made him look like a Greek god, and mine was almost as bad."

Privately, Oliver had concluded that under the smudges this princess in disguise was probably quite adorable, but he forbore comment.

The princess continued, "I was supposed to have an escort, but when we switched places I had to come up with an excuse to send all my countrymen back. We hired all new servants, too. No one who knows me will be here for the ceremony."

Oliver considered. "So, what happens if the false Ginevra marries the prince? Is it legal?"

The real Ginevra shrugged. "Probably not, but who will ever know? I was never really interested in court life, so even my father's ambassador doesn't know me. If I could just get away, I'd happily leave the prince to Trudy. I'd even be glad to work as a servant for the rest of my life, just not for her."

Oliver surprised himself. "You could come with us!" he offered suddenly. "Someone told me we get to ask a boon of the king, as favored guests, you know. If I asked for you in front of a lot of people, the false princess couldn't say a thing. Besides, why should she? You'd be gone, and not coming back, at least not as long as our adventure takes, and the way things are going that'll be years."

"I don't know. What if it doesn't work? If the king doesn't ask for my head, Trudy's bound to be worse than ever."

Oliver grinned. "We've been looking for an adventure, so if the king refuses we'll kidnap you. Or something. Come on, it's worth a try, isn't it? What have you got to lose?"

She thought about it. Oliver watched with an unaccustomed tightness in his chest that relaxed suddenly as hope dawned in the princess's eyes, and an answering smile spread across her face. "You're right," she said simply, and stood, shaking out her soggy skirts. "Anything's better than this."

"Great. You'd better lead the way, Your Highness, as I am totally lost." Oliver bowed deeply and swept an imaginary hat along the floor. "After you, milady."

The princess giggled, more in relief than at Oliver, and he smiled to show he knew it. "Thank you, kind sir," she said in her best princess voice, sweeping a deep curtsy before taking his arm regally. In her normal voice she added eagerly, "But do, please, call me Ginny."

Fortunately, the princess knew her way back to the main part of the castle. The grand stairway might lead nowhere, but tucked underneath it a nondescript door opened onto a twisty little passageway that snaked along the irregular contours of some oddly shaped rooms.

"I think this part of the castle got blocked off when they did some remodeling," she said. "I don't know how Trudy found it, but it's very like some similar passages at home, except there aren't as many spy holes here. Too busy with fashion to bother spying on each other, I guess. The biggest intrigue I've heard the servants discussing yet is the way Lady Montaigne bribed the dressmaker to sew bright yellow ruffles on Countess Daisy's puce ballgown."

"Is that bad?" Oliver asked innocently.

"Not if you're colorblind," Ginny laughed.

It was not quite three hours past noon, according to one sundial, when Oliver and Ginny reached the gamers' rooms. Tracy, already decked out in a lacy confection with wide hooped skirts that would have had Scarlett O'Hara wild with envy, gaped in dismay when Oliver introduced the princess and explained what he wanted to do.

"I thought we were going to ask for something to help with our quest," she complained, looking Ginevra up and down like a prospective purchase. "I figured if we made the request general enough, he'd give us an all-purpose weapon, or protective charm, or something useful. What can we do with a princess in disguise? For that matter, how on earth are we going to get her cleaned up and dressed in time for tea?"

Oliver put a reassuring arm around Ginny, and told Tracy sternly, "Her life is more important than some stupid gift for a quest we haven't figured out yet. Maybe rescuing a princess is part of it."

Reluctantly, Tracy agreed. "You get to explain it to the others, though. Especially Hali. She's not here yet, but I bet she'll have something to say."

Somewhat sourly, Oliver agreed. "First, though, we need to get dressed. We've got more than an hour still. That's enough for Ginny to wash up, and she can borrow one of those dresses you got. You're not going to wear that thing, are you?" he asked, looking pointedly at the wide skirts. "How are you going to sit down, anyway?"

Tracy stomped one foot, setting her skirt to swaying. Angrily, she stilled it with her hands and told Oliver, "I am too going to wear it; I've been practicing all afternoon. The maids tell me this is just the thing for tea, and I think it's beautiful."

To Oliver's surprise, Ginny supported her. "She's right,

you know. King Benton makes a regular ritual of these teas, and everyone wears these silly things." She slipped out from under his arm, and looked him up and down. "You have to change, yourself. While you're gone, I'll wash up, but I won't change. You're asking for a lowly servant, not a princess, remember."

A manservant in elegant gold livery helped Oliver into silk stockings and shirt, a skintight pair of powder-blue satin knee breeches, flowing silk shirt with ruffles at neck and wrist, a white vest embroidered all over in blue bachelor's buttons, and a blue satin jacket edged with gold scrollwork entwined with forget-me-nots. "Such a fine fit!" the valet enthused, tweaking the skintight jacket to make it sit just right. "Such a romantic design on the 'broideries, don't you think? The flowers evoke the image of the forlorn lover. You'll have all the ladies sighing over you."

Revolted, Oliver was on the verge of telling the servant to find him another outfit, when it occurred to him that the image of a lover might be useful. It would certainly explain his odd request for a serving girl, at least to the frivolous minds of the court. True love overcame all odds in the fairy tales, didn't it? Reconciled, Oliver even allowed the manservant to dress him in a powdered wig, and deck him out in rings and pins of gold and sapphires, though he drew the line at face paint and patches. Ginny was a nice girl, but Oliver wasn't painting his face to look like a mime, not for any female. He consented to just a touch of white powder on his face, feeling like a fool, but was reassured by a look in the mirror. He looked like something out of an old Three Musketeers movie, but not totally effeminate.

Meeting Leo in the hall, Oliver was even more reassured. Leo had adopted this latest fashion wholeheartedly, and the results were, to say the least, colorful. From his elaborately curled, high-topped wig to the jeweled heels on his shoes, Leo went to the extreme in every detail, and in every color of the rainbow. His jacket and breeches were of cloth of gold, almost buried under the heavy embroidery depicting gay flowers and birds, most prominently a fanciful phoenix with jeweled tail (nothing like the drab, stuffed bird they'd seen earlier) rising from a border of multihued flames that licked all around the bottom and cuffs of the coat. The waistcoat was covered with the same fiery pattern. For jewels, Leo had chosen flame-colored stones in every shade, from clearest yellow to deep red, so that sparks seemed to fly every time he waved his ring-encrusted hands. His face was painted white, his lips bright red, and two dark beauty spots graced his chin and cheek. In one softly powdered hand, he waved a fine painted fan.

"I don't think we're Victorian after all. This is more—pre-Revolutionary," he lisped.

"American or French?" Oliver asked.

"Whichever," Leo said, dropping the accent, looking down at his own finery. "If the rich folks dressed like this all the time it's no wonder the peasants revolted—either from jealousy or good taste."

An outraged animal scream had both boys running down the hall, only to be bowled over by a powder-drenched Bernie, tearing out of Hali's room like a giant powder puff on legs.

"Hey, watch it!" Leo shouted, straightening his wig. "You've got powder all over my outfit."

"Your outfit!" shrieked Bernie in outrage, hopping up and down and sneezing as he tried to shake off the powder. "That fiend picked me up and dumped me in a whole box of the stuff!" Still sneezing, he rolled on the floor, trying to rub the white coating from his face.

Oliver found a bath towel and started brushing powder away from Bernie's eyes and nose. Soon, the wombat's natural dark grey face peered out from the surrounding white cloud. "This stuff is kinda sticky," Oliver observed. "Did they oil you first or something?"

"Yeah," growled Bernie. "Told me it was hair oil. I thought it was to make my fur shiny. Can you get it all off?"

"Not without a lot of soap and hot water," Oliver said.

"Bat wings and spider bites!" Hali exclaimed behind them. "What happened to you?" she asked the wombat sternly.

Bernie cringed. "They powdered my hair. It wasn't my idea and, gee, Hali, you wouldn't consider undoing it for me, would you? Pleeeease? Pretty please? Oh, stop laughing. It's not funny."

"You're all dressed so nicely for tea, I wouldn't dream of changing a thing." With a last cackle, Hali went into her room to change her dress.

"Crud," Bernie muttered. "Oh, well, at least they didn't try to make me wear doll clothes this time. By the way," he looked up at Oliver and Leo, "where are the others? They are here, aren't they?"

"Tracy's here and ready to go," said Oliver. "I haven't seen Jamison."

The three went to check Jamison's room, where an attendant reported no sign of the missing critic.

"Oh, boy," said Bernie, worried. "What time is it? I hope he turns up soon."

Jamison still hadn't shown up several minutes later when Hali reappeared, in a slinky white dress made all of lacy spiderwebs. Her hair, all silver now, was piled high on her head, and decorated with gleaming bats carved in jet, chasing tiny diamond flies.

"Wow," said Tracy, coming into the room, careful to move gracefully as she came closer to examine the dress. "The spiderwebs are great, but shouldn't you be wearing hoops?"

"Me?" Hali asked calmly.

"No, I guess not. Oh, yeah. We have a little problem." She turned to Oliver, who shrugged. "Ginny, come on out."

Princess Ginevra came out of Tracy's room nervously. Her clothes were a bit drier, but no more presentable. Her face, however, was fresh-scrubbed and glowing, her skin fair and smooth, with a dusting of freckles over the nose. Her hair, still slightly damp, curled wildly around her face. A few dry strands gleamed bright, coppery red. Oliver smiled, and stepped forward to take her hand.

"Your Highness." He bowed, careful of his wig. "I knew you'd clean up beautifully."

She smiled faintly. "You shouldn't call me that," she reminded him. "I'm just a maid."

Tracy hurried to explain, and Hali listened patiently. When she'd heard the whole story, she went up to Ginevra and examined her like an odd scientific specimen. "Ha! A princess in disguise, hmmm?" She peered in Ginevra's eyes, then took her hand and examined the palm. "Sleepwalker if I ever saw one," she muttered, dropping the girl's hand, and turned back to the waiting gamers. "Well, it's your adventure. If you want to add her to the party, that's fine by me. You get to explain to the king," she told Oliver, poking a finger in his chest.

"Now, where's Jamison?" she asked. The others exchanged glances, then as one shrugged.

"He went out on his own," Tracy said. "He knew about the tea."

"Hmmph," Hali grumbled, glancing out a window to check the time. "He's got about fifteen minutes before I turn him into a toad in white ruffles."

With barely five minutes to go, Jamison arrived, whistling and jauntily swinging an ebony cane. He looked a trifle sinister, dressed in a form-fitting suit of fine black leather with tall black boots and a tricorne trimmed at the edges with fur.

"About time," growled Hali. "Spent a little too long at the tailor's?"

Jamison swept her an elegant bow. "Hardly. The suit—elegant isn't it?—was acquired early this morning. I'm afraid I was delayed somewhat by a visit to one of the many elegant bawdy houses to be found in this amusing little town. Unfortunately, I didn't realize yesterday that the houses do not open until midafternoon. As a reviewer, I felt it my duty to see just how detailed this little world of yours gets in the areas of adult entertainment." Smugly, he brushed a bit of imaginary lint off of one shoulder.

"Well?" said Leo finally, irritated with himself for giving Jamison the satisfaction, but he was bursting with curiosity. "How detailed does it get?"

"Quite," said Jamison. "There was a particularly charming little redhead . . ."

"If I'd only had some money," mourned Leo.

"That's disgusting!" said Tracy. "We went out and bought useful stuff and he went and bought himself a fancy suit and a prostitute."

"Well, really," Jamison said, looking down his nose at her. "How can I review this game properly if I don't explore all the possibilities? Quite a few computer games call themselves 'adult entertainment,' but this one has a potential in the area I had hardly suspected. It's certainly not covered in any of the brochures, but perhaps there's some fail-safe in the program that prevents *children*"—his tone left no doubt that he considered his fellow gamers such—"from having such encounters. It might be worth testing." He cocked his head and considered Leo briefly before shaking his head in exaggerated despair.

"You're not testing anything, you're late," said Hali. "We have to leave; there's no time for you to change. I'll have to do it for you." With a wave of her staff (now covered in rhinestones, spiderweb lace, and fluffy white feathers) she gestured at Jamison, and his slick black leather transformed into an absolutely charming little sailor suit, with powder-blue shorts and middy blouse and a jaunty little white cap perched on a head full of glossy ringlets.

"My clothes!" Jamison wailed, as the others began laughing.

"They're still there," Hali told him. "It's just an illusion, and it will have to do. Now, march—we don't want to be late."

CHAPTER
12

USING her staff as a goad, Hail kept the gamers moving at a good clip all the way to the king's tea chamber. Just outside the door, she gave them a minute to straighten their outfits, then nodded to the waiting butler, who announced them all by name.

When he got to "Trudy the Serving Girl," conversation stopped dead, and for a moment the gamers were the cynosure of all eyes. Then a ripple of little shrugs ran through the room, and the sound of gossip swelled quickly to a muted roar. Tea might be more exclusive than dinner, but it was still well attended, and the somewhat more intimate confines of the tea chamber were crowded with exquisitely attired guests.

The gamers' initial impression of the room was one of manic lace, whirling, flouncing, and fluttering from every chair and around every table. Most of the ladies wore dresses covered with lacy ruffles, looking like over-decorated wedding cakes with too many layers. Fans of feathers and lace fluttered; lace-trimmed handkerchiefs whisked in and out of pockets and sleeves. Even the chandeliers of intricately spun glass looked as if they had been tatted out of ice.

The king came forward, his expression determinedly genial as he held out his hand in welcome.

"Hali, dear lady," he cried, taking the witch's decidedly limp hand and holding it within an inch of his lips in a faint-hearted kiss.

Hali snatched her hand back, and the stout little king jumped back as if she'd hit him. Recovering quickly, he tugged at his elegant white and silver waistcoat, fluffed up the lace at his throat, and greeted the rest of the party with an amiable but incoherent mumble before moving on to greet still more last-minute arrivals.

At Hali's quiet urging, the gamers moved to the tables. An elegant young lady gracefully served tea, keeping up a discussion of the latest tourney results with her grandmother, a fragile, whitehaired old lady in gold lace who sweetly offered a choice of coffee or cocoa between her observations on the fights.

"These modern fighters don't know how to kill. Now in my day, when a knight went for the throat, he got a good gush of arterial blood going to please the crowd. None of this breaking their necks, with nothing to show for it."

Quietly, but quickly, the gamers moved away to a large buffet table spread with a small feast. Leo helped himself to a heaping plateful, while the others watched their fellow guests to make sure they did not take too much, though Tracy declined to imitate the most fashionable ladies, who limited themselves to minuscule amounts of food, which they then left largely untouched.

"It's a scam, isn't it? They eat elsewhere, right?" Tracy asked in a fierce whisper.

Amused, Ginny nodded. "Ethereal is in this season," she said. "The ideal lady subsists on dew and moonlight."

Oliver bent over to whisper, "Is that 'Princess Ginevra' over there? The chunky brunette in the silver and yellow who's glaring at us? Tracy, don't look."

Ginny nodded, not having to look. "That's her, and she's furious. I hope you can carry this off."

"At least she didn't raise a fuss right off. She's on the defensive. That's good," Tracy said, craning her neck as she tried to find a way to look at the false princess without being seen. "I think I'll just circulate a bit," she said airily, and flounced off.

Leo settled himself on a corner seat near the buffet table, next to a portly gentleman who appeared to share both Leo's appetite and taste in clothes. Bernie, banished from the ladies' immaculate laps because of his powdered fur, settled for rubbing catlike against every nonwhite silk stocking he could find, blazing a white trail that went largely unnoticed in the crowded room. Oliver and Ginny whispered together briefly, then took their plates to a quiet corner, where they fed each other choice morsels, laughed together at private jokes, and otherwise presented every appearance of being deeply, sickeningly in love—though not so deeply they couldn't fend off Bernie when he reached their corner of the room.

"You've managed to get most of the powder off," congratulated Oliver, "but don't think you're going to lose any on us."

"Wouldn't think of it," said the wounded wombat. "I just wanted to see what you two are up to. All lovey-dovey, aren't you? Isn't this pretty sudden?"

"Why Bernie," Oliver said. "I thought this was a land where fairy tales come true. Don't you believe in love at first sight?"

"Yeah, but I thought you were smarter than that." Shaking his head, Bernie wandered off looking for more virgin legs to despoil.

Deeply embarrassed by his childish attire, Jamison decided to present a bold front, and teacup in hand proceeded to introduce himself to the glittering personages holding court in the center of the room. He was taller than most of the men in the room, and in his shorts looked painfully thin, but he could toss his curls with a superior disdain that quite impressed the ladies. He was also more than willing to tell amazing tales of Outworld life, pandering to the ladies' taste, turning movie stars into lords and ladies, exaggerating the artistic qualities of television, and claiming that every home had not only hot and cold running water but also swimming pools and saunas.

The false Princess Ginevra was one of those charmed by his discourse. She took advantage of her rank to demand a private conversation with the Outworlder. Flattered to have royal attention at last, Jamison let her lead him to a quiet spot. A large woman, with strong, dark coloring, she was forceful, voluptuous, and not in the current mode at all. Her very stylish tea dress seemed designed for a more delicate form, straining visibly at the seams. The volumes of honeycomb lace (to go with the gold and silver bees embroidered all over the yellow bodice) gave her more the appearance of an undomed hive than the fanciful queen bee the designer intended. Jamison actually found her attractive, if poorly dressed, but he was unable to satisfy the princess's curiosity regarding Ginny's presence at the party.

"When one is at the mercy of a witch's caprice, there's no telling what may happen," Jamison observed, gesturing at his own garb, but his companion clearly found this response unsatisfactory.

From behind them, Tracy managed to observe the false princess quite closely. She also managed to gush and exclaim her way to an introduction to "a real-life prince"— Ginevra's intended, Osbert.

Shortly thereafter, she joined Oliver and Ginny in the corner. "Jamison's being an ass, the false princess hasn't a clue, and Osbert's even worse than you said. He managed to leer at me and pretend I wasn't even there at the same time. Reminded me of that dreadful elf lord we met, except Osbert's so pale and fishy. You'd have to drown the elf and leave him in the water for a week to make him look that bad."

Since she was technically on the job, Hali refrained from making passes at any of the elegant gentlemen in attendance, but that didn't stop her from intimidating a few with her undivided attention. Tracy made the acquaintance of Queen Griselda, an unfashionable figure in a narrow skirt, but "a very savvy lady," Tracy decided. Leo, in the meantime, had literally bumped into King Benton, and the two became the best of buddies, sharing a plate of macaroons as they traded stories of their mistreatment at Hali's hands. All in all, Tracy was well satisfied with the tea party's progress.

"Unless Leo manages to really blow things, the king's going to be on our side, and glad to give us anything he thinks will annoy Hali," Tracy reported to Oliver and Ginny.

The party's charm had begun to pall when Hali finally gathered the gamers. She led them to the king, who was cheerfully recounting the more personal details of his encounters with Hali's goats to Leo. King Benton spotted Hali and paled, his sprightly narrative suddenly reduced to mumbles.

"Well, Benton," Hali said. "Fun's fun, but these kids have a boon to request of you."

The round little king cheered up immediately. "Boons I can handle. I'd be delighted to hear your request." He stood up and gestured across the room to the tall seneschal. In seconds the room was quiet, and the center of the room cleared for Benton and the gamers. There, they were joined by Queen Griselda, who stood silently just behind her husband.

The seneschal raised one hand, and announced to the watching guests, "Our honored Outworld visitors have a boon to ask of the king." He paused to let excited murmurs die away, and bowed to Hali. "You may make your request."

Hali eyed the king skeptically, just long enough to see him start to squirm, then turned her glance on Oliver, who was standing with Ginny's hand on his arm. "Think you know what you're doing, do you, boy? It's all yours." With a theatrical cackle, she stepped back.

Oliver bowed, and stepped forward, leading Ginny. "Your Majesty, we have a boon to ask, and it may be a bit unusual. We would like your permission to take this servant with us on our quest. She is Gertrude, known as Trudy, a lowly serving maid to Princess Ginevra."

"You want a maid?" King Benton said in disbelief. "Are you sure? Usually questers want magic items, not janitorial services."

"We considered asking for a magic item to help us, but so far we haven't even found a proper quest," Oliver admitted. "Then, as I was exploring this magnificent castle, I stumbled across this lowly servant, scrubbing an abandoned stairway. She looked up, and it was love at first sight for both of us." He sighed deeply, and turned to gaze deeply into Ginny's eyes, ignoring Leo's faint gagging noises.

The gamers found this display of affection decidedly overdone, but the courtiers gathered about sighed in delight—all except the false princess, so red-faced with fury she looked ready to burst. She pushed into the center of the circle and confronted the king.

"That's my maid! You can't give her away," she shrieked.

"Now, now," Benton tried to calm her. "We have plenty of maids here in the castle."

"I'm very attached to her," said the false princess.

"Then why do you make her dress in rags and scrub floors in abandoned parts of the palace?" Tracy asked indignantly.

"Yes, do tell," Queen Griselda interjected. "The major-domo has mentioned this matter to me; he considers it a gross waste of manpower, and an insult to his management. I must say, I don't want visitors thinking we can't afford to dress the staff decently."

"Good heavens, no," the king agreed. "That wouldn't do at all. What is your explanation, my dear?"

The false Ginevra glared at the real princess, but responded politely enough. "The poor girl suffers from delusions, Your Majesty, and refuses to change out of her familiar garb. I feel responsible for her, as I brought her with me all the way from my parents' home, but I didn't want her disturbing the other servants with her odd ways. I thought that a simple, out-of-the-way task would keep her busy, and happy, as happy as it is possible for such a disturbed creature to be."

Ginny smiled sweetly at the false princess, and curtsied to the king. "Your Majesty, it is true that I have acted oddly. I was unhappy to be separated from my home, and frightened by the grandeur of your magnificent court. But now I have found my true love, and I know that as long as I am with him I can be happy."

The king harrumphed, looking back and forth between Ginny and the furious false princess. "Well, I must say the girl looks happy enough now," he observed. "I say she should go. Be good for her, fulfill the boon, get her out of the castle so nobody's upset. This group won't be coming back here, though," he explained kindly to Ginny.

"I understand," she told him happily. "Much as I have admired your castle, it is much too grand for the likes of me. Even if the future forces me apart from my beloved Oliver, I will never return. I'm sure my princess understands that I could never be happy here. I would never willingly do anything to distress her," she added, glancing meaningfully at the false princess, "but I must go."

The more romantic souls in the audience sighed deeply, and even the false Ginevra appeared much struck by this argument. "You would leave me like that, just go and never return?" she asked, eyeing Ginny suspiciously.

"I would," confirmed Ginny. "May you marry your prince and live happily ever after, with nary a worry about me, Your Highness, for I have found mine own true love."

"Your Majesty, I cannot stand in the way of these lovers," Princess Ginevra said, with a gracious wave of her hand. "Though I cannot understand it myself, if my maid truly wishes to leave your court forever, she has my best wishes."

"Well, then, it's all settled, and everybody's happy," King Benton beamed. He shook Oliver's hand, kissed Ginny's, patted Tracy on the cheek and Bernie on the head, and was about to clap Hali on the shoulder before he thought better of it, and called for a toast instead.

The tea party ended two hours before dinner. "Just time enough to dress!" one lady wailed in despair at this hectic schedule.

"Must be sheer hell in winter when the sun sets at five," Leo observed on the way back to their rooms. He was still considering the possibility of becoming a wizard's apprentice, but even more than sweeping floors the prospect of staying at this court through even one winter was daunting. Wizards obviously didn't rate high enough to attend teas, or perhaps they had the option of refusing, which would be a plus, but Leo was getting tired of watching his manners. Dressing up was fun as long as you had servants to attend to every detail, but he was quite sure apprentices didn't. Visions of casting lightning bolts, taming dragons, and impressing village maidens were fading before the much more mundane reality of brooms, court manners, and the frightening prospect of a life spent studying mathematics and this world's version of physics. He hesitated to ask Hali's advice, and Bernie refused pointblank to comment, leaving Leo to brood alone.

Reminded, Bernie waddled off to fill Hali in on the wizard's offer. "I don't think the kid's going to go for it," he said. "It's too much like work, and he knows it."

"Blast Endymion," Hali said. "He should know better. I wouldn't mind having the kid off my hands, but Bentwood would throw a fit. If the kid turns out really talented, we won't be able to let him go home. Can you imagine the havoc he could wreak with magic in the Outworld?"

"Well, go give the kid some kindly advice. You do it so well. Tell him he'll be so busy that the first few years will just zip by before he even has time to think of learning spells."

"Mmm," Hali agreed absently. "Now that I think about it, maybe we *should* leave the kid here for two, three years. Just long enough to have him begging to get out, not long enough for him to even light a flame Outworld."

"That's cruel," said Bernie. "I like it, but I'm pretty sure he won't go for it." He glanced over at Ginny and Oliver, walking with their hands conspicuously clasped. "By the way, are you sure that girl's a sleepwalker?"

Hali nodded. "Can't mistake it. She's an Outworlder, all right. Must have been dreaming hard about her handsome prince to get here."

"She and Oliver are getting pretty mushy together," Bernie said. "Shouldn't we warn them about waking her up?"

Hali shrugged. "The dream's got to end sometime, but if you want to warn them, go right ahead. Won't do any good, though."

"So call me a romantic. If they gotta break up they might as well know ahead of time."

"Just remember: she really thinks she's a princess. You tell her she's dreaming, she might wake up anyway."

"I'll try to avoid that detail."

A little later, Bernie tracked down Oliver and Ginny in Oliver's room, discussing which outfit he should wear for dinner. Bernie cleared his throat. "We need to talk," he said.

"Huh?" Oliver turned to look at him. "What's up?"

Embarrassed, Bernie shuffled his feet. "I don't know precisely how to put this. Remember what Hali said when she first saw Ginny?"

"Yeah. Something about sleepwalking. Didn't make sense," Oliver said.

"Well, it's a technical term some of the witches use.

It . . . well, there's something odd about Ginny, besides being a princess in disguise."

"Something odd?" Ginny asked. "What do you mean?"

Bernie scratched his nose, hoping for inspiration. "You don't know it, but you're . . . under an enchantment. Yeah, that's it, you're under a spell. It's like being asleep, that's why they call it sleepwalking. The problem is, if you wake up, you'll be magically transported far away from here, and we'll never see you again."

"What do you mean, wake up?" Oliver asked. "She's not really asleep, so how can she wake up?"

Bernie sighed. "It takes a major shock to wake a sleepwalker. Dying usually does it—almost dying, I mean. But what I really wanted to warn you about is sex."

"Sex?" Oliver asked, slightly shocked. He looked at Ginny and blushed.

Bernie was beginning to wish he'd kept his mouth shut. "Look, I don't know if you've been thinking of having sex, though the way you've been making goo-goo eyes at each other I wouldn't be surprised. I just wanted to warn you. For some reason, having sex wakes females up. It's not as effective for guys, don't ask me why. You know all those fairy tales where Prince Charming wakes up the princess with a kiss? Those are the cleaned-up versions. It's not just a kiss that wakes her up."

"We're not really in love," Oliver said, a little too firmly in Bernie's opinion. "That was just an act, so the king would be on our side. Right, Ginny?" The princess smiled at him sweetly and agreed.

Still somewhat dubious, Bernie returned to Hali's room to report his progress. "I should have kept my mouth shut. I think I just gave them new ideas," he groaned.

"Huh," Hali grunted, looking up from the map she was studying. "It's hard to give teenagers new ideas in that area. If their minds don't think of it, their bodies will. I wouldn't worry. It's not like we really need an extra player in this little game anyway."

Bernie stood on his hind feet to get a better view of Hali's map. "That where we're heading? The ol' enchanted forest?"

"Yep," Hali confirmed, rolling up the map and putting it away in her belt pouch. "Can you think of a better place for an adventure?"

"Not a bad place for house hunting, either," Bernie noted.

Dinner was a repetition of the previous two nights, but for the addition of Ginny at the high table. The servants had found a fine gown for her, and she carried herself like a princess. Oliver attended her with every gallant flourish he could think of, and many a lady gave a heartfelt sigh as the couple passed. Jamison had obviously had an impact on the court, as well; more than one ambitious courtier had his hair in ringlets, and wore a flat straw cap with ribbons. One even had a middy blouse and shorts.

"Someone must have been sewing hard," Tracy observed.

"Nah, it's probably magic," Leo said. "That's about all it seems to be good for around here."

"Does that mean you're not going to become an apprentice wizard?"

Leo just growled in reply, but as soon as dinner was over he sought out the jolly wizard. The two talked together for some time, but even watching from across the room Tracy could tell that Leo was turning down the job. She felt surprisingly ambivalent about Leo's decision. She hated to see anyone turn down such an opportunity, and, in many ways, she thought Leo was a liability in the game. Having him parked in the castle would have saved some bother and worry. On the other hand, he was oddly likable, and though she felt a little bad about it, his incredible bumbling made Tracy feel better about her own performance.

Leo chose not to discuss his choice. Not feeling particularly sociable that night, the gamers returned to their rooms early, planning on an early start the next morning. They got up early, but by the time they'd eaten, raided the kitchen for fresh food, and figured out anew how to harness poor Whitenose to the cart, the sun was well over the horizon and halfway to noon. After a slow trip down the winding road to the gate, they were on their way. Rested and relieved of the burden of their packs, the gamers stepped lively, following the river road with a fresh sense of adventure.

CHAPTER
13

THE track the party followed led upstream along the broad, slow-moving river, and passed a large lake, across which they could see the towers of the untimely city of Anachronopolis. Instead of following the road around the lake, Hali turned off onto a narrow lane edged in high brush that soon turned into trees, and finally a thick wood. There, the road branched. One arm skirted the wood, following a crude wood fence; the other branch led directly into the deepest, darkest part of the forest, passing through a simple single-barred gate in the fence. Beyond, the smooth litter of dead leaves on the path made it clear that this was the road less traveled.

"What do you want to bet we go through the gate?" Leo muttered.

"No bet," said Oliver.

As they expected, Hali went to the gate, lifted the bar and swung it wide.

Peering into the murky spaces beneath the trees, Leo balked at the gate. "Hey, can we go through this? Isn't that trespassing?" he called.

Hali looked up. "The gate's to keep livestock out, not people. Come on, you're holding us up."

"Yeah," Bernie chimed in from his seat on the cart. "Haven't you ever seen an enchanted forest before? This place is oodles of fun. Let's go!"

The trail, little more than a path of beaten earth, wandered through the forest. Tall and dark, the trees grew so close together that no light passed through unfiltered to the gloomy, leaf-littered floor. The air was filled, not with the rare bird calls, but with the eerie, high-pitched screams of branches and trunks rubbing together in the restless breeze. What little underbrush there was looked black and deformed, covered with lichen and fungi. The only brook they crossed ran icy clear over a streambed black with glistening chunks of coal.

Subdued, the gamers clustered close to the donkey cart, while Hali strode cheerfully some yards in the lead. Whitenose walked along amiably enough, pulling steadily over muddy spots and through brush that overgrew the trail, but he refused to be hurried, even when a spot of light appeared up ahead.

To the gamers' relief, the light turned out to be real sunlight, falling on a clearing filled with tall grass and cheerful meadow flowers. In the center of the clearing stood a colorful cottage, its warm brown walls decorated with colorful designs and what appeared to be white snow and icicles on the roof.

"Snow? In this weather?" Jamison asked, peering at the little house.

Leo snorted. "It's icing, dummy. Icing! On a gingerbread house. A real gingerbread house. I don't believe it." He ran toward the building, catching up with Hali by the front door, where she stood, arms akimbo, studying the cottage carefully.

"Hey, is this real?" Leo asked her, bouncing from foot to foot with excitement. "Can we eat it? I've wanted to have a gingerbread house to eat since I was a kid. Think of it. Enough junk food to last for weeks!"

"Take it easy, Leo," Tracy advised, pulling Whitenose behind her. "The witch who lives here wouldn't bother to wait to fatten you up."

"She a friend of yours?" Leo asked Hali. "I mean, wouldn't she be willing to offer a snack to a friend of a friend?" Struck by a thought, he scowled. "Or is this an adventure? Are we supposed to play Hansel, Hansel, Hansel, Gretel, and Gretel, and defeat the wicked witch?"

"I'm not enough, you want more?" Hali snapped. "Only one witch to a customer. Well, one at a time," she amended, thinking about it. "Anyway, this place is vacant. The last owner had a baking accident."

"I'll bet," said Tracy. "Can we go inside?"

"More important, can we eat it?" Leo insisted.

"Go ahead, go ahead, eat and explore," sighed a weary, hollow voice overhead. The gamers looked up to see a scruffy brown owl squinting back at them.

"You must be the agent," Hali said, stepping back for a better look.

"What is this?" Bernie objected, hopping down from the cart. "Hali, you hate gingerbread, you've told me so a dozen times."

"It doesn't hurt to look," she told him. "Besides, I thought the children might like to see it. Go ahead," she said, waving the gamers on, "check it out."

Leo had already pulled off a bit of gingerbread trimmed with red and white peppermints. Tracy cautiously picked off a tiny sugar icicle, and nibbled at it, stepping into the cottage behind Hali, while the others explored the exterior looking for a particularly tempting bit. Whitenose sampled the doorjamb, shook his head at the spicy flavor, and settled for the lush meadow grass. Grumbling, Bernie sniffed at the gingerbread with distaste and waddled into the cottage.

Inside, the owl described the built-in conveniences, which primarily consisted of huge ovens set into one wall. Tracy opened one of the chest-high doors set into the wall, and gaped at the space inside.

"This is great. You could bake four large pizzas at once in here," she said. "Why would a single person want such huge ovens?"

Hali snorted, and Tracy looked at her impatiently. "I know, I know, witches are supposed to bake little children in these ovens, though if you ask me it'd be better to tie 'em on a spit over that huge open fire."

Hali cackled appreciatively. "The ovens are for the gingerbread, girl," she explained, and pointed out huge, flat metal baking sheets hanging on the walls, and a shelf full of giant mixing bowls. "You can't make a house out of pure magic, not if you're a witch. It'd fall apart the first time you tried a major spell. So, you use real materials, and just use magic to augment them. Since this place is meant to be nibbled on, it has some major spells supporting the walls, making them grow back when necessary. If too much of the structure becomes magical, though, it becomes unstable, so you have to keep patching. Not only am I a lousy cook, I can't stand the taste of humans, or pork, so I usually avoid this sort of place. No offense," she added, with a nod to the waiting owl.

"None taken," he said, and sighed with a cooing whoo. "The upkeep is terrible, worse than thatch, and I'm afraid almost no one has the patience for this sort of craftsmanship anymore. Gingerbread is out of fashion at the moment, as well. One day I shall find a witch who appreciates the magnificent workmanship of the place, but at present the market is terribly slow."

Bernie and Tracy amused themselves by pretending to be trapped in the combination chicken coop and prison out back, while Hali admired the sturdy construction, but the gamers were a bit shocked to find human bones (many cracked to release the marrow) strewn about the backyard between the compost pile and the outhouse.

"Kinda grim," Tracy observed, eyeing a row of skulls impaled on the posts of the garden fence.

"Overdone, if you ask me," Jamison observed. "As I recall from the story, all the witch's victims had been turned into gingerbread men, and were released from the spell when the old crone died."

Bernie snorted. "That's got to be a cleaned-up version, again. I don't believe what people do to perfectly good stories to make then 'acceptable' for kids. Did you really think, even for a second, that Hansel was going to be turned into a cookie? Of course not, but you want a nonthreatening happy ending—as if kids don't think up worse on their own. Then folks come here and expect everything to be sweetness and light."

"As to that, I haven't seen anything truly frightening, yet,"

Jamison observed. "A clumsy ogre and an irritable toll-taker, however ugly, do not constitute a major threat. The game designers do much better at stage settings than at actual plot and adventure. Look at this place—it's quite nicely done, even tasty, a multisensory treat, but there's nothing happening here, only a suggestion of past horror that I find highly inadequate, if not unnecessary."

"You want me to let something kill you?" Hali asked. "That could be arranged."

Enjoying himself, Jamison waved an elegant hand. "I hardly think so. I begin to suspect that our psychological linkage to the computers generating these images is so close that they don't dare let us die in the game, for fear of causing actual trauma, or death, in our physical bodies."

Jamison's reasoning, however faulty, had led him too close to the truth for Hali's comfort. Before she could think of a proper retort, Leo jumped into the fray.

"We may not be able to die," he said wryly, "but I've got blisters enough to prove we can suffer plenty. Besides, you ask me, this house is the best thing we've seen yet." He pulled a bit of decorative trim from his pocket, and took a big bite. "Looks great, tastes good. What more can you ask?"

Jamison sniffed. "It may taste good, but it's in the worst possible taste, a blatant appeal to the lowest common denominator."

He continued to expound on this subject as they continued down the road. When his fellow gamers demonstrated a definite lack of interest in his brilliant analysis, Jamison walked ahead with Hali, who gave him no more encouragement, but at least refrained from calling him "a big bore" and worse. Besides finding the game lacking in action (a flaw Hali secretly agreed with, though she was at a loss for a guaranteed nonfatal remedy), he deplored the inconsistent theme or style of the world, harping on the rococo elegance of the palace at Fairehaven, as opposed to the Germanic gloom of the current forest. Always, he returned to the little gingerbread cottage as a symbol of Grimmworld's failings.

"Unimaginative, unoriginal, and terminally ticky-tacky," he judged, writing furiously in his little notebook.

Finally, Hali broke. "I'm no fan of gingerbread myself," she snarled, "but that's a matter of taste, not a flaw in the stupid game. Is that all a reviewer does, look for the manure around the roses? Well, fine." She raised her staff and the wind rose with it, whipping around them with a fierce whistle and setting the trees to tossing against each other with agonized squeals. Alarmed, the other gamers hurried to catch up, pulling and pushing at Whitenose and the cart for more speed. By the time they got to Hali, the wind was already dying, and in Jamison's place stood a beetle, six feet tall on its spindly hind legs.

"Darn, we missed the fun," Bernie mourned.

"What happened?" asked Tracy.

"Is it dangerous?" Oliver asked, drawing his sword and placing himself between the others and the shiny black beetle.

"Hey, don't!" Leo shouted. "That's Jamison! Look, the bug's shell has the same design that flashy leather outfit had. It is him, isn't it? He won't hurt us, will he?" Leo asked Hali.

Hali looked at the beetle, which bent toward her on its long, thin, slightly bowed hind legs. It clacked its heavy, multiply pronged forearms together and chittered in apparent confusion.

"It's Jamison, he's harmless, and he's now a modified scarab, also known as a dung beetle," Hali informed the group. "It seemed appropriate."

She refused to answer any further questions, and insisted the group push on. Jamison appeared to accept his new status immediately, though it was hard to tell since he could no longer talk. The rest of the gamers had more trouble with his new appearance and kept watching him out of the corners of their eyes. However, coaxing the donkey to walk anywhere near the upright beetle kept them busy, and Jamison followed along amiably enough, clicking to himself occasionally. They soon got used to having a giant insect for a companion, and only his habit of collecting manure kept them worried, particularly with the discovery that nervous donkeys tend to void their bowels with embarrassing frequency. Fortunately, Jamison formed the dung he collected into a tidy little ball, rolling it along the road somewhat awkwardly with his hind feet. The ball quickly acquired a thick coating of dust that sealed out the worst of the unpleasant odors.

Bernie, in the meantime, decided to walk, and made the extra effort needed to dog Hali's heels as she strode ahead of the rest.

"What's with the bug?" Bernie asked. "Not that he wasn't asking for it, but aren't we supposed to be keeping these guys happy?"

"Trust me, he's a happy insect," Hali said. "This form's as true to his nature as the other, and this way he can't talk."

"And we all appreciate that," Bernie assured her.

"Besides, he's the one who wanted something to happen. The antidote's the usual—easy to find, if he wants it."

"True love's kiss?" Bernie asked, amused. "That one's not going to find true love outside a mirror."

Hali shrugged. "Not my problem. I'm more worried about the action Bentwood's promised to arrange."

"You let Bentwood arrange something? Don't you think that's dangerous?"

Hali scowled. "Potentially embarrassing, maybe, but not dangerous. Bentwood's scared to death of losing one of his precious gamers. I talked to him on the castle line, and he swore he'd come up with something exciting, but not too demanding. He wouldn't give me any details, though."

"Oh joy, such thrills," the wombat intoned with a noticeable lack of enthusiasm. "Don't you just love surprises? Should I warn our little friends about the boogeymen in the woods?"

Hali shrugged. "Can't hurt."

Bernie dropped back, got Oliver to boost him back on the cart, and whiled away the rest of the afternoon telling stories about the various unfriendly denizens of the woods.

So it was that when a black horse with glowing red eyes appeared before them, only Whitenose showed any inclination to go nearer, in the interests of equine unity. Tossing its head playfully, the heavyset horse pranced around the cart, sidling up to the girls and trying to nudge them into mounting.

"Stop that," Tracy insisted, after being jolted into the side of the cart by a particularly insistent nudge. "You're a big, bad pooka, or whatever, and we're not going to fall for this harmless horsie bit." She swatted the insistent horse on its sensitive nose, and it jerked back, ears twitching and a hurt look on its face.

"What's going on here?" Hali demanded, swatting the horse on the rump with her staff. "Move over, you big lummox," she added, as the stallion moved coquettishly in front of her.

"Bernie was just telling us about the black pookas, the horselike beings that plague travelers, and this thing appeared," Oliver explained. "We can't get rid of it."

Hali looked at the horse, which nodded its head eagerly. "This one's a kelpie," she said. "They drag unwary riders underwater with them. Go away, fellow, we're not interested."

The kelpie snorted, and pawed the ground fiercely.

"You're kidding," Hali said, and pulled a map out of her pouch. "No look, there's nothing here." She spread the map against the cart, and pointed to a spot. "See. Nothing."

Shaking its head, the kelpie neighed loudly. Startled, Whitenose let out an echoing bray that sounded like rusty pipes being tortured at the bottom of an empty well, and all the gamers jumped.

"Don't make a fuss," Hali told the horse. "I believe you, but I'm not interested in some rundown, off-the-track hovel. Particularly not underwater."

"Cripes," Bernie muttered. "Don't tell me this is another real-estate agent."

"You guessed," Hali told him sourly. "Apparently there's a nixie's nest nearby he wants us to look at."

The kelpie let loose a loud raspberry, and stomped a back foot.

"All right, all right, a palace in a swamp. Lake. Whatever. Look, I'm not interested in underwater residences. It's just not my style."

"Mine either," said Bernie. "Wet fur really gets me down."

The horse stretched his neck and nuzzled the wombat,

blowing at his fur, and turned to look at Hali, who laughed shortly.

"He says you'd make a great beaver," she translated.

"No, no, no, no, no!" Bernie shrieked. "I've barely gotten used to being a wombat! Besides, I don't know how to swim. And don't think you're going to teach me, either," he told the black fairy, holding up one paw with the claws out and ready to scratch.

Hali held firm, and the kelpie finally desisted, though not without many tempting offers of discounts and handy financial arrangements.

"Geeze," Tracy said as they were leaving. "I never knew real-estate salesmen were such a threat. You know, if I didn't know better, I'd say we were house hunting, not having an adventure."

Bernie snorted, trying not to laugh. He waited until Hali walked ahead far enough to be out of earshot, then called Tracy close and explained. "Hali made management promise to get her a new house if she baby-sat you guys. So, as long as we don't have anywhere better to go, we're going house hunting."

Openly listening in, Leo snorted. "Too bad Jamison can't comment anymore. If he thought the plot was lame before, he would really have loved this."

Bernie shrugged. "Believe me, these places are a lot more fun if the witches aren't in residence, but if you want major action, you're going to have to find it yourselves. Keep a sharp eye out; there's plenty of things worse than real-estate salesbeings out there."

Her shopping instincts piqued by the prospect of house hunting, Tracy was more interested in establishing parameters for the search. "I can see why gingerbread might not be Hali's style, but what's wrong with an underwater palace? Sounds really fantastic; it's probably covered with watery things like freshwater pearls and gold dust. I wish we'd gone to see it."

Leo laughed. "Can you see Hali playing Lady of the Lake? I don't think that's her style at all."

"Actually, the water dwellers are usually pretty dangerous,

sex-offender types," Bernie said. "You know—they look beautiful and lure young people underwater for cheap sex. Some like to drown people just for kicks; others keep them in their luxurious underwater palaces until they tire of them. If the young victims ever escape, they find out that a hundred years have passed, and then all of a sudden they age and die. Hali's never been real good at luring men, even if she makes herself look young and sexy, and really, she's more into the crone bit."

"How can you get into being a crone?" Leo asked. "What's so interesting about grey hair and wrinkles?"

Bernie sighed. "Can't say I completely understand, myself, but the witches really get into it. Like a saying they've got: 'Wisdom must be wizened.' Their oldest members are called Wisdoms, you see."

"Hali must be pretty young then," Ginny observed.

"Nah," Bernie denied. "She just hasn't aged as badly as she'd like. She spends a lot of time in front of her mirror desperately hoping to find a new wrinkle or two. The bony ones don't wrinkle as well as the witches who start plump, and Hali never could gain weight. Lots of would-be witches put on the pounds while they're young, then try to lose it when they get older and the skin loses its flexibility, so they'll have all these folds of skin. City witches, like the charm sellers and palm readers, often get really fat, and never manage to lose it. No willpower, I guess; the more successful witches wouldn't be caught dead living in a city, anyway. A proper witch is a scrawny, wrinkled crone who lives in a secluded hut.

"Hali's got the seclusion down, but her hut's a prefab plastic thing that somehow got here from your world, and she's desperate for a new one. That's why we're house hunting. Back when I was a crow, I was hoping for something with a lot of windows and one of those fancy roofs with lots of peaks and gables to perch on. Now the wombat in me wants something dark and underground, but I'm hoping to go back to being a bird sometime."

"Hard to think of something to fit both a bird and a burrower," Tracy agreed.

"Easy. Just make sure the place has both a basement and a roof," Leo said.

"Basements aren't big around here," Bernie said. "I don't want to make do with a root cellar, and dungeons are too grim, not to mention damp."

"How about a hobbit hole in a high cliff?" Oliver suggested.

Agreeing that cliff dwellings of some sort sounded promising, the gamers continued down the road behind Hali, arguing over the ideal room arrangements and building materials for a witch's hut. In the middle of a rather loud discussion of the merits of art nouveau, as opposed to traditional fairy-tale Gothic, the goblins struck.

Oliver had just opened his mouth to tell Tracy that her amulet was glowing when the first goblin landed on his head, wrapping its scrawny, green-skinned arms around his mouth and nose. Oliver tried to pull it off, but its grip was too strong. In the meantime, more of the creatures dropped out of the trees and sprang from the bushes onto the gamers and their cart.

Bernie managed to dodge one goblin, and with a fast swipe of his paw managed to knock another, squalling furiously, onto the road. Oliver reached his sword before the goblins' busy hands could grab it, and slapped awkwardly at the goblin on his head. Somehow, he must have connected, for the goblin screeched and let go, but not before others had grabbed hold of Oliver's arms and legs.

Between two and three feet tall, though strong for their size, the goblins would have been more nuisance than threat if not for their numbers. As it was, neither Oliver nor Tracy could get free long enough to make good use of their weapons. Tracy had her bow with her, but a couple of goblins jumped on her quiver and emptied the arrows onto the road. Tracy's staff was in the cart, where Leo was able to grab it and lay about him to some effect. Seeing the threat, the goblins mobbed him, grabbing at the staff.

Off balance, Leo knocked the staff into Whitenose's legs. Kicking in surprise, Whitenose caught one goblin in the chest, sending it flying. More goblins moved in, but after some initial surprise, the beleaguered ass started stomping the annoying little monsters with enthusiasm. His long white teeth proved useful as well, and he bit with vigor. Bernie tumbled off the cart, and made use of his bulk by charging the flimsy goblins again and again.

Jamison, however, was the hero of the day. His slick black carapace made him invulnerable to the goblins' sharp little teeth and claws, and when he dropped down onto all six legs, the armored prongs on his forearms raked through the crowded goblins with devastating efficiency. With outraged shrieks, the goblins who could retreated, leaving their wounded to make their own escape. It was over in seconds; by the time Hali ran back, alerted by the noise, the only goblins remaining were either unconscious, dead, or captive.

Whitenose's forceful hooves were responsible for the three actual deaths, but another five battered goblins lay moaning in the dirt. Leo knelt on one goblin lying facedown in the road; Tracy held another captive with one of its arms behind its back and her dagger at its throat. Oliver held another at swordspoint, backed against one of the tall cart wheels.

"What's going on here?" Hali demanded, surveying the scene.

"It's not fair, that's what it is," Oliver's captive retorted in a surprisingly deep voice. "Ganging up on an innocent bunch of goblins. There we was, going about our business as usual, and even the ass sticks a foot in. What happened to the good old days, when a goblin horde could take on single, lonely travelers in a fair fight?"

"Hey, that one talks," Tracy noted.

"It's been known to happen. Nothing in the job description says a goblin can't express himself now and again. Thinking, now, that's something else again. Thinking on the job's definitely not allowed, but there's the odd coffee-break philosopher among us, and no one can say we're not entitled, on our own time. Though to tell you the truth, the next time I see a group like yours wandering about I'm going to be mighty tempted to think once, maybe even twice, about attacking, I can tell you." He looked down at the tip of Oliver's sword, and his eyes crossed. "Now, if you could see your way to removing this thing, me and my fellows will just be taking ourselves off, and no harm done."

"No harm done!" Tracy said in disgust. "You attacked us, my tunic's shredded and—I'm bleeding!" she shrieked, pulling one sleeve back to reveal extensive bruises and dots of blood welling from a series of tiny puncture marks. "You bit me!" she said, waving the injured arm in front of the voluble goblin.

"Not me, personally," the goblin explained. "Besides, you gave as good as you got. If I took the time to think about it, I expect I'd say you came out ahead, what with several of my boys dead, and all those wounded. Too bad about them, really. We'll miss them. You really ought to put them out of their misery, if you've got any kindness in your hearts. I don't expect you do. Humans are funny that way."

"If you mean we won't kill defenseless creatures just because they're wounded, you're right. I feel bad enough about the dead ones," Oliver said, carefully keeping his gaze away from the ground at his feet where one of Whitenose's victims lay, his skull split open and face pulped. Now that the battle was over, the goblins' small size and apparent sexlessness made them appear uncomfortably childlike.

"See what I mean?" the goblin appealed to Hali. "No mercy in 'em. What good's a goblin who can't keep up with the horde? Might as well be dead: will be soon enough."

"Fine," Hali said, and gestured with her staff; with a blinding flash the unconscious and dead goblins disappeared. "Happy now?"

"Much better, your witchiness," the goblin said. "Now, if you'll just tell this young gentleman to remove his sword . . . "

Hali waved Oliver back. Released, the goblin calmly brushed himself off, and surveyed the scene, waiting until Tracy and Leo released their captives as well. Then the little leader nodded to Hali.

"We'll be reporting this, you know. The union will have something to say about this sort of behavior—leading armed groups in an enchanted forest without previous clearance. Our contracts say we attack one adult or two juveniles at a time, no more, and you have no business putting more in our way. What's the world coming to when hard-working goblins have to think about who to attack? It's unheard of."

"Goblins have unions?" Leo asked skeptically.

"This is a union forest, I'll have you know. No scab labor here. We're dues-paying members of IMP: Insignificant Monsters and Pests, Local 7. What our members lack in weight we make up in numbers. IMP's the most powerful union next to OGRE, the Organization of Giants, Reprobates, and Elementals. They're the real heavies, and when it comes to a violation like this they might just side with us little guys."

Hali squinted skeptically at the goblin. "IMP and OGRE? I thought it was Big Monsters Union and the Organization of Little Pests."

"That's another thing," the goblin complained. "I understand management insisted on the change. Something about cute acronyms being good for business. No one gave the rank and file any say, either, and as long as I'm thinking anyway, I have to say I don't think that's right. Maybe it's time we made our feelings known."

"Look, take it up with Bentwood," Hali said. "If you don't quit with the threats, I'll just blast the healthy as well as the injured, and there won't be anyone to complain, will there?"

Taking the hint, the goblins melted quickly into the forest. A faint cry of "We'll go on strike!" came back to the gamers as the goblin leader had the last word.

"I told you Bentwood didn't square this with the unions," Bernie muttered under his breath while Hali examined his badly torn ear.

"That's his problem," Hali said shortly, concentrating on the ear. "You're missing some skin here. This is going to heal a bit ragged."

All of the gamers had bites and scratches, but none were serious, and rather than expend the energy to heal them all magically, Hali opted to stop early at the next stream, where she boiled up a pungent herbal broth with which the gamers washed their wounds. For all their aches and pains, the gamers were feeling cheerful about their success in battle—even if Bernie did express the opinion that there was nothing easier to fight than goblins, except maybe a furious swarm of butterflies. By the next morning, the Outworlders were even a bit cocky, eager for the next battle, whatever it might be.

CHAPTER
14

THE morning dawned fair and bright, with a gentle breeze that tossed the treetops, scattering dappled sunlight on the trail below. Wandering in and around a series of gentle hills, the road took the gamers through a surprisingly varied landscape. They passed from the dark depths of an old oak grove to a rocky stretch that boasted only a few twisted pines, warped by the wind until they appeared almost human, like tortured souls with arms outstretched, begging for release. The resemblance was enough to make Tracy shudder, but not enough to quell the gamers' ebullient spirits.

Even Jamison seemed remarkably cheerful, having adapted quite well to his new insect identity. He trundled along the road, rolling his ball of dung, adding to it at every opportunity. Fortunately, such opportunities were scarce; the gamers met no one on the road, and the few droppings encountered were old and dry.

The travelers made good time, held up only by Hali's determination to explore every empty hut and hovel on the way. The first they encountered was a tiny tumbledown shack, surrounded by nettles, briars, and lichen-covered fruit trees. Blackberry vines encroached on an abandoned orchard, having already taken over the ornamental shrubbery where overgrown roses fought a last desperate battle for space. A few valiant lilacs still lifted their fragrant flowers above the thorns; brave narcissi and hyacinths poked their heads out from under the bushes and around the shack's foundation.

Everywhere, the seasons mixed madly in this wild garden. In the orchard, some trees were bare of leaves, while others were heavy with fruit: one contrary apple tree was in riotous bloom. The shack itself, though quite picturesque from the outside, was quite plain within, and in tediously good repair. It boasted three rooms—one large room in front, a kitchen in back, and a small loft under the roof—with nothing magical in any of them.

After a couple of such undistinguished houses, the gamers quickly lost interest in the basic Grimmworld domicile, with its one or two rooms built of bare, weathered wood planking, crude stone fireplace, and possibly a sink and luxurious indoor pump. Hali found a promising shack, at the edge of an odorous marsh, that had—in addition to its highly desirable location—an infinite number of rooms magically tucked away inside. Unfortunately, the house had been stripped of its furnishings and any distinctive decor, leaving a series of almost identical rooms in which the gamers got thoroughly lost. By the time she managed to track the last one down, even Hali was a little annoyed with the building's idiosyncratic floor plan.

Halting for lunch in a pleasant glade, Hali spread out her maps, fighting the breeze which threatened to carry them off. "Get over here and hold this down," she snapped at Bernie. "You might as well see this yourself. There's no point in our looking at every cottage and shack along the way—we'd be at this forever."

While Bernie squinted at the map, Tracy wandered over and squatted beside him. "Where are we now?" she asked.

"Here," Hali pointed to a spot on the edge of the map. "We've already seen these places." Abruptly, she pointed out several squares, circles, and triangles that marked habitations.

Puzzled, Tracy studied the map, tracing the road on it with one fingertip. She looked sideways at Hali, who was busy studying another map. "Hey, Bernie," she said quietly, leaning toward the fuzzy paperweight. "Where's this road on this map?"

He looked up at her quizzically. "You're pointing at it," he said.

"It can't be," Tracy said. "We've been following this road straight from one house to another, but they're all over the map. I thought it was odd that all these witches lived so close together, but the houses look far apart on the map, and some of them aren't anywhere near the road, even. What's the deal?"

"Oh that," Bernie said, finally understanding. "This is an enchanted forest, remember? There's only one road, and it goes where you want it to. Grandma's house, the Black Woods, the swamp, wherever. Even out the other side, if you're lucky. Distance is meaningless in here, and with all their practice in visualization and concentration, witches can force the road to go where they want, as fast as they want.

"Ordinary folks like you and me have more trouble. Their subconscious leads them astray. Teenagers tend to keep wandering until they find their true love, for instance. Or their fears get the better of them, and the road takes them right to the monster they most want to avoid. People living near the wood tell some great tales intended to keep their kids out of the forest, but the tales tend to backfire on anyone who has to go in for some reason. If you're sure the boogeyman will get you, he really will, in this forest."

"Yuck," Tracy shuddered. "I saw a TV show once where they made the hero face his greatest fear, and I wondered what mine was, but I don't think I want to find out by facing it in person."

Bernie snorted. "Well, don't go wandering off alone and you won't have to find out. Besides, worrying about things is almost always worse than actually facing them. Look at all those folks scared of the New York subways at night. I was never scared of them—of course, I was ripping off other people myself. I admit, I got nervous any time some tough punks came along in an almost-empty car, but I got beat up a few times and finally decided the fear was worse than the pain, and quit worrying about it."

"You were a mugger?" Tracy exclaimed loud enough to attract the attention of the other gamers.

"You're missing the point," Bernie said, annoyed, as the others gathered around.

"I got the point. 'The only thing to fear is fear itself,' right? I'd rather hear about you mugging people." The others agreed eagerly, clustering closely around the wombat to avoid annoying Hali.

Gingerly lifting one paw off the maps, Bernie scratched his nose in embarrassment. "I wasn't a mugger, exactly; I'm not really the violent type, no gang member or anything. Mostly I was a pickpocket. Not a very good one, but it's a living. Or at least it was, right up to the time I tried to pick the pouch of this scrawny out-of-towner in a crowd.

"It was Hali, of course. I figured her for a tourist. How was I to know she was a witch? I got hit by a bolt of lightning, and the next thing I knew I was looking up at everyone, and every time I tried to talk all that came out was a squawk. Before I even figured out that I was a bird, Hali had picked me up and stuffed me into that pouch of hers, and it's dark in there. I just went to sleep. That's the one big drawback to being a bird, really; we're helpless in the dark. Well, except maybe for owls—I don't know how they do it."

"Wow, a real thief," Leo said, impressed.

"How long have you been here?" Oliver asked.

"Hard to say," Bernie admitted. "Time runs funny here. It seems like I've been here for centuries, but I know only a few years have passed Outworld. Hali's taken me with her on a couple of trips Out, but the trips have to be kept really short, to avoid losing too much time here—and to keep the Outworlders from going on witch hunts. Hali in a real snit could put an end to decades of rational thinking, I'm afraid."

"Hmmph. As if I would," Hali snapped, rolling up her maps with a yank that sent Bernie rolling. "Well, while you've been gossiping, I've decided on the next few stops. They should at least be more interesting than what we've seen so far."

The next bit of real estate they visited was a round tower perched on top of a tiny, barren hill in the middle of a particularly dense bit of woods. The gamers scrambled eagerly up the hill ("Like a pack of particularly obnoxious puppies," Hali muttered) and circled the tower, looking for the entrance.

"Hey, there's no door," Leo called.

"Of course not," Hali sniffed. "If there was one, anybody could get in or out, now couldn't they?"

"I get it," Tracy said. "It's Rapunzel's tower! You have to climb her hair to get in."

"Nonsense," Hali said, looking up at the only window visible, some thirty feet overhead. "Who's got hair that long? Or wants to have it yanked out by the roots that way? All it takes is a little magic. A waste of energy, if you ask me, but some people like the ostentation."

"You mean there's no Rapunzel?" asked Leo. "I always liked that story, especially when the prince landed in the thorns and scratched his eyes out."

"You would," Tracy said.

"The only rapunzel I've ever heard of is a kind of salad green. Weird name for a kid," Hali mused. "There're plenty of these towers about, though. Kings in particular find them very useful for hiding away unwanted relatives, or to keep their daughters virgin."

"That's disgusting," Tracy said. "What a sexist idea."

"Never works anyway," Bernie offered. "Sooner or later a prince always shows up."

"I'd rather go find my own prince than sit waiting in a tower to be rescued," Tracy snapped back. "That's the trouble with most of these old tales—all the girl gets to do is wait to get rescued."

"Most of them learn to lie back and enjoy it, though," Bernie said.

"There's actually quite a few stories where the princess gets to rescue someone. Usually a brother or other relative, though," Leo said, unusually thoughtful. "Then she gets a prince for a reward. It is kind of silly, but look at the cultures the stories come out of. Feminism's too new a phenomenon to have had much effect on fairy tales."

"And all the people who used to write down folk tales seem to have been male," Tracy pointed out fiercely. "All the ones I've ever heard of anyway: Andersen, the Grimms,

Perrault. I bet among themselves, women told different kinds of stories, the sort men probably didn't think were important or interesting."

"Forget the fairy tales," Bernie told her. "As long as women can get pregnant, and men can't, princesses will end up in towers. Around here men like to think they have some control in matters of childbirth. For that matter, don't most fathers have this weird idea of protecting their daughters from other men? This kind of prison is just a last-ditch, desperate measure."

"And it never works," Hali snorted, shaking her head. "These things attract princes the way rotten meat attracts flies. Nice stone work on this one, though."

"Maybe what they need around here is better birth control," Oliver suggested.

"Maybe they shouldn't make them so phallic if they're going to hide princesses inside," Leo said. "This way, they're like sex beacons."

"How do you make a tower look anything but phallic?" Tracy asked reasonably.

"And what else would you keep a princess in?" Ginny added timidly. "Towers are traditional."

"Handy in my business, too," Hali added. "I don't mind making teenagers suffer a bit, but I certainly wouldn't want to be stuck with them forever. Lock a girl up in a tower like this, and I'm sure to have her off my hands in no time."

"It still sounds awful to me," Tracy insisted.

Bernie agreed. "I sure wouldn't want to be stuck in one of these unless I had wings," he said, with a meaningful glance at Hali. "Fortunately, there aren't many who can afford something as useless as this. Once the girl's married off—or has run off with her handsome rescuer—you're stuck with a tower no one can get into, and remodeling to add a door would be a real struggle." Bernie stuck out a claw and tapped the solid stone foundation of the tower.

"Well, anyway, how are we going to get in?" Tracy asked.

"There's no caretaker about," Hali said, "so I'll just fly up and take a quick look."

She held her staff horizontally, and left it floating gently in midair a few feet off the ground. Hiking her skirts slightly, she sat down on the staff in a most ladylike sidesaddle position, and floated gently upward. At the window ledge she halted the staff with a curt command and stepped off into the room. A few moments later she was back, and floated down the way she'd gone up.

Hali shook her head when the gamers asked to see the inside, too. "No point," she told them. "Two rooms, no view, very boring."

From the tower, the road—now little more than a broad dirt path—led through a pleasant wood with young trees and considerable undergrowth. Numerous bushes bore a variety of berries, from a few wild strawberries low to the ground to the tall sprays of wild elderberry far overhead. Hali pointed out the edible fruits, though she added an ominous warning against straying from the path in search of more. Though Oliver and Tracy kept a sharp eye on Leo, they had no trouble gathering as many berries as they could eat on the march, from the bushes that often closed in on the trail like tall hedges.

For a while, the undergrowth thinned, and from the top of a rise the gamers could see a densely wooded valley ahead. On the far edge of the valley a castle stood, hedged about with a tangle of roses that completely covered the outer walls.

"That one's occupied," Hali said, checking her map. "Though it's got a hundred-year lease that's almost up, the current tenant has a renewal option—if she wakes up in time. Too big for my taste, anyway."

"Besides, she's never had much luck growing roses," Bernie confided in a loud stage whisper. "They get mold, and she hates pruning."

The road turned away from the castle, and soon the woods ended completely. A wide, grassy flat stretched ahead, leading toward a tall structure that glittered brightly in the afternoon sun.

Shading her eyes, Tracy tried to make out the building ahead. "That looks like a glass-walled skyscraper," she said indignantly. "One of those fancy triangular ones. What's something like that doing here?"

"It's too bright," Oliver said. "I can't make it out clearly, but it's not that tall. What the heck is it?"

"Maybe it's the original glass house—you know, the one whose owners shouldn't throw stones," Leo suggested, peering ahead.

Bernie couldn't make out more than a flash or two of light, even from his perch on the front of the donkey cart. He hopped down to the ground to lope after Hali. "I really don't want to live in any glass houses," he told her nervously. "I know you like some occasional flash and glamor, but let's not, huh? Even if I were a crow, I'd be scared to death. I've seen birds smash their brains out, flying into plate glass."

Hali looked down at him through slitted eyelids. "Another phobia, Bernie?" she asked. "Relax, it's not that bad."

Up close, the gamers began to make out details of the structure before them, but it took Leo to identify the shining mass. "I know this story. This is the glass hill the knights had to ride up to win the princess at the top. See? There's a tent up at the very top."

Peering against the glare, the others could indeed make out an elegant pavilion of vivid blue and scarlet, with a tall peaked roof and many banners. It perched jauntily there at the top of a mound of clear glass so slick it looked as if it might still be molten, but proved cool and very solid to the touch. The gamers could make out numerous scratches and scuff marks at the base of the hill, and a few just above their heads, but the upper reaches of the hill appeared untouched.

"Can you imagine trying to ride up this on a horse?" Leo asked. "It's way too steep to walk up, too slick to climb, and too tall to jump, no matter how fast a run you took at it. It's got to be, what, six, seven stories tall at least. A horse wouldn't have a chance. There must have been some spectacular falls. I bet a lot of men died on this hill. Horses, too."

"Don't be gruesome," Tracy told him. "At least they didn't get that high up—maybe some of them managed to jump down."

"Get real," Leo told her. "Look at the marks. Can't you just see the horses flailing about and falling, the knights caught underneath them, their steel armor gouging these deep lines?" With morbid glee, he traced a deep scratch with his fingers. Suddenly, he snatched his hand away, as if stung. "Aaack! I think I got a sliver!" he cried. "Of glass! I'll never find it. I'm gonna die. Help!"

"Serves you right," Tracy told him.

The group had to wait while Hali probed the wound with a needle and a sinister-looking pair of tweezers, but the crisis was soon over. The gamers circled the hill, finally finding a stairway cut into the glass on the far side.

"I wondered how the princess got up there," Leo said, sucking gently on his damaged finger. "If you're going to climb it I think I'll wait down here. I'm wounded, after all."

The steps proved rather slick, but Tracy, Oliver, and Ginny decided to scale the heights. Waiting below, the others could hear a few exclamations from the climbers when they reached the top, but sound echoed oddly off the glass hill, making communication impossible. Finally, the three returned.

"Anything up there?" Hali asked.

"There's a great view," Oliver offered, "but mostly just more forest, and some hills in the distance."

"The tent's great," Tracy said. "All velvet and pillows and plush rugs and stuff, like something out of *The Arabian Nights*. I could just imagine some princess lying there in luxury, watching all those knights make fools of themselves. It's in great shape, too. Why do they just leave it out here?"

Hali looked up from the map she'd been studying. "The hill's something of a landmark in this area, and every now and then someone rents it out for their daughters. It's been on the market forever, but no one really wants to buy it, even though some king paid a fortune to have the wizards put it up. I gather the glass hill was the daughter's idea. She didn't want to marry, but her father insisted, so she gave her suitors some impossible conditions to fulfill. The thing's supposed to be magic-proof, but no wizard yet has come up with a security system another wizard can't break. Thank goodness, or we'd have far too many unmarried royals wandering about."

She folded her map with a brisk rustle. "However, it's much too frivolous for me. Now, this next place looks much more interesting."

The warmth of the afternoon was fading by the time they reached the last stop of the day. Hali pushed the gamers on, despite lengthening shadows that increased the gloom of the increasingly tangled forest. Vines and fallen branches littered the road, making progress slow.

"This place is creepy," Leo complained when yet another obstacle blocked their path. "I don't want to be stuck here overnight."

Hali glared at the fallen sapling that prevented the donkey and cart from passing. The tree was a little too large and too well tangled in the undergrowth to be easily moved aside. Oliver offered to have at it with his ax, but Hali waved him aside. She scowled in concentration until the sapling turned to sawdust with a loud "pop."

She waved the cart on. "It's not much further, now. We might be able to stay overnight at the place coming up. At the least, we can camp out in the yard."

The ground grew rough and rocky, and the trees thinned out, growing tall and bare as they reached for the last rays of the sun. Soon, to the gamers' relief, the road came to a clearing where the slanting sunlight actually reached the ground.

Frowning, Hali looked at her map, and said, "This should be it." She looked around.

The clearing wasn't large enough to miss a house, if there had been one, but all the gamers could see was a well, a garden full of scraggly weeds, and a picket fence adorned with skulls.

"More skulls. How predictable," Leo offered for Jamison, though the hard-shelled critic was too busy patting his precious dung ball—now the size of a small beachball—to notice.

"Now where did that house get to?" Hali muttered to herself, going through a gate in the fence.

A beaten path led to a rough square of dry, packed earth. An extraordinarily large black and white housecat lay stretched out on a large stone doorstep, snoozing in the last rays of sunlight.

"Cat!" snapped Hali.

The dozing beast yawned, and got slowly to its feet. "I

suppose you're here to look at the house," he said mournfully. "Well, it's not on site."

"I can see that," said Hali. "Where is it?"

"Oh, it's around, I'm sure," the cat said. "Things just haven't been the same since the old lady left, you know. She heard about something called perestroika and Russia opening up, and went off in her mortar to check it out. She hasn't been back in years. She even took the pike from the well to sell on the black market. It always comes back, you know, but this time it never returned.

"Management found out and says it's her fault for going Out, heaven knows when she'll be back, and they won't pay for upkeep anymore. The house is still sulking about somewhere in the woods. Just follow the tracks—they're hard to miss."

"Tracks?" asked Tracy.

"Giant chicken tracks," the cat explained. "The house has a huge stride, of course, so they're usually quite far apart."

"Houses have legs?" Leo asked dubiously.

"This one does," said Hali, scanning the softer ground near the edge of the clearing. "Here, this one looks fresh," she said, pointing. She set off into the woods.

"Yoicks, away!" Leo hollered, trotting after her. "This is my kind of house-hunting!"

After one incredulous glance at the four-foot-long footprint, the rest of the party followed at a run, spreading out as they searched for more tracks. In the rapidly dimming light, prints were hard to see. The inexperienced trackers soon found themselves hopelessly lost, and started shouting back and forth to each other. Oliver stumbled over a low bush, and sat down hard in a patch of soft soil. From this position he could see that the shrub he had tripped over had been recently crushed, and a closer look revealed another giant footprint. He shouted, and soon the rest of the house hunters came crashing through the brush to join him. With Hali in the lead, they moved off in the direction of the track, scanning the trees for any sign of a fugitive house.

It was Leo, tripping over a large root, who made the next discovery. The knobby root was an odd yellow color, with a scaly bark, and Leo looked to see what kind of tree he had stumbled on. It was a tree with knees, he realized, and there were two such trees, quite close together. Peering into the branches thick overhead, he finally made out a small grey hut, perched on tall yellow legs, frozen in place in a desperate attempt at camouflage.

He backed up quickly, away from the legs, and hollered. "Guys, guys! It's here. It's huge. It looks like one of those walking tanks in *The Empire Strikes Back.* Oh no, you don't," he shouted as the nervous hut tried to inch away. With a vigorous leap, he wrapped himself around one of the long legs, shrieking for assistance as the hut started to move, dragging him through the brush. Suddenly, the hut stopped dead.

Leo looked around to see Hali standing in the hut's path. "Just what do you think you're doing?" she demanded sternly.

Leo looked up at the hut, which shifted uneasily, apparently equally unsure as to which of them the witch was addressing.

"You," she pointed at Leo with her staff. "Get down and stop scaring the poor thing. And you, house, back where you belong."

Meekly, the house turned and headed back to its yard, stepping gingerly over the treetops. The gamers had to run to keep up. They arrived back at the clearing to see the house settled neatly in place, looking for all the world as if it had never moved at all. The cat waited on the doorstep, calmly washing his paws.

"Your donkey's eating whatever's left in the garden, and that bug seems to be following him," the cat said, washing one ear. "Odd creature, that. Doesn't appear to talk."

"That was the primary reason for the transformation," Hali said.

"Whatever," said the cat, dismissing the subject with one fluffy paw. "Do you want to see Izbushka now? It's getting rather late."

"Actually, we were hoping to stay the night, if that's acceptable," Hali said.

The cat shrugged. "If you like. Open up, Izbushka," he

called over his shoulder. The door swung open. "Come on in," the cat said, and led the way inside.

"We're going in that?" Tracy asked. "Izbushka, is that its name? I don't think I want to go inside a house with legs."

"Yeah," said Leo. "It probably has one heck of a digestive system."

"Suit yourselves," Hali told them. "I just thought you might like to sleep in a bed tonight." She entered, followed by Bernie. After a second's hesitation, Oliver and Ginny braved the house, and reported back when they came to fetch their packs.

"It's just a house," Oliver said.

"In fact, it's quite nice inside," Ginny added.

Unconvinced, Tracy and Leo started to make camp by the garden, but the light was fading fast, and as it did, the eyes of the skulls impaled on the fence began to glow deep red. Suddenly, Whitenose's sleepy company seemed small protection against the terrors of the night. A pair of bats flitted by, just visible against the twilight sky, and Leo and Tracy were banging on the front door before the startled bats had a chance to nab their first gnat.

Inside, the hut was indeed quite ordinary in appearance, though somewhat better kept than many, with some elaborate woodwork. It was also completely furnished, even cluttered. It appeared the owner had just stepped out, and fully intended to return. This didn't stop Hali from examining the place in detail. She was particularly fascinated by the large standing cupboards, which held something different every time they were opened.

"A great organizer, if you can remember where you put things," she observed, opening the cupboard on a selection of herbs. Closing the door again, she examined the lock with interest: shaped like a mouth, it snapped fiercely at anyone who tried to open it without the proper key. "Nice touch." She opened the door again; this time she found a collection of lacy lingerie. "Who'd have thought it of the old girl," she muttered, shaking her head.

Bernie had uncovered a cache of edible food, including sausages and hams in good condition, hung out of the cat's reach but easily available to determined young humans. The cat put the sausages in a pot with water, and started a savory stew. Bernie bustled out cheerfully into the darkness to see how many edible roots remained to be unearthed in the garden.

With a fire crackling on the hearth, and a hot, filling dinner inside them, the gamers forgot all about the ambulatory nature of the hut. Unchallenged by the others, Hali claimed the luxury of Baba Yaga's own bed, but there were two smaller beds in back, and the cat managed to find several extra mattresses and blankets in the depths of the cupboard, so all the gamers spent the night in relative comfort.

CHAPTER
15

THE next morning, the gamers bid a cordial farewell to the cat and the hut Izbushka, which stood up politely to see them off.

"It's a lovely place, truly unique," Hali told the cat, "but your mistress is bound to return, and I can't help but think that she'd be a bit annoyed to find squatters on her turf."

"She does a lovely temper tantrum, doesn't she," the cat said nostalgically.

"Legendary," Hali affirmed. "Now, if she'd left that oversized mortar and pestle she flies in, I might not be able to resist. There's a high-powered vehicle for you." She sighed and patted the cat on the back. "Hang in there, she'll be back. Maybe you should talk to Bentwood about a temporary job, though. You've done your bit guiding kids around."

"Yeah, but never without the old lady to play the bad guy," the cat said. "It's an idea, though. Better than sitting around waiting."

For a little while, the terrain stayed rocky and rough with the tall, spare trees that had seemed so unnatural the evening before. An easy walk brought the gamers into a pleasant wood, full of low twining maples and straight-trunked aspen, interspersed with small clearings and sparkling ponds.

Occasionally, they encountered pastures fenced with tall hedges and low stone walls, but the livestock in the area proved as elusive as the local deer, darting away as soon as sighted.

The first sign of habitation was a simple footpath lined with bushes, leading from the road. Hali stopped, and eyed the donkey cart coming up the road behind her.

"That cart won't fit," she said.

"Are we leaving the road permanently, or is this another house you're looking at?" Oliver asked. "If it's just another house, I'd just as soon stay here and keep an eye on the cart."

"I'll keep you company," Ginny offered. "If you don't mind."

Hali eyed the couple for a moment, then nodded. "Fine, but I'm not leaving you two unchaperoned, and the bug won't do. Bernie, you stay and keep an eye on them."

"Oh, geeze, how embarrassing," Bernie muttered, but he stayed behind as Hali led Tracy and Leo down the path. Jamison chittered briefly in confusion, looking from one group to the other, but settled happily enough with his ball at the side of the road where Whitenose browsed.

The footpath led to a small, grassy meadow, but no house. Instead, a quaint well stood in the center of the clearing. A peaked wooden roof covered the stone-walled well, and a large crank jutted from the roof's supports, connected to a round crossbeam. Wound around that beam, a sturdy rope depended into the depths.

Her hands on the waist-high wall, Tracy leaned over the well, trying to make out the end of the rope. "There should be a bucket but I can't see one, or water."

"I'll get it. I could use a cool drink." Leo started to turn the crank vigorously, knocking Tracy aside and almost into the well.

"Take your time," Hali told him, holding Tracy back before she could do him damage.

Leo's cranking slowed quickly, and soon Tracy had to move to help him. "This water had better be something really special," she muttered.

"It's heavy enough," Leo panted.

When it appeared, however, the wooden bucket was

empty but huge. At Hali's instruction, the two gamers raised the bucket until its top edge was even with the top of the wall around the well.

"It's big enough to hold all three of us," Tracy said. "No wonder it was so heavy. But where's the water?"

"No point in getting wet," Hali said, setting her staff in the bucket. Gathering her skirts, she sat neatly on the top of the wall and swung her legs inside. "Get in, get in, we haven't got all day."

Tracy and Leo let go of the crank cautiously, but to their surprise the bucket didn't move. Quickly, they scrambled over the wall and into the bucket. Once all three were inside, the bucket sank smoothly down the dark shaft of the well. Soon, they were beyond the reach of the sunlight, and then even the faint glimmer of light from above was gone. The bucket kept falling and only Hali's silent calm kept either of the gamers from panicking.

Finally, with a little jolt, the drop ended. In the complete darkness, the gamers held their breath. The only sound was a rustle of skirts as Hali swung out of the bucket the way she'd entered. "Come along, quickly now," she called, disappearing into the darkness.

Leo and Tracy scrambled to follow, moving as best they could in the direction of Hali's voice. Suddenly, they found themselves blinded by sunlight so bright it made them stumble. When they could see again, there was no sign of well nor bucket. Instead, they found themselves alone in a beautiful field full of thousands of flowers: daisies, wild asters, foxglove, and more nodded their heads in the soft breeze. It was an idyllic scene, but neither Leo nor Tracy could enjoy it. Hali was nowhere to be seen, and if anyone had passed that way recently they had somehow managed to do so without trampling a single blade of the luxuriant, waist-high grasses.

"Oh, great. Now what?" Leo asked, wading experimentally through the grass.

"You've got me," Tracy said. She turned and looked about, seeing nothing but grass mixed with wildflowers on every side. Finally, she pointed.

"Look, I think there's something over there, some kind of

lump on the horizon," she said. "Maybe a building. We might be able to find out where we are."

"It's not like we've run into anybody in this weird forest yet," Leo grumbled. "Maybe we should stay here. There's no point in getting any more lost than we are already."

"I don't think we're in the forest anymore," Tracy said. "Obviously, that was a magic well. We could be in another land, like Wonderland, for all we know. Besides, we'll be visible no matter where we are on this plain, if anyone comes looking. Come on," she said, pushing through the grass.

Sighing, Leo followed, concentrating on his feet as more than one clump of grasses threatened to trip him up. Despite being in better condition, Tracy also found walking through the tall grasses difficult, and both were panting by the time they reached their destination, an odd domed structure built of large yellow bricks and plaster. There were no windows, but on one side Tracy found several small doors set at different heights in the wall.

"Reminds me of the ovens in the gingerbread house," she noted.

"Ow! It's hot enough," Leo said, having tested the walls rather rashly. With a frustrated frown, he blew on his burnt hand. "Hey!" came a cry from within the structure. "Take me out, take me out, or I'll burn! I've been baking long enough."

Gingerly, Tracy tested the handle on the door from which the cry seemed to come. Quickly, she yanked it open, letting go immediately, and peered inside. A dozen loaves of bread, all a golden brown, sat inside what appeared to be a large baking chamber.

"*It is* an oven," she exclaimed.

"What else would it be?" said one of the loaves grumpily. "Now take us out, will you?"

"How? It's too hot," Tracy explained.

The loaf sighed with a small whistle of escaping steam. "There should be a paddle somewhere around, and a cooling rack too. Now hurry, before I'm overdone."

Sure enough, a quick search revealed the paddle, a wooden device shaped much like a flat snow shovel, hidden in the grass. Leo then stumbled on the wire cooling racks, and managed to free them from the plants that had grown up between the wires. Tracy managed to scoop the loaves up with the paddle and slide them onto the racks with only minimal damage to the bread. Unfortunately, once freed from the oven, the bread was no longer inclined to talk. Even threatening to eat it brought no response, and the gamers began to despair of finding their way out.

"You know, though," Leo mused, "this is starting to sound familiar. I bet if we keep going in the same direction, we'll find more tasks, and then finally the witch's house."

They walked on in the same direction they'd taken before, and soon a tree appeared. A bit nearer, they could make out the gleam of hundreds of red apples weighing down the branches. Closer yet, the tree began to talk.

"Shake me!" it cried. "My branches are breaking under all these ripe apples. Shake me!"

"I don't know," said Leo, hands on hips. "I think we should negotiate. How about some information, first?"

"Shake me! Shake me!" the tree repeated, and neither Leo nor Tracy could get anything more out of it.

"Stupid tree," Leo muttered. "Let's leave it and go on."

"I don't think we should skip a magic task," Tracy told him. "Besides, it really does look pathetic, weighted down like that."

"It's too much work. That tree's too solid to shake easily."

With a look of disgust, Tracy turned her back on Leo and set both hands on the tree trunk, pushing firmly. The tree trembled, and its branches rustled encouragingly, so she set to with a will, pushing again and again in sharp little jolts until the uppermost branches began to whip back and forth. One apple fell, then another and another, and suddenly Tracy had to duck for cover as dozens of apples came raining down all around the tree.

"Neat!" Leo said. He grabbed a still-drooping branch and tugged hard, setting a whole section of the tree to bobbing, and freeing another storm of apples. After a brief exclamation of annoyance, Tracy retreated to the other side of the tree, and grabbed a large branch of her own. In no time, they had the ground covered with bright red apples, and most of the branches, relieved of their burdens, had sprung up out of reach. A few stubborn apples still clung here and there despite their best efforts, but at least the tree no longer complained. Tracy and Leo decided they'd done enough, and sat down in the grass to snack on the juiciest of the fallen apples.

"They're bruised," Tracy noted, examining a soft spot on her apple. "Shaking isn't the best way to get apples off a tree."

"At least it's fast," Leo said, munching away. "Maybe you could use them for cider or applesauce."

"It does seem a waste to just leave them here to rot. I can't think of anything to do with them, but it seems awfully pointless."

"We helped the tree—that has to count for something."

Having rested, they continued on their way, Leo with his pockets full of apples. Soon they came to a small cottage.

"Huh," Leo grunted around a bite of apple. "I thought tasks were supposed to come in threes."

Tracy laughed nervously. "Maybe we have to sweep out the stables, or something. I don't care, just as long as there's someone who can help us."

As boldly as she could, Tracy walked up and knocked on the door. It swung open quickly, and Hali stood there, frowning furiously.

"There you are. Stop lollygagging and come in."

Busy inspecting the cottage, a rather pleasant place with several rooms, Hali listened with only half an ear to stories of ovens and trees. When Leo mentioned a third task, Hali grunted. "Fluff the featherbed," she said absently, examining a kitchen cupboard.

Already bored by yet another ordinary house, Tracy and Leo decided to do just that. "My aunt has a feather comforter," Tracy said. "It packs down flat, then fluffs up to three or four times its usual size. I can't imagine a whole mattress like that."

They found the feather mattress in the largest bedroom, atop a boxy bed built into the wall. Essentially a large sack of feathers, the mattress was limp and rather lumpy when they found it, and only a few inches thick. Dragging it from the bed, Leo and Tracy soon had it fluffed up so much it made a cushy-looking bed almost four feet high.

"Now, that looks comfy," Leo declared, and threw himself

onto the newly made bed, falling with a soft "whoomf" in the middle of the mattress, sinking almost out of sight.

Tracy grabbed a pillow and hit him. "We just got the bed made, and you ruined it. Look, it's all flattened in the middle now."

"Who cares," Leo said, grabbing another pillow and striking back. Nothing loath, Tracy renewed her attack, and soon the two were bouncing back and forth across the room in vigorous battle.

Like the mattress, the pillows were filled with feathers, and soon bits of down began to escape from the seams. Then a stitch gave, and then another, and soon the air was filled with flying feathers. The two combatants kept swinging until their pillows were almost empty. They dropped the limp pillows and collapsed on the floor, laughing hysterically.

"Can't leave you alone for an instant, can I," Hali remarked dryly from the doorway. No expression crossed her face, but she drummed her fingers on her staff with one hand while the other waved feathers away from her face.

Tracy blushed and Leo blustered briefly, but both got to their feet and stood in front of Hali, awaiting sentence.

Hali's silence became oppressive. "We'll clean up the mess," Tracy offered.

Hali shook her head and sighed. "No, I think I'd better get you out of here before you make things worse. This way."

Leo and Tracy followed obediently. Hali led them down a hall, stopping in front of a large door neither of the miscreants had noticed before.

"Out," said Hali, opening the door. "Go straight to the others and stay put."

"But . . . " Leo started, jumping backward as Hali raised her staff in a clearly threatening gesture.

"Out," she repeated, pushing Leo backward with the staff. Choosing the better part of valor, Tracy hurried through the door after him.

"Yeah, but how do we find them?" Leo shouted as the door slammed shut behind them. "Geeze, it's cold out here."

Tracy shivered, and looked around. Where the well had been pitch black, this place was glaringly white. She took a step, then pulled back at the familiar crunch underfoot. "It really is snow," she exclaimed. "No wonder it's so cold. At least the sun's out."

"Where the heck are we, the Arctic?" Leo asked.

"Might as well be," said a muffled voice nearby.

Turning quickly, Leo and Tracy found themselves facing their cart, half-buried in snow. Whitenose stood nearby, his ears frost-tipped and drooping dejectedly, a snow-encrusted blanket draped over his back. Calling out, they found their friends huddled together on the clear ground under the cart. Bernie popped up in front of them from under the snow, where he'd been burrowing.

"Hi, guys," he said cheerfully. "Great weather for a fur coat, huh?"

"Give me my cloak," Tracy forced out between chattering teeth, "and then I'll think about it. What happened, anyway?"

Oliver laughed, crawling out from under the cart with Tracy's cloak. He stood up, handed it to her, and shook snow from his clothes. "About half an hour ago, it started snowing all of a sudden. At first, there were just a few white flakes, and we could hardly believe it. I mean, it was warm out. I thought it was summer here, didn't you? Then it got colder, and just started to dump on us, huge fluffy flakes falling so fast you couldn't see a foot in front of your nose. All this fell in just ten minutes or so, then stopped just before you guys showed up." He gestured at the two-foot-deep snow piled all around, then looked up at the sky. "It's really crazy. Look, there's not a cloud in the sky, and it's already getting warmer."

The sun shone brightly on the pristine snow, which slumped and dripped and melted away in minutes. The gamers spent some time rescuing their equipment from the dripping slush, but in the warm sunshine even the soggy cart promised to dry out quickly. Hali appeared to be taking her time underground, if that was where she was; Tracy and Leo recounted their adventures, to the amazement of their companions. During the telling, however, Leo suddenly remembered why the encounter had seemed so familiar.

"I've read this story," he told the others. "A girl falls down a well, rescues some bread, shakes a tree, and runs into a witch who makes her fluff a bed until the feathers fly and make it snow. We made it snow! Isn't that great? We should have gotten gold or something; I wonder if we get points for this?"

"Considering the mess you made of things, making it snow out of season, I wouldn't be surprised if you lost points, if there were any, which there aren't," Oliver said. He and Leo argued this technical point while Ginny, no gamer herself, listened in amused incomprehension.

Tracy, however, felt somewhat embarrassed to have made such a mess. As well, she was bored. Instead of staying to listen to Leo bluster, she decided to take a walk. Promising Bernie that she would stay in sight of the cart, she wandered down the road.

A long straight stretch ahead offered a safe stroll of some length, and Tracy enjoyed the warm sunlight. Not far from the cart the road was bone dry, even parched, and the foliage on the trees and bushes showed no sign of a recent freeze. Apparently the blizzard had been not only short-lived, but also a strictly local phenomenon.

Tracy reached a bend in the road and was about to turn back when she noticed a large terra-cotta pot of flowers beside the road. Crossing over to take a look, she noticed that the flowers, a tightly packed clump of small ruffled pinks, were wilting badly. Digging her fingers into the soil in the pot, she found it hard and dry.

"Poor things, you really need water. I wonder if there's a stream or anything near here." She listened for the sound of water nearby, but heard nothing. However, a quick glance at the surrounding woods showed her a clearing nearby, with a low stone structure in the center.

"I don't believe it," she said. "Another well. Maybe this one has water in it." Hefting the flowers in their container, she pushed through the underbrush at the edge of the road and into the clearing.

Though lacking any sort of pulley or crank, the well did indeed have water in it, and a bucket on a rope with which to pull it up. Tracy set the pinks on the edge of the well and watered them carefully, waiting for the water to drain through and then watering them again.

"You guys were really dry," she said, watching water pour

from the pot. "Maybe I should water you one more time, just to make sure it sinks in."

She was pulling up a second bucket of water when she noticed a woman entering the clearing. Tall and ethereally slim, the lady wore a long white dress and an elaborate headdress that framed her face with rolls of green velvet wrapped with gold cord.

"Oh, how beautiful," Tracy breathed, then blushed.

"Thank you, child," said the lady. "Are those your flowers?"

"These? Oh, no, I found them by the side of the road and thought I'd better water them before they died. They aren't yours, are they?"

"Regrettably, no. They belong to a young lady, a friend of my son's—I was hoping you might be she."

"I'm afraid not," Tracy said. "I don't know any boys from around here."

"How unfortunate." Sighing, the lady cupped a few of the small blossoms in her hand, and bent to smell them. "They've almost lost their scent. If you hadn't come along, they probably would have died. You have my thanks, young lady."

The lady's manner was so elaborately formal, Tracy felt impelled to curtsy, though the unfamiliar movements made her awkward. "It was nothing, really. I couldn't leave flowers to die like that."

The lady smiled gently. "Nonetheless, I am grateful, my dear. I have one request, however. Could you return the flowers to where you found them? I still have hopes that their owner will return for them someday."

"Oh, sure," Tracy said. "Just let me water them one more time—they were so dry the water went right through the first couple of times."

There was no answer, and when Tracy looked up the lady in white was gone.

Shrugging, Tracy finished watering the flowers, and carried the pot, now much heavier, back to the roadside. She looked around, but there was no one in sight. In fact, she realized suddenly, she couldn't see her friends. Remembering Bernie's warnings, she started running back the way she came. To her immense relief, the cart came into sight immediately. She didn't stop running until she reached it, and found her friends seated on the grass just behind it.

"You don't know how glad I am to see you guys," she panted, leaning against the cart. "I was sure I'd gotten lost. Why on earth are you all staring at me like that?"

Two gold coins dropped at her feet, falling on a pair of long-stemmed red roses.

"Hey," Tracy said. Another rose dropped to her feet. "Where are they coming from?" she asked, puzzled, and two coins fell.

"They're coming out of your mouth," said Leo, staring at her wide-eyed. "Don't those roses hurt coming out?"

"Don't be silly, they're not coming out of my mouth," Tracy said, producing a white rose. "Oh my god, they are!" she exclaimed, clasping her hands over her mouth just in time to catch a gold coin. One hand firmly over her mouth, she held the coin in the other, examining both sides.

"It looks real," she said, wonder in her voice. This time, she caught a lovely pink and white bloom half out of her mouth. She held it there a moment, but finally pulled it all the way out.

"This is really weird," she said, scowling as yet another rose and coin fell. "I can't feel them in my mouth, but if I don't let them all the way out, I can't close my mouth at all." She lifted her arms in despair as more money clinked to her feet, and stomped into the middle of the road, where she started pacing frantically back and forth.

"How do I stop it?" she cried in desperation, spewing a giant pink cabbage rose.

"I don't think you can," Bernie said, amused. "You've run into a witch, haven't you?"

"I don't want to talk about it!" Tracy stomped her feet in exasperation as more gold fell.

"Hey, if you don't want the gold, can I have it?" Leo asked. He'd already scooped up the coins near the cart, and was eyeing those in the middle of the road.

"Oooooh!" Tracy shrieked with fury from between tightly closed lips. It didn't help; with a funny look on her face, she spat out a tightly closed rosebud.

"I think that means, 'hands off the gold,'" Bernie told Leo.

"You don't want it to go to waste, do you?" Leo asked ingenuously.

"Pile it in the cart if you must," Bernie told him. "I have a feeling we're going to be seeing a lot more of it, though."

He turned back to Tracy. "This sort of thing is pretty common," he told her. "It's really hard to cure, though usually folks with your sort of affliction don't want to cure it.

"You might as well tell us—what exactly happened?"

Sighing, Tracy gave in and came over to sit beside the cart with the others.

"I found a pot of flowers sitting beside the road. They were so dry they were dying. I saw a well nearby, so I decided to water them. While I was pulling up water, this really beautiful lady came by, and said something about the flowers belonging to her son's girlfriend. She thanked me for watering them, and then just disappeared when I wasn't looking.

"What I can't figure out is why she didn't water the flowers herself if she was so worried about them. In fact, she asked me to put them back where I found them, so I did, and that's when I came back here." With a somewhat bemused expression, Tracy sorted the gold from the roses that had piled up in her lap.

"Really pretty, huh?" Bernie asked. "What color was she wearing?"

"White, a white dress."

Bernie nodded. "A white lady, then. One of the fairies. Well, they're a kind of elf, really, but more polite, even friendly sometimes. This one's probably caught up in some sort of spell involving those flowers. Maybe her son's been turned into a potted plant, and needs his true love to set him free. The spell would be set up so his mother couldn't interfere without making things worse. You might have saved her son's life by watering those flowers. That would explain the big reward she gave you."

"This is a *reward*?" Tracy asked, mournfully eyeing the velvety red rose that the words produced. She tossed the rose into the road, then scooped up the rest and tossed them after it. "I don't want it."

"Well, the roses aren't so hot, but what about the gold?" Leo pointed out. "Keep talking, and we'll have enough money to buy you all the dresses and horses you want."

"Not to mention a certain magic sword," Oliver added.

"Hey, if we can afford it, why not?"

"Because it's not your money," Oliver told him. "It's Tracy's, and she gets to do what she wants with it."

Keeping her mouth firmly shut, Tracy rolled her eyes.

"Well, do you want it or not?" Leo asked.

"Of course I want it," Tracy snapped, then covered her mouth with both hands.

"Well, how about the roses, then?" Leo asked. He pointed. "Jamison's adding the ones you tossed out to his ball."

"Good," said Tracy, giving up on silence. "Maybe it will smell better. I don't want any stupid roses. At least the gold's worth something." She tossed two more flowers at Jamison, gathered the gold coins from the ground, and dropped them into her pack.

Leo watched the gold disappear with evident longing. "You know," he said, getting up and wandering out into the road, "I could use a drink of nice, fresh water about now. Maybe I could water those flowers again, make sure they've got enough to last for a while."

Whistling tunelessly, he started walking briskly down the road, while the others exchanged shocked glances.

"He wouldn't," said Oliver.

"Want to bet?" Tracy asked.

"No bets! We've got to stop him," Bernie cried, and took off at a surprisingly speedy trot. Oliver followed close behind. They caught up easily, and between them dragged Leo back to the cart.

"What's the big deal?" he whined. "I just want my chance at a reward, too. You guys don't want me to have any of the good stuff in this game."

"If you've read the stories, you should know it doesn't work that way," Bernie told him sternly. "Good deeds have to be done out of the goodness of your heart, not out of greed. There's lots worse things you could end up spewing than roses and gold."

"Oh sure. Like what?"

Bernie considered. "Oh, vipers and toads, spiders, nettles, you name it."

"That wouldn't happen to me, anyway. You're just jealous," Leo said, unconvinced.

"Jealous of what?" Oliver asked a wide-eyed Ginny in a stage whisper, making her giggle.

"I'm not going to stay here and be insulted," Leo huffed.

"Oh yes you are," Bernie told him, grabbing Leo's nearest leg in a fierce bear hug. "Hey, help!" he shouted as Leo started off anyway, dragging the disgruntled wombat with him.

"Sheesh," Oliver said in exasperation, exchanging a rueful glance with Ginny before going to help Bernie.

By the time Hali returned, the group was seated by the cart, sharing some of their road rations. The tranquil effect of this roadside picnic was somewhat spoiled by the sight of an indignant Leo lying prone with Oliver seated on his back and Bernie cheerfully sprawled across his legs.

Already raised, Hali's eyebrows rose even higher. She bent and picked up a small golden coin. It gleamed brightly in the sun as she examined it.

"Fairy-made, but permanent," she observed. "What's been going on here?"

Bernie explained, with Tracy's reluctant assistance. Hali asked for a more detailed description of the lady at the well, and considered the answer—and resultant roses—most carefully. Finally, as if to herself, she nodded.

"Don't know the lady in question, but things could have been a lot worse," she said. "You did a good job keeping our fat friend here out of it."

"Hey!" Leo shouted, only to find himself ignored. "Don't I get to have any fun around here?" he muttered indignantly.

"What I want to know," Tracy told Hali meanwhile, "is what I have to do to get rid of this spell."

Hali smiled very slightly. "What makes you think you can?"

And with that, she started briskly down the road, swinging her staff in time with her determined strides.

CHAPTER
16

DESPITE the eventful visit underground, it was still morning when the party moved on. Hali led at a brisk pace through some of the thickest and darkest woods yet. Tall, dark evergreens dripped with moss and lichens. Beneath the trees, only bright toadstools and pale mushrooms dared to grow. Though insects buzzed and burrowed in the thick carpet of fallen needles, bird calls were few, and muffled by the heavy branches of the conifers.

Deep in these woods, Hali stopped briefly at a dismally dirty cave. From its appearance, some rather slovenly animals had recently been in residence. A rancid odor wafted from the entrance, keeping any would-be spelunkers in the party from exploring. Hali ducked inside for a quick glance, but backed out quickly. Only Bernie was able to accurately decipher the scowl on Hali's face as one of puzzlement rather than distaste. His own curiosity piqued, he would have questioned her, but was distracted by a fresh outbreak of squabbling among the gamers.

Tracy still spewed flowers and gold every time she opened her mouth. Leo followed close behind, watching eagerly for overlooked coins. When he wasn't trying to snatch a coin through stealth, he argued loudly for a share in the wealth,

invariably provoking Tracy into making some rash statement—rash because it would produce more coins and roses,
further irritating her already inflamed nerves. To Bernie's
wary eye, she was near breaking.

Jamison at least did not add to the problem. With every
appearance of cheerfulness, he rolled his ever-growing ball
along and industriously added every rose Tracy left in her
path. The ball was becoming more rose than dung, to the
point that Jamison had to occasionally resort to using mud
and damp clay to cement the roses together. Fortunately, the
beetle followed far enough behind the rest that Tracy hardly
noticed. Oliver and Ginny were too wrapped up with each
other to even notice the mounting tension, so Bernie cast
himself in the unlikely role of peacemaker. Nursing hysterical adolescents had never been his favorite chore, but with
Hali around it was necessary often enough.

As he stepped in between the battling teens for the
umpteenth time, it occurred to Bernie that for the entire trip
Hali had been rather well behaved, suspiciously so, in fact.
At the moment, though, she appeared annoyed, which was
normal, and edgy, which most definitely was not.

She was also leading the feckless gamers deeper and
deeper into the darkest reaches of the forest, into a deep hollow where ancient trees twined their gnarled limbs together
in an impenetrable canopy. Shut off from the light, the trees'
lower limbs and branches died, some falling to the forest
floor, others hanging lifeless and withered from the trees.
Even mushrooms hesitated to sprout in these woods, though
deep piles of leaves and deadwood fostered plenty of smaller
fungi like mold and mildew, turning the floor of the forest
black with damp and decay. In addition, dark lichens and
moss covered the trees, making the overall color scheme a
grim and depressing black. The smell of rot filled the air, to
go with the festive spiderwebs strung between the trees.
Chill breezes swept through with an eerie whistle, changing
directions unpredictably while the trees creaked and groaned.
Only the distant, raucous cries of crows pierced the constant
susurrus of the wind.

At least these drear surroundings finally made Tracy forget her problems. Fear took their place; all the gamers closed ranks with their weapons in hand.

"This is too much like *The Hobbit*. I don't think I can handle giant spiders," Tracy said, her voice near breaking. She carried her bow strung and ready, but more often used it to swipe nervously at nearby webs.

Hali still strode ahead, nonchalantly using her staff to clear spiderwebs from her path, but to Bernie there was a particular alertness to her bearing. Something was up, he was sure of it, but whether it would be another staged attack or something more serious he couldn't say. He wasn't eager for a fight with spiders himself, though he was more worried about the small, poisonous variety than the big ones. Wombat hide appeared unusually tough, but in case he needed protection from falling arachnids he dragged a heavy blanket from its resting place in the cart, and covered himself with it. He peered out from under this improvised shelter, ears cocked, alert to possible danger.

He sat that way for the better part of an hour, watching the forest grow darker, the webs thicker, and Hali more anxious. As they traveled, the wind picked up and the creaking noises from rubbing trees grew louder and more ominous. With every passing minute the tension grew, and the gamers were starting to jump at every shriek and groan from the trees. Chill drafts whistled past, tugging at the gamers' hastily donned cloaks and even penetrating Bernie's thick fur beneath his blanket.

The chill decided him; shedding his cover he jumped down from the cart and loped ahead to join Hali.

"Hey, what's up?" he said. "This looks like a bad neighborhood. You sure we ought to be out strolling with the kids like this? We might run into some trouble."

"You'd think so, wouldn't you," Hali grumbled.

Bernie turned that over in his mind a few times before deciding some clarification was in order. "You want trouble?"

"Just a little action," Hali said. "Right now, I'd settle for a couple of irate banana slugs for this group to battle. They get into more trouble when they're bored than in combat, unbelievable as that may seem."

"Well, how about calling Bentwood and setting something up, instead of taking chances like this."

Hali glared at him. "What do you think took me so long at the last place? I set it all up once I got rid of the kids. We should have had an unfriendly encounter long since. Two ogres share that cave back there, but they weren't home, haven't been for a couple of days, I'd say. This stretch of woods harbors goblins, giant spiders, a good-sized albino serpent, a will-o'-the-wisp, even an enchanted bear—and we haven't seen a one. Even if Bentwood screwed up completely, we should have run into something by now."

Bernie scratched one ear. "If we don't run into something, are we going to stay here till nightfall?"

Hali's scowl had a wistful edge to it. "Well, we'd be sure to have a battle on our hands, wouldn't we?" More seriously, she shook her head. "No, of course not. These kids would be eaten alive by the nightcrawlers. What with trying to protect this lot, we'd be lucky to survive ourselves.

"We'll head out of here now. There are a few less risky spots nearby where I know monsters lair. We should be able to get a quick battle in and still make camp before dark."

Bernie returned to his post on the cart, determined to keep an eye out for trouble. At the same time, he encouraged the gamers to relax a bit, hoping to keep them from jumping at shadows and injuring themselves. This worked only until a strange, high-pitched giggle floated down from the treetops.

Instantly, everyone in the party was on the alert. Even Whitenose pricked his ears, and Jamison stood upright on his hind legs. Hali fell back to join the group, scanning the trees with narrowed eyes.

Something giggled again, this time on the opposite side of the road. Branches stirred against the wind; the sounds of small claws skittering across wood reached the gamers who had clustered together, backs to the cart and facing out into the gloomy wood.

For several minutes, the high-pitched laughter continued. Either the giggler moved with astounding speed, or a group of creatures surrounded the party. Then the laughter stopped, and the only sound to be heard was the rushing wind and the creaking and groaning of the trees.

"Sneaking cowards," Hali shouted, to the sick astonishment of the gamers. "Come out and show yourselves! Fight, you miserable scuttlers!"

This evidently struck the hidden watchers as funny. A fresh burst of giggling broke out from all sides, and branches rustled furiously.

"In a way, I wish they would attack and get it over with," Tracy whispered to Ginny.

"Don't worry," Ginny said, holding her bow ready. "Oliver will protect us."

Though somewhat surprised, Oliver lifted his chin slightly. "I'm certainly going to try."

On the other side of the cart, Leo risked a glance over his shoulder. One look persuaded him that the ex-princess was serious.

"Get real," he told her. "Oliver's no fighter, none of us are. We managed to beat those goblins more by luck than by skill."

"Stop it," Tracy told him urgently. "There's no point in scaring her."

"Why not? We're all going to die, anyway. She's got as much right to be terrified as the rest of us, even if she is just a character in a game."

"Not another word." Hali moved to face Leo. "Not about gaming, or dying, do you understand?"

It was a measure of Leo's desperation that he even considered arguing. After a second, he nodded and mumbled assent.

Ten minutes passed with no sign of attack. The manic laughter stilled, though there was no evidence that the gigglers had left. Another ten minutes passed in silence. Finally, Hali set one end of her staff on the ground, leaned her forehead against the upper end, and sighed heavily.

"All right," she said. "Looks like the little buggers aren't going to attack. We'll move out slowly and stay together. Oliver, you take up the rear and keep an eye out for a sneak attack."

Hali led the way slowly, but with grim determination. The gamers moved with a peculiar twisting, sideways gait as they tried to keep an eye on the trees above and beside them.

Even at the crawling pace that resulted, the company soon reached the edge of the forest. Trees thinned and the ground grew damp; soon the gamers found themselves surrounded by dead spars and wiry swamp grass. Grey clouds, so low they almost touched the ground, filled the sky, casting gloom over the land, though after the black forest the misty light seemed almost blinding. Visibility was limited to the immediate area, an enchanting vista of dew-drenched spiderwebs that persisted beyond the borders of the wood, spanning the dead trees and effectively fencing in the road. Finally, even the webs thinned and disappeared as the road led deeper and deeper into the swamp.

Despite water on every side, the road ran smoothly on a narrow stone causeway. Gases bubbled in the thick mud at the side of the trail, and strange splashes and plopping noises kept the gamers jumpy, but at least the gigglers no longer followed. Leo swore he'd seen huge, bulbous eyes floating on the water, but as no one else saw them, his report was dismissed by all but Hali, who scowled and increased her speed.

Less on guard, the gamers made good time. In less than an hour, the land began to rise. As the swamp fell away, trees appeared. The clouds thinned and the sun broke out. Soon the group was climbing a pleasant hill covered with oak and rowan.

From the top of the hill, the gamers saw another steeper mound ahead. They elected to stop for a rest, and broke out some food. Hali paced while the others ate, keeping an eye on the hills ahead. As soon as the gamers had eaten, she pushed them on the trail again.

The road headed steeply upward. Despite Hali's urging, the pace slowed. Whitenose struggled with the cart. At Tracy's insistence the gamers donned their packs again to reduce the weight of the cart. Under protest, Leo took Jamison's pack, since the uncommunicative bug showed no interest in pushing or carrying anything but his ball of dung. Bernie walked, as well, but even so it soon became necessary for the humans to help push the cart up particularly steep inclines. Before long, Tracy stopped, sat down, and took off her pack.

"I don't need this gold after all," she said, spilling dozens of coins on the ground. "It weighs a ton, and it's not like I can't make more." As if to demonstrate, three more coins and a white rose joined the rest as she spoke.

Leo dove for the pile, tossed the rose aside, and scooped the coins into the pack he carried.

"You'll be sorry," Tracy warned him.

"I'm not going to pass up a fortune just because it takes a little effort," he replied smugly.

Within ten minutes, however, Tracy caught Leo dropping coins surreptitiously into the bottom of the cart.

"You're not going to make poor Whitenose carry those coins," she exploded. Furious, she leaned into the cart, grabbed a handful of coins, and tossed them in Leo's face. "You want them, you've got to carry them."

"There's not that many of them—the donkey won't notice a couple extra pounds."

"Just like you didn't?" she asked scornfully. "The poor little fellow's hardly making it up the hill as it is. Making him haul more than absolutely necessary is cruelty to animals. I won't let you do it."

"Oh, listen to Miss Goody Two-Shoes," Leo scoffed, but he put the coins back in his pack, picking them up off the ground as Tracy indignantly tossed them out of the cart.

After that, Tracy kept one eye on him, but he made no effort to sneak the coins back aboard. In fact, he dropped some way behind the cart, where Jamison was busy rolling his burden uphill. The dung ball was considerably larger, more than three feet in diameter already, though Tracy would have sworn they had not passed that much manure on the road. Initially, Jamison had had a difficult time rolling the ball uphill, but then he started walking backwards on his sturdy forelegs, rolling the ball ahead of him with his hind legs. This method worked much better, and from the jaunty angle of his knobby head he seemed quite pleased with himself for having thought of it.

Meanwhile, Leo stopped to open his pack again. Tracy watched, prepared for subterfuge, but with sincere regret on his face Leo proceeded to empty the coins on the ground, along with a couple of pieces of clothing Jamison no longer needed. As long as Leo didn't dispose of the pack itself,

Tracy decided not to interfere, and turned away. Leo shouldered his lighter pack and hurried to catch up with the others.

Neither noticed that Jamison, too, found the coins interesting. Clicking gently to himself, he tossed his old clothing aside, and examined the small pile of coins carefully. Somehow, in his buggy mind, the coins must have qualified as excrement (certainly, they were a sort of human waste), for he quickly scooped up the coins and forced them into his ball before moving on.

The road wound steeply upward, forcing the group to rest frequently. Every time they topped a rise, another hill appeared beyond, higher yet.

"We're not going to make it," Leo moaned when a particularly tall peak was revealed. He sat down on the ground and pulled out a water bottle; the others joined him.

"I hate to say it, but I'm beginning to agree," Oliver said. He stood and shaded his eyes with one hand and scanned the rather barren hillside ahead. "There's not much shade out there, either."

"It feels like we've been climbing all day," Tracy protested. "Isn't it almost time to camp for the night?"

"Nonsense," Hali said, having dropped back to see what was keeping the gamers. "There's hours yet to go."

The gamers groaned.

"You're too soft," Hali grunted. "The exercise is good for you."

"Have a heart," Leo moaned. "What good is exercise if it kills us?"

Hali didn't relent, and soon the group was moving again. To the gamers' relief, the road wound around the hill ahead, with less of an incline than they'd expected. Despite the steep and rocky terrain, the road was wide and well-maintained, and their pace actually picked up a bit.

Hali's latest destination proved to be a cave, tucked away in the middle of some sheer and rocky cliffs. Large boulders and smaller rocks littered the hillside, but Hali and the gamers were able to pick their way across to the entrance of the cave. Then an errant breeze stopped them in their tracks, still several feet from the cave.

"Phew. What is that?" Tracy asked.

"It smells even worse than that other cave," Ginny added.

The stench, a compound of well-rotted meat and the un-buried droppings of large carnivores, kept most of the gamers from going closer, but Leo decided to investigate fur-ther. He covered his nose with his sleeve, and moved closer.

"Hey!" Tracy called. "What if there's a bear in there?"

"From the smell, it's probably dead," Leo called back. "Or maybe this is a dragon's lair. Don't be so chicken." Deciding that a little discretion was called for, however, he paused to toss a rock into the cave. They could hear a sharp crack as it hit a rock wall, then a softer thud, but no enraged beasts came roaring out to complain. Leo tried again, with similar results. Grinning back at the others, he entered the cave—and backed out quickly. He stumbled blindly over boulders until he was several feet away, then fell to his knees, gagging violently and trying not to throw up.

"What is it?" Oliver asked in concern.

Hali had followed close on Leo's heels. Staff held ready, she entered the cave. She lasted a few seconds, but soon emerged as well.

"No one's home," she said grimly, her jaw set. "But they left very recently. There's a fresh kill impaled on a stalag-mite right by the entrance."

"It looked human," Leo gasped, sitting up very carefully and holding his head as if it were about to fall off.

With little sympathy, Hali looked down her nose at him. "That's what ogres do, you know."

"Ogres! What if they're still close by?" Tracy had relaxed on the mountain climb, but she had her bow strung and ready in seconds. Pulling an arrow from her quiver, she turned quickly to survey the cliffs.

"Your amulet's not glowing," Oliver pointed out.

Carefully transferring both bow and arrow to one hand, Tracy picked up the pendant in the other hand and held it in her palm where she could see it.

"Fat lot of good it's done us so far. By the time it detects anything, it's too late."

She turned in a circle, holding the amulet out as if it were some sort of scanner.

"At least there's nothing nearby," she said, relaxing slightly.

"What's the range on that thing, girl?" Hali asked. She moved toward Tracy, jumping briskly from boulder to boulder.

Behind her, Bernie scrambled valiantly around and over the jumbled rocks. Between grunts, he sang to himself, "'Oh, for the wings, for the wings of a crow,'" in a deep monotonous rumble. Wombats were not meant to sing, he decided, but continued anyway. It took his mind off whatever it was that had Hali on edge, not to mention man-eating ogres. Even if wombats tasted bad, no one was going to find out until it was much too late.

Tracy couldn't remember the amulet's range. Oliver thought that range had never been mentioned when they bought it; Leo opined, from the evidence of the goblin raid, that the range couldn't be greater than ten feet. Hali, having taken the amulet from Tracy, held it in front of her face and concentrated fiercely.

"I'd say, more like thirty feet," she said, looking up.

"How can you tell?" Leo asked, doubt evident on his face.

"That's how high the cliffs are," Hali told him. She displayed the pendant, now glowing brightly, and pointed overhead.

The gamers' eyes followed her pointed finger up the cliff to the very top.

"I don't see anything," Tracy said. Nevertheless, she had her bow drawn and ready, aiming at the cliff top.

"Oh, geeze," Bernie moaned, shading his eyes with one paw. "Those two particularly lumpy rocks up there are ogres."

The two lumps ducked back suddenly, then reappeared. Apparently realizing they'd been spotted, the two ogres stood up to full height. One thumbed his nose; the other stuck his thumbs in his ears and waggled his fingers derisively.

"Booga, booga, booga!" he shouted hoarsely.

"Nyah, nyah, nyah, nyah, nyah, nyah," the other chanted in a childish sing-song. "We're not gonna play with you."

"What?" Hali shouted. "You get down here and fight, you ugly blobs of lard!"

"Try to make us," shouted back the ogres.

"Hey," Leo said, plucking nervously at Hali's sleeve. "Don't get them mad at us. Let's get out of here."

Yanking her arm out of his grasp, Hali glared at him. "I thought you wanted adventure."

"There's a body in that cave! I'm not staying around here." Stumbling over the rocks and boulders, Leo headed for the road where Whitenose and the cart waited. Moving quickly, Oliver grabbed him by the shoulder.

"Don't panic. We've got to stay together. They can't do anything to us from up there, anyway."

"Oh yeah?" Leo pointed upward, where the shouting ogres were jumping up and down. One held both arms straight over his head, holding a small boulder in a most threatening manner. "They can throw rocks. Big ones. I'm out of here."

Before the ogre could toss the rock, his companion cuffed him fiercely about the head, making him drop the rock. It bounced once and fell harmlessly down the cliff, but startled Tracy into firing. The arrow flew straight and fast, barely missing one of the ogres before bouncing off a piece of jutting rock. Both ogres dove for cover with startled squawks.

"See if we ever play with you guys again!" one shouted.

"Cowards! Chickens! Thick-skinned, moth-eaten, miserable excuses for a couple of monsters!" Hali howled. "Come down here and fight like the disgusting creatures you are."

"Uh, Hali," Bernie attempted. "Everyone's looking at you like you're crazy."

Muttering to herself, Hali ignored him. "Stupid ogres. I bring them a bunch of eager adventurers to fight, and they give us less trouble than a crew of construction workers would give a bunch of passing females."

Tracy edged away from the angry witch. "They have construction workers here, too?" she asked Ginny in a whisper.

"Someone has to build the palaces," she answered.

As best she could on the rocky ground, Hali paced back and forth furiously, keeping one eye on Tracy's amulet, the other on the top of the cliffs. Several minutes passed with no sight of the ogres, though the amulet insisted they were still nearby.

Finally, Hali stopped pacing, and turned to stare at the

ogres' cave. "All right!" she shouted over her shoulder. "If you won't play fair, neither will I."

She leveled her staff at the cave entrance. A shaft of light burst from the end of the staff and roared into the cave with a blast of white noise. Shedding white sparkles as it went, the light poured into the cave. Soon a backwash of those glittering bits of light came rushing out of the cave, filling the sky with thousands of points of light that swirled like sparks up and over the cliffs.

This brought the ogres' heads back into view. Peering cautiously down at their cave, the ogres howled in anguish.

"Our home! What's she doing to our home? You can't do that! That's our cave," they cried in futile protest.

"All right," said Hali, stopping the flow of light and lowering her staff. "Now it's time to get serious."

She tapped the end of her staff against the ground, and suddenly she was holding a twisted, handmade broom. "Broom, get sweeping," she instructed.

The homely household instrument supported itself upright on its bristles, then began spinning like a top. Faster and faster it spun, until it began to move, skipping over the stones on its way, careening like a drunken dervish into the cave.

"Bernie, you get in there and start cleaning, too," Hali ordered.

Bernie looked at her over his shoulder. "In there?" he asked. "With a dead body? You want me to go in there?"

"Dead never bothered you before."

"I was a crow."

"And you didn't like caves. Now you're a wombat. You should feel right at home."

"Wombats don't like meat. Or blood. Or ogre droppings, for that matter," Bernie shuddered.

"The place has been fumigated," Hali told him. "Any bodies in there are ash. Now get in there and start cleaning. You too," she told the gamers, waving toward the cave. "Get moving."

Hali overrode all protests, and the gamers reluctantly entered the sanitized cave. Fine ash lay in layers over every surface, holding on with a fierce static cling, but the broom was busily sweeping every nook and cranny, even zooming up the walls and across the ceiling. Under Hali's orders, the gamers set to clearing out the few solid objects that remained, mostly bones so clean that only Leo had trouble handling them. Many of the bones were broken and splintered beyond recognition. The whole skulls found were mostly animal, with a few at least humanoid, though none definitely human.

"They must not have been able to catch many humans out here in the middle of nowhere," Leo said. "Now that we've destroyed their food, I bet they're just waiting to get their hands on another nice, plump human." He started edging toward the cave entrance.

"Hold it," Hali told him, barring his exit with her broom. "We're not done yet."

Hali's formidable presence held the gamers in the cave, despite the possible imminent arrival of outraged ogres. That didn't stop anyone from wondering at Hali's actions. Brow furrowed in concentration, she transformed loose rocks into lace doilies, which the gamers placed on every flat surface that might serve as a table or shelf. Concentrating even harder, she leveled and polished the cave floor until it gleamed like finest marble. A fluffy, flowered rug sprouted in the center of the floor. Turning the broom back into a staff, Hali used it to blast a round window into the side of the cave. More transformed rock made delicate white curtains trimmed with ruffles. For a final touch, more lacy ruffles, these apparently carved in pure white stone, sprouted at the base of every stalactite and stalagmite.

"How precious," Leo said when Hali paused to take a satisfied look around the cave. "Even my kid sister would puke at all the lace."

"Good," said Hali. She turned and stalked out of the cave, staff held militantly before her.

The gamers clustered at the cave entrance, waiting for sounds of battle.

"Well, what's keeping you now?" Hali asked from outside.

One by one, the gamers emerged into the afternoon sunlight. Where boulders had covered the ground before, Hali stood on a neat path of crushed gravel, bordered by bright flowers, that led straight from the cave to the road.

"Our cave! Our beautiful cave! What have you done to it?" sobbed one ogre from the top of the cliff. His friend patted him consolingly on the back, while shaking his fist at Hali.

"You'll hear about this!" he shouted. "We're taking this to the union."

"Fine," Hali shouted back. "I've got a few words for your union myself."

"Do that. You'll find out. This is no wildcat strike. No monster in the land will attack you now. Why don't you just send those Outworlders back where they came from?"

"Oh no," Bernie groaned. He rolled up into a ball and rocked back and forth, making deep grumbling noises. "Please, no. Not a strike. Bentwood's done it to us again."

CHAPTER
17

HALI accepted the news of a strike with equanimity. "Get up, wombat, or I'll knock you about like a croquet ball," she threatened mildly. The staff tapping his behind did more to convince Bernie to uncurl than Hali's tone of voice.

He unrolled just enough to peep out with one eye. "Aren't you upset?"

Hali glared at him. "Of course I'm upset, but I was beginning to suspect something like this. You should have known—you're the one who's been moaning about Bentwood and the unions all along."

Bernie sat up, and scratched his belly pensively. "So, what are we going to do now?"

Hali rubbed her chin. "See what the story is. See if I can get the truth of the situation out of Bentwood. Huh." She grinned down at the worried wombat. "Fat chance of that, I know. Maybe we should try old Humbert."

"The dragon?" Bernie squeaked faintly.

"A dragon?" Leo echoed. "You mean, a big lizard with scales and wings, breathes fire, like a real dragon?"

"Not *like* a real dragon," Hali corrected him. "Humbert *is* a real dragon. Very real, very old."

"Very cranky," Bernie added helpfully. "Likes his dinners well cooked, with that special flavor of fear. If you've ever seen a cat playing with a mouse, you know how ol' Humbaby treats his visitors."

"Nonetheless," Hali said imperturbably, "I think we should visit him. His lair's not far." She pointed overhead at a tall peak that peeped over the edge of the cliffs.

"Let's get moving," she said, prodding Bernie into motion with her staff.

The gamers groaned, but Hali was not interested in their opinions. Rather, she seemed to have every intention of keeping the gamers too busy to ask questions. In minutes, they were on the road again. Tracy reclaimed her amulet from Hali, and kept a wary eye out for ogres, but the group hiked on undisturbed.

When they reached a trail that branched from the main road, leading directly to the craggy peak above, Hali persuaded the gamers to leave the cart and much of their supplies at the fork. Tracy refused to leave Whitenose behind, lest he become prey to the ogres, but the unburdened donkey proved willing and quite nimble as they climbed the hill. Not nearly so spry, Bernie had to accept an occasional lift from Oliver when Hali ignored his pleas to slow down. Though apparently untiring in his insect form, Jamison lagged further behind, having some serious difficulties as he rolled his ball up the rough places in the trail.

The afternoon was well advanced by the time the group neared the peak, though a glance back down the slope showed the exhausted gamers that they had come a long, long way—almost straight up—in a relatively short time.

"Wow. What a view," Tracy said, looking out at the panoply of valleys, forests, and distant mountains laid out before them.

"No kidding," Leo said, looking straight down at the steep, bare slopes before them. "I never thought I'd go mountain climbing in my life. Once is enough, if you ask me, but it is something to see. So where's this dragon?"

Still panting heavily, Bernie shuddered. "Don't be so eager to die, kid. It's not natural."

Leo shrugged. "What's to worry? If all the monsters are on strike, he's not going to hurt us."

Bernie shook his head sadly. "That's what Hali's counting on, I'm sure, but dragons are all individually contracted, like witches. This one might honor the strike, or he might not. The way things are now, you can't count on anything."

"Sowing disaffection in the ranks?" Hali asked, having just come up behind Bernie.

Bernie jumped, and turned to face her, his fur on end. "Don't do that," he said irritably. "I'm jumpy enough about this dragon. I don't need you on my tail."

"You don't have a tail," Leo said.

"Yes I do," Bernie snapped. "It's tiny, but it's there, and no, you're not going to feel around to find out." He snarled, baring his long teeth.

"Calm down," Hali instructed.

"Calm? Who can be calm just outside a dragon's den?" Bernie yelled.

"Good question," a new voice interrupted. Deep and throaty, it oozed warm confidence. "I was just wondering that myself."

Bernie shrieked wordlessly, and started running for the downhill trail. Her staff suddenly a shepherd's crook, Hali caught him around the neck and hauled him back.

"Stop that," she said sternly.

Eyes bulging, Bernie gibbered briefly, his claws scrabbling uselessly against the rocky ground. Echoing his sentiments, Whitenose brayed, a tormented metallic sound that echoed off the hills even as the terrified donkey bounded down the hill, back the way they'd come. Too late to catch him, Tracy stood at the edge of the trail, debating the wisdom of giving chase to an animal doing an excellent, if unexpected, imitation of a mountain goat.

"What do you know, my charm works," Oliver observed, showing Ginny the glowing dragon detector he'd bought in Fairehaven Town.

"It's the dragon!" Leo whooped, waving his arms and jumping up and down. "Look, there, behind you!"

"Glad to see me, are you?" asked the dragon, a rumbling chuckle in his voice.

"Show some manners, boy," Hali snapped at Leo. "Calm down, all of you, and be polite."

Leo grumbled, but backed up behind Hali and gestured for her to precede him. Nodding skeptically, Hali took the lead, and bowed to the dragon, who perched on a large, rocky ridge beside the trail, where he was dramatically silhouetted against the sky. At first his hide appeared black as midnight, but when he nodded regally to Hali, the sun glinted off his scales, revealing subtle hints of bronze and purple.

"Polite?" Leo grumbled sotto voce behind Hali's back. "It's a dragon. We should kill it and get its hoard."

Tracy hushed him urgently, and whispered. "Dragons have wisdom, you dork. We need information. Don't screw things up now."

"Quite," said the dragon amiably, craning his neck to peer over Hali at the gamers clustered behind her back. His huge, bony head loomed ominously over them, his golden eyes glowing. "Oh, and a tip to the wise might be in order—dragons have quite extraordinary hearing."

"I told you to be polite," Hali snapped over her shoulder at Leo. "You want to fight dragons, you wait until we're done here, and the rest of us have gone."

"Oh, I wouldn't bother," the dragon boomed cheerfully. "I have no intention of fighting today. There's a strike on, you know."

"That's what I wanted to talk about," Hali started to explain, but Leo pushed her aside. Finding himself free, Bernie headed for the protection of some large boulders. Exchanging a quick glance, Tracy, Oliver, and Ginny followed hot on his furry heels.

Peering out from between two large rocks, Bernie held his breath. Hali stood as if turned to stone, her expression frozen somewhere between fury and incredulity as she stared at Leo. The overweight gamer stood with legs spread and chin thrust out, shaking one fist and glaring up at the dragon.

"Jamison was right!" he declared. "This monster is just like the others. He couldn't eat us if he wanted to—this stupid game is programmed to keep us from getting hurt at all costs."

Having just caught up with the rest of the company,

Jamison peered over his dung ball at the odd confrontation in progress. Apparently surprised, but gratified by Leo's support of his ideas, he clacked his forearms together in stiff applause. The old dragon craned his neck for a look at the odd creature and snorted a puff of high-pressure steam that threatened to send the dung ball rolling downhill, forcing Jamison to turn all his attention to protecting his treasure. Nodding in satisfaction, Humbert turned his attention back to Leo, bringing his head down to meet him eye-to-eye.

"If that statement was meant as a challenge, I would normally be more than happy to oblige you, but you see, I've given my word," he rumbled ominously.

The dragon's breath was hot, his craggy head longer than Leo was tall, and from up close his teeth could be seen to be needle sharp and numerous, the longest fangs a glistening three feet in length. Leo took an involuntary step backward, then another, before he turned to look at his friends. It took him a second to locate them behind their rocks.

He snorted in disdain. "Cowards! This dragon's no danger at all—he says so himself."

"Well, if you're not worried about the dragon, you might consider Hali," Bernie called from behind a sturdy chunk of granite. "I think she's about to explode."

Peering over their boulders, the others could only agree. Leo, suddenly realizing what he had done, turned slowly to face the witch. One look at her face, and he, too, took shelter behind some rocks, just as a sparkling beam of light splashed across them. The rocks disappeared, leaving a pile of small green frogs in their place, Leo cowering on the ground behind them. He stared for a moment at the bewildered amphibians, then bolted, disappearing behind a thick outcropping of stone. A second beam of light spattered against the rock. It lost a bit of surface (converted into a cluster of small grey lizards that quickly scurried out of the way) but otherwise resisted Hali's attack.

"Hmmph." Hali glared at the stone, but refrained from striking again, turning to the grinning dragon looming above her.

"Ah, Hali, you're such a delight," he boomed, stretching his dark, membranous wings wide, and flapping them twice in enthusiasm, raising a breeze that briefly sent dust devils racing down the trail. "I haven't been so entertained since those dwarves tunneled into my caverns by mistake. Tasty little fellows they were, too. Ah, well, I'll have to forgo that pleasure this time, though that plump one looks quite tasty."

"Too old," said Hali, calmly. "They get tough once the testosterone gets flowing, you know."

"With my teeth, I hardly have to worry," the dragon told her. "I find, though, that a good marbling of fat really does add to the flavor."

"Well, I couldn't let you have him, anyway," Hali said with a regretful sigh. "Bentwood made me promise to bring them back alive—the kid's right about that much."

"Mmmm," the dragon mused. He cocked his head inquisitively at Hali. "You really think you could stop me in a fair fight?"

Hali snorted. "You're not going to start that again, old lizard. We could argue the point forever, but I don't want to put it to the test any more than you do."

Humbert chuckled nastily. "If it suits you to believe that, it's fine by me."

"Don't tempt me," Hali snapped back. She started to say something, stopped, and shook her head. "I don't have time for pleasantries. We've got to talk."

Humbert seemed disappointed. "Ah. Hmmm. Well, if we're going to be civilized, then let's go to my cave," he offered. "Humans too, if you think they can behave themselves. I assume they're housebroken?"

Hali nodded curtly, and Humbert turned and hopped off the ridge on which he sat, gliding behind it and out of sight.

"Well, come on," Hali told the gamers. "We don't have all day." Without a look behind her, she clambered up and over the ridge.

"Hey, wait up!" hollered Leo, popping up from behind a rock. "Guys, did you hear that? A dragon's cave! Just think of the treasure we can steal."

"Oh, right," Bernie moaned. "Give him an excuse to eat us, why don't you. He won't even have to go to any work to catch us. Trapped like rats, we'll be." With a heavy sigh and dragging feet, he started after Hali.

"So, why are you going?" Tracy asked, scrambling up the rock ridge, and giving the awkward wombat a boost. "There's no way Jamison can get up here with that ball of his—you could stay with him."

Perched precariously on a small ledge, Bernie eyed her mournfully. "Given the choice between a dragon's word and a witch's wrath, I'll take the dragon anytime—but it's not much of a choice."

From the top of the ridge, rough steps carved in the stone led down the other side. The gamers sidled down them carefully, finding themselves at the top of a long, sheer cliff. The primitive stairway led to a ledge that ran along the face of the cliff, finally ending at a broad ledge wide enough to make a decent landing pad for one large dragon. A large cave opened onto the ledge. A stream ran out of the opening, pooling briefly at the edge of the cliff before diving to the rocks far, far below.

Leo got down on hands and knees and crawled to the edge of the ledge, watching the water as it fell in white ribbons down the cliff. "Wow, look at that. I bet if you fell from here you'd really go splat when you hit the ground. Funny, though, the cliff looks like it's got icicles all over it where the waterfall runs."

Over by the pool, Tracy frowned. "It's this water, it's weird. The edges are all crusted over. The rim's all white and slick like ice." She touched it gingerly, and snatched her hand back quickly. "Hey, it's hot!"

Concerned, Oliver joined her. He took a close look at the water and laughed in relief. "It's a hot spring. They've got ones just like it all over Yellowstone Park."

"What's it doing way up here?" Tracy asked.

Oliver shrugged. "Must have something to do with this cave being here."

"Mr. Know-It-All comes up dry, huh?" Leo taunted him. "Come on, I always wanted to explore a cave."

"Wait!" Bernie shouted desperately. "You can't just barge in there."

"We've been invited," Leo reminded him impatiently.

"Well, let's take it slow. And polite."

"Politeness is as politeness does," Hali snapped, appearing

in the cave entrance. "You're late for tea, and Humbert gets crabby when his guests aren't prompt. Move it!" Wielding her staff like a broom, she swept the gamers into the cave.

Inside, a long wide tunnel followed the stream into the dark heart of the mountain. Once the gamers' eyes adjusted to the interior gloom, they could see that the path was actually dimly lit by glowing globes placed at every turn, turning the tunnel into a shimmering, glistening tube of crystalline white stone, its walls etched here and there with abstract patterns and touched with subtle colors only barely visible in the dim light. Echoing loudly, the tinkling, gurgling sound of rushing water filled the cave, and the air was warm and moist, with a faint mineral tang. The walls of the cave dripped with sweat, but the warmth made the atmosphere comfortable, even cozy, like a bathroom filled with steam after a shower.

Without warning, the tunnel opened onto a great, brightly lit cavern, and the gamers, stunned, stood and gaped at the dragon's splendid lair. Crystalline rock lined the walls, and seemed to glow with its own internal light. Around the walls, gleaming stalagmites and stalactites met to form great archways and pillars that ran in rows, like marble columns in a huge, extravagant cathedral. The center of the cavern was clear of all such obstructions, and overhead the naturally vaulted ceiling rose a good three stories from the floor. At the far end of the chamber, small waterfalls cascaded down the wall, flowing over a steplike series of glistening ledges before coming to rest in a large, deep pool that reflected the golden light that filled the cave. Smaller tunnels and rooms led off at strange angles and heights from the main cavern, their entrances for the most part dark and uninviting.

The nook to which Hali directed the group, however, was well lit, and formed a pleasant sitting room for the dragon, just large enough for him to curl himself in one corner, while his guests made themselves comfortable on convenient stone outcroppings. The very solid rock formations in this chamber had a deceptively lacy appearance, and the dragon's fine silver teapot and elegant china looked quite at home.

"I see where Hali got her inspiration for the make-over of the ogres' den," Ginny whispered to Tracy. The girls giggled, earning them a frown from Hali and an indulgent smile from the dragon, who passed them a tray of small cakes.

"I hope you don't mind fruitcake," he said apologetically. "I'm told this brand is quite tasty, and it keeps well, you know. I so seldom get human visitors, but I do try to keep something on hand just in case."

Politely, Tracy said, "This is fine, thank you." A gold coin and a tiny pink rosebud fell from her mouth.

Humbert quirked one scaly brow. "Very elegant. I always appreciate good manners."

Hali poured tea very precisely, handing cups to the gamers with a cautionary glare. For the dragon, she filled a matching soup bowl that he cupped delicately in his claws as he sipped at the tea.

"Ahhh. Hmmm. A lovely blend," he sighed, nodding at Hali.

"Glad you like it, it's King Benton's favorite," Hali said. "Look, I hate to be rude, but the day's almost gone, and we need some information."

Looking as hurt as a dragon can, Humbert sighed. "Ah, foolish me. Here I thought you would have a little time to visit with an old friend."

Hali glared at him.

"I wouldn't hear of your leaving this late. I insist you all spend the night here," Humbert said with a toothy grin. "We'll have plenty of time to talk."

Off in his corner, Bernie moaned. "I know it. Talked to death and then eaten. What a way to die."

"Bernie, knock it off," Hali snapped. "Look Humbert, I appreciate the invitation, but I need to know what's up."

The dragon shrugged, spreading his neatly manicured (and well-honed) claws expressively. "It seems to me we're on opposite sides. Now, hmm, I wouldn't object to sharing a bit of gossip with an old friend, but if you insist on sticking to business, well, there's not much I can do for you."

"There's always a price with you, isn't there?"

"Mmmmm. A point of pride with us dragons."

"Sounds like a good deal to me," Leo said, stretched out comfortably on the floor. "These are the best accommodations we've seen since the palace."

Humbert grinned at him toothily and turned to Hali. "So, do we have a bargain? You stay here in luxury, I'll feed you all well, and we chat over dessert this evening."

Hali eyed him skeptically. "You're not going to try any of your new recipes on us, are you?"

"How often do I have a chance to test them on real humans? I'm generally considered a fine cook, but my repertory is of necessity limited. It's very hard to be a gourmet when one's natural diet consists strictly of raw meat taken in large quantities two or three times a month. It's a pleasure to be able to try something a bit more delicate than a whole cow or sheep, and with a knowledgeable audience."

Hali snorted. "Last time I took you up on the offer of dinner, you confused ginger for potatoes. It was scalloped very nicely, but a whole casserole full was a bit much."

Humming absently, the dragon scratched his nose with one long, polished claw. "One exotic root looks like another to me, I'm afraid," he apologized. "I thought it was quite tasty, actually."

"You like heartburn. You live for it, as far as I can make out. If we're going to chance your cooking, you'd better have some really good gossip in return."

"You have my word on it," Humbert promised, blinking solemnly twice, then touching his forked tongue to the end of his nose. "Dragon's honor."

"Sounds good to me. How bad can his cooking be, anyway?" Leo asked.

"Bad enough to make you wish it was you being eaten, I'm sure," Bernie grumbled.

"Stop it, you two," Hali said. "All right, Humbert, we'll risk your hospitality, but you'd better make it worth our time."

"You won't regret it," Humbert vowed, and excused himself to go gather the ingredients he'd need for dinner.

Left to their own devices, and recovered from their hike up the mountain, the gamers decided to explore. Hali showed them how to find and remove glowing chunks of stone from the walls, and armed with these lumpish lights, the gamers disappeared into the caves that adjoined the dragon's lair. Despite their best efforts, they were unable to get lost; even the longest tunnels eventually wound back to the main cavern, though the gamers were willing to swear they had gone straight in the opposite direction, or gone downhill for miles without ever climbing back up. They encountered strange rock formations, bats, an underground river that ran icy cold, glowing fungi, and a pile of old, well-chewed bones—but no treasure nor even a storeroom full of old furniture to pilfer.

Humbert returned, hauling a dragon-sized string bag in his claws. It was filled with gourmet goodies, and even some fresh fruit and vegetables. "Those silly villagers persist in trying to give me virgins," he grumbled. "I've told them over and over that it's only olive oil I want in that condition, but they always put up such a fuss. Here, take this, will you?" Letting Oliver and Leo carry the bag between them, Humbert led the way to a side chamber the gamers had yet to explore. With their entrance, the walls began to glow, revealing a shining kitchen full of white cabinets and steel countertops.

Humbert directed the boys to put the food on a center table. Cautiously, Hali poked through the groceries. She held a glass jar up to the light, and squinted at its contents, which appeared to include a purple tentacle or two. "Considering the quality and scarcity of some of this stuff, it's probably cheaper for them to scrape up a few unwanted females than to keep you in munchies," she observed.

"Oh, I don't eat this stuff," the dragon explained. "Usually, I just raid their herds for the occasional sheep or steer, and the locals don't complain too much. They will raise a fuss if I chase the milk cows, but otherwise we get along quite well, actually. No one's bothered to send a prince or a hero in, hmmm, a century or so now. No, this food's all for you people."

"We have to eat this?" Tracy asked, eyeing a bleeding calf's head dubiously.

"In some circles, calves' heads are considered quite a delicacy," Humbert assured her, dropping the head into a pot.

"I'll keep an eye on him and make sure it's at least safe to eat," Hali assured the skeptical gamers. "Go explore some more, or something."

"There's nothing to see," Leo complained. "All the tunnels lead back here."

"Or up to those balconies and choir lofts," Tracy added.

Hali glared at them. "I suppose you wanted to get lost, instead?"

"Well, it would certainly be more interesting," Leo said mutinously.

"And now you want to be entertained." Hali drew herself up, and pointed to the kitchen entrance. "Out! Right now, and stay out of our hair until you're called to dinner."

"All right, all right, we're gone," Oliver said, pushing Leo and Tracy ahead of him back into the main cavern.

Realizing that they'd missed the kitchens completely, the group checked out other nearby nooks and crannies, but found nothing more than before. Their enthusiasm for exploration completely exhausted, the gamers were too tired to do more than collapse and speculate on dinner. They had walked almost continuously that day, and welcomed Tracy's discovery that the large pool in the cavern, though scalding in the center, was cool enough at the edges for them to soak their feet. Despite Bernie's worried warnings, the young people soon shed most of their clothing and soaked the rest of themselves as well. Ginny kept her knee-length undertunic on, but the others shed everything down to their underpants.

"It may not be modest," Tracy told Bernie, who was pacing the edge of the pool, clearly distressed to see her topless, but not quite sure how to put it, "but it's not like I have much to hide anyway." She gestured at her almost-flat chest.

"It's the principle of the thing," Bernie grumbled. "Good girls don't go around without shirts on."

"You've been here too long," Leo told him. "My mom tells stories of swimming nude at church camp back in the sixties."

"That doesn't prove anything; the preacher's kids were always the worst, even back in my day," Bernie replied.

"Come on. Nudity is natural. People ought to be able to go around without clothes and be comfortable together—it's only society's artificial rules that make clothing such a big deal."

"I bet you try that line on every girl you meet, too," Bernie snorted.

Leo smirked, and Tracy splashed water at him, but the

warmth of the hot spring kept everyone too relaxed for conflict to continue long. In comfortable silence, they enjoyed the unexpected luxury of the dragon's indoor mineral spa.

Eventually, Hali appeared poolside, eyeing the largely undressed and increasingly embarrassed gamers in grim silence.

"I suppose this means dinner's ready?" Leo finally asked, deliberately nonchalant.

Her eyes like slits, Hali nodded. "I suggest you dress for dinner, however. Humbert prefers a somewhat formal style of dining—unless of course this was meant to be an orgy, in which case I'm afraid he would be seriously unimpressed."

Despite their limp muscles, the gamers managed to scramble out of the pool and into their clothes, doing their best to make themselves presentable. Ginny even helped Tracy put up her hair, for a formal look.

"I wish all our other clothes and things weren't down at the bottom of the hill," Tracy sighed. "Gee, I hope Whitenose is OK."

"I wouldn't worry," Oliver told her. "Jamison's bound to follow him for the manure. It's too bad we had to leave him behind, but at least as a bug he's pretty tough."

Dinner proved quite tolerable, if exotic. The gamers picked their way carefully through the various dishes, finding enough identifiable items to more than satisfy them. For dessert, Humbert produced gingerbread, warm and fresh from the ovens and so spicy that Ginny gasped when she first bit into it.

"Breathe through your nose, not your mouth," Tracy advised, washing her own first bite down with a swig of tea. "The air makes the heat worse. This isn't bad, actually," she told the dragon cheerfully. "My mom likes hot food. She'd love this."

Hali wolfed her portion down, drank her tea to the dregs, and sat back. "All right, Humbert, we've played your game, and lived. Now give."

The old dragon shrugged. "What's to tell? There's a strike on."

Hali leaned forward, her eyes glittering nastily. "That's it?"

Bernie crept cautiously behind one of the more solid stone seats.

"Hmmm, hmmm, well, there are a few more details I could give you."

"You promised good gossip, dragon."

"Yeah," said Leo. "Hali's counting on you to explain away this problem with noncombatant monsters, like a good plot device."

"I beg your pardon?" the dragon said politely, moving his head to stare the gamer in the eye. "I don't believe I was addressing you."

"Oh, right, never mind us," Leo said, with a weak little wave. "We're just flies on the wall, that's all."

"Mmmm. See that you don't buzz loudly," the dragon said.

"Now, Hali, what can I tell you?" Humbert scratched his chin delicately with one claw. "As I understand it, our friend Bentwood decided to usurp power, claiming an energy crisis as sufficient cause to set armed groups of Outworlders, with magical assistance, on missions to attack innocent monsters throughout the land. On top of that, he's got every available construction worker, dwarf, and wizard out building a phony city—an obvious fake for tourists, hardly livable—on that plateau out by administration headquarters. I haven't seen any sign of this energy crisis, but I do know that project of his is killing business everywhere else. There's so much money tied up in this scheme, there's nothing left for ordinary folks who need loans, no construction going on, and no jobs except at Grimmworld. The local cattlefarmers are driving their herds up there because the money's better—no one else can even afford beef these days."

Hali pounced on that last point. "Now we get to the root of the problem. You're just upset because you have to fly a little further to steal dinner."

"Phooey," Humbert said. "That's just one of the symptoms I've observed. Our company here is another, though frankly," he eyed the gamers carefully, "I can't see them as much of a threat to even one halfway-competent ogre."

"Why, you . . . " Leo gasped out, before Oliver got his hand over Leo's mouth.

Humbert chose to ignore the interruption. "For that matter, Hali, I would think you in particular would object to the extra work. He's got you guiding a whole group of maladroits about the countryside, not to mention this ridiculous requirement of keeping them alive. What did Bentwood offer you, anyway?"

"That's not important," Hali said firmly. "I agreed and signed in blood, so I have to go through with this. Besides, how do you know there's not an energy crisis? I've talked to Endymion, King Benton's wizard, and he thinks it's all too likely. I know things have certainly gotten slow in my line of work. I'll thank you not to mention this to Bentwood, but with business so slack I've taken some unscheduled time off and gone Out a few times recently. Things have changed there—life's too easy for a lot of people, though to listen to them you wouldn't think so. Whole countries have forgotten what real famine and plagues are like. Folks don't have the same sort of uncertainty about the world they used to, either. They believe in science, not magic, and live in big cities away from nature. Instead of worrying about witches and ogres, they worry about their neighbors these days."

"We've got a plague, it's called AIDS," Tracy interjected.

Hali shook her head. "I do keep an eye on the latest diseases," she said. "This AIDS is tricky, but it has nothing on the old diseases, like smallpox and bubonic plague, that wiped out whole towns at once. Your modern medicine got them all pretty well licked. Now this new one spreads so slowly, it's not much better than leprosy. Now there's a classic incurable disease for you. It's still around in the backwaters, but you'd hardly know it in the civilized areas.

"More to the point, people in the Outworld believe that science can find a cure for anything these days, even this AIDS. They don't believe in magic; although quite a few go in for miracles and faith healing, that's not really our sort of operation. I've run into witches Outworld, but not many, and they run more toward religion than magic, too. Oh, some burn a few candles and herbs and think nasty thoughts about their straying boyfriends, but that's about it."

Gesturing earnestly, she leaned toward Humbert, poking him in the chest. "If the wizards are right, and we're a reflection of

Outworlders' dreams and desires, then the culture that gave us birth is almost gone. Who's to say we won't follow?"

"Oh, piffle," the dragon responded. "Really, we've survived centuries of social change. I don't see any evidence that things have changed—nor have any of my fellow dragons. I certainly haven't noticed any diminution of energy around here. My lights burn as brightly as ever."

"Are you sure you'd notice a very gradual change—before the lights went out completely?" Hali asked. "I'm not sure I want to take the chance, if there's something I can do about it."

"I would be more likely to agree if the first word of this so-called crisis hadn't come from a troll, one who stands to benefit if we take his word for it. Maybe there's been a slight shift in energy levels, but who's to say it's a trend? It might be a natural variation that no one's ever noticed before. There's no point in letting Bentwood stampede us all over something unproven, anyway. Give a troll an inch, and he'll take a league, you know that. Dreadfully anal little buggers."

"Anal?" Hali asked, one eyebrow raised.

"Umm, yes, well, I've been reading Outworlder psychology texts of late. Fascinating, the ways they've found to classify personalities. I must admit, they do have a tendency to analyze all the mystery and romance out of life. Still, that's beside the point. Anal personalities want to control and organize everything, and never let go of anything they can get their hands on. Describes trolls to a T, don't you think? Anyway, what with all the trolls in high positions these days, someone has to protect defenseless monsters from a decidedly unethical administration."

"Has it escaped your notice that both the major unions have trollish advisors running them?"

"You expect goblins, ogres, and the usual brain-dead giants to negotiate contracts on their own? Better to let the trolls take on each other—at least both sides have a chance that way. Besides, if the money-grubbing little buggers won't stay under the bridges where they belong, this at least should keep them out of trouble."

"So we end up with trolls running everything. I think the ogres and goblins could do just fine, particularly with the giants on their side. They'd settle for plenty of meat, nice caves, and decent odds in every battle. If they don't like the way things are run they can go work somewhere else, or put up a fight. I think your average ogre would be perfectly happy to do without union dues and these ridiculous contracts no one but the lawyers can interpret—though most of the lawyers these days are trolls, anyway."

"However you feel about it, the organized monsters have gotten quite upset over the issue. They feel the administration has taken advantage of them, and they're simply refusing to cooperate any further. They can't stop construction on the plateau, but they're certainly not going to let your little friends here count coup on them just for fun."

"So, who do I talk to? Who's really in charge of all this?"

"Hmm." The dragon scratched his head in sincere puzzlement. "Hard as I find it to believe, two generally reliable sources tell me that a witch is at the back of all this, a real rabble-rouser with a serious grudge, but no one seems to know who, or why. Any thoughts?"

Hali sat back, thinking out loud as she stared at the ceiling. "Most of my colleagues are lousy at social situations, particularly crowd control, which is why once a community gets up in arms witches usually get burnt. If there's a witch behind this, she's got to be really mad, and unusually persuasive. Maleficent's out of commission, Uglina's settled down lately, old Nettles couldn't rouse a rabble if her life depended on it—I can't think of anyone else with a major grudge against the administration, though there's a few private feuds. There's plenty of second-raters who're bitter about not making the grade, but if they can't concentrate enough to pull off the big magic, how the heck would they manage something like this?"

"This is silly," Leo said, and yawned. "We're not getting any closer to a good battle, you're just coming up with more reasons why we can't. How 'bout we go ogre hunting, and make them fight?"

"You're bored? You want to go ogre hunting?" Hali asked solicitously. "Fine. That sounds like an excellent idea. Tomorrow, we go ogre hunting."

CHAPTER
18

HUMBERT insisted on cooking a large breakfast, delaying Hali's hoped-for early start until nearly noon, but at least the gamers got a lavish feed to support them on their ogre hunt. Though the food was unusual, it all proved quite tasty, particularly the chocolate cream–filled omelettes.

"I brought ingredients for a souffle, but I couldn't find the proper pan for it," Humbert explained. "Dragons don't eat that often, and I'm afraid I don't get much chance to cook, so I haven't stocked as many kitchen utensils as I'd like."

"No problem," Leo assured him around his second serving.

"Crepes would have been more traditional," Hali said.

"No crepe pan," the dragon told her. "You know how hard it is to get good imported cookware. If I can get the specs, I'm thinking of having one made."

"It wouldn't kill you to use an ordinary fry pan."

"There's no point in cooking unless it can be done right," Humbert informed her loftily.

Hali held up a forkful of omelette, watching the chocolate filling drip down in heavy, dark glops. She raised one eyebrow scornfully. "This is 'right'?"

Sniffing, Humbert made an elaborate show of preparing a fresh pot of breakfast tea.

When it came time to leave, Humbert escorted the group to his cave entrance. Hali could not escape without a parting gift of several dozen coffee-bean cookies, but retaliated with a large packet of King Benton's Special Blend Tea, unearthed from the depths of her belt pouch. The old dragon actually wiped away a tear as the gamers made their goodbyes. Finally, the gamers made their escape back down the hill, stopping every few yards on Hali's command to wave farewell to the dragon, who watched from his perch on the ridge, silhouetted sharply against the grey morning sky. Finally, a turn in the path hid him from sight.

"Thank god," Bernie said with a sudden access of devotion.

To their relief, the party found Whitenose and Jamison both waiting patiently beside the cart, neither the worse for their night alone together. Soon the cart was rolling, and Hali led the way down the track.

Back on the main road, however, Hali turned the lead over to Bernie.

"What? Why me?" he asked. "I'm the slowest one in the group. I don't even know where we're going."

Hali smiled. "We want to find the leaders behind this strike—I figure the best way is to let your anxieties lead the way. You're the one who's been sure we're in for union troubles all along. Just keep worrying, and we'll find them for sure."

Bernie moaned. "We're doomed."

"Good, good," Hali encouraged him. "You're doing fine. Just think 'unions.' "

"Think strikes," Tracy added.

"Picket lines," Oliver offered.

"Thugs and scabs," Leo chimed in.

"Aaaagh!" Bernie wailed, curling into a ball in the middle of the road.

"Scabs?" Hali asked.

"You don't want to know," Bernie growled, the words barely making it past his tight-packed belly fur. "I'm not going any further."

"Scabs are nothing to the wounds you'll get from me if you don't get moving." Hali thumped him solidly with her staff. When that had no effect, she tried again, only this time there was an electric crackle when the staff connected, followed by the smell of singed fur.

"Yeow!" Bernie yelled, unrolling enough to rub his bottom and glare at Hali. "You don't have to get vicious, I'm going. Yeesh." Grumbling under his breath, he picked himself up and trundled down the road without a single look back, his head hanging like that of a condemned man on his way to the gallows.

Trying not to laugh, the gamers followed, waved ahead by Hali. The witch strolled along in the rear, occasionally wielding her staff to give Jamison a hand over the rough spots with his ever-growing ball of dung and roses.

Bernie shuffled slowly but steadily down the center of the road. The road ran up and down along the hills, gradually working its way downward. The barren slopes of the higher altitudes were replaced first by sparse strands of evergreens, then by lush meadows and occasional clumps of graceful, leafy green trees. The sun burned through the early overcast, leaving a bright blue sky filled with fluffy white clouds blown about by a light breeze. Any confrontation with the unions seemed far off, and no real threat. The gamers carried their bows unstrung, used their staves as jaunty walking sticks, and generally enjoyed their stroll through the foothills.

The party stopped for a midday meal beside a mirror-bright little lake cradled between two steep brush-covered hills. Between the extravagant lunches packed by Humbert and the charming setting, the meal took on the air of a picnic. Even Bernie relaxed enough to enjoy the fresh roots provided for his delectation, though he muttered darkly that the dragon was just trying to fatten him up.

When they started up again Bernie took the lead without prompting. The road soon left the mountains behind, winding into a lightly wooded valley, full of sunny meadows and shady green dells.

Tracy jogged up to Bernie, Leo tagging along behind. "This is really beautiful," she said, one gold coin and a magnificent white rose dropping from her mouth. "It's like a big park, with flowers all over. So what happened? I thought we were going to run into your worst nightmare."

"Not if I can help it." Bernie gave her as dignified a glare as he could manage from his low vantage point. "I'm thinking 'peaceful negotiations,' 'contract settlements,' 'nonviolent protest'—none of that head-bashing, cement overshoes type of thing. Makes me shudder just thinking about it." A demonstrative shudder rippled his fur.

A cloud shadow swept down the trail, and Tracy shivered slightly in the sudden chill, looking up at the fat grey clouds suddenly filling the sky. "Looks like we're in for a change in the weather," she observed.

"Oh, no," Bernie groaned, and stared about him, wide-eyed. "Nettles!" Fur on end, for a second he glared at the tall clump of nettles growing beside the trail. Then, with a high-pitched squeal, he bolted down the trail, running into deepening shadows beneath dark trees.

"Hey!" Tracy shouted, and started running after him. "What's wrong with nettles?"

Curious, Leo followed Tracy, jogging heavily. He sped up slightly as the girl and wombat both disappeared beyond a bend in the trail, where it skirted a huge, moss-covered outcropping of rock. Just before Leo reached the turn, he heard a loud, yodeling war cry behind him. He turned around just in time to see three club-wielding ogres burst from behind the clump of nettles and descend upon the donkey cart.

Dumbfounded, Leo stood in the center of the trail and watched with mouth agape as the ogres grabbed Ginny and Oliver and disarmed them before they could raise their staves to defend themselves. From behind, Hali shouted and ran forward, leveling her staff at the intruders. A brilliant beam blazed out of the staff, catching the ogres squarely in their ample midriffs. The light spread out, covering the ogres in a glittering layer that made the monsters twitch as if they were being tickled. Despite a giggle or two, the two holding Oliver and Ginny never loosened their grip on the wriggling gamers.

The third advanced on Hali, grinning as another beam of light splashed harmlessly on his chest. Carefully battling her staff aside with his club, he grabbed Hali's wrist roughly, forcing her to drop the staff.

"I'm reporting this!" Hali snarled as the ogre hauled her off her feet by one arm. "You can't do this!"

"Hey, if you can cheat, so can we." The ogre chuckled. "You started it, by ganging up on us. Anything goes now."

"You've got spell protection!" Hali accused, still hanging in midair. Her own transformation spell had disappeared, leaving her looking pathetically thin and ordinary, though her fine hair stood out wildly. With a snarl, she kicked the ogre in the side with the pointy toes of her black button-top boots.

He grunted and dropped his club. With both hands free, he managed to stick Hali under one arm, both of her arms pinned down firmly. Behind him, her legs kicked helplessly. "Stop that," he growled. "We're going to see the boss."

"Well, it's about time!" Hali snapped. "I've been wanting to talk to someone who knew what was going on. Put me down and I'll go willingly."

The ogre shook his head. "You're not putting anything over on me," he said. "We were warned about you. Without your staff, and with this spell on me, you're helpless as long as I keep a hold on you."

"Oooh!" Hali snarled and kicked in frustration.

"So, is this it?" asked the ogre holding Ginny. He looked her over skeptically. "I was expecting more than a couple of scrawny kids. Seems like a lot of fuss over nothing."

The ogre holding Hali looked around. Just in time, Tracy pulled Leo behind the rock where she'd been hiding. Seeing nothing of interest, the ogre turned to Jamison and eyed the tall beetle and his five-foot dung ball dubiously. "I guess this is it," the ogre said. "There were four in the party, but word was the witch transformed one—that's the bug. She must have done the donkey, too. We don't need to worry about the livestock. Let's go."

Tracy, Leo, and Bernie scooted quickly around the rock until they were out of sight of the trail and held their breath. Singing a rough marching chant, enumerating all the various ways to cook a full-grown human, the ogres passed them by without a pause.

Leo, Tracy, and Bernie emerged cautiously from behind the rock. Tracy went to Whitenose and rubbed his velvet-soft muzzle in reassurance. Leo checked out the contents of the cart, while Bernie morosely nosed at Hali's staff lying forgotten in the dust of the road. Jamison rolled his ball carefully up to the cart and left it there, coming over to poke with mild interest at the staff, losing interest as he decided it was too big to add to his ball.

"I don't think they took anything," Leo said. "Now what do we do?"

"This is all your fault," Bernie told Tracy.

"My fault? What do you mean, my fault?"

"You distracted me. Broke my concentration. I had us following the primrose path, and you made me think of the stuff I didn't want to."

"We were supposed to be looking for the strike bosses, anyway," Leo pointed out.

"I was hoping for a nice, reasonable negotiator type. Not a bunch of angry rank and filers."

"Why would anyone in a monsters' union be particularly reasonable?" Leo asked. "You were probably looking for a nonexistent person. That's probably why we went nowhere so long."

"Give me a break," Bernie muttered.

Leo refused to touch Hali's staff, but with reassurance from Bernie, Tracy picked it up, dusted it off, and set it in the bottom of the cart, carefully wrapped in Oliver's cloak. If a couple of tiny tears escaped to run down her cheeks, Bernie and Leo managed to ignore them, and to manfully refrain from joining her in a good cry. For several minutes, they stood around the cart, none willing to make a decision.

Finally, Tracy stated the obvious: "We've got to follow them." A couple of small, wilted, and rather greenish rosebuds fell from her mouth.

"Oh, right," Leo scoffed. "The flower girl, the fat boy, and Bernie the Wonder Wombat are going to rush right in and rescue their captive companions from the ogres' den."

"Don't forget Jamison," Tracy said. "He's good in a fight."

The giant scarab bobbed his head and clicked in apparent

agreement, before scooping up the roses and gold that had fallen from Tracy's mouth.

"Right. We don't even know for sure how much he understands," Leo said. "How much can you expect from a guy who lives to collect manure?"

"Well, you've got to admit he's good at it," Bernie observed, considering the dung ball seriously. "There's more stuff in that ball than ever came out of our one little donkey." He shook his head. "But that's all irrelevant. We've got to get to Hali. She's our only hope. Without her, I don't think we're going to be able to get out of this forest alive. Only perfect fools, total innocents, the brave, and the pure of heart survive here, and we're none of those things—though we come close in the fool category. We don't have a choice. We've got to follow. Come on."

With grim determination, Bernie lumbered down the trail. Resigned, Tracy and Leo coaxed Whitenose into following at a reluctant trot. Clicking anxiously, Jamison brought up the rear, following more closely than usual and pushing his ball so fast it threatened to break away from him more than once.

Even at Bernie's top speed, they saw no sign of the ogres. The road wound through the forest, weaving in and out around a series of rock outcroppings that grew thicker and taller the further they went. Eventually, the trail ran over the top of a huge rock shelf. Whitenose's hooves skidded on the mossy rock, and the huge cart wheels found little purchase on the stone. Tracy and Leo kept busy trying to hold the cart steady as Whitenose pulled—and trying to keep out of the path of Jamison's ball.

"That thing's dangerous," Leo gasped at one near miss. The ball of dung rolled past him and smacked into a scrawny pine, shaking the entire tree and threatening to uproot it.

Bernie spared a glance back, and grimaced. "Don't let it hit you," he warned. "With all that gold in there, that thing must weigh a ton."

"Just what we need, more dangers to worry about."

The rocky trail climbed gradually, but steadily. The trees found little purchase on the rocks, and thinned out quickly. Soon, bright sky ahead promised the end of the forest. Hoping for a view of the trail ahead, Bernie put out an extra burst of speed, but almost instantly skidded to a scrabbling stop in the sunlight.

"Whoa!" he shouted urgently, peering down at something. "Go slow, guys."

"What is it?" Tracy asked softly, hurrying forward carefully, bow in hand. "Ogres?"

"No, a cliff," said Bernie, still looking down. He gestured with one paw. "What a view!"

The trail turned sharply where Bernie had stopped. In front of him, the gamers could see nothing but empty air. They moved closer, and looked straight down at the rocks below them, tons of fallen boulders and gravel come to rest in steep mounds at the foot of the cliff.

"Geeze, we almost ended up down there," Leo said on hands and knees as he peered over the edge.

"I don't even want to think about it," Tracy said. A gold coin fell from her lips, bounced once on the brink of the cliff, and fell in a bright, shining arc over the edge. It hit an outcropping, bounced high, and kept falling, flashing brilliantly once or twice before Leo and Tracy lost sight of it.

"Wow. It must be miles to the bottom," Leo exclaimed.

"Don't look at the rocks," Bernie said impatiently, pointing again. "Look out there."

Obediently, Leo and Tracy looked further from the cliffs, which curved in a massive semicircle around a barren plain that sloped down steadily for nearly a mile until it met a river. On the near bank of the river stood a huge castle with dozens of rounded towers glistening black in the afternoon sun. A road ran along the river to the castle, where two tall fang-shaped towers framed a gate of two sharp incisors.

"What a great castle!" Leo said. "It looks like a mouthful of teeth. Something's weird about the color, though. I swear, it keeps flickering white, like a bad hologram."

Beside him, Bernie shuddered. "Whatever it is, I don't like it. There are spells in the air, big ones. And I'll bet you a million bucks that's where the ogres have taken Hali."

Hali's reaction on seeing the castle was different. "Look at that thing. Oh, poor Marj. How could Bentwood do that to her?"

"What do you mean?" Ginny asked. Draped over an ogre's shoulder, she had to crane her neck to see the castle.

"I know the witch who lives here, Marjoram as was—she's calling herself Sinestra now. Those teeth could mean only one thing. Somehow, Bentwood's gotten her to take over the job of tooth fairy. She's done a brave job of adapting, but you can see the color's not stable—those teeth would revert to white in an instant if she didn't have a self-renewing spell on them. See the flicker? I don't know how Marj can stand it."

Ginny and Oliver both squinted at the castle, but neither saw the irritating flicker. "Is that where we're heading?" Oliver asked.

Hali shrugged.

Oliver managed to jab an elbow into the ear of the ogre carrying him. "Hey—big, fat, and sweaty! Are we going to the castle?"

The ogre grinned, displaying sharply pointed teeth in crooked rows. "You bet. Eager to arrive, are you, dinner-boy?"

"Dinner-boy?"

"You prefer to be called 'lunchmeat,' maybe?" ·

"My name's Oliver."

"Don't like it. Sounds too much like olive loaf, and I don't like olive loaf," the ogre hauling Hali under his arm noted. "Lunchmeat has a real ring to it."

"Well forgive me, but I don't like the sound of it at all," Oliver snapped. "You can't eat me."

"Why not?" asked his carrier reasonably. "Eating people's what we do."

"Bentwood won't like it," Hali muttered morosely, "but I have a feeling that's a point in its favor."

"You bet," said the ogre holding her. "You're so scrawny, I wouldn't even bother eating you otherwise."

"Well, don't put yourself out for my sake," Hali snarled. "Let me go now, and I'll go murder Bentwood for you. He told me he'd cleared things with the unions!"

The ogres found this joke particularly funny and laughed loudly, a painful sound that reminded Oliver of air bubbles caught in water pipes. The laughter led to joking, and then to what passed with them as singing. To the tune of a raucous marching song (the words to which involved counting the number of ways, some of them quite inventive, in which bones could be broken) they marched briskly along the cliffs, down a rocky stair at the far end, and on to the black castle, where the tall gates swung open to greet them, and swung shut with an ominously final clang behind them.

Unaware of the stone stairway's existence, the uncaptured gamers traveled slowly, picking their way along the cliff edge. With the castle clearly in sight, Leo grew impatient. "We're not getting any closer this way. Maybe we can use the cart to slide down the cliff. It sort of angles out at the bottom, like a giant slide, see?"

Tracy stared at him in horrified disbelief. "You've got to be kidding. It's too steep—we'd be crushed into pulp!"

Bernie sighed. "We'll save the suicide attempts for later, if you don't mind," he told Leo. "And stay further back from the edge. We don't want the ogres to spot us."

Some time later, they came to a jagged crack that split the cliff. The trail, what there was of one, went around, but Bernie stopped and spent some time examining the fissure from different angles.

"What's up?" Tracy asked. "Looks to me like we have to go around."

Bernie looked up at her smugly. "That's what ogres would think, too. They're too big to fit in here, but I think we can make it. We can climb down here."

On hands and knees, Leo peered down into the crack. "You've got to be kidding. I'd rather sled down."

"You'd be right in plain sight of the castle," Bernie pointed out, "if you survived the fall in the first place. This'll be a little work, but it gives us a chance to get down unobserved. If there's an easy way down, it won't be unguarded. Even the ogres aren't that dumb."

"Sure they are," Leo said.

"Oh, come on," Tracy told him. "Maybe they're that dumb, but there's obviously someone behind this, an evil sorcerer or something. How else would they get the spells to defeat Hali?

"Even so," she told Bernie, "I don't think this is going to work. What about Whitenose, and the bug?"

"The bug should manage better than me, if we can get him to leave the ball behind," Bernie said. "We'll have to leave the cart and the donkey for now. He wouldn't be comfortable walking on all that rock, anyway. His hooves've been slipping around as it is."

Tracy insisted on finding Whitenose a spot with some scrubby grass and a spindly tree for shade. "There's no water anywhere up here," she complained, patting the little ass sadly. "What if we can't get back?"

"Tie him loosely and he'll pull his way free if he gets thirsty or hungry enough," Bernie told her. "Right now, we've got to worry about our skins, not to mention Hali's and Oliver's and Ginny's."

The crack they planned to climb down was jagged, with sharp-edged rock faces. It looked as if some giant had taken the cliff and tried to pull it apart, succeeding only in ripping a small tear in it at that point.

"Are you sure this is safe?" Tracy asked Bernie. "It looks like the cliff could close up behind us any minute."

"If we get an earthquake on top of everything else, fate's really out to get us, and we might as well give up anyway," Bernie told her. "I'm more worried about falling, but it's a tight enough fit we should be able to work our way down, no problem. I'm the creature least well adapted for climbing here, and I don't expect much trouble. I sure wouldn't mind having my wings back right now, though."

"Well, at least we've got rope," Leo said. "Oliver left his in the cart."

"I hate to say it, but we'd better bring Hali's staff along, too," Bernie told him. "The ogres couldn't take it, but there's no telling who might come along if we leave it. It's going to be murder to climb with, though; it's too long. Maybe you can tie it with the rope and we can lower it ahead of us. Tie a couple of the water bags with it, too. We're probably going to need them."

"What about us?" Leo asked. "We ought to tie ourselves together."

"Do you know how to do it?" Bernie asked dubiously.

"I've never gone mountain climbing, but it seems to me there's got to be a trick to it. Otherwise, how do you keep one falling body from dragging all the others with it?"

"I'd rather take my chances alone," said Tracy, pointedly looking Leo up and down.

He flushed. "What makes you think I'm the one who's going to fall? You're the one who sounds scared."

"Scared?" Tracy asked indignantly. "I'm just being cautious. We're not prepared for this sort of thing."

"That's what adventures are all about," Leo retorted.

"I notice neither of you is getting any closer to the edge," Bernie sniffed. "I'm lightest, and smallest; I'm probably going to need a boost from time to time, so I'll go last. The bug should go first, if we can get him to go." He eyed Jamison dubiously. "How about it?"

Leo stepped forward, and put a chummy arm behind the bug's back and started steering Jamison toward the crack. Jamison chittered nervously, and tried to turn back to his ball, but Leo insisted firmly. "You first," he told the bug. "We'll come back for the ball."

To everyone's surprise, Jamison clicked a couple of times anxiously, then turned to the rock he was to climb. His long limbs gave him good purchase in what would otherwise have been a precarious position; after a brief scrutiny he disappeared quickly headfirst down the crack.

Leo followed with Hali's staff, dropping it as far as it would go on the rope he had somewhat belligerently tied around his waist, then hesitantly lowering himself feet first into the crevice. "It's not too bad," he declared with relief, just before disappearing from sight. "There's plenty of hand- and footholds."

Steeling herself, Tracy followed. "I've never done anything like this before," she told Bernie. "I'm probably going to kill myself." Nonetheless, she found the climbing easy enough, and descended until her head was well below the top of the cliff.

Bernie had a harder time. First headfirst, then hindfeet first, he made several false starts before settling on the tail-first approach. Holding on to the top of the crevice with his sturdy claws, he scrabbled with his hindfeet for a hold. "Oh blast," he muttered under his breath. Considerably louder, he hollered, "Help!"

"Oh, no," Tracy wailed, spitting out a pair of slightly wilted white roses with particularly thorny stems. She looked up, whitefaced and holding on to the rock next to her with a white-knuckled death grip. "Are you falling? What can I do? I don't think I could catch you, Bernie."

"Calm down," Bernie snapped. "I'm not falling, I just can't reach a foothold. Just climb up a little and put one hand on my rump, and keep me from falling until I can reach that little ledge there."

"I guess I can do that," Tracy told him, starting to edge up to the wombat. Two gold coins spilled from her mouth and fell with sharp pings, ricocheting on their way down the rocky channel.

"Yow!" came the outraged cry from Leo, out of sight below. "That hurt. Keep your mouth shut while we're stuck in here, will you?"

Barely restraining herself from making a pointed, and probably thorny, remark, Tracy shut her mouth and proceeded to climb down, stopping from time to time to give Bernie a hand. Though the rock occasionally jutted out in angles that proved awkward to bypass, and progress was slow, the gamers had little trouble descending the cliff. Leo barked his shin, Tracy scraped her knuckles, and tempers were wearing correspondingly thin by the time they finally made the bottom.

Leo sat on a hip-high boulder, panting heavily, his face beaded with sweat. "I didn't think I'd make it, there at the end. No way I'm going back up that."

"The ogres will make sure of that if you don't get down," Bernie told him. "We've got to stay behind the rocks, out of sight."

"Sheesh," Leo complained, but he did as he was told.

Having effectively taken command, Bernie chivied his troops into ragged order. What had appeared a smooth, flat plain from the clifftop was, on closer inspection, a rough terrain of giant rock shelves and massive flows, separated by the occasional crevasse or jumble of broken black slabs. Avoiding the smoother areas for the cover of the more uneven stretches, the team picked their tortuous way across the plain toward the side of the castle.

With his extra legs, Jamison maneuvered with a stability the others could only envy. They appreciated his willingness to help, however, as the oversized insect threw his body into service more than once to make a bridge over some of the wider rifts. The gamers trod cautiously, but the beetle's chitin shell was tough and more waxy than slick, making an excellent surface for safe crossing.

By the time they reached the wall of the castle, the afternoon had advanced to early evening, with the sun just hovering over the horizon beyond the castle, leaving the gamers hidden in the stretching shadows. Nonetheless, they rushed from nearest cover to the castle and cowered there, backs pressed firmly against the wall as if they could magically blend into it, invisible. Bernie was the first to relax, uncurling from his protective ball.

"No alarm so far. Come on, let's see if we can get to the gate," he hissed.

"We're not going in there, are we?" Tracy whispered urgently.

"Not on your life," Bernie whispered back. "But it's going to get dark fast, and I want to get the lay of the land so we can make plans."

The humans edged cautiously along the wall, and Jamison, after a few quizzical clicks, imitated them. Bernie trundled forward with his usual gait, more concerned with keeping quiet than with being seen. Rather than succumb to the ever more urgent need to panic, Tracy kept her mind busy guessing at the castle's total size. By her best estimate, the gate was more than a block away from their first point of contact, and their slow pace gave her more time than she really wanted to consider the total number of ogres one could pack into a square block, in a building approximately the height of her high school, not counting the taller towers.

No outcry heralded their approach to the gate. Getting there was easy; getting a good look without being seen was nearly impossible, with two imposing guards posted outside the gate on either side. More guards were barely visible at the top of the dental parapets. All were ogres, more impressive than the usual shambling hulks, however. They were decked out in stiff and gleaming armor made of shining, hardened leather covered with teeth—all kinds of teeth. The helmets had boars' tusks for cheekguards, and crests formed by long, discolored baboon fangs, set in crooked rows. Neater rows of shark's teeth stood, point out, on oversized shoulder pads, while molars of indeterminate species studded at the rest of the armor.

"How the heck do they sit down in those getups without getting bit?" Leo asked under his breath, earning himself angry glares from his angry companions. Bernie shook his head, and motioned for the others to return the way they'd come.

Back where they'd started along the castle wall, the group took advantage of the advancing dusk to dart to the rocks beyond the castle, finding shelter in a region of rough, jutting slabs of basalt. Crowded but out of sight in a nook between two opposing slabs of stone, they settled down to confer.

"It's getting dark," Tracy noted nervously. "How are we going to get back to the cliff?"

"We aren't," Bernie told her flatly. "There's no way we could make it."

"We can't stay here," Leo cried in outrage. "We didn't bring any food."

"We've got water. We'll survive," Bernie said. "What choice do we have? In the morning, we'll take another look at the wall. So far, I haven't got any ideas about how to break in. You?"

The others shook their heads. Morosely, the group resigned themselves to an uncomfortable night in the rocks.

CHAPTER
19

T HE morning dawned clear and bright. Tracy woke to a strange scratching sound. Stiff from sleeping propped up against a slab of stone, she crawled awkwardly out from the rough shelter, and blinked against the bright morning sun. The scrabbling sound came from the castle walls. Keeping her head as low as possible, Tracy scanned the dental ramparts, but not an ogre or other grim guard appeared. There was, in fact, no sign of movement whatsoever. A thin, cool breeze blew off the hills, but there were no bushes nearby to explain the steady scritch-scratch scraping. Finally, Tracy lowered her sights to the foot of the castle wall. There she spotted Bernie humped over in a furry ball, digging frantically, if futilely, at the foot of the wall.

In her best imitation of a soldier crossing a battlefield under fire, Tracy scuttled across the uneven rocky surface to the castle wall.

"What the heck are you doing?" she hissed at Bernie, keeping one hand just under her mouth to catch any coins before they could fall. "The ogres'll hear you."

Bernie ignored her.

"Well, is it doing any good?" she asked.

His front paws still flying, Bernie tilted his head just long enough to glare at her, then went back to digging with a grunt.

"Bernie!" Tracy snapped, as forcefully as she could in a whisper spitting out a fat gold coin in the process. Before she could catch it, the coin struck the ground with a sharp clink. She glanced fearfully up at the walls. "Bernie, we've got to get out of here."

"I've got to try," he grumbled. "Go get the fat kid."

"What?"

Bernie paused in his efforts and examined his claws, still formidable despite the rather extreme sanding they'd just undergone.

"Look," he told Tracy in an undertone, "first, ogres make noise, lots of noise. No one's going to notice a little scratching out here. Second, we've got to get inside somehow, and I don't think we want to waltz through the front gate. Now, get Leo."

Sighing, Tracy quickly picked her way back across the rocks. Ducking carefully under the jagged slabs that formed the cozy shelter, she found Leo curled, comfortably oblivious, in the center of the floor.

"Hey, wake up," she hissed. Leo muttered briefly, but failed to stir. With several mornings' experience behind her, Tracy mercilessly jabbed Leo in the ribs. With a jerk, he rolled over in the cramped space, banging his head on a rock.

"Ow!" he muttered, and rubbed his head. Blinking muzzily, he sat up slowly. Finally, he focused on Tracy. "What happened?" he asked. "Are we under attack?"

"No, and keep your voice down, you idiot," Tracy told him. "Bernie wants you. Outside. At the castle. Hear that scratching? He's trying to dig his way under, I think."

"You've got to be kidding," Leo said. "That's solid rock."

"You know that, and I know that," Tracy said impatiently, "but Bernie apparently thinks otherwise. If he doesn't give up soon, someone in the castle's bound to notice. You'd better go humor him."

"Jeesh." Even slower than Tracy, Leo crawled out of the shelter. For a few minutes, he lay blinking in the bright sunlight. "I'd give anything for a cheese Danish right now," he muttered before crossing to the wall, half stumbling and half crawling over the uneven terrain. He bolted across the last few feet of clearer ground and pressed himself, panting, against the wall.

Bernie stopped digging with a sigh, and sat back on his haunches to look at Leo. "This rock is too solid," he commented in a dry undertone. "I can't quite convince myself it's mostly air."

"What?" Leo asked, confused.

"You know," Bernie told him, gesturing at the ground. "What you were explaining to Hali back at the beginning of this trip. Molecular theory, and all that stuff. I can't even find a decent fracture line here around the base of the castle—it's like someone melted all the rock and set the teeth in before the rock could set."

Leo grinned. "Looks more like gums that way, doesn't it?" he whispered.

"Well, that's a big help," Bernie told him. "All we have to do is figure out a way to give this castle a bad case of gum disease, and wait a year or two. I was kind of hoping you could speed the process along a bit."

"Me?" Leo squeaked, surprised.

"You know, by zapping the rock, the way you did by the campfire."

Shamefaced, Leo shrugged, hands wide. "I thought you knew. I can't do that on purpose," he confessed.

"I'm desperate," Bernie told him. "Hali's been in there overnight, now. We're connected somehow, I think I'd feel something if she died, but I don't know that for sure. I do know that if there were anything she could do, she'd be out of there by now. If she's still alive—if your friends are alive—they're not going to be much longer. Ogres aren't noted for their patience. We've got to do something. Look, I don't expect that much, but just try, will you? A little gum disease, a nice big cavity, I'll take whatever I can get."

Leo eyed Bernie skeptically, but the wombat easily won the resulting staredown. Throwing up his hands, Leo sat down heavily and crossed his legs. Leaning forward, he placed his palms flat against the wall in front of him. Nothing happened. Leo frowned in concentration, but the wall remained firm.

"Try relaxing," Bernie suggested quietly. "Maybe a little Zen is what you need. If you zone out a little, just experience the stone, it might come easier. We know you can do it. You just have to find the right state of mind."

"What do we know he can do?" Tracy asked quietly, coming up behind the two suddenly with Jamison in tow.

"Don't do that!" Leo hissed in surprise, falling forward suddenly. "Hey!" he exclaimed as several inches of rock crumbled beneath his hands. "I can do it!"

"Shush," Tracy reminded him urgently, pointing upward.

"But . . . look, I did it," Leo exulted in a whisper, pointing at the partially collapsed patch of suddenly friable stone that had appeared beneath his hands.

"Let's see how far it goes," Bernie muttered, moving into position. With swift and efficient strokes of his powerful foreclaws, he swept the crumbling rock, now softer than chalk, from the castle wall.

Leo and Tracy held their breath, but were in no danger of asphyxiation. The roughly oval cavity revealed by Bernie's claws was barely eight inches deep, and a mere two feet at its widest point.

"Well, it's a start," Bernie said, sitting back on his haunches to inspect his work. "Try again, kid."

"Yeah. I'll be through there in no time." Eagerly, Leo knelt before the hole and put his hands against the wall.

An hour later, the sun beat hot against the black basalt plain, and the shining black castle walls were still marred only by that first touch of decay. Sweat rolled off Leo's face as he concentrated for minutes at a time.

"I can't do it," he gasped, dropping his hands from the wall. Solicitously, Jamison bent over and tenderly took Leo's limp hands, placing them against the wall as Leo groaned.

"Don't keep saying that. You did it once, you can do it again," Bernie insisted.

"I can't," Leo wailed. "I've tried everything I can think of. You guys get to just lie there while I do all the work."

Tracy shaded her eyes and leaned back against the wall. "What work? All I've seen you do so far is sit there and make funny faces. Yeah, we just love lazing around getting sunstroke while you whine."

"I'm trying to do magic," Leo told her. "You wouldn't understand." Stung, he set his jaw, leaned into the wall, closed his eyes, and concentrated fiercely.

"I wouldn't mind getting out of this sun, myself," Bernie observed. "This isn't ideal weather for a fur coat. But if we don't get Hali out, I don't see much point in going anywhere else. Just relax and try to enjoy the experience."

In response, Leo squinched his eyes closer together and leaned further into the wall, his shoulders tensed.

"Relax," Bernie coached.

Leo frowned fiercely, sweat beading on his brow as he pushed against the wall.

"He never listens, does he?" Bernie observed. Quietly, he leaned over and extended one forearm, claws extended. With a swift jab, he plunged one thick claw into the fleshy portion of Leo's calf.

"Aaagulgg!" Leo almost screamed, catching himself quickly. Snatching his hands from the wall, he turned on Bernie and plunged his hands into the wombat's thick neck fur.

"I'll kill you!" Leo whispered hoarsely, shaking Bernie back and forth, trying to get a good stranglehold.

"Stop that." Tracy slapped him lightly on the head. "Look, the wall's crumbled again."

Sure enough, the hole had crumbling edges. Quickly, the gamers cleared the softened stone, revealing a hole significantly wider and several inches deeper than before.

"Aack," Bernie choked slightly, and cleared his throat. "As I thought. You were trying too hard. All you needed was a diversion, and I provided that."

"You didn't have to stab me!"

"It worked, didn't it?"

"I don't believe this. I work the magic and you abuse me."

"Look, guys, I hate to interrupt," Tracy said, "but you're starting to raise your voices. We don't have time for this, anyway."

"I sure don't," Leo grumbled. He folded his arms across his chest. "Count me out of this game. I quit."

Bernie snickered. "Great. You'd better find the referee and let him know before the other team gets its hands on you."

"Better them than you," Leo muttered mutinously. He turned to Tracy. "I'm not playing with this stupid wombat. If we both quit, they'll have to cancel the game."

Tracy looked up at the toothy tops of the castle walls. From time to time that morning, ogre guards had been heard laughing heartily at unheard jokes.

She sighed. "I don't think I want to count on that."

Jamison chittered in agreement, and gently but firmly lifted Leo's hands from his chest.

"Stop that," Leo hissed. He struggled, but the bug's manipulating members held him as firmly as iron shackles. With a firm click of admonition, the beetle placed Leo's hands against the wall again, and held them there.

"All you've got to do is eat a hole through the wall," Bernie encouraged him. "It can't be more than seven or eight feet deep."

"It's not like I have a choice, is it?" Leo groaned. In a gesture of total despair, he leaned his forehead against the wall, only to have a few more inches of rock crumble at the point of contact. "Well, what do you know?"

A new enthusiasm carried Leo for another futile half hour of efforts before Tracy tried the effects of goosing her fellow gamer. That resulted in another six inches of depth, but no more width, and left Leo braced against further surprise attacks.

After another two hours, even Bernie conceded that Leo wasn't going to make it through the wall. Even when startled or despairing, Leo managed to eat through only a few inches of rock at a time, and the radius of the destruction seemed to be shrinking. Moreover, Leo himself was starting to look drawn, a worn-out, slightly faded appearance that Bernie associated with Hali's more drastic magical efforts.

"I think that's it," he patted Leo on the back. "Time to give up."

Leo promptly collapsed onto his back, limply spread-eagled against the sun-heated stone. "You couldn't call it quits ages ago, no, you had to make me keep trying for hours and hours. And for what?" He waved one arm limply. "Nothing. We're no further ahead than when we started. My sacrifice was pointless. I might as well just die."

"Well, I'm glad you're all right. I was worried about you, but if you have enough energy to complain like that, you've got enough to make it back up that cliff."

Leo didn't have quite enough energy to sit bolt upright so he settled for rolling his eyeballs in outrage. "Why bother? We don't have anywhere to go."

"We've got to get some food," Tracy pointed out. "We left it all in the cart."

"That too," Bernie agreed. "But while we're at it, I've got an idea."

"Nooo," Leo moaned. "Spare me."

"Come on," Bernie urged him. "The sooner we get off this plain, the sooner we'll find some real shade."

"Big deal."

"How about food?" Tracy asked.

"Well, now that you mention it . . ." Leo rolled over, and pushed himself upright. "I guess I could go for some lunch."

"If we hurry, we might make a midafternoon tea," Bernie said doubtfully, eyeing the sun, still slightly short of zenith. "Thank goodness we got such an early start. Come on, we've got quite a climb ahead of us."

"Great," said Leo. "That'll give you plenty of time to explain this 'plan' of yours."

Bernie rolled one dubious eye to focus on Leo. "Thank you, but I prefer to save my breath. Let's get moving."

Hali, Oliver, and Ginny spent a slightly more comfortable night. On arrival, the ogres headed straight for the kitchen, a huge room with giant ovens and open spits lining one wall. Tossing the gamers on the giant butcher's table at one end, the ogres quickly searched their captives, carefully removing (and pocketing) any potentially dangerous or useful objects. With considerable rough handling, they stripped Hali of her belt, pouches, and cloak. Then with quick efficiency the ogres shoved their three prisoners into a small room, just off the kitchen, its walls lined with empty shelves.

"Hey!" Hali shouted as the ogres turned to leave. "Don't we even rate the dungeons?"

"Sorry, babe," the leader chortled. "We took those for ourselves. Lots of slime, bones, some tasty rats and lizards. Too good for guests like you. No, you guys get to stay here in the pantry. Boss had us clear it out just for you. It already had strong spell-warding on it, enough to keep us ogres out, so it should keep you folks in just fine. Not to mention it'll keep you handy for later. Like dinnertime." With a rasping guffaw, he turned and slammed the heavy door shut behind him, leaving the trio in the dark.

" 'Like dinnertime,' " Hali mimicked him ferociously, and kicked the door. "I don't believe it. Nobody shuts Hali in a stupid pantry and lives to laugh about it. There's not even a window in here."

Moving carefully in the dark, she gestured. A small flicker of light appeared in her hand and promptly went out.

"Blast. This room's been damped. Probably to keep the food from spoiling, but it has the same effect on spells." Feeling her way along the walls, Hali picked out a spot and sat down.

"I thought that using magic would wipe out other spells," Oliver commented. "Can't you fight it?"

Hali shook her head absently, then remembered that the others couldn't see her. "That works for illusions and stuff conjured out of nowhere. The spells here are an integral part of the room, probably built in. I imagine that's why they stuck us in here. Without my tools, there's not much I can do. We'd probably have as much chance looking for secret passages."

"Maybe we should," said Oliver, reaching between the shelves to knock on the walls. "There's some kind of backing here. Maybe the whole shelf unit pulls out from the wall."

"Oh, sit down," Hali told him. "No one builds secret passages in pantries."

"All the more reason to have one here. No one would ever suspect. Besides, if there's nothing better to do, we might as well look," Oliver reasoned.

He and Ginny proceeded to tug, push, and knock at the walls, shelves, and even the floor. For the most part, Hali suffered their work in silence, stirring to make a sarcastic comment only when Oliver tripped over her in the dark. It didn't take long to survey the room, even working by feel, and Oliver had to admit that if there were any secret panels they were well-enough hidden that only luck or accident would reveal them.

The ogres did not disturb them, a mixed blessing at best, with no dinner forthcoming, nor water or even sanitary facilities. A corner was designated as the bathroom, a necessity that greatly discomposed Oliver. The two females with him approached the matter with a pragmatism he found daunting. In this matter at least, he was quite thankful for the total darkness; even the sound of Hali urinating set him blushing so hard his cheeks felt feverishly hot, and dry enough to crack. In this more realistic fantasy game, blood and blisters hadn't particularly fazed him, in fact he'd expected them, but until now he'd never really considered the truly awkward, and cruder, aspects of dungeon confinement—even if this wasn't a proper dungeon per se. He wasn't able to keep his feelings on this matter entirely quiet, either, leading Hali to opine, rather acerbically, that his mother must have been overstrict in his toilet training.

With little else to do, the group decided by default to sleep. Morning's arrival was signaled only when all three prisoners had awakened and, unable to sleep further, given in to the need to use their "bathroom."

"It's getting smelly in here," Oliver observed unnecessarily.

Neither of the women felt obliged to answer.

"I'm hungry. Aren't you?" Oliver asked Ginny, sitting next to her on the floor.

"Mmm," she agreed.

"Thirsty, too," he added, encouraged to get any response. "Do you think they'll bother to feed us today? They could at least provide a little water. My mouth is really dry."

"I'd rather not discuss it," Ginny told him. Oliver groped for her hand, and found it; she pulled it away.

Oliver sighed, and sat quietly where he was. Finally, Ginny relented, and found his hand again.

"I don't see any reason to worry about what we can't help," Ginny told him quietly. "We should be planning a way to escape, but I can't think of any. I doubt we'd be able to physically defeat one of those ogres, even if we took him by surprise. The only weapons we could use might be the shelves—we could probably rip them apart if we tried—but I doubt a blow from the heaviest board any of us could lift would do more than make one of those hulking creatures blink."

"That's a great idea, though," Oliver said. "I never even thought about taking the shelves apart. At least it would give us something to do. C'mon."

He tugged Ginny to her feet, and with a shrug invisible in the darkness, she joined him in using their combined weight to wrench the shelves one by one from the wall.

"You'd think they'd be smooching and fondling like any normal couple," Hali muttered to herself, moving out of the way. She was too busy formulating and discarding her own plans for escape to give them much heed, despite the formidable amount of noise produced by the tortured wooden shelves being ripped from their frames.

The destruction was hindered somewhat by the darkness; the second time he tripped over boards lying on the floor, Oliver decided to stack them by the door, to have them handy in case the ogres showed up. Since the door opened outward, the pile of lumber wouldn't block the ogres, but it might at least trip them up a little, giving Oliver more time to strike.

As it happened, Oliver and Ginny were both caught off guard, working at a particularly stubborn shelf, when the door opened suddenly with what seemed a blinding burst of light. An ogre popped in and promptly stumbled over the piled shelves, scattering boards around the half-dismantled pantry.

"What the hell is going on here?" he roared, kicking aside the last couple of boards.

"Well, obviously we enjoy indirectly inflicting pain upon ourselves," Hali muttered sourly, pushing one of the shelves off her lap, where it had landed with a particularly vicious thump, apparently in vengeance for its own recent pain.

"Stay down!" Oliver yelled at her. Grabbing one of the loose shelves, he advanced on the ogre, swinging wildly. With a sigh, Hali flattened herself, keeping one wary eye on the ogre, who stepped forward and brushed first the board and then Oliver aside with a negligent swipe of his arm. Flung into the wall where he'd so recently been at work, Oliver slumped helplessly to the floor. With an exclamation of alarm, Ginny rushed to his side. Oliver grinned weakly and waved her away, leaning against the wall as he pushed himself upright.

"It could have been worse. At least we removed all the shelves first."

Half in tears, Ginny hugged him fiercely, and kissed him quickly on the cheek.

"You wrecked our pantry," the ogre scowled, "and now you want to play kissy face? You're supposed to be screaming and begging for mercy. A little useless struggle, maybe, but let's not have any of this mushy stuff. Come on, the boss wants to see you."

"Don't we even get breakfast?" Hali asked from the floor. "I'm no good in the morning without my breakfast."

"Don't give me any trouble," the ogre told her. "The boss said not to feed you. Leave you in the dark, maybe soften you up a little."

Hali frowned fiercely; the ogre shrugged. "You don't look any softer to me. You're pretty bony, could use some fattening up, but what do I know? Come on, get up."

With one big hand he grabbed Hali's wrist and pulled her up off the floor and into the air. He let her dangle uncomfortably there for several seconds, then with a rumbling chuckle he tucked her under his arm, careful to pin her arms against her sides in the process. With Hali settled, he gestured to Oliver and Ginny.

"All right, you two, get a move on. We've got to go see the boss."

He turned and headed out, knocking Hali against the doorjamb as he exited, and chuckling even louder when she complained. Two more ogres appeared in the doorway, grinning widely as they escorted Oliver and Ginny from the confines of the pantry.

Morning light slanted dimly through high-set windows into the spacious kitchen, revealing walls darkened by soot and grime, and filthy floors heaped with refuse. Bones, hair, and scraps of rotting animal skins scrunched and squished underfoot.

"You guys aren't getting enough vegetables in your diet," Hali commented, scrutinizing the debris from her vantage point beneath the head ogre's arm.

"You witches, all alike," he scoffed, jerking Hali roughly. "I wouldn't worry too much about our diet, if I was you—if we want that roughage stuff, we eat scrawny old birds like you. Cleans out the system in no time."

"Urg," Oliver gurgled, turning slightly green.

"Whassa matter, lunchmeat?" the ogre next to him asked. "All of a sudden, the idea of being eaten makes you sick?"

"N-no," Oliver gasped. "I'm discovering that I don't like thinking about human bodily functions. Just the thought of ogre shit . . . "

The ogres found this excruciatingly funny.

"You gonna get firsthand experiences of ogres' 'bodily functions' if we got any say in the matter," cracked one when he could finally stop laughing long enough to speak, only to send himself into further gales of laughter.

"Firsthand experience. That's a good one!"

"Gotta remember to tell the boys that one," his buddies cheered.

"Well, at least they're not angry at us," Ginny observed, as the joking ogres pushed the three much smaller humans along.

The castle seemed to consist, Hali decided with detached architectural interest from her rather awkward position, of a series of giant, hollowed-out teeth. At least, that was the best explanation she could think of for the rounded-off corners and vaulted ceilings in almost every room of any size. From the outer edges of the windows they passed, Hali judged the buildings to be made of the same enamel-like substance that coated the outer walls, even to the same annoying flicker in color.

The ogres led their captives up a stair chipped out of the same hard enamel, along a thin, incisorish hall, and through a series of rather Gothic arched towers. (Carved-out fangs, Hali decided.) Finally, they entered a large chamber similar in size to the kitchen, but much more elegantly appointed.

Black predominated in the overall color scheme, with the occasional bit of silver or grey for variety. Elaborate carvings covered every inch of the ebony walls, which had the gloss and texture, if not the color, of fine ivory. Carved black ivy twined around the baseboards, and crawled up the walls, supporting a host of strange creatures, all fur and fangs, some easily identifiable, others more mysterious, but every one showing mouthfuls of needle-pointed teeth chiseled in dangerously sharp detail. Weasels and rats skulked at ground level; hungry cats and fat snakes prowled the higher levels. But the region from the high windows to the soaring arches was the sole domain of bats, sleek ebony bats sculpted in all sizes and varieties: some hanging, some flying, others crawling across the multiply vaulted ceiling. Definitely an inside-out molar, Hali decided, craning her neck for a good look at the arches overhead, though probably not a human one, since it had six rather regularly spaced vaults.

From her position under the ogre's hamlike arm, Hali had a far better view of the floor, an expanse of black marble polished to a finish so glassy smooth it seemed at times as if the gamers could see right through it, with occasional iridescent gleams giving the impression of depth. On the surface, inlaid ribbons of silver ran the length of the room, forming elaborate borders and arcane designs. One broad path outlined in fine filigree led from the large entrance to a very tall throne at the end of the room.

On the throne, dwarfed by the jet and hematite-studded pillars that supported the black velvet canopy, sat a very disgruntled fairy, a cross between a cartoon-style evil queen and some frill-fascinated designer's image of the tooth fairy. A tall, thin woman with a fierce and angularly regal face, she wore a spangled net tutu skirt with a lacy low-cut bodice, all in black. She leaned forward slightly in the throne to leave room for the flutter of her delicate, undersized silvery-purple wings. In one hand, she held a small wand topped with a glowing, sparkling light, shining against the dark walls like a bright early star in the winter night. This was an eclipsed star, however, always partially obscured by a magical dot, absolutely black and light-sucking, that somehow managed to follow the end of the wand where it moved—and it moved a lot. Waiting for the ogres and their prisoners, the dark tooth fairy tap-tap-tapped the unlit end on the arm of her throne, in an irritable and apparently unconscious gesture of impatience.

"What took you so long?" she demanded ungraciously as the ogres deposited their charges at the foot of the throne.

Saluting hesitantly with his left hand, Hali being still under the other, the head ogre explained.

"It's not our fault the kitchen's so far from anywhere."

The fairy frowned.

"Besides, the prisoners made trouble. They just about took the pantry apart, they did, and tried to do us in with the pieces."

"Since when do ogres have to worry about what a few weak little humans do with a bunch of shelves?" the fairy demanded. "Oh, never mind. And put her down." She pointed her wand at Hali. "She's no threat here."

"Gee, thanks," Hali said, carefully straightening her skirt, which had hiked up dreadfully during her ride. "I just love being reminded how helpless I am." She looked up and quirked one eyebrow. "But you, you've really come up in the world these days, haven't you, Marj?"

"That's Sinestra!" shrieked the fairy, bouncing to her feet. "You never could remember, but you will now!"

"Oh, really? I'm shivering in my shoes already," Hali drawled. "From wicked witch to tooth fairy—that's quite a jump, don't you think?" she asked the ogre next to her.

He gave Hali a look that questioned both her sanity and her continued existence, and stepped back quickly to a position beside the throne, well out of the line of fire.

"Hmmph," Hali said. "You just can't get good help these days," she observed to the advancing fairy. "I suppose you had to get rid of your familiar—what was its name? A sheep, wasn't it? No, it wouldn't have gone with the new job at all."

"Murgatroyd is a chamois, dammit," Sinestra spat in fury. "You never could remember anybody's name for long, you bush-brained imbecile."

"Oh, right, that big old billy goat. So what did you do with him, turn him into polishing rags?"

"A chamois is an antelope, not a goat," the fairy told her

coldly, "and he's currently staked out in the back garden. This castle is really quite well equipped. Not like that cute little cottage you call home."

"Cute!" Hali sputtered.

The fairy knew she'd hit a nerve, and dug a little deeper. "Oh yes, *très* cute, with that quaint blue plastic roof? What else could you call it?"

This attack was a mistake. On familiar ground, Hali stiffened. "You may call it what you will. I'm getting a new place, anyway."

"So that's why you fell in with Bentwood's new schemes," Sinestra crowed. "He promised you a new house. What a sap."

"What do you . . . hold on here. You must have agreed to playing tooth fairy somewhere along the line. At least I had enough pride to avoid that."

"I didn't have a choice!" the outraged fairy shrieked. "I wanted to do the evil queen bit—I needed a castle. Bentwood got my signature on the contract before I realized what the 'slightly-altered services' clause meant.

"Business was slow anyway." She shrugged. "I thought maybe I was going to have to curse a few kids at christenings, that sort of thing. I never, ever, suspected he meant this!" Her gesture encompassed wand, skirt, and wings.

"It's a great castle," Ginny offered timidly before Hali could stop her. "Could use some cleaning, but this chamber is magnificent. Very elegant."

Finally, out of the corner of her eye she caught Hali's shushing gestures. "Elegant in an evil sort of way, I mean."

Slightly stunned, Sinestra heard her out, then exploded. "Stay out of this! How dare you . . . I don't know how you can stand to work with these pathetic creatures," she said to Hali. "Worms know more about what's going on!"

She looked Ginny and Oliver over contemptuously, then turned to the head ogre.

"Tell me, oaf, why there aren't more of them. I distinctly recall telling you that there were four of these Outworlders!"

"Whoa, now," the ogre backpedaled quickly. "But you told me one was a bug and not to worry about it. The only other critter with these three was a fluffy little donkey. I was sure . . . I mean . . . I thought you wouldn't want that!"

"What in all the darker worlds gave you the idea you could think!" the fairy screeched, waving her arms, slapping the ogre about the head with her wand. The black spot seemed to hurt more than the light; wherever it touched a bright red mark appeared on the ogre's skin.

"Ow, ow, please, I'll never do it again," the ogre promised, crossing his arms high to protect his head. "You want, I'll go get that cute little critter right now. Won't take more'n an hour or two. Maybe three or four if it's strayed far, but . . . Ow!"

"Stop babbling," the fairy told him. "Not only are we missing at least two humans, however modified, there's an experienced witch's familiar out there, just aching to cause trouble. You still got that crow, right? Beanie, wasn't it?" she asked Hali.

"Bernie," said Hali calmly.

"So set up a watch for a crow," Sinestra ordered the head ogre. "Any been seen this morning? He's bound to turn up, and I want him the minute he shows his smart beak around here."

"No crows," said the ogre. "And we've kept an extra sharp watch on the sky, just like you told us yesterday. Birds avoid this place—we'd spot one in no time."

"That's odd," mused the fairy, eyeing Hali speculatively. The air around the prisoners seemed to thicken suddenly. Ginny and Oliver shifted nervously; Hali faced the suspicious fairy with an imperturbable expression.

"So, where's that familiar of yours?" Sinestra asked Hali, who stood silent.

The air pressed even more firmly on the prisoners.

"Talk!" insisted the fairy, waving her wand in Hali's face.

The pressure increased steadily. Oliver held his nose and tried to pop his ears inconspicuously. Ginny shook her head against the pressure, but could get no relief.

She tried opening her mouth to yawn, and to her horror found herself talking instead. Information poured out against her will, but she found quickly that the more freely she spoke, the more control she had. Babbling a mile a minute, she did her best to avoid revealing any more than she had to, but the most damaging information came first.

"Bernie's not a crow. I don't know precisely what he is, really, no one ever explained exactly what he's supposed to be now, but he's not a crow. I know what crows look like, and I've never seen one with fur, oh dear, but Bernie's definitely got fur now. He talks, though, and everyone calls him Bernie and I think, yes I really think I did hear him complaining about not having wings anymore and I did wonder about that but I suppose he must be the same Bernie, unless Hali names all her familiars that . . ."

"Oh, be quiet!" the fairy ordered, slapping Ginny with the wand. The black dot clung briefly to Ginny's cheek, then pulled loose with a sucking sound, leaving a red weal. Ginny put one hand to the spot quickly, and cradled her cheek.

"Are you hurt bad?" Oliver asked anxiously, putting one hand on her shoulder.

Ginny shook her head silently. Tears ran down her cheeks.

"That talking spell must have transferred to me," Oliver observed. Words flowed steadily from his mouth. "I don't seem to be able to stop talking. This is really weird. Not very effective, though. That witch-fairy hasn't gotten anything very useful yet. I get the feeling I could talk myself to death at this rate, though. Never had anything like this happen to me in a game before; I wonder if there's any way to break this spell, like kissing an enchanted princess. Hey, it's worth a try, anyway."

Suiting his actions to his words, he bent to kiss Ginny, but couldn't stop moving his lips against hers as he kept talking, mumbling into her mouth.

"So much for cures, but we should try again, don't you think? There's nothing else I'd rather do right now. I can't think of anything, anyway. You wanna try again? Maybe this time, no, that doesn't work . . ."

Both witch and fairy watched this tender exchange with almost identical expressions of disgust on their faces. Finally, the fairy broke.

"Quiet, both of you!"

Instantly, Oliver fell silent.

"Stop that. Hugging and kissing all over the place, that's disgusting," the fairy howled and stomped her feet.

Ginny stuck her tongue out at her and smiled sweetly.

"Take these two Outworlders back to the pantry," the irate fairy ordered.

"OK," said one of the ogres, "but no kissing on the way back, we don't hold with kissing. Rubbing a few elbows and knees with a lady ogre, tossing a few rocks at her, maybe, but none of this revolting mouth-to-mouth business."

CHAPTER
20

SINESTRA put an arm around Hali's shoulder, and led her to the throne. Tossing a pillow onto the dais, she gestured for Hali to sit, grandly taking the throne for herself.

"You could be sitting in a throne, yourself, if you play your cards right," she declared grandly.

Hali raised an eloquently skeptical eyebrow.

Sinestra waved her hand in a dismissive gesture. "Or terrorizing villagers from a proper tumbledown shack on a cliff, in the classic style, if that's what you prefer. You certainly deserve to be done by better than Bentwood's ever managed. That house of yours is an indignity. No witch should have to tolerate such treatment! You've suffered from Bentwood's incompetent administration—now business is down, times are hard, and Bentwood's blaming outside influences beyond his control. And this latest scheme of his! You've seen first-hand how hopeless this project with Outworlders is.

"The problem isn't with us, it's with management. Pandering to Outworld fads won't help—that's what's lost us our power in the first place. It's time for a change, time to get back to basic values, back to the blood and gore that bring a chill to children's spines—and we want you with us."

"Me?" said Hali mildly. "I've never been the political type. In fact, I've always gone along with management. What makes you think I'd join in some wildcat strike?"

"This is no mere strike!" the fairy declared grandly. Her little wings beat in rapid excitement, shedding a cloud of silver fairy dust. She leaned forward and dropped her voice dramatically. "This is *revolution*."

"Oh, sure," Hali said. She folded her arms and leaned against the throne nonchalantly, ignoring the lumps of the black gemstones set into the dark metal. "You might consider that I've got a contract signed in blood to worry about, and if those precious little wings of yours are any indication, so do you."

"Yes, exactly!" the fairy cried, her eyes alight. "Unfair contracts that force witches to do things never mentioned in our job descriptions, things no witch should ever have to stoop to. You can't tell me you approve of taking bloodthirsty groups of maladjusted teens on pointless treasure hunts. Do you?"

"No, although I'm beginning to think the process has potential as a form of group therapy. I prefer to work one on one, of course, but I'm not convinced Bentwood doesn't have a point. For one thing, the drop in clientele can't be all Bentwood's fault—business has been falling off for a long time, now."

"Bah!" Sinestra scowled. "I know perfectly well that you take unauthorized jaunts Outside—that's how you picked up that smart-mouthed familiar of yours. You must have noticed what Outsiders have done with the old stories, getting rid of the sex and gore, making those ghastly moving pictures with prettified witches and sappy happy endings. I've seen them; we've got some here."

"You've got movies? Whole movies? That's some weight allowance you travel with."

"They've got them on lightweight magic disks now—I wish I could figure out how they do that—but even so, we wouldn't have managed to get them if Bentwood's wizards hadn't brought them back for us. We've got supporters on his staff, I'll have you know. It took his team of wizards months to figure out how to get the images to show, and it still takes a ridiculous amount of power to display a full two hours' worth, but such images! Sweet little singing mice and frumpy fat fairies, and such happy endings as would make any realistic person gag, much less a decent witch! Great stuff for rabble rousing, though. Even the ogres know we can't let Bentwood bring us down to that level—though they *like* the idea of musical comedy, unfortunately.

"More important, that's precisely the sort of thing that's lost us power. Bentwood thinks we exist because the Outworlders believe in us, but how do we know that it's not the other way around? Maybe they believe in us because we exist. Maybe our greatest horrors and wonders somehow seep through into their dreams and stories. We lost our edge and they cleaned up their fairy tales in response. We've got to put real horror back into our world to get their belief back."

Hali looked up skeptically. "I'm not entirely convinced that Bentwood's theory is correct, but yours doesn't quite set my cauldron bubbling over, either. I'd love to believe that we exist independently of the Outworlders. Even better if we're the source of their ideas and dreams, not the result. But how do you know you're not indulging in wishful thinking, Marj?"

"That's Sinestra!"

"Sinestra, sorry. Anyway, they've got horror enough of their own. Bluebeard had nothing on what they've got going for themselves Out there. I'm not inclined to try to compete."

"I should have known. You're a wimp, Hali, you always have been. More power than you know what to do with, and all you want is a stupid hut on a hillside. When's the last time you actually ate a human brat?"

"That's not my style. You know that, Marj."

"Oh, right. You think making a kid sweep the floor is some kind of torture."

"It works for some."

"Think big for once. We've got both monsters' unions with us. We've got wizards, even inside Bentwood's operation. His heavy-handed management techniques have won us a lot of support—so much we're just about ready to go open with the revolt."

"How many witches do you have?"

Sinestra frowned, and thumped her armrest in vexation, making the star on her wand vibrate madly and cast a strobelike light on Hali. "So far, only a couple of our esteemed colleagues have given their outright support. Dozens of noncontract witches have expressed interest, but most of the cowards are waiting to see how things fall out—they won't commit to the movement until they're sure we'll win."

She leaned forward and spoke earnestly. "That's why we need you, Hali. You've got a rep, and you've toed the company line so long, people will sit up and take notice if you join. With you on the team, we might even try recruiting a few dragons. So far, they've honored the strike, but they're the real wildcards in this game. I've been leery of revealing our complete plan to them, but you—you've got connections.

"Join us, Hali, and we'll have a spring housecleaning like Bentwood will never believe."

Almost against her will, Hali's lips quirked. "Put that way, it almost sounds appealing."

On their way back to the pantry, Oliver and Ginny also got an earful on the revolution.

"That witch sure is pushing it," one of the guards complained. "It's bad enough she orders us around, she does the same thing to our captain. 'Kill the knight, trash the village, lean on the goblins, don't fight the Outworlders, capture the Outworlders, wrestle the witch, bring back the donkey'—she never stops. I mean, this was supposed to be a union action; the old witch is supposed to be helping us, not running things."

His buddy agreed. "Yeah. Just because we need her brains, it don't give her the right to walk all over us."

Oliver wanted to hear more. "You mean she's not the boss here? You sure could have fooled me. Why do you let her get away with it?"

"Hey, don't ask us," the first ogre growled. "We're just flunkies. They don't tell us rank and filers what's going on. We trust the union organizers to take care of us."

"They're ogres, then."

The two guards found this highly amusing.

"Hooh. You got a great sense of humor, kid. Ogres, running an organization? Nah, we hired the best."

"Best?"

"Trolls, of course. No one bargains tougher than a troll, except maybe a dwarf, but them dwarves won't have nothing to do with us ogres. A troll'll do anything for enough gold."

"Yeah!" the other ogre agreed. "We tell 'em the more we get, the more they get paid."

"Works like a charm."

"Yeah, but aren't the same guys running the unions and the administration?" Oliver asked. "Sounds like a conflict of interest to me."

"Conflict of interest . . . you mean like battling banks, or something? Sounds dull. No gore, just red ink. I like a little action in my battles."

"No, no," Oliver explained. "I mean, what if the trolls got together and made a deal? The trolls in management might offer to split their profit with your trolls if your trolls agreed to lower wages."

The ogres exchanged worried glances.

"You got a warped and twisted mind, kid. You sure you ain't got troll blood in you?"

"Don't be stupider'n you have to," his buddy told him. "Lunchmeat here ain't green. He's nice, pink, and tasty looking, not stringy like a troll. " 'Sides, who ever heard of two trolls working together? They don't trust each other any more than we trust them."

"Oh, yeah, right. I forgot."

"Well, I think maybe we'd better have no more talking. I don't like the way this appetizer here spreads unpleasant ideas, if you know what I mean."

"Huh?" his companion asked.

Rolling his eyes, the marginally more intelligent of the two closed his lips firmly together and pushed Oliver and pulled Ginny along the elegant halls, down some stairs into ever more dingy rooms, until they finally arrived back at the filthy kitchen and noisome pantry. With a grunt, the ogre tossed the two humans into the pantry, sending them stumbling and falling over the dismantled shelves. With a solid thunk the heavy pantry door closed behind them, leaving the two slightly bruised and disconcerted in the dark.

They stacked the shelves along one wall, making themselves a low seat. Seated in the dark, they carefully felt each other's more inaccessible bruises, making sure there was no bleeding or serious swelling. Remembering Bernie's warnings, though the memory seemed months, even years, old, Oliver restrained his initial impulse to kiss Ginny. She had her own ideas. Oliver nobly tried to redirect her thoughts, with only limited success.

Soon enough, the pantry door was flung open in a blaze of light, and Hali was literally thrown in, landing on her bottom with a loud smack. Several ogres outside the door guffawed noisily as the door was slammed shut, leaving the group in darkness once more, and muffling the sound of raucous laughter.

"At least we don't have to listen to their jokes." Hali got up stiffly, rubbing her rump with a rustle of fabric.

"What happened?" Ginny asked.

"Yeah. What did that fairy say?" Oliver echoed. "Oh, hey, we've got a sort of seat over here."

Hali felt her way to the wall and sat down gingerly on the piled boards. "Ow. Those food preservation spells are playing hob with my usual healing powers," she muttered.

"So, what did she say?" Oliver asked.

Hali sighed. "Much what I expected. The monsters' unions are upset with having to face groups of fighters. Not that I'd really say you guys qualify as fighters, mind you, but these union types get all caught up in technicalities. Anyway, they've got an illegal strike action going—though I doubt they've bothered to officially notify Bentwood yet. Marj is really pissed at having to play the tooth fairy, and my guess is she's behind the whole thing."

"So?" Oliver prompted.

"So, she tried to talk me into joining, too."

"And?"

"And I told her no," Hali told him flatly. "Marj is a flake, always has been. Can't be happy just being an ordinary witch, she has to go for the whole evil bit: the name, the castle, the excessive outfits, they're all of a piece. The evil look's been the fashion for a few centuries now, but Marj got carried away, as usual. The tooth fairy uniform, tutu and all, looks better on her than some of the getups she's come up with for herself. But look where it's gotten her: associating with ogres, of all beings. I'd rather have a horde of goblins in my basement, personally. Not that some ogres aren't real pros, but in general, they're a sorry lot."

At that thought, she sat up rather suddenly, and stared at the pantry door as if by sheer force of will she could see right through it. The pantry's various spells thwarted that effort, but Hali was thinking too furiously to notice.

"Ogres," she declared pedantically, "are of low intelligence. They have little appreciation of metaphor, and a strong tendency to take words very literally."

In her normal voice, she added, "It makes for rotten cocktail parties—I hate to think what their dinner-table conversation is like."

Oliver and Ginny shuddered at the thought.

"Of course, if we don't get out of here, I don't think we have to worry much about conversing at the dinner table," Hali observed. "We're more likely to be the entree. I wasn't too polite to Marj, there at the end. I suggested she needed counseling—I don't know why the pros in this business always take that advice so poorly."

"Urk." Oliver choked. "Isn't it a bad idea to tell crazy people that they're crazy?"

Hali shrugged. "Some want help. Some don't. Megalomaniacs usually get upset if you even suggest there's a problem. I knew that, but I felt I had to offer."

"You couldn't just play along long enough to get us out of here?" Even in the dark, Oliver had a good idea that Hali was glaring at him. "I mean—now we're going to get eaten. How long do you think we have?"

Hali thought. "The windows here are all so high, it's hard to tell, but from the change in shadows going and coming, not to mention all the ogres grabbing meat off the butcher's table, I'd guess it's just past noon, now. Ogres usually save their big meal for just after dark. That's the only meal for which they bother to cook their food, and I'm sure Sweet Sinestra wants us broiled live on spits. Since ogres aren't much for advance preparation of their food, we've got several hours at least."

"Oh, joy," Oliver groaned.

"There must be something we can do," Ginny suggested timidly to Hali. "Even if it's just committing suicide so they can't torture us."

Hali snorted, half in laughter, half in disgust. "It won't come to that if I can help it. What kind of adventurers are you, anyway?"

"Tasty ones," said Oliver.

"You're starting to sound like Bernie," Hali observed. "Be patient. I have a plan, but we need to wait a little longer, till the guards are definitely through with lunch. I want as few ogres out there as possible. If you want to help, sit with one ear to the door, and tell me when it's really quiet out there."

Glad to have anything to do, Oliver hurried to the door and glued his ear to it. He heard faint thumps and bangs, as of furniture being knocked around, and always over it the metallic hoots and screams of ogre laughter. Finally, the sounds got briefly louder, then passed by the pantry.

"I think they're leaving," Oliver said.

"We'll wait a little longer," Hali told him. "I want the ogres on guard duty to be bored. Really bored. Ogres are too dumb to bore easily but we've got time."

Time passed slowly, and Oliver passed his boredom limit long before Hali.

"My ear's going to sleep, and there's nothing going on out there," he complained. "How much longer?"

"Not too long. Let me know if you hear anything."

Oliver had no idea if minutes or hours had passed, but finally he heard something worth reporting.

"Sounds like someone's torturing a big dog right outside the door," he told Hali urgently.

She made her way to the door and stooped to listen. "Perfect! He's singing."

"Singing?" Ginny joined the other two at the door.

"Only one voice," Hali said. "Let's wait; if there's another one out there he'll join in. I've never met an ogre that could carry a tune in a bucket, but they seem to find singing irresistible."

They waited, through a chorus, a verse, and a second chorus.

"Perfect!" Hali breathed, as if unable to believe her luck. "There's only one out there."

She stood up, straightened her clothes, and mussed her hair as best she could without a mirror or light. "All right, here goes. You guys just keep quiet."

With that, she knocked firmly on the door.

The raps sounded loud inside the pantry, but the singer hardly paused in his song. Hali grunted and knocked again, a little harder.

This time, there was a definite pause in the song, but after a few seconds the noise started again.

"Open this door!" Hali shouted, kicking instead of knocking. The hard heels of her boots hit sharply against the door: rap, rap, rap.

The song ended abruptly. There was a second of silence, the rattle of a lock being removed, and then the door opened just a crack. A wide, bloodshot eye peered in.

"You knock?" asked the ogre cautiously.

"Well, it's about time," Hali told him. "Look, I want to give you a little advice."

"Me?" the ogre squeaked in surprise.

"Well, it's just that I wouldn't want a nice fellow like you to get in trouble. You sing so nicely."

"Aw, shucks." The ogre let the door fall open a little wider, just enough so the prisoners could see him blushing shyly. "It's just a new little song from those moving pictures."

"All about going to work, wasn't it? It's nice to see a monster so dedicated to his job."

"Gee," the ogre looked about him nervously. "You won't tell the other guys, will you? It's a dwarf song, really. I don't want the guys to know I was singing that one. They might think I'm . . . *dwarfish* or something."

Hali stepped up to the ogre and patted him on the shoulder, in the process edging the door open a little wider. "I won't say a word, honest. But that's not what I wanted to talk to you about."

The ogre eyed her suspiciously. "What, then?"

"I just wanted to let you know that you're making a terrible mistake," Hali told him. "The others would be really angry if they found out."

A worried look crossed the guard's face. "What mistake?"

"Well, you know we're supposed to be the main course tonight."

The ogre grinned happily, and nodded. "Big feed, a regular party, the boss says."

"Well, everyone will be very disappointed if we spoil before then."

"Spoil?" the ogre asked, puzzled.

"You know, get smelly and moldy and rotten? So bad you can't eat us?"

"I like my meat rotten."

"Sinestra won't, you know, and if she's really mad she won't let you eat us, either."

"Ooh. Yeah."

"And then your friends would get mad."

"Oooh. That's bad." The guard thought about it some more. "But you won't go bad before dinner. Meat takes days to get really ripe, the way I like it."

"We wouldn't normally, but you put us in a pantry, you know."

"Uh . . . so?"

"Hasn't anyone ever told you that meat doesn't keep in a pantry?"

"No."

"Well, have you ever seen anyone store meat in a pantry?"

"No."

Hali patted the confused ogre on the shoulder again. "Take my word for it. Meat just doesn't keep in pantries."

"I never knew anyone with a pantry before," the ogre mused.

"Look," said Hali, edging out the door to lay a chummy, consoling arm over his shoulders. She had to stand on tiptoes to reach, but the ogre seemed to appreciate the gesture. "There's an easy solution."

"There is?" the ogre asked hopefully.

"A very easy solution," Hali told him. "Just let us into the kitchen. We'll keep much better there. See those carcasses on the meathooks over there?" She pushed the door open wider, and turned the ogre around to point out a pair of deer and a half-skinned boar hanging along the wall.

"Those are for dinner, too," the ogre told her, drooling slightly.

"See, that's where we should be, to keep properly. You don't even have to bother with the meathooks; we'll just look after ourselves." Behind the ogre's back, Hali waved Ginny and Oliver toward the kitchen stairs. Quietly, the two edged around the door and past the ogre.

"I dunno," the ogre said. "I'm supposed to be guarding you."

"Oh, well, I wouldn't worry about that," Hali told him. "Where could we go? There's no way we could escape this castle, not with all you brave ogres guarding the gates."

"That's right," the ogre nodded. "I guess it's okay."

"I'm so glad I was able to help. Why don't you go join your buddies, since you don't have to keep an eye on us?"

"Sounds good," he agreed. "Gee, thanks for the help."

"No problem," Hali assured him. "I'm always glad to give a little good advice. That's what witches are for."

Patting him on the back again, she ushered the cheerful ogre to the outside door and saw him on his way. When he finally disappeared into the bright sunshine, she shut the door behind him and breathed a sigh of relief before hurrying across the kitchen to join Oliver and Ginny, who were peering cautiously down the kitchen stairs.

"Come on, let's find my pouch," she told them. "All these ogres are spellproofed, and this castle's got some major enchantments on it. The minute I use magic, Marj'll know it. I want to be armed and ready, and then we're going to really sweep up around here!"

Dripping sweat and panting hoarsely, Leo pulled himself up out of the crack onto the top of the cliff. He dragged himself away from the edge and then, shuddering with the effort, pulled up the rope tied around his waist. The other end led down into the crevice, tight with considerable tension. He shook the rope and with a scrape, a clunk, and finally a clatter, Hali's staff popped out of the crevice. Immediately behind the staff, Jamison's head poked up. He grabbed the edges of the cliff with his forearms, and hoisted himself up in one swift movement. He straddled the opening on all six limbs and peered down, chittering inquisitively. Finally, he reached down with one of his heavy, pronged forearms, and withdrew it slowly and carefully with Bernie clinging to it, eyes closed, holding on for dear life. Jamison carefully moved away from the edge on five legs, and deposited the trembling wombat safe on solid ground, several feet from the edge. Last, Tracy pulled herself up and collapsed, panting, inches from the cleft.

"I don't believe you made us move that fast," Leo gasped. He rolled over to glare at Bernie, who lay flat on his belly, panting hard.

"I don't believe we managed to get up here at all," Bernie wheezed. He flopped over on his side and groaned. "But we have to move fast if we're going to save Hali. It's already midafternoon."

"Oh god," Tracy moaned from flat on her back. "I can't move. I don't think I'm going to be able to save myself, much less anyone else." As she spoke, roses and coins appeared at her mouth. Two coins rolled down her chin, but a rather wilted yellow rose clung to her lips. Making a face, Tracy brushed the rose aside and sat up. She pulled up the waterskin at her side, unscrewed the top, and took a quick sip. With resolution, she recapped the waterskin and set it aside.

"I'm thirsty, we're almost out of water, and there's none available anywhere. Can things get much worse?" Several coins and a rosebud dropped from her mouth. She picked up the rose and examined it. "Even my roses are turning brown."

"You're thirsty?" Leo groaned. "I'm dying."

"You shouldn't have drained your waterskin dry before we even reached the cliffs," Tracy told him.

"I have more bulk. I sweat more. I need more water."

Bernie sighed loudly and pulled himself to his feet.

"If you've got the strength to argue, you've got the strength to keep moving. Come on, get up. We've got to find Jamison's ball."

"What?" Tracy asked. "I thought we were going to get Whitenose."

"No, no, we don't need the donkey," Bernie told her. "We want that ball. Jamison, go get it. We'll follow."

Happily, the giant beetle set off away from the cliff. With moans and groans, the others stumbled along in his wake, over the rocks and into the scrubby trees and bushes. Jamison scuttled nonstop over obstacles the others could barely climb, but they managed to keep the eager scarab in sight. Finally, a happy bray greeted them, and Whitenose came clattering over the rocks. He stopped briefly to bump noses with the bug, then dashed on to come to a bouncing stop in front of Tracy. His long, fuzzy ears wig-wagged back and forth quizzically, and the rope on his halter dangled just in front of Tracy, as if the little ass were willing, even eager, to be caught.

Tracy seized the rope with a little sob. "Oh, Whitenose, you pulled loose," she laughed, burying her face in the dusty fur at his neck. "I don't know why I'm so glad to see you, you silly little creature."

"I know why I'm glad," Bernie said. "You think you can get me on his back? My wobbly little legs weren't made for this kind of exercise."

"Your legs?" Leo sputtered. "What about mine?"

"They're a lot longer than Bernie's, if nothing else. I wouldn't ask Whitenose to carry that kind of weight, anyway," Tracy told him. "Come on, let's get Bernie up. My arms feel like limp spaghetti right now, but maybe we both can manage."

By dint of much effort, and a few slips, they managed to get Bernie perched on the donkey's back. Tracy led on in the direction Jamison had taken, while Leo held on to Whitenose's mane with one hand, and steadied Bernie with the other. Over a little rise and around a few rocks, they found they were back at the cart, with Jamison's dung ball still parked nearby. Jamison himself was busily crawling up and over the ball, adding bits of fresh manure and patting the ball into shape.

Leo eyed the ball warily. "I swear it's gotten bigger while we've been gone."

"The bigger, the better," Bernie told him. He slid off of Whitenose, who looked around in surprised concern, but Bernie waddled past him in quick determination. He walked around the ball, scrutinizing it closely.

Close up, the ball had a warm, sickly sweet scent, a compound of manure and roses overlaid with the dry smell of dust. Bernie stuck out one long, solid claw and tentatively tested the ball with it. Even with firm pressure, the claw penetrated barely half an inch.

"Perfect," Bernie muttered to himself. He tested the ball at another point, this time barely getting past the surface before he made contact with metal. "Lot of coins. Very good." He put his shoulder to the ball and tried pushing with all his strength, but it didn't even rock in place.

"What?" Leo asked. "What's the big deal with the ball?"

"Hmmm?" Bernie said absently. "How many gold coins do you suppose are in here? How many does Tracy produce, anyway?"

Leo scowled. "Why are you asking me?"

Bernie gave him a skeptical look worthy of Hali. "I had this idea you were paying attention there for a while."

"Well, maybe," Leo shrugged. "The way she talks, there must be hundreds of gold pieces in there. Maybe thousands."

"The way I talk? What about you?" Tracy asked indignantly. Three more coins fell and bounced on the hard, dry ground.

Jamison chittered eagerly, dropped down from his position on top of the ball, deftly scooped up the coins, and promptly returned to add them to his collection.

"See what I mean?" Leo said.

"Most of those coins are well under an ounce," Bernie mused, "but there's plenty of them in there, plus rocks and dirt. Jamison's got this ball packed really tight, too."

"Come on," he told the beetle, who was listening attentively. "We need to get this ball to the edge of the cliff. Can you handle it?"

Jamison stood erect and saluted proudly, clearly thrilled to see his dung ball get the attention it deserved. Turning with a snap, he strutted to the ball and stood on his forelimbs, putting his two hindlegs up on the ball. Seemingly without effort, he had the ball rolling on its way.

The path back to the cliff was of necessity more round-about. Jamison, moving backward, used considerable trial and error to avoid the obstacles he'd previously crossed without effort. Leo and Bernie followed not far behind. Tracy stayed behind to hook Whitenose up to the cart, despite Bernie's urging. With every bit of speed she had managed to develop in her several days' experience, she had Whitenose harnessed up and hitched to the cart in seconds. Leading the donkey, she brought up the rear, moving as fast as the little ass would allow. Once they caught up with the others, both Leo and Bernie took the opportunity to rest their weary feet, and hitched a ride in the back of the cart.

CHAPTER
21

A FEW feet from the cliff edge, Bernie jumped out of the cart. "You wait here," he instructed the others. "We don't want someone in the castle spotting us up here. If you have to come forward, keep low."

"Hey, yeah," Leo said. "Like Indians on the ridge looking down at the helpless wagon train below. We don't want them to see us until we're ready to attack, put a little fear in them."

"I don't think fear is precisely the emotion we'll inspire," Bernie snapped. "Just stay down while I scout out the territory."

Bernie followed the very edge of the cliff, moving at a surprisingly speedy gallop. Every so often, he paused to peer down at the side of the cliff, then the castle, as if measuring the distance between them. For a few minutes, he disappeared over a slight rise, then reappeared, running fast and low to the ground.

"I found the perfect spot," he gasped as he skidded to a stop. "Leave the cart, but bring a couple of the quarterstaves. Oh, and you'd better bring Hali's staff, too. And keep low, guys. C'mon, Jamison, let's get your ball set up. Careful, now. You don't want it rolling over the cliff."

Jamison clicked in agreement, upended himself and set his

legs to push. Bernie practically bounced in impatience as he backed cautiously up the trail, guiding Jamison along the cliff. Somehow, he kept his voice calm. Progress was slow, but finally Bernie called a halt.

"This is the perfect spot?" Leo asked. "Looks the same as the rest of this cliff."

"Look over the edge," Bernie said over his shoulder. "That's what I was looking for."

On hands and knees, Leo peered over the edge and down the cliff. Turning his head, he scanned the rock walls on either side.

"I still don't see what the big deal is. It's a little smoother here, but that's it."

Bernie shook his head. He gave Jamison a last few careful commands, and finally declared himself satisfied. The huge sphere perched precariously just inches from the edge of the cliff, looking like a misplaced balancing rock. Nervous, Jamison kept one eye on the drop-off and the other on his precious ball. Bernie moved over to where Leo lay on his stomach and sat down.

"I'm surprised you haven't guessed. I got the idea from you," Bernie told Leo.

"Really?" Leo said, gratified if still confused. "But you still haven't explained."

Tracy, having taken the time to unharness Whitenose and tie him nearby, now cautiously joined the two on the edge.

"Explained what?" she asked.

Bernie looked over his shoulder surreptitiously, making sure Jamison was out of earshot. Sure that the bug was still busy with his ball, Bernie explained.

"See how this cliff slants out at the bottom? And how smooth the plain is between here and the castle?" He waved a paw at the scenery below.

The two gamers peered at the rocky landscape below them.

"Yeah," Tracy said slowly. "You aren't planning to slide down the cliff, are you?"

"Hey, that was my idea!" Leo exclaimed.

"*We're* not going down there. It's too steep," Bernie said patiently. "But the dung ball's another matter. It's so solid, it should survive a bounce or two, and with any luck at all it'll roll down the cliff, pick up some incredible momentum, smash into the castle, and just maybe go right on through the walls. This whole area is really a giant bowl, with the land all slanting toward the castle; we can't miss it. If we get really lucky, we'll hit the part of the wall we've already weakened. See, the smooth area leads straight to it."

Leo and Tracy squinted, but the distance was too great to make out the low, shallow hole, now in the afternoon shadow.

"Take my word for it," Bernie assured them. "I was careful to note the position of the teeth before we left. Remember? This clear area was right in our path, but we had to avoid it because we would have been too exposed."

"I remember," said Leo. "My skinned shins and banged-up knees remember, too. I just loved going out of our way to climb around all those boulders."

"Well, your memory's going to get refreshed right away," Bernie told him. "We've got to get to the castle as fast as we can."

"You want us to go back down? Now? We just got up here," complained Leo.

"Well, what choice do we have?" Bernie asked. "If the ball smashes through the walls while we're still up here, all we'll have managed is to stir up the castle, like kicking an anthill. By the time we got to the hole, there would be ogres all over the place.

"Tracy, you stay up here. We'll use the staves to rig a lever, so you can get the ball rolling. We can't do a test run, so I'm counting on you to be here to figure out how to get Whitenose to push or pull, somehow, if the lever doesn't work. Just give us time to get down to the walls."

"Why can't Jamison do it?" Tracy asked, her voice tight and face pale.

"I'm not sure I could explain it to him," Bernie said. "I don't even know if he has any sense of time. Most important, I don't think he'd be willing to give up his ball."

"He's also the best fighter we've got," Leo added.

"I can fight. I'm not afraid," Tracy said angrily. "You

shouldn't try to protect me by leaving me behind just because I'm a girl."

"We've got to leave someone behind," Bernie said. "Someone's got to take care of the donkey, too, and I'm sure if he had a choice he'd pick you."

"Well . . . " Tracy seemed willing to be persuaded.

"Besides, you don't like fighting, and ogres freak you out," Leo added.

Tracy set her jaw mulishly. "I don't want to be left out. I'm a lot better fighter than Leo."

A hoarse cry from some distance away put an end to the argument. The gamers turned to see a band of ogres hiking along the edge of the cliff. The leader was pointing in their direction with his club, and shouting something that sounded oddly like, "The donkey! The donkey!"

"Oh, no," Bernie moaned. "Maybe we should try sliding down the cliff."

The ogres started running, shouting hoarsely and waving heavy clubs as they came. Their stubby legs weren't built for speed, but they worked steadily. For several seconds, the gamers watched in horrified indecision as the ogres came closer and closer. Jamison took up a defensive stance in front of his dung ball, clearly prepared to defend it with his life, but the others in the party were more inclined to take their chances on outrunning the advancing monsters.

"If only we could fly," Bernie whimpered, seeing his plan fall to pieces before his eyes. "We can still roll the ball down the cliff, but there's no way we can get down there ourselves. Oh, for a pair of wings!"

Jamison turned to look at Bernie, and chittered inquisitively. Suddenly, the shiny wing cases on his back parted, and pairs of translucent wings appeared. With a whir, Jamison's wings went into motion. The beetle lifted a few inches off the ground and hovered.

"I didn't know he could fly," Tracy breathed.

"Me either," Leo said. "I wonder—did he?"

"The real question is, can he carry us?" Bernie said.

"All of us? Off the cliff?" Tracy looked over the edge and gulped. "I don't think I want to try it."

"I don't think we've got a choice," Bernie snapped, one

wary eye on the rapidly approaching ogres. "Jamison, get down. Let's get your dung ball rolling before the ogres can steal it."

Chittering worriedly, Jamison landed quickly on his forelimbs and efficiently pushed the ball with one swift kick. The giant brown orb hung for a breathless second at the very edge, then started to fall, seemingly in slow motion. Then it struck the side of the cliff and started to roll. Like a giant's bowling ball it rumbled down the slope, steadily picking up speed as it raced toward the castle.

The gamers had no time to watch their weapon in action. As soon as the ball went into motion, Jamison had his wings out and fluttering. With a scooping motion of his heavy forearms, he urged the others to get on. Recklessly, Leo grabbed Hali's staff barehanded and managed to mount, finding a seat on Jamison's heavy shoulders, in front of the wings. With Leo's help, Bernie climbed up and found himself reasonably secure in the young man's lap.

"Hurry, Tracy," urged the wombat.

"There's no way he can carry all of us," Tracy shouted over the buzz of wings and the cries of the rapidly closing ogres. "You're not getting me on him."

"It's this or the ogres," Bernie shouted back. "We've got to try."

"They're almost here!" Leo screamed, looking behind him. "Take off! Let's go!"

"I can't!" Tracy shrieked. "I hate heights. I hate this place. I can't do it."

The ogres were almost on them. Jamison's wings beat faster and faster. Then the lead ogre headed straight for the donkey, with a hoarse, exultant cry.

"We've got the donkey!"

Whitenose brayed and kicked in protest, but the ogre holding him merely chortled wickedly. Almost effortlessly, he picked the little donkey up, and slung it over his shoulder.

"No!" Tracy shouted involuntarily. Aghast, she clapped one hand over her mouth and took a step backward.

The lead ogre turned, spotted the rest of the group, and gestured his patrol forward. "Those must be the missing humans. Get 'em, guys!"

The ogres rushed forward, brandishing their clubs eagerly. With a shriek, Tracy ran for Jamison, falling over Leo's legs and on top of Bernie.

Wasting no time, Jamison beat his wings furiously. When he failed to take off, he turned, wings still beating, and ran off the edge of the cliff before Tracy could even catch her breath to scream.

Wings working at full speed, Jamison struggled to maintain altitude. He was losing the battle, but slowly, and flew doggedly after the ball still rolling inexorably toward the castle.

"Yee-haw!" Leo yelled exuberantly, waving one arm like a cowboy riding a bucking bronc. "Look at that sucker go!"

Tracy only moaned. She was clinging tightly to Jamison's carapace with her eyes screwed shut, and she had no intention of looking at anything until she was back on solid ground.

Bernie managed to worm his way out from under Tracy's midsection, and dazedly shook his head. "What sucker? Where?"

Leo pointed eagerly. "The dung ball. It's moving fast. It's almost at the castle walls already!"

Still feeling somewhat dazed, Bernie looked down. It was a mistake; the ground not only swept by but also came closer at a dizzying pace, making him feel decidedly queasy. Automatically, he shifted his gaze toward the horizon, finding the castle in the process.

"Yahoo!" he yelled, spotting the speeding dung ball. "It's working!"

The dark sphere had picked up plenty of momentum, enough to send it into the air whenever it hit an uneven spot in its path. Such jumps did nothing to diminish its speed, however, and with a crash that echoed off the cliffs the ball slammed into the castle walls, knocking out one tooth completely, and pushing several more askew.

The ball itself did not survive the collision. Smashed into pieces, chunks of packed manure and vegetable matter flew into the air, in the process spilling out hundreds of gleaming coins that shone so brightly even the gamers could see the sparkles. Shouts rose from within the castle, and soon ogres appeared, tiny in the distance, jumping up and down like excited little dolls as they gathered the golden treasure. Jamison chittered angrily, and found the strength to fly a little faster.

The extra speed was a mistake. Too soon, he began to falter, dipping and weaving. Tracy moaned in terror. Leo called in alarm, "He's getting hot! I think he's overheating."

Bernie leaned forward and touched a bare patch of chitlin, finding it feverishly hot. He looked ahead, trying to judge their rate of descent. There was no way they could make it over the wall, but they would at least make it close to the castle.

"Jamison! Try to land us near the hole in the wall," Bernie shouted.

The exhausted bug didn't waste energy responding, but put new effort into flying a straight path to the wall. He dipped lower and lower, at times almost grazing the rocky surface, but somehow he managed to keep airborne just long enough to land within easy running distance from the wall. The rough landing threw Jamison onto his abdomen, and sent his riders sprawling. Uninjured, they picked themselves up quickly, ready to run, but the castle guards were too busy digging through the dung and fighting each other over the gold to pay attention to such insignificant attackers.

The humans paused, not sure what move to make next, but Jamison had no such doubts. Though exhausted, his every instinct told him to fight to defend his ball and if his wings were too weak to move, his legs, at least, were rested. The angry beetle made a dash for the ruins of his ball, and crashed headlong into the middle of a group of angrily shouting ogres.

"Let's go while they're distracted!" Bernie shouted, streaking for the gap in the wall.

The two humans looked at each other, both aghast. Leo shifted his grip on Hali's staff, bringing it up in fighting position, and started for the wall. Having no intention of battling the ogres hand-to-hand, Tracy looked around in desperation, but saw nothing that would make a decent weapon, not even a rock of reasonable size. With no time to find one, she shrugged, pulled out her small belt knife, and followed.

Inside the castle, the search for Hali's pouch led quickly into a bewildering series of rooms. Ginny found a stairway into the depths, but a foul stench arising from the opening confirmed to Hali's satisfaction that the ogres had taken over the dungeon.

"No one would trust ogres with anything valuable," she said. "Sinestra knows better than to leave anything of mine in their hands. Let's search the upper levels first."

The ground floor proved dauntingly empty, not only of ogres but of any inhabitants, and even, in many cases, of furniture. Though the searchers carefully ducked inside each new doorway, they moved faster than they had originally expected, though they also found it hard to keep as quiet as they had intended.

Looking into what might have been a waiting room, had there been any chairs, Hali sniffed. "I knew Marj was trying to develop a taste for austere magnificence, but this is ridiculous. Not a desk or cupboard in sight."

"At least it makes searching easier," Ginny offered.

"We're in the wrong part of the castle," Hali decided. "Let's try one of those tusk-towers in the center."

The castle rooms seemed joined together without thought to convenience. Often one room led directly to another, requiring inhabitants to pass through each room to get anywhere. The rare hall or walkway more often than not led nowhere, with dead ends hidden around corners so a mere glance told nothing; each avenue had to be explored. Past the first few rooms, there was a total lack of access to the outside, as well. The explorers could divine no clue to the proper path from one point to another, and the lack of doors and scarcity of low windows made it almost impossible to tell where one tooth-building was in relation to another. Twice Hali climbed up on Oliver's shoulders to peer through windows placed just out of reach, and each time she scowled, finding her target in a different direction.

"I'd swear these stupid teeth were set in a spiral," she muttered at one point. "I get the feeling we have to walk through every room to get to the center. Maybe Marj uses those wings for more than just show."

"At least we aren't running into any more ogres," Oliver said. "It'd be real easy to get trapped in one of these stretches without doors."

"Don't remind me," Hali grumbled. She studied the view from the window closely before dropping to the floor with a thump that sent her to her knees. She stood with an exasperated sigh and brushed off her skirts.

"Let's keep going. Watch for a big, wide window. I want to get a better look."

Several minutes later, Ginny spotted a large, arched window. A twisted pillar divided the opening's width, but even so it was large enough for two humans to stand side-by-side on the substantial window sill.

"It's a little high," Hali said, "but it's the best candidate I've seen recently."

She climbed up on Oliver's shoulders, but the window was beyond her reach. Hali looked down at Ginny, at the window, and at Ginny again.

"Do you think you could climb up here on my shoulders?" Hali asked doubtfully.

"Urk," Oliver muttered, staggering slightly as he turned his head to look at Ginny, who smiled slightly and shook her head.

"I wouldn't know where to start," she said apologetically. "I'd probably bring all of us down if I tried."

Hali grunted. "Don't know if I'd be able to hold your weight, myself." Awkwardly, she climbed down off of Oliver's shoulders, landing heavily. "My knees aren't what they used to be, either. I don't know how Marj stands having all these spells running all the time. My ears are ringing."

Ginny cocked her head. "Maybe there's a spell on us, or on this part of the castle, to keep us from finding anything."

Hali looked at her with a peculiarly sour expression. "Don't teach your grandmother to suck eggs," she snapped. "Of course there's a spell. The problem is figuring out how it works, so we can get around it." She glowered at the window overhead. "If I could get my head out of the window, past the edge of the walls, I could at least tell if the spell is part of the buildings. This pile seems to have been designed with security in mind—doesn't a tooth fairy have something to do with money?"

Not knowing where to start, Oliver explained reluctantly. "The tooth fairy goes around taking baby teeth and leaving cash in their place."

"You're kidding," Hali said skeptically. "All the baby teeth in the world? Before or after they fall out?"

"Um, they fall out and you put them under your pillow and in the morning the tooth is gone and the money's there instead. I don't know if it's the whole world, or just the United States, or what."

"Poor Marj," Hali said quietly, shaking her head. "Well, there's nothing I can do about that now. We've got to get to that window. I'll work back, you guys look ahead; see if you can find a table or chair or something we can stand on. Oh, and keep an eye out for something we can use as rope. We can rip up rugs or wall hangings, but I don't remember how far back we last saw any. Do you?"

Oliver shook his head.

"I looked behind a large arras with black dragons on it," Ginny offered, "but that was miles back."

Hali grimaced. "I don't want to separate that long. Move quickly, and we'll meet back here in about ten minutes."

At a quick jog, Hali located a spindly side table she'd vaguely remembered some six rooms back. She shook it, leaned on it, and finally got on her knees on top of it. Balancing carefully, she stood up and rocked back and forth, and finally jumped up and down with increasing vigor until the little table overturned and dumped the witch with a clatter on the floor. Somewhat embarrassed, Hali froze, but after a few seconds with no sound of outraged pursuit, she scrambled to her feet. She grabbed the table and checked it quickly. Finding no more damage than a few scratches, she picked it up and ran back to meet Oliver and Ginny.

They arrived at the meeting point a few minutes later, without a more sturdy support, but with their arms full of heavy black drapes, and several lengths of silver bullion rope.

"We found these drapes held back with the silver rope,"

Ginny said triumphantly. "We should have no trouble tying enough together to get up the wall."

Hali grunted, pulling out one of the drapes. Laid out straight on the floor, it was easily twice as long as the witch was tall. "Up and down again on the other side, if necessary," Hali told her. "Start tearing, but leave the strips wide."

While Hali and Ginny worked with nails and teeth to tear the heavy fabric, Oliver laid the stiff, twisted silver ropes end to end and carefully knotted them together.

To Oliver's annoyance, Hali checked his work carefully. "I know the difference between a square knot and a granny," he complained.

"A granny?"

"A weak knot, like an old lady would tie."

"I'd watch that kind of talk. Grannies around here wouldn't appreciate the allusion," Hali told him sourly. She gave the ropes a last tug, then quickly started adding lengths of curtain to the end, knotting with a speed and skill that a sailor would have envied.

Not sure whether to be annoyed or embarrassed, Oliver shrugged, and went to check out the little table under the window. With Ginny providing a stabilizing shoulder, he climbed up on it, and accepted the coil of homemade rope Hali handed him.

She tied the end of the rope loosely around her waist, and, with Ginny's assistance, managed to climb up on the table, barely fitting her feet beside Oliver's. Fighting a degree of embarrassment at finding himself pressed so closely to the feisty witch, he stood silently as she proceeded to hoist herself onto his shoulders, using his knees and hips for footholds on the way.

Once on Oliver's shoulders, Hali reached the window easily, and pulled herself up onto the ledge. She knelt there, and, with both hands, grasped and wrenched at the column that divided the window. Finding it solid, she removed the rope from around her waist and tied it firmly to the column. Then, holding on to the column with one hand, she cautiously stuck her head outside the walls, into the sunshine. A quick glance revealed no watchers in sight; Hali leaned out as far as she could, examining the exterior walls of the castle, both above and below her.

Pulling herself back, she leaned inside and waved Oliver and Ginny to her. "We're getting out of here," she told them with a grin. "Get yourselves up here."

Oliver traded places with Ginny, and gave her a boost up to the window ledge. By that time, Hali had disappeared from the ledge, so Oliver was able to pull himself up without worrying about room in the window. He stood up on the ledge, and peered out. The window was surprisingly far above the ground, several stories at least; it was hard to tell with all the dark shadows around the bases of the dark towers. There was no sign of Hali.

"Where is she?"

Ginny pointed straight overhead. Grasping the column for balance, Oliver managed to lean out far enough to get a good look at the wall—and Hali's petticoats and black and red striped socks.

"How come I never noticed those socks before?" he asked, slightly dazed.

"Must have been magic," Ginny told him. "What I want to know is how she's climbing the wall."

Oliver looked closely at the wall above him, then ran his palm over the exterior surface. "There's ridges, really shallow ones, but she must be using them somehow."

He watched Hali's technique carefully. "See? I think she's using the pressure of her fingertips against the ridges, and bracing herself with those pointy-toed boots."

Hali reached a little ornamental ledge some fifteen feet above them. She clung to it with her hands, then started to work her way sideways along the ledge, always looking up. Several feet over, she pulled herself slowly over the little ledge, and then disappeared beyond it. In seconds, she reappeared, looking down at Oliver and Ginny.

"Found a new window," she called. "Toss me the rope."

It took only two tries to get the rope within her reach. Braced against the window frame, Hali anchored the rope. Both careful not to look down, Oliver and Ginny followed quickly up the wall.

Hali reeled in the rope, and left it lying on the floor. "No point in leaving clues to where we've gone."

She stretched her arms vigorously. "I knew all that rock climbing would come in handy some day, but boy, are my arms tired."

Oliver snorted. "Just like flying."

"I beg your pardon?"

"Where now?" Oliver asked quickly.

Hali frowned. "With any luck, we've escaped the enchantment maze."

Looking around the room, Ginny observed, "At least this room looks like someone really lives here. There's rugs and chairs and even a magazine on that table, and even a little color."

"Very little," Hali grunted, observing the sprinkling of scarlet accents about the room. She picked up a black throw pillow embroidered with tiny, bright red hearts, each pierced with a silver nail. With a sigh, she tossed it back on the over-stuffed black armchair.

"Marj never could resist the sentimental touch," Hali observed. "Let's get searching."

Oliver and Ginny threw themselves into the work, and soon no unattached cushion or drawer remained in its place. Hali checked behind a couple of wall hangings, then moved to the next room, a bedroom. From there, the trio found themselves in a round room bare of fixtures except for a stairway leading up and down.

"Excellent. We're in the center of a tower," Hali observed. "We'll split up and search all the rooms on this floor, and then we'll head up."

In minutes, the searchers had wreaked havoc on a linen closet, two more bedrooms, and a surprisingly modern bathroom. Finding no sign of Hali's pouch, they rejoined at the stairs.

"This is going to take forever," Ginny gasped.

"Then there's no time to lose, is there?" Hali led the way up, taking the stairs two at a time. At the first landing, she stopped briefly, wrinkling her nose.

"Should we start searching?" Ginny asked.

Absently, Hali shook her head. "No, I'm starting to pick something up. Hold on, I'm going to try listening for my bag. If it's close, I should be able to pick it up without disturbing any of Marj's spells."

She closed her eyes and stood there for several seconds. When she opened her eyes, she pointed upstairs. "We're in luck. It's up there, somewhere. Keep climbing."

Hali raced upward. The stairs wound around and around the central core of the tower, the only light coming from narrow, irregularly placed windows, little more than archer's slits, and the occasional open door on the landings. Hali passed each landing without a glance, leaving Oliver and Ginny to struggle after her.

Leaning against the wall at one landing, Oliver watched Hali bound upstairs in amazement.

"How old did she say she was?" he asked.

"Hundreds of years, I thought," Ginny said, panting hard. "Pretty well preserved, isn't she?"

Oliver could only groan as he pushed himself off the wall and headed shakily for the next flight of stairs.

On a landing several stories up, Hali stopped and tilted her head, listening intently. Suddenly she spun around, and ducked into a room. Oliver and Ginny were too far behind to see where she went, but once they reached the landing they had no difficulty finding the witch; they just followed the rhythmic sound of bureau drawers being drawn, dumped, and thrown on the floor with a clatter.

"What took you?" Hali snapped the minute they entered the door. "Never mind, get looking. It's around here somewhere, but I can't tell where. There's too many spells."

Neither Oliver nor Ginny was surprised. Wide windows provided plenty of cheerful light, but the room was filled with arcane paraphernalia: long stone-topped tables covered with oddly shaped pots and glassware; jars filled with powders and herbs, and burlap bags filled with charcoal, sulfur, and rock salt. Several large cabinets and sets of drawers lined the inside wall, and it was here that Hali methodically searched. Avoiding the flying drawers, Oliver and Ginny split up, taking opposite ends of the room.

An open fireplace filled one wall. Finding it cool, Oliver checked the ashes, and then climbed high enough to feel the area above the flue. Sooty but determined, he moved next to two small ovens that sat against the outside wall. One was charcoal fired and the other wood, he discovered, but neither concealed Hali's purse. Nor did the sacks of fuel, which he upended and emptied with a certain glee.

At the other end of the room, Ginny quickly eliminated a heavy stone sink (the drain simply led outside, she determined with a glance out the windows). Huge ceramic jugs on shelves above the sink held water, drained through a siphon system. Ginny removed the spring clamps that held the siphon tubes closed. Having set the jugs to drain, she moved on to large urns sitting on the floor. These held a variety of crystals, powders, and even grains. Careful not to touch the contents, Ginny emptied the urns onto the floor, one after another, with as much speed as she could manage.

"Aha!" Hali cried, standing at the open doors to a squat cupboard. She rubbed her hands gleefully as she scanned the colorful, closed compartments inside, each painted a different gaudy color, with designs in silver and gold scattered over the whole.

"This thing's got magic seals all over it. One touch and alarms are going to ring all over. Now, which one is it?"

Oliver and Ginny dropped the containers they were searching and picked their way across the rubble to Hali's side.

"Alarms?" Oliver said nervously.

"Right," Hali said absently. "We won't have much time once I open the first drawer, so I'd better get it right the first time."

Without quite touching the surface, she ran her hands over the compartments, paused for a second, then started again. Each time her hands came to the lower left section of the cupboard, she paused. Finally, she held her hands over just that section, narrowing her search to two compartments large enough to hold her belt pouch. Wiggling her fingers, she hesitated over the two. Finally, she set her jaw, and touched the compartment on the left edge of the cabinet.

With yellow sparks, a tiny puff of smoke, and a musical tone, a drawer popped open.

"Yes!" Hali crowed, snatching her purse from inside.

Suddenly, thunder rolled in the room, deafeningly close, and Sinestra appeared in a cloud of oily smoke.

"What do you think you're doing?" she screeched, pointing her wand at Hali.

"What I should have done at the start," Hali told her calmly, and reached into her bag.

CHAPTER
22

HALI pulled her closed fist out of her purse, and with a quick snap of her wrist threw a handful of grey dust at Sinestra. As if in fear, the black fairy stepped backward and held up her wand in a desperate warding gesture. The dust spread out into a glittering fog that threatened to envelop Sinestra—but the black dot that followed the tip of her wand cut a quick swath through the cloud, sucking up the dust as if it had never been.

"Ha!" Sinestra crowed. With a grand, sweeping gesture, she crossed her wrists above her head. Fire poured out from her fingertips, racing to envelop Oliver, Ginny, and Hali in glistening webs of magic. Oliver and Ginny found themselves completely immobilized by impossibly strong strands of light. Hali fought the web, and for her the strands became elastic, allowing her to move only so far before snapping back into place with an electric crackle.

"Did you think I wouldn't be prepared?" Sinestra laughed triumphantly as Hali writhed. "I put spells on everything, everywhere I could think of, before you even got here. I can't hurt you magically, you're too strong for that, but all I have to do is hold you physically, and keep you from using your own talents. Then all I have to do is affect the things around you—the air, for example—and there's nothing you can do about it.

"I've been thinking about this for a long time, you know. You've been a thorn in my side since school. Most girls your age would have still been at home, or at best starting an apprenticeship with a local witch. But you! You turn your mother into a pig, and as a reward they send you off to Hexmont—something most girls only dream of, an honor reserved for the most talented and deserving."

"It wasn't a reward, believe me," Hali rasped out. "I was too young to know what I was doing."

"Silence!" Sinestra sent another bolt of magic at Hali. "You showed us all up from the start. And you didn't care! You could have gone on to higher studies, you could have ruled the world."

Busy fending off the glittering ring of spellstuff that now spun about her head, threatening to strangle her, Hali only grunted in protest.

"You could tell Administration what to do, even now. You know Bentwood's afraid of you, of what you could do. But just as before, you turn away from your power, your responsibilities!"

"I gave you a chance," Sinestra said quietly, suddenly calm. "I asked you nicely to join us. You turned me down."

On her knees, Hali had both hands inside the magic band that circled her face. Sweat ran down her cheeks as she wrestled the rubbery substance away from her nose and mouth. "I don't want to run the world, even if I could, which I doubt," she snarled. "I just want to be left alone to do my work."

"You have one more chance," Sinestra told her, coming close to lean over Hali and enjoy her humiliation. "One more chance. Join now, and I'll let you live. I want your oath, sworn in blood on the rising moon. I can't trust you anymore, I see that now. You have to swear or die. You're too dangerous to me alive."

In the background, Oliver gurgled as he strained against his restraints. Hali's eyes darted to him quickly, then back again to the insane fairy looming over her.

"What about them?" she gasped.

Sinestra's gaze never wavered. "Oh, them?" she said

lightly, with a wave of her wand. "If you agree, I'll let them live. Why not? They're no danger to me."

Frozen in their glistening cocoons, Ginny and Oliver waited wide-eyed for Hali's decision. Sinestra smiled widely.

"Well, what do you say? You really haven't any choice." She held out one hand, palm up, to Hali. When there was no response from the kneeling witch, the fairy's grin grew stiff. Slowly, carefully, she closed her hand into a fist, and as she tightened it, the ring about Hali's face also tightened, closing in on her nose and mouth.

Hali kept her hands, now curled into fists, within the ring. For the moment, she held the ring at bay, but the pressure was turning her knuckles white, and grinding her fingers into her cheekbones.

"Give up!" Sinestra howled, waving her clenched fist in Hali's face.

"No," Hali grunted, eyes closed.

"Yesss," hissed the fairy. "You can't hold out for long."

Hali didn't respond.

Sinestra glared. "I can wait," she said. "I've waited a long time already. A few minutes more can't matter."

Several seconds passed, the only sound the dripping of water in the sink. Sinestra kept her eyes fixed on Hali.

"Dear, dear, your arms are trembling!" the fairy told Hali in a treacly voice. "Don't you think it's time to give in?"

Eyes still closed, Hali made no movement or sound to suggest she'd even heard the fairy. Her face was pale and contorted, the strain evident in the hunching of her shoulders.

"Tsk, such a tantrum," the fairy joked, but her gaze never wavered from Hali's face.

Suddenly, a deep rumbling filled the air, followed by an explosive thump that set the tower walls to vibrating.

"What!" exclaimed the dark fairy, snapping her head toward the windows.

In a flash, Hali was on her feet, wrenching at the strangling spell spinning around her head. With a snap, the ring parted, and Hali used the momentum to fling the broken bits at the fairy, who had already turned back, dismay at her mistake written in her face. The magic band smacked Sinestra in the face, and started sparkling madly, quickly growing to cover her entire head.

With a furious screech, the fairy ripped the rubbery substance from her face, but not before Hali had grabbed the wand out of her hand.

"Well, now," Hali said mildly, leaning nonchalantly against the wall and toying idly with the wand. "This puts quite a different complexion on things, doesn't it?"

Only the angry red and white marks of her knuckles, still visible on her face, reflected Hali's recent ordeal. Her expression was benign, her voice gentle, but even so Sinestra began backing away.

"Hali, girl, don't do anything you'll regret later," the fairy babbled. "We've always been friends, I only wanted to make you see. It was all in your best interests, I swear. Perhaps I got a little carried away...."

"Hey!" Oliver, freed in the instant Hali broke loose, had run to the windows to check on the disturbance. Now he was leaning out, waving frantically. "It's our guys! Look, down there. They blew up the walls!"

"What?" Hali and Sinestra both cried in astonishment.

Ginny ran to the windows and peered out. "It is them! Jamison's attacking the ogres. And there's Bernie and Leo. They're attacking, too."

"Oh, no," Hali sighed. "Just what I need, a bunch of dead heroes."

That instant, the room lit with a bright flash and thunder rolled. Sinestra disappeared in a dark cloud of smoke.

"Marj!" Hali howled, and shook her fist at the ceiling. "You can't get away now. I've got your wand."

Coming back to herself, Hali shook her head. "Blast. Lose my concentration for one second, and see what happens. Now ..."

Turning around, she eyed the room speculatively. She raised the wand and spun it over her head so fast it scribed shining circles in the air. Light spread out in spiraling waves from the central circle. Whatever the light touched began to glow with a light of its own; the spell-locked drawers in the open cabinet burst open with showers of sparks, while several jars burst noisily on their shelves. The light spread into the walls themselves, and beyond. At the windows, Oliver and Ginny could see black buildings turning into shining white teeth wherever the rings of light passed.

"You two, over here, by me," Hali ordered.

Oliver and Ginny rushed to comply. Once they were within the orbit of the spinning wand, Hali snapped her fingers, and the three faded swiftly from the room.

Down in the courtyard, Jamison barreled into the ogres attacking his dung pile. Using his heavy forearms as a furious moose might use its antlers, he started scooping up and tossing ogres right and left. Despite his recent flight, he fought with tireless speed, but with limited effect. Too heavy to throw far, the ogres with their heavy muscles and bulging bellies tended to bounce when they hit the ground. With gold to win, they came back fighting. Only those ogres unlucky enough to hit a nearby section of the wall went splat with sufficient force to render them unconscious.

However, the bug and the gold together provided a considerable distraction for the ogres. Carefully but quickly, Bernie, Leo, and Tracy sneaked through the gaping hole in the wall, picking their way through the manure-strewn rubble while keeping as far as possible from the battle of the dung heap. Then an ogre came flying at them, feetfirst and screaming. Tracy managed to duck, but Leo was caught off balance. By luck, he had been holding Hali's staff up and away from the wall; the ogre caught one end of the staff between his legs, driving the other end into the wall. The ogre screamed in agony, the staff sizzled, and Leo yelled as the heavy ogre slammed into the wall, knocking the gamer off his feet and the staff out of his hands.

Leo scrambled to the staff. He pulled at it, but it was stuck under the groaning ogre. Staying as far as he could from the writhing monster, Leo worked the staff back and forth until it finally came free with a little spark.

"Come on!" Tracy urged, pulling at his shoulder. "The ogres have seen us."

Leo looked up and realized that several ogres were pointing in his direction from their vantage point atop the dung heap.

"Oops," he said, and started to run for the clear space of the castle courtyard, with Tracy hot on his heels.

They didn't get far. More ogres, off-shift latecomers to judge by their lack of armor, appeared on the far side of the courtyard. Not yet distracted by the presence of gold, these ogres were ready to do battle. They raised their clubs, and, shouting rude war cries, rushed at the gamers.

More by instinct than by plan, Tracy and Leo stood back to back and waited, Tracy facing the dung-heap ogres, Leo the newcomers in the courtyard.

"We're doomed," Tracy yelled over the ogres' clamor. "Where's Bernie?"

"I don't know," Leo called back. "I hope he gets away."

"Hey, the ogres aren't chasing us," Tracy cried in astonishment.

Leo risked a lightning glance behind him, and saw that the ogres behind him had indeed stopped, and were standing uncertainly at the edge of the dung pile, greed warring with duty in their brutish faces. Greed appeared to have the upper edge in the conflict, and with renewed hope Leo turned back to meet the ogres rushing toward him.

"Talk fast!" he told Tracy. "Talk fast, and start throwing gold at the new ogres."

"What?" Tracy asked incredulously, catching the small coin she spit out in the process.

"Throw the gold, any gold. Divide and conquer," Leo gasped out quickly, and raised Hali's staff to take the first blow from the oncoming horde.

To his surprise, the ogre's club struck the staff and rebounded with an electric crackle. The blow was solid enough to sting Leo's hands, but not enough to make him drop the staff. The ogre wasn't so fortunate. With an angry howl he dropped his club and blew frantically on his smoking palm. Then, shaking his injured hand, the ogre shrieked in outraged warning, "Magic, magic, magic!"

By that time, Leo had lashed out, almost without thinking, striking two more ogres on the head and shoulder. The blows had not been heavy enough to disconcert either ogre, but to Leo's amazement the two danced about screaming, with wisps of smoke rising from the spots where Hali's staff had struck.

"Yee-haw!" Leo yelled, eagerly dashing into battle, knocking brawny ogres aside as easily as if they had been straw dummies. Unfortunately, unlike dummies, the ogres seemed inclined to take offense once they were over the first shock.

Behind Leo, Tracy let words gush forth, saying anything that came to mind: the Pledge of Allegiance, prayers, scraps of nursery rhymes. She caught coins in one hand and threw with the other, letting the roses fall where they might, and not pausing in her rapid-fire babble even when she ran out of things to say. She wasn't entirely sure she wanted the ogres to identify her as the source of gold, but several had already started scrabbling in the dust for the coins (providing Leo with easy targets in the process) so Tracy kept talking, hardly heeding what she said.

However, she had the presence of mind to keep one eye on the dung heap, and thus happened to be looking upward when strange bands of light came spiraling down from the castle's tall central tower, spreading along the walls and finally over the dung heap. Jamison was barely holding his own against the avaricious ogres, but as the light swept over him, Tracy was horrified to see the beetle fading into man.

The wave of light hit him head first. As the wave passed over him, he looked at the human arms with which he was futilely trying to pick up an ogre, and his suddenly human head screamed in pure anguish. Before the stunned ogre could react, though, Jamison's scream turned to fury. Almost instantly, his fingers turned back to heavy prongs, then his wrists and arms. In a blink of an eye, he was all beetle again, and the unfortunate ogre went flying.

Tracy felt nothing as the light passed over her, and Leo hardly registered its passage—until he realized that Hali's staff was no longer a staff but now a homemade broom. Nor did its touch cause small burns when it struck the ogres; now the lightest touch of straw or stick sent ogres flying, leaving them stunned or unconscious where they fell.

"Wow, this is great!" he shouted. "I knew all I needed was a magic weapon. We're sweeping up!"

"Yeah, right," Tracy growled from immediately behind him, just as a tiny black arrow buried itself in the dust at Leo's feet. "Tell that to the guys with the bows."

"Drop your weapons and put your hands up," a squeaky voice called from the rounded toothtop battlements of a nearby two-story molar. Leo, and those ogres still standing, looked up to see a horde of black imps dancing over the glistening white building.

"Hey, the flicker's gone." Still holding the broom like a quarterstaff, Leo gaped at the building.

"Pay attention," an imp screeched. "Drop the weapon or you'll look like a pincushion."

Shaking their fists at the imps, the ogres jeered. "What a bunch of spoilsports. We had these guys on the ropes."

"Yah, yah, yah!" the imps mocked, jumping up and down. "Big dumb ogres couldn't beat a chicken before it hatched."

Her back pressed against Leo's, Tracy whispered, "Jamison's probably arrowproof, but we've got to get to cover while they're distracted."

"Right."

As the ogres and imps exchanged insults, Leo and Tracy sidled toward the edge of the courtyard. But before they could escape the battlefield, a high-pitched command to stop sent them running for their lives.

"All right, you asked for it!" shrieked one imp, indistinguishable from the rest. He raised his bow, arrow nocked, and then screamed as a plummeting black object struck him in the chest, knocking imp and arrows off the top of the building.

The black object split off on widespread wings, revealing itself to be a large black crow. The ogres and imps shouted in outrage, and prepared to follow as the bird and gamers disappeared around the nearest corner.

They sped between two buildings. At the first crossing, the two humans hesitated, debating which way to go. "Left!" ordered the crow, and they darted into a dark series of accessways at the base of the castle towers. The humans were soon winded. At Leo's urging they ducked into a dark doorway for a breather. Leo peered cautiously back the way they'd come, and the crow landed on his shoulder with a harsh scream.

"Aaagh!" Leo shrieked, batting at the bird.

"Hey, let up, it's me, Bernie," the crow snapped, beating back at Leo with his wings.

Leo froze. "Bernie?"

The crow cawed in laughter. "Told you I was really a crow, didn't I? I was looking for an entrance into the castle when the spell front caught me, and Whammo! I was a bird again.

"That was a good idea, by the way, distracting the ogres, but we can't avoid them forever. We've got to get into the castle and find Hali if we want to get out of here with our skins intact."

"Where do we look?" Tracy asked, looking up at the central tower, its shining enamel white against the blue sky. "This place is huge."

"Well, if you'd hold still for any length of time . . . " Hali's voice came out of the air. The startled trio looked over their shoulders, trying to find the source of the sound.

With a faint pop and rush of air, Hali, Ginny, and Oliver appeared before them. Over his shoulder Oliver held the black tooth fairy, sputtering threats and kicking furiously. Despite the feet waving in front of his eyes, Oliver ignored her, except to occasionally push her stiff tutu out of his face. With glad cries, Ginny and Tracy embraced, while Leo and Oliver grinned at each other.

"Hali!" Bernie crowed ecstatically, flapping over to land on her shoulder. "I hate to say it, but I missed you. Have to say though, that's an awfully silly replacement you've got there for your broom."

"Quiet, bird," Hali snapped, tapping him on the head with the twinkling wand. No longer obscured by the wandering black dot, the wand was brightly pretty, a precious toy. Hali eyed it sourly. "It's not mine, it's Marj's. By the way, I'll take that back, now." She reached out for her broom.

Leo hugged the broom tight for a second, then with a re-signed sigh handed it over. "Works great on ogres," he said meekly. "Who's that Oliver's got?"

"I guess you'd call her the wicked witch." One eyebrow

raised, Hali examined her broom closely. "Hmmph. Seems to be all right." Quickly, she detailed the failed tooth fairy's role in the revolution, and her defeat.

"Once we had her wand, it was easy to track her down and take her in hand. So, now it's all over except for the mopping up. What did you do with Jamison?"

Tracy pointed back the way they'd run. "We left him back by the hole in the wall."

"You left him to fend for himself as a human?" For a second, Hali looked just a bit alarmed.

"He's still a bug," Tracy reassured her. "He seemed to be able to take care of himself."

"I missed that," Bernie said, curious. "How did he escape the light wave that dewombatized me and the broom?"

"It hit him, and he halfway changed," Tracy explained. "But then he screamed and changed back."

"That light was a spell neutralizer," Hali explained. "It took the color and space distort off the castle, and should have taken the spell protection off the ogres."

"No wonder the broom zapped them harder than the staff. The ogres lost their protection," Leo said, wistfully eyeing the dangerous cleaning implement.

"I'm surprised the staff was effective," Hali said.

"Wherever it touched, it gave the ogres a little zap and burned them," Leo said.

Hali reexamined the ends of her broom with tender concern. "No spell warping, thank goodness. I grew this broom, tree and straw. Combined with your talent for destroying things, it's got enough magic built into it to short-circuit the ogres' defensive shields. Marj here probably designed the warding spells to defeat my talents in particular, so you had an unexpected edge. Protection and transformation spells are generally temporary, and easily removed by contact with outside magic, but sometimes there's feedback—that's the zap. It can be really tricky to undo someone else's transformations."

"But why didn't Jamison change permanently?" Tracy persisted.

Hali just shrugged. "Some people simply can't let go of a spell. When it fades, a certain amount of magical force is released, and in that instant almost any effort of imagination or determination can redirect that energy. He must really like being an insect."

Leo snickered. "I guess it lets him be himself."

"Exactly." Hali nodded. "The same for Bernie. He's a flighty, irresponsible scavenger by nature, so—a crow." She ruffled his neck feathers fondly. Bernie considered complaining, but Hali was so seldom this mellow he decided to get his pleasure while he could, and stretched his neck out for a good scratch.

"I don't want to disturb this tender reunion," Oliver broke in, "but this witch is getting heavy."

"One moment." Hali held her broom and the witch's wand in front of her and tapped them together three times. Then, sticking the starry end of the wand on the ground, she broke the shaft with a sharp blow of her heel. The captive fairy groaned, and sagged against Oliver's shoulder. Hali stooped to pick up the pieces of the wand and turned to Oliver.

"All right, you can let her go."

Oliver carefully deposited the fairy on the ground, but she had gone limp and pale; even Sinestra's tutu had lost its stiffness, hanging sadly around her spindly legs. Oliver had to keep one hand under her elbow to hold her up.

"You always were too dependent on your props and magic," Hali told the fairy, dropping the pieces of the wand into her trembling hands. "The least you could do is use real starch."

The fairy sobbed quietly over the pieces of her wand.

Hali rolled her eyes. "Let's go find the beetle."

Bernie led the way back to the battle site, darting ahead and swooping back with giddy joy. Hali followed at a brisk walk that had the others jogging to keep up, Ginny and Oliver dragging the bedraggled fairy between them. They encountered a pair of guards not far from the wall. Stunned to see their quarry approaching voluntarily, in augmented numbers, the wary ogres approached slowly. Then they got a good look at Oliver's captive, and Hali's frown, and decided discretion was definitely the better part of valor.

The courtyard battle had progressed to mudslinging, with the imps' verbal ammunition proving sharper than the ogres' handfuls of manure, though the roses' thorns provided some distraction. Jamison had chased the ogres off the main body of the dung pile, but not before the bulk of the visible gold was gone. Now furious but exhausted, he fought futilely to stem the ogres' depredations on the outer edges of the pile.

Hali stopped at the edge of the courtyard and watched with raised eyebrows. The few ogres who noticed the group of humans quietly crept away. The rest fought on, interspersing attacks on the imps with the occasional ogre-to-ogre scuffle over a freshly revealed coin.

More than a minute passed in this manner before Hali sent Leo into the fray to collect Jamison. The beetle protested, but weakly, and Leo managed to get him away from the dung heap and over to Hali without any trouble.

Hali shook her head. "Such accomplices, Marj. Is this what you were reduced to?" She lifted her broom, transformed it back into an iron-shod staff, and brought one end down on the pavement with a crack of thunder. Three times she struck, and on the third blow the heavens—sunny only seconds before—opened, and rain sheeted down in torrents upon the combatants below.

Wet imps are miserable imps; the castle's contingent surrendered without a fight. The ogres were not disturbed by the water, but were impressed by the flood as a demonstration of power, and those that couldn't sneak away dropped their weapons and raised their arms.

"Hali's always had a knack with weather," Bernie confided to Tracy, shaking his tailfeathers dry. "Such a show-off."

"I wish she'd stuck to lightning," Tracy complained. "I didn't think it was possible, but wet ogres smell even worse than dry ones."

The gamers collected the weapons, and Hali escorted the ogres into the dungeons before calling up Bentwood in a handy mirror. She made short work of the three receptionists who in turn insisted that Bentwood was unavailable, ill, and in conference. Finally, the troll appeared, his haggard visage a pale lavender streaked with green, more wanly froglike than ever.

"Bentwood, you look like death warmed over. Having a bad day?"

The troll grinned weakly. "Hali, sweetie, how are ya? Listen doll, I'd love to chat, but no time. Let's do lunch one of these days."

Hali waggled one admonitory finger at the mirror. "You're not avoiding me that easily."

Bentwood fidgeted with his cravat. "Look Hali, I'm hip deep in problems here."

"Like a little strike?"

Bentwood started nervously. "Strike? I told you, there's no problem with the unions, no problem at all. I can't imagine where you'd get an idea like that."

"Like maybe I ran headfirst into a bunch of union thugs? Bentwood, you held out on me."

"Look, I've got it under control. Trust me."

"About as far as I can throw you, troll. *I've* got the situation under control for you. If you're interested, send a reliable security crew over."

Hope was just beginning to dawn on Bentwood's face when Hali wiped her hand over the mirror, breaking contact. Hali chuckled. "That'll bring 'em."

CHAPTER
23

HALI waited for the security troops to arrive and take custody of Sinestra, then gathered her gamers together in the courtyard. Even Whitenose was present; the patrol that had chased the gamers off the cliff made its way back to the castle only to find it under enemy control. Outnumbered, the patrol meekly surrendered the donkey, and joined their comrades in the dungeons.

Jamison had spent the wait hard at work, and refused to leave his resurrected dung ball behind. Not only had he scraped up the dampened sludge from the courtyard, he also added bits of offal and excrement from some heaps found rotting behind the kitchens. What the resulting ball lacked in size and weight it made up in juicy smell, and the giant scarab was more than satisfied with the result.

The other gamers had trouble waiting quietly. They found themselves, in the aftermath of battle, filled with an energy that made it impossible to hold still. Hali declined to explain why they waited, ignoring even Bernie's badgering. Finally, a section of the courtyard began to glow. A group of dwarves and a human wizard in full regalia appeared. The wizard pulled some sticks out of his sleeve and tossed them on the ground. As they hit, the sticks transformed into flat boards and poles, quickly seized by the dwarves. With bustling efficiency, they constructed a raised platform. The wizard produced scraps of cloth that became a canopy and a magnificent, gold-edged red carpet. The dwarves stood aside, the wizard gestured, and, with an impressive fanfare of invisible trumpets, a scrawny troll appeared in the center of the platform, dressed in a black silk smoking jacket and looking quite smug.

"Hali, doll, good to see you," Bentwood crowed, stepping down from the platform. "Couldn't believe my ears when the boys told me what you'd done. You've solved a sticky situation, let me tell you. Can you believe old Marj? I give her an important, influential job like tooth fairy, and how does she respond? Is that gratitude?"

"I think it was about as much gratitude as you deserved," Hali observed.

"That's my girl, always joking," Bentwood laughed and slapped her on the back hard enough to shake Bernie off her shoulder.

"Gee, Bentwood, got a death wish all of a sudden?" Bernie asked nastily, flapping back to his perch.

"Bernie, don't make fun of the mentally deficient," Hali told him sternly.

Blushing a bright green, Bentwood turned to the rest of the company, arms open wide. The sight of Jamison stopped him for a second, but he recovered quickly. "Well, here are our valiant gamers. Congratulations to you all! You've far exceeded our highest expectations. I can't tell you how grateful we are. You've saved our little world from a terrorist rebellion. How can we ever repay you?"

"Who is this geek?" Leo asked.

Bernie cawed. "Bentwood's head paper pusher and chief petty nuisance around here."

Sudden comprehension dawned on the gamers' faces. "So that's a Bentwood," Oliver murmured. "Such a small creature to cause such trouble, and so—amphibian."

With as much dignity as a frog-faced troll could manage, Bentwood ignored the hecklers in the crowd. "Friends, as a small token of our gratitude, we want you to be our guests at the new Grimmworld Theme Park."

Startled into laughing, Hali quickly covered her mouth and converted the sound into a cough. Bentwood glared at her suspiciously, but when she made no further comment he continued, "In fact, you'll be our first guests. The park hasn't officially opened yet, so you'll be having a special preview of the greatest vacation spot ever invented. I guarantee you'll get the red carpet treatment you deserve as real heroes. Hali, if you will do the honors?"

Hali shrugged, and gestured the gamers onto the platform. With a brief hitch while the dwarves helped Jamison get his dung ball up on the platform and Tracy persuaded Whitenose that the red carpet wasn't some exotic variety of serpent, the gamers assembled in the center of the little stage, with Bentwood squeezed uncomfortably in between Jamison and his ball. Hali quietly walked in a circle around the group, then joined them. With a nod of her head, the group faded out of the castle courtyard and reappeared on a larger, permanent platform in front of a magnificent rose-covered gateway of wrought iron that read, in huge gilded letters, "Grimmworld."

The gates swung open without visible assistance, and the gamers walked through into a quaint medieval village, from which they had an excellent view of the huge park beyond, filled with dozens of castles, lakes, and even an artificial mountain topped with a huge mechanical dragon that periodically flapped its wings and breathed out a jet of bright orange fire.

"Wow," Leo exclaimed. "A cleaned-up version of the game. Why bother, though?"

Bentwood chuckled, and smoothly went into his official spiel. "We're thinking big, here at Grimmworld. Once the game takes off, we expect more people will want to participate than our computers can handle. The theme park will provide an additional outlet for those who want to share the experience, particularly families with small children who wouldn't be able to handle the game itself."

He waved at the park laid out before them. "All this is actually the computer model for the real-world park we're building. Since we have the computer capability to bring a world to life, we decided to do our planning here, where we can test various designs. As long as you're already here in Grimmworld, I thought you might like a look at our little project. I'm looking forward to your input."

Bentwood led the group to a quaint inn, where they checked in for the night and arranged stabling for Whitenose and incidentally for Jamison, who declined to leave once he found the highly authentic dung heap out back.

Bentwood proudly escorted the rest of the group on a stroll around the village. Ogres in cute polka-dots shorts and beanies walked the quaint cobbled streets, hawking souvenirs that included goblin masks, artificial elf ears, and little stuffed trolls that bore a strange resemblance to Bentwood. Bernie was tickled to find a porcelain rendition of Hali with staff and dramatic cape, looking just as she had when the adventure began.

"Well, maybe a bit bigger in the chest," Bernie chortled, pointing out the statuette. Hali wasn't quite so amused, but neither was Bernie when Tracy impulsively spent one of her gold coins on a life-sized stuffed wombat with a collar clearly labeled "Bernie, the Witch's Friend."

"I don't suppose we can take these back with us," Tracy said. "But I just couldn't resist."

"Actually," Bentwood reassured her, "souvenirs purchased here will be replaced with identical real-world objects when you leave. As the first group through, you won't be charged." He beamed at Tracy, highly impressed by his own generosity.

Bernie hopped onto a nearby booth to examine his namesake. "Friend?" he squawked, reading the label. "It's bad enough I had to be a wombat, I can't be a familiar anymore?"

Bentwood shook his head, checking to make sure the gamers had moved out of earshot. He spoke quietly. "Bad connotations. We're fighting an antiwitchcraft prejudice, here."

"Witches are OK, but familiars aren't?"

The troll shrugged. "That's what the guys in marketing research say. And by the way, you're out of uniform, bird."

"Tough," Bernie told him. "The adventure's over, remember?"

"You'd better be back in fur before the next one starts."

"Next one! This one was a total fiasco. There's not going to be another one, is there? Hali!"

The day had been a long one for the gamers, and they were soon ready to return to the inn. Their rooms in the elegant Trollbridge Suite featured balconies from which they had an excellent view of the park—and the truly spectacular fireworks show.

The next day, Hali and Bernie cornered Bentwood for a little chat, leaving the gamers to their own devices for the rest of the day. Jamison showed no inclination to leave his ball, so he was left behind to happily putter around the stable dung heap. Armed with an illustrated guide map, the others took off to explore, Leo and Tracy in the lead. Attracted by the odd buildings at the edge of the park, they took a route past the ziggurat and Egyptian pyramid, and across a series of canals to an Aztec temple, where a sign offered "Sacrifices at Noon Daily." Leo noted the place for later, and the group moved on. Tracy pushed Leo firmly past a Greek temple with beckoning maidens on the porch. The miniature Enchanted Wood caught the group's attention, with its dark pathways and gibbering beasties in the shadows, but overall the gamers felt it lacked authority.

"No danger, nothing on the real thing," Leo judged, thumbing his nose at a giant, hairy grey spider dangling on a thread just beside the path. But even he was impressed, and Tracy ecstatic, when a unicorn, glimmering white in the gloom, leaped across the path and disappeared into the brush.

Even a unicorn could not divert Tracy long from her ultimate goal—shopping. With unerring instincts she led the way to the Country Fair, where minstrels and tumblers entertained and merchants hawked their wares, though Tracy was somewhat disappointed to find their wares ran mostly to souvenirs. The group lost Leo briefly to a stall selling meat rolls, but once sated, he caught up again and threw himself into the shopping with frightening enthusiasm.

He paused in this orgy of shopping to join Oliver at a shooting range, where players could shoot at a variety of authentic Grimmworld monsters with magical self-loading crossbows. Tracy joined them briefly, and with her first arrow shot an ogre in the chest. She watched its dramatic death throes in dismay, and sighed with relief when it finally disappeared with a little flash of light. "This is silly," she said, putting down her crossbow and accepting a cheap medallion on a chain as her prize. "They can't be real, or the unions would really be complaining," she pointed out to Leo as he snapped off two quick shots and pegged a pair of goblins before they could race across the stage to safety.

"Besides, it's too easy," Oliver complained. "It doesn't feel right."

"Oh, phooey," Leo muttered, missing a tricky shot at a dancing black imp. "But it's nice to get a shot at them out in the open for once." With regret, he put his bow down and took his prize, a small plaque proclaiming him a champion archer. "At least the prizes are classy."

Laden down with souvenirs, the gamers decided to return to the inn and drop them off before continuing further. After a little discussion, Oliver and Ginny decided to split off on their own.

"This is our last day," Oliver said. "We'd like to spend it together. By ourselves. Right?"

A little sadly, Ginny agreed.

"Well, here, take some of these coins. Prices are steep here." Tracy passed out several coins each to Ginny and Oliver.

"Great!" Leo said, taking Tracy by one arm. "Now let's you and me see what trouble we can get into."

"How romantic. Just you, me, and my gold?"

"You got it," Leo admitted cheerfully. "There's no way they'll let us take real gold with us—let's see if we can't spend it faster than you can spit it out."

Late in the afternoon, Hali sent Bernie winging across the park to collect the gamers. Taking the opportunity to do a little sight-seeing, the crow flew up to the top of the dragon on the park's central peak. He landed on the dragon's head and pecked at it, the hollow ring reassuring him that the incredibly detailed reptile was indeed metal.

From his high vantage point, Bernie had an excellent view of the grounds. Though he would rather be plucked than admit it, he thought Bentwood and his crew had done a good job with the park. The odd architectural mix Bernie had seen the first time through was only one edge of the park, the buildings designed to serve as luxury hotels and office space. The rest of the city-sized layout mixed parklands, tall castles, a noisy country fair, and several tiny villages, all in different styles. A lazy river wound its way around the park, magically flowing smoothly back into itself where it started. Gaily colored boats trimmed with waving banners floated gently on the current, ready for tourists. Spotting Oliver and Ginny in the bow of one of the boats, Bernie nodded to himself. Leo and Tracy, however, eluded him.

With little metallic clanks and groans, the dragon underneath Bernie sprang to life. Bernie took flight, dropping backward quickly as the mechanical monster opened its eyes, turned its head, and roared straight at the startled crow. The dragon then flapped its wings and spat flame, just as it had before, but Bernie was willing to swear that the bronze dragon had actually winked at him.

"There's worse things to be than wombats," Bernie decided with a shudder.

Recalled to his duty, Bernie headed straight for Oliver and Ginny's boat and told them to return to the inn. Neither had any idea where the others had gone, though Oliver suggested the zoo, since Tracy had expressed an interest in the griffin exhibit. Ginny recommended Bernie check the Truly Gruesome Torture Chamber, which Leo had wanted to see. However, Bernie finally tracked the two down deep under Dragon's Peak, dancing with gnomes in the crystal-studded Hall of the Mountain King.

"Better than a disco," was Leo's verdict.

With dozens of gnomes waving good-bye, the gamers headed back to the inn. There, Hali waited with Jamison and Whitenose. The donkey carried two large baskets filled with souvenirs.

"I packed for you so we could get going quicker," Hali said. "Been doing a bit of shopping, have we?"

Tracy blushed, and hurried to hide a porcelain witch under a pair of Grimmworld T-shirts. "Well, Bentwood said we could have souvenirs, and I had all that gold to get rid of. . . . "

"Yeah. I got myself a great enchanted sword. Did you

pack it?" Leo pulled the sword in question out of one of the baskets, and drew it from its sheath. "See, says right here, 'This sworde be magik.' At least I'll have something to show the guys."

"Besides the Grimmworld underwear, socks, slippers, cap, bath towels, and, oh yes, the official souvenir chamber pot?" Hali held the offending item, decorated with delicate images of unicorns and elves, at arm's length.

Leo snatched it from her. "Hey, I thought the sanitary conditions around here were the most convincing part of the whole scenario. Do you know, I was even a little disappointed to find modern plumbing in our inn. I'll treasure this, believe me." He stuffed the pot back in the basket, carefully padding it with a pair of official Grimmworld scarves. "And don't forget the wombats." He pointed out four of the stuffed creatures at the bottom of one of the baskets. "We couldn't pass up those precious reminders of our visit."

Bernie sniffed. "Why four of them?' he asked suspiciously.

"I bought one, and then Leo got one this morning," Tracy said. "One must be Oliver's."

When Oliver and Ginny arrived a few minutes later, Oliver blushingly confessed to having bought one wombat. Giggling, Ginny claimed the other.

"I bought it for Jamison," she said. "I figured he might want a souvenir or two, besides the manure, once he stopped being a bug."

"Ultimately, the manure's more useful," Hali observed, "but you may have a point. All right, let's get going. It's time to head home."

After the exertions of their adventures, the walk to the meadow where they had originally entered Grimmworld was but a pleasant stroll. Tracy unloaded Whitenose and gave him a tearful farewell hug, letting go only after exacting Hali's promise to see the little ass well cared-for. Bentwood arrived and genially asked the gamers their opinions of the theme park.

"Could use some more exciting rides," Leo suggested, "something guaranteed to make kids throw up, like a high-flying dragonback ride."

The other gamers exchanged slightly embarrassed glances, and politely murmured assurances that the park was all they could desire. Bentwood grinned broadly, a truly impressive sight considering the width of his mouth, and made a short farewell speech exhorting the gamers to spread the word of Grimmworld's glories. Finally, nothing remained but for the gamers to depart.

"Hey, wait a minute," Leo protested. "This is a game, right? So who won?"

"We all won," Hali said. "The forces of good defeated the forces of evil. Isn't that enough?"

Shaking their heads, the gamers informed her that it wasn't. The lone dissenting voice, Tracy, spoke up.

"What does it matter who won? We had a real adventure, more real than anything I ever experienced before, and I think maybe I learned not to fantasize so much, and to face up to reality."

"Oh, so you *learned* something," Leo scoffed.

"I did. The elves were a real disappointment, but at least they were real. Everything was, and we survived anyway. It means something to me, anyway."

Leo ignored this argument. "You're just sore 'cause you didn't do so hot in battle. Now, I thought, since I managed to fight off so many ogres, I should win on hit points, at least."

"You didn't actually kill any," Tracy told him coldly. "Besides, Jamison did more damage than anyone."

Waving his arms and clicking his mandibles, Jamison signified his agreement. Not only did he fight best (demonstrated with a bit of shadow boxing) but he had certainly gathered the most treasure. In conclusion, the beetle stood erect and struck a proud pose leaning against his dung ball.

Laughing, Oliver conceded that by the usual criteria, Jamison had indeed won. "But I think I won. I rescued a princess and found true love—I just wish it weren't just a game." Smiling bravely, Ginny turned to him and took his hand. He brushed a tear from her cheek, and bent to kiss her. Just as their lips touched, Ginny faded away, leaving only a small cry of distress and disappointment quivering in the air.

"Well, that puts a damper on the festivities," Hali muttered, shaking her head. She went over to Oliver, who stood looking lost and bewildered. "Look, kid, you were warned. Bentwood, talk to the other kids for a minute. Maybe they can give you more pointers for the park."

Putting one arm around Oliver's shoulder, she steered him away from the others. "Look, I don't think I'm supposed to tell you this, but there's still a chance for you two. Ginny's an Outworlder like you. She was dreaming. That's how she got here. She may not remember you when she wakes up, she may not look quite the same, but there's a chance you two can meet."

"How?" Oliver asked, his voice filled with despair. "I don't know her real name, or where she's from—and you say I might not even recognize her if I found her."

"She might find you, if you can jog her memory. Bentwood's eager for publicity, and I suggest you make the most of it. Using the incredible communications systems you Outworlders have developed, Bentwood's henchmen will plaster your picture all over the world, if you let them. If she remembers, she might just find you, if for no other reason than to try to dispel a disturbingly vivid dream."

For a second, the possibility gave Oliver hope, and then a realization struck him. "But this is just a game," Oliver told Hali with a new anger. "You don't exist. She doesn't exist, except in the mind of a computer. I'm in love with a subroutine."

Hali started to speak, then thought better of it. She considered possible explanations, then shrugged. "You're young, you'll get over it."

"Gee, that's reassuring. Thanks."

"Don't try sarcasm on a master. I don't care how you explain it; she was as real as you, even if she didn't get here the same way. If you find her, she won't believe it either. But what does it hurt to try?"

"I don't plan on wasting the best years of my life chasing a girl from a computer game."

Hali sighed. "You're so young."

Oliver stiffened and pulled away. Hali followed him back to join the other gamers.

"Well, the game's definitely over," Hali said. "Leo fought ogres . . ."

"And used magic!" Leo added.

" . . . and used magic. Oliver nobly rescued his princess in disguise. Jamison fought ogres and accumulated enough gold to stave in the wall of a castle. But that gold came from Tracy, who did a good deed for a fairy and earned one of their highest rewards."

"Some reward," Tracy muttered, looking cross-eyed as she watched a white rose fall from her lips.

Hali laughed. "You have to watch out for the kindness of fairies," she conceded. "But at least the spell won't work in your world." She waved her broom in the air, first over Tracy's head, then over the others' in turn. As she passed, she left the players dressed in the clothes in which they'd arrived, ending with Jamison. The beetle faded away, and the man stood in its place.

"Excellent!" the man exclaimed, pulling out his notepad. "I must make notes immediately. Ingenious, transforming players that way. Very convincing, and an amusing, if contrived, way to add strength and useful talents like flight to an otherwise weak party." He started writing furiously, and looked up only when it was his turn to walk up the two steps to the glowing doorway through which the gamers returned to the real world.

"You had to transform the reviewer, didn't you," Bentwood grumbled to Hali, who sat beside him at the bar in Black Buck Inn.

The witch grinned. "He enjoyed it, didn't he?"

"A great selling point: 'Come to Grimmworld, be a bug. Play in real manure.' "

"And eat it, too."

"Hali, you're joking. Aren't you? Please tell me you're joking."

"Well, what else would a beetle do with a ball of dung when there are no females around to court? I assure you, they don't normally go around storming castles."

"Great. One game, and we need damage control already."

Hali looked down at the agitated troll, and took pity on him. "Relax, Bentwood. Jamison will remember his visit fondly. They all will."

Bentwood looked up with hope. "A spell?"

"No, human nature. Not only your publicists but all their friends are going to make a fuss over them for being the first to come here. The stories will get better with each telling, and in a few days the gamers will have forgotten the uncomfortable and embarrassing bits. Well, I expect Leo will get extra mileage from all the hardships he's endured so stoically, but that just demonstrates the 'realism' that's your big selling point. Next time, though, we'd better have a real adventure planned. We can't expect to luck into a strike again."

"Such luck." Bentwood stirred his drink. He didn't much like alcohol; it disagreed with troll metabolism, but he felt it was expected of him as a producer. Even cut with stumpwater, it tasted foul.

"It gave us a plot, didn't it?"

"Big enough to be buried in."

"Which reminds me . . . about my house."

Bentwood sighed. "Believe me, I've learned my lesson. No more messed-up employee relations. You can have any place you want," he said bitterly. "I'm not going to give you any cause to break your contract. Of course, if you want Marj's—sorry, *Sinestra's*—place, you gotta take the job, too."

Hali shook her head. "You've got a winning way about you, Bentwood."

"I'm a troll trying to do a high-profile job. It's not ideal, but no one else volunteered."

Hali waved that objection away. "Anyway, I wouldn't take that toothsome bit of architecture—it would take forever to clean, particularly the flossing. No, I rather liked the little underground job with the well access and those potent feather beds."

"Mother Holle's?" Bentwood asked, surprised. "I didn't know that was back on the market. Funny you'd go for her old place, what with the similar names and all."

"I don't think I've heard of this Mother Holle. Who is she?" Hali asked suspiciously.

Bentwood shrugged. "Before my time, but there's lots of stories. Some say she was an earth deity, or maybe a death goddess, before the god market dried up. So, she ended up working as an underground witch before she finally retired ages ago. Sad. That's the sort of thing I worry about happening to us."

"We're anything but gods, I'm glad to say,"

"Speak for yourself, old girl," Bentwood grinned. "I have plans."

Hali sighed, and took a fortifying swig of cider. "You always do, Bentwood. You always do."